C000005537

The Devil You Know

Terry Tyler

©Terry Tyler 2015

This is a work of fiction. All names, characters, places and incidents are either products of the author's imagination or used fictitiously.
Any resemblance to actual events, locations or persons, alive or dead, is entirely coincidental.
No part of this publication may be reproduced or transmitted in any form or by any means, electronic, mechanical or otherwise, without the express written permission of Terry Tyler.
All rights reserved.

A big thank you to my dear husband, Mark, and everyone who enjoys my books, past, present and future.

Prologue

February 2016

On the rare occasions she'd pondered on such a thing, Dora had imagined the moment of her death to be profound, intense, even beautiful—a flash of joyous memory, a vision of God, the face of her beloved mother welcoming her into the next world. But as the realisation dawned that this man was actually going to kill her, she saw only her brother, begging her not to believe Valter's promise of a job in a hotel when she got to England.

She'd laughed at Petras, mocked him. "Just because you've got no ambition—do you think I'm stupid? I'm the one playing *him*, silly! You know he's sweet on me; he'll get me anything I want."

But as soon as she entered her new home, a huge dormitory shared with many other girls, Valter changed.

The room was high up, with thick walls, bricked-up windows and locked doors, and the only favour he granted her, as a nod to the friendship between their families back in Ragožiai, was to weaken her dose of the *heroinas* with which the girls were injected regularly, to keep them dependent on the men. Valter told her he was giving her 'a fighting chance', because he had a soft spot for her brother.

"Not so soft for you, though!" He laughed when he said this, and winked at her; she didn't know why.

She found out, later that night, when he forced her to her knees and indicated how she should show her gratitude.

Why hadn't Petras tried harder to stop her?

(*He did, though. He hid your passport, stood in front of the door. He even cried.*)

But she had always gone her own way. Never listened to advice. Her mother used to say it would be the death of her.

The other girls told her it was best to stay in the house, where it was safe, and you could call for the men if a punter got rough. *Never work the street,* they said, *it's not worth it. If they find out, the men give you a beating, and you have no protection. You're on your own.*

But Dora knew better, so she sneaked out via the rickety fire escape.

Most of the girls had fallen into dependency on the drug with open arms. They had no spirit, and would never get away. The small amount of money they were allowed to keep went on extra hits and cigarettes, chocolate, make-up and the postage for letters home that Dora was sure were never sent. Dora never bought anything. She was no weakling who would put up with being treated like a chicken in the coop in her grandmother's back yard. The money she made out there on her own was added to the meagre escape fund accumulating in the slit in her mattress.

She would reclaim her passport if she had to kill the boss to do so, and then she would be off, back home to Petras and her grandmother, but first she would go to the police and tell them about this terrible place.

Bad stuff only happens to other people. Girls who weren't as quick-witted as her. She told herself this every day.

But now the man's hands tightened around her neck as he pumped in and out of her. He was only her second punter that night, and she'd thought, when he pulled up at the kerb, that he, of all people, would be kind to her.

He was the only man who had been, since she'd arrived in this hell.

Once safely in his car, she'd pointed out the alleys where the girls took their men, but the smile fell from his face and he ignored her. He sped out into the dark countryside where there were no people, no well-lit streets. She'd cried and begged to be let out, but he'd slammed his arm back against her neck and told her not to try anything. At a junction she'd tried to open the door and he'd pulled her back by the hair, tied her hands together behind her head, then turned up the music to drown out her sobbing.

Pretty girls, the sunshine in their hair, the perfume that they wear—

She knew it, from a CD that Petras had, at home. *Sounds of the 70s.* They used to dance to it.

Oh, Petras.

The ground was hard and cold. As she struggled to breathe, tears for her own foolishness streamed down her face, just as they had when Valter's men locked her into the house. Bad stuff could happen to anyone, especially if you were crazy enough to give it a helping hand.

She stared into the brute's dark eyes, willing him to remember her, forever.

The last thing she saw as she blacked out was not God, or her mother, but his triumphant face—and her last coherent thought was *I curse you. One day, you will pay for this.*

Then, nothing.

PART ONE

Down by the River

February ~ September 2015

Chapter One

Juliet: The Wife

Kirton, South Lincolnshire

One year earlier ~ Friday, 6th February 2015

"Good afternoon, this is your lunchtime news. The discovery of a third body in the River Lynden in the Monk's Park area of Lyndford has sent shock waves around the area and raised the question: is this the work of a serial killer?"

Juliet Tully had just applied arnica gel to her bruises, though she wasn't sure if it did any good. Paul said all homeopathic remedies were placebos, artfully packaged to attract gullible middle-class housewives who had nothing better to do than look for new ways to waste their husbands' hard-earned money.

"The same goes for any product with the word 'artisan' in its description, and ditto quinoa, goji berries, or whatever else you've been told is this month's must-have *superfood*." The way he spat out the words made her feel even more silly than the words themselves.

A plain tuna and cucumber sandwich and a glass of organic apple juice waited for her on the coffee table, untouched; it seemed wrong to eat whilst watching an account of a brutal murder. As if she was relishing the gory details. Instead, she picked up the tube of gel, felt under her blouse and made another careful application to the painful place at the top right of her rib cage where Paul's fist had landed the night before.

She'd been waiting for the attack, the first of these episodes for a while, because she knew the pattern. Afterwards he treated her with great consideration for a few weeks but, gradually, his irritation would return, building up and up until any ill-chosen word might spark him off.

Years ago, when it began, she'd thought his remorse was genuine and meant he'd never do it again. Later, she just learned to enjoy the good times. For a while (how ashamed she was to admit this!) she'd even considered it worth getting clobbered now and again, because afterwards Paul would behave like an attentive, loving husband, however briefly. Now, the feeling of dread grew with every passing day of bright smiles, offers to wash up, soft kisses at bed time. And the periods of calm were shorter.

Today brought back that only too familiar sensation of being *wounded*, bruised all over, inside and out; perhaps she should buy tubes and tubes of arnica gel and bathe in it. Swallow the wretched stuff. If only there was someone to put strong arms around her and make her world right again, but there was nobody she could tell except Lara, and Lara couldn't do anything. Juliet wouldn't let her.

Buried beneath that thick blanket of pain, struggling to be heard, was a tiny spark of anger, and she knew that anger was healthy, but mostly she just felt so terribly, terribly sad and lonely.

Tears filled her eyes as she watched the on-the-spot, Barbour-clad reporter leading the camera down to the place by the river, just ten miles away in Lyndford, where the body had been found. The day was cold, dreary, the ground muddy. Around the reporter were yellow police lines, and people in those funny white space suits. A female, thought to be in her early twenties, they said. Juliet's face quivered, and she let the tears fall down her cheeks. That poor girl, a life unlived. Her poor mother, too.

Juliet cried for the dead girl, for those who loved her, and her sadness mixed with grief for herself, and for her own mother, dead for some years now, and how she would have felt if she'd known her daughter would end up getting knocked about by her husband. But her mother was of the upbringing that considered a good marriage the be all and end all of a woman's life, and twenty-four years ago Paul Tully had seemed like a reasonable if not ideal choice, especially as Juliet was not inundated with offers. Her mother reminded her of this, and accepted Paul into the family even though his money came from property developing rather than a profession. ('It means he buys cheap houses, does them up even more cheaply, and sells them on at a profit', Juliet's father explained, a hint of distaste on his face.) Not the barrister, lecturer or medical consultant they'd hoped to welcome for Sunday lunch, but at least Juliet was 'settled' ("implication being that you can't be 'settled' without being married," Lara said, with a snort).

The local news handed back to the studio, where the glossy young presenter provided the information (with no small excitement in her voice) that this latest incident was 'hot on the heels' of the discoveries of two other young girls in similar circumstances over the past six months. A source within the police confirmed that the three could be linked by the same M.O., she said.

Pictures of two other girls flashed up on the screen. Jodie Walker, a 'sex worker', and Leanne Marsh, a hairdresser.

Juliet wondered if the presenter, who looked scarcely older than those two poor girls, knew what 'M.O.' actually stood for, and thanked God she had sons. Big strong boys in their late teens, Sam and Max were chips off the old block, just like their father. Fledgling alpha males, good at sports, sailing through their 'A' Level years despite a lax attitude to their studies, assured of their place in the world. Mini versions of their father, male chauvinistic pigs in waiting. She wondered what they would think if they knew Paul hit her.

Later that night, in front of the television once more, Juliet saw the dead girl named as twenty-one-year-old Kayla Graham, a prostitute who'd worked the red-light district out by Monk's Park industrial estate on the edge of town. The report suggested that the area had been adopted because of its proximity to a truck stop on the dual carriageway, the distance from the busy town centre where kerb crawlers' cars might be recognised, and the large blind spots between CCTV cameras. Miss Graham was thought to have been dead for three days, and had, like Jodie and Leanne, been strangled during or just after sexual intercourse.

Because she was alone in the house Juliet felt safe to cry again as she watched; no one would come in and ridicule her for being over-emotional ("Mum cries at *everything*!") When the picture of Kayla as a laughing, teenage schoolgirl flashed onto the screen, she wept as if the girl had been a part of her own life.

The announcement of Kayla's identity was followed by a fuzzy film of the 'sex workers' plying their wares under yellow street lights, vulnerable girls dressed in hot pants and high-heeled boots, some wearing short fur jackets in the cold winter's night. Juliet shuddered. They were so *young*. She pulled her dressing gown around herself more tightly, and shoved her feet under a cushion.

She was alone in the house because Paul was having a drink with a potential client. Sam and Max were out at a 'party', which was likely to be a cover for a night spent in the town centre bars of Lyndford. Sam was not eighteen for two weeks and Max had only just celebrated his seventeenth birthday, but she knew they both had fake ID. She suspected they lied to her about where they went much of the time, as Paul did, and she doubted whether such falsehoods ever caused any of them a moment's guilt. How

Juliet felt mattered not; all three cared only about doing what they wanted, when they wanted, without restriction.

The boys lying to her was not such a problem. She knew more or less where they were, if not the exact details; out drinking in horrible, noisy bars, or, in Sam's case, at some girl's house having sex (she was sure Max wasn't doing that yet, not her little Max). More painful was her husband's deceit. In her darkest moments she pondered the possibilities (gambling, strip clubs, another woman, other *women*, even), but a confrontation never went down well, so mostly she tried not to think about it.

"I'd bloody well have it out with him," Lara would say to her.

"I know you would. But I'm not you."

Paul didn't like Lara. She spoke her mind in a way Paul considered unfeminine, and caused Juliet to question the stability of their family life.

She kept Lara and Paul apart whenever possible, which made her sad, too. Lara was all she had.

Juliet missed her mother, so badly.

She blocked such thoughts from her mind, and snuggled up on the sofa. The presenter of the news programme introduced a special guest, an expert on serial killers. Oh, so now it was official, was it? A serial killer! Wincing with the pain that the arnica gel had done nothing to relieve, Juliet listened to the confident young woman (how could you be an expert on anything at her age?) holding forth on the possible personality traits of the man who'd done what he did to Kayla Graham, Jodie Walker and Leanne Marsh.

Leanne had not been seen since she left work one chilly, dark evening last October.

Her mother. Her poor mother.

Their pictures flashed onto the screen, all three of them alike with their long, dark hair and pretty faces.

"Serial killers might be attention or sensation seekers, with the need to control and a lack of true remorse. They feel justified in what they do, to the extent of a God complex, in some cases," said Little Miss Expert, shiny copper hair catching the light, manicured hands gesturing expansively. "They may appear quite normal to the rest of the world—charming, even. The most well-known example of this is Ted Bundy, of course, for whom the term 'serial killer' was introduced. Now, Bundy, he actually worked on a suicide crisis helpline." She waited for the gasp of incredulity from the programme presenter. "Yes, amazing, isn't it? The mask of sanity is very common."

"So the killer could be someone from an ordinary family, even?"

Miss Expert nodded, pleased to have been fed the right line. "Indeed, yes." She looked at the camera, and, thus, into the homes of the viewers. "And he could be sitting with that family, watching this, right at this very moment."

The presenter gave an uncomfortable smile. "Not that we want to start a national panic, do we?"

The girl smiled. "Sorry, I didn't mean to worry anyone! But the point I'm making is that he might be popular, well-liked—take John Wayne Gacy from Illinois in the US, multiple killer of young men, lauded for fundraising within his community; he used to dress up as a character called Pogo The Clown to entertain children. Or Fred West, the likeable odd job man. Harold Shipman, a doctor trusted by his patients. With any of them, though, you don't have to look far beneath the veneer of normality to unearth serious psychological damage. Many serial killers suffered abuse—sexual, physical or emotional— when they were young. They might have been bullied or ridiculed by their peers. These forms of abuse can result in behavioural dysfunction. Some serial killers have a history of vandalism or theft, or have displayed sadistic tendencies from an early age, such as the torture of animals."

The psychologist went on to describe more common personality traits of the average homicidal maniac, but Juliet had heard enough.

She muted the smiling woman's voice and sat back, staring at the screen.

No. Stop it.

She looked down at the carpet. There were crumbs under the table, from her lunchtime sandwich. How could she have missed them, earlier? Damn it, she'd have to get the hoover out.

She stood up, too quickly, and her head swam. Eyes closed, she clutched the arm of the sofa.

No. No.

She sat down again. No one but her would care about those few crumbs. She could pick them up with her fingers, no need to get the hoover out at this time of night—

Didn't work. The niggle in her head wouldn't go away, however hard she concentrated on the crumbs.

Come on. Take a reality check, as Sam would say.

This was no different from looking up symptoms on the internet and finding out that for the past twenty years you'd been suffering from half the types of cancer known to medical science, Legionnaire's Disease, irritable bowel syndrome and Alzheimer's.

In isolation, none of the traits Miss Expert had listed meant anything.

But they weren't in isolation.

Juliet shut her eyes, ticking off the list of traits in her mind, the copper-haired young woman's voice as clear in her head as if she was saying the words to her out loud, now, in the room.

A need to control.

A lack of remorse.

Abused when young.

Bullied or ridiculed by peers.

Can believe self to be untouchable—a God complex.

Sadistic tendencies.

Appears to the rest of the world to be quite normal—charming, even.

Wears the mask of sanity.

Oh, yes, and the killer could be sitting on the sofa in a normal family home, right now.

Oh dear.

Little Miss Expert, with her crisp white blouse and shining white teeth, had just described Paul Tully. Juliet's husband.

Aside from the fact that Paul wasn't sitting on the sofa in their normal family home, because he was out. Again. And, as usual, Juliet wasn't entirely convinced that he was where he said he was.

Neither had she been three nights before, on the night Kayla Graham was murdered.

Paul had been out until after midnight, and he hadn't told her where. When she enquired, as casually as possible, he made vague noises about drinks and a curry with Oliver Carroll, his bank manager and good friend.

"Oh. You don't smell of drink." Nervous laugh. "Did Oliver get you to do the driving again?"

"Well, yes, obviously, if I haven't been drinking."

In bed, when he leant over to give her his customary peck on the cheek goodnight, she noticed that he didn't smell of curry, either.

"No, because I had a chicken korma. You know, the mild one. More cream than spice. What's this, a bloody interrogation?"

(Lara would have said, yes, you're my husband, I have a right to know where you are until after midnight. But Lara wasn't married; she didn't know how this stuff worked.)

When Juliet picked up his shoes from the bedroom floor the next morning, to polish them—she kept the shoes of the whole family polished, they'd never bother to do it themselves—the spaces between the ridges on the soles were caked with mud and grass.

(Mud and grass, like on riverbanks.)

Last night she'd plucked up the courage to ask him again where he'd been, and his answer was brusque, dismissive. When she mentioned the condition of the soles of his shoes, he grew angry. Very angry. When she dared to insist that he told her why they were so, he hissed, "Don't you ever shut up?" and pushed her against the wall. As a reflex she picked up the first thing that caught her eye on the draining board, which happened to be the potato masher, and wielded it at him.

He laughed. He actually laughed and said, "What's the matter, have you forgotten to take your tablet today, or what?"

She pushed him back and shouted that if he wasn't such a pig to her, she wouldn't need the bloody happy pills, which was when he punched her.

She yelled in pain and he said, "Don't blame your crazies on me," and walked out of the room as she sank to the floor.

Of course, Paul hadn't been hitting her since the beginning of their relationship, or she would never have married him, but when the violence first occurred, she realised it had been waiting in the wings for some time.

Did men like him consciously seek out women like her, who had little self-confidence? Did they 'see them coming', or did they connect with them via instinct? Women who could be manipulated into thinking that everything was their fault.

She often wondered that.

Juliet didn't talk about the violence. She tried not to even think about it, let alone say the words out loud. She felt *ashamed*. Embarrassed that she stayed with a man who caused her physical harm, yes, but, more than that, shame that her marriage was not a success, that she couldn't make Paul happy, make him want to care for her, instead of hurting her.

Fear that she was such an infuriating, silly, useless idiot that the one person who was supposed to love her above all others was driven to hit her.

She didn't understand how badly damaged he was until some time after they met, and even then, she never imagined he would take his pain out on her. She was an unworldly twenty-four-year-old when they were introduced at a friend's party, and Paul was twenty-eight.

After they got engaged, she asked him why she'd appealed to him, and he remembered to mention her looks, warmth and engaging personality only when he saw her hurt reaction to his first answer.

"You're just the sort of woman I've always imagined myself marrying," he'd said, going on to cite her good education, her solid, traditional, middle-class background.

Juliet's father was the chief executive of their county council and her mother a housewife who took for granted that the word 'husband' was synonymous with 'provider'.

Juliet's father was a Mason, of course.

Paul did not tell Juliet much about his own upbringing until he felt sure of her unconditional love. When he did, she was scared by the bitterness in his voice.

"Grandfather was a drunken layabout, and Dad followed suit, except that he thought he was better than his dad because he dragged himself into work every day at the shoe factory, hangover or not. He used to stink of drink in the mornings, I could smell it the minute he walked into the kitchen. Nothing worse than the smell of stale whisky when you're trying to keep down your cornflakes, especially when the milk's off. Mind you, the estate where we lived was so bloody depressing, I think I'd have turned to drink if I'd stayed there, too. Mum worked in Woolworths when she could be bothered; she buggered off with the bloke down the road when I was sixteen, and Dad died a few years after I left home, of lung cancer, probably due to smoking forty Woodbines a day for his entire adult life. Our house reeked of them."

Juliet felt completely out of her depth. "You lost them quite young, then. It must have been awful," she said, trying to sound comforting, fearing he would think her a spoiled little princess who knew nothing of real life.

He didn't answer her, but swigged back his red wine and stared at the wall; they were sitting by the fire in her flat at the time. "Mum was one of those women who have a big mouth but nothing intelligent to say, and nagged Dad into the pub most nights, then nagged him when he came home again. She sat there drinking cider with her mates every night, and sometimes in the afternoon; I'd come home from school and there'd be no tea on the table, and Mum would be lying in front of the telly, snoring. Then Dad would get home from work and she'd wake up and rant at him about us living in a shit hole. He was hen-pecked, so he took it out on me. I got caned if I didn't do well at school, but he didn't really care about my future, he was just venting his general anger about life. Apart from Mum's nagging, he got passed over for promotion at work, again and again. When I say 'promotion', I'm talking about foreman at the factory. Foreman in a fucking shoe factory! That was the extent of his ambition. If I hadn't got into posh school, I would've ended up stitching bits of leather and getting wankered down the club five nights a week for the rest of my life, too."

Juliet learned, during other wine-fuelled true confessions, that his scholarship to the 'posh' school had not been the life-improving experience anticipated by the teacher who'd put him forward. He was bullied by his classmates because he was the council house kid. Despite his gift for figures, his unhappiness at school resulted in academic failure, but he was strong and hard-working with an aptitude for the practical, and his careers master suggested the building trade, with day release to learn quantity surveying.

Paul soon gave up on the day release; he had bigger ideas. The building trade was clinging onto the tail end of the 1980s property boom, and he bought his first terraced house at auction while still living with his father, made the improvements himself and sold it for a tidy profit. He bought another, and then another, acquiring a girlfriend who worked at a property auctioneers along the way; she was able to tip him off about houses up for foreclosure and, thus, going for a song. By the time Juliet met him, his small business was thriving, despite the downturn in the market, with one of his rental flats in Lyndford transformed into the office of Tully Developments.

Their first marital home was a three-bedroomed 1930s semi, for which Juliet's father provided a hefty deposit. Paul hadn't liked what he saw as interference, but Juliet soothed his bruised pride.

"It's Daddy's way of showing his approval," she said, and congratulated herself on the wisdom of her words. Ten years and two moves later, their home was the four-bedroomed detached house in the village of Kirton.

Paul's humble beginnings were consigned to the past, never to be mentioned.

With the influx of immigrants from Eastern Europe in the new century, legal and otherwise, Paul found that a cheaper labour force came with its own problems.

He arrived on site one morning to find that his gang of Albanian labourers had disappeared, along with a brand-new van and all of his tools.

Later that day he drowned his anger in whisky, and hit Juliet for the first time.

When she was still recovering from the shock he said sorry and bought flowers, but even then, even as she comforted him (because he was so very distraught about what he'd done), she knew he wasn't really, truly sorry, not in the way she would have meant the words; he just wanted her to stop being upset.

His sorrow was not shame that he could do such a thing to her, his beloved wife, but disappointment at his own lack of control.

Juliet was a slight, physically weak woman. Fair, rounded, feminine. Paul was tall, strong, athletic.

The second time came a few months later, when a buyer pulled out of the purchase of a Victorian edifice he'd developed into flats, at the last minute, deciding to invest elsewhere. 'Elsewhere' meant a property owned by a fellow Mason, and Paul was not a part of that elite. Although he formed connections with bank managers, estate agents, and the council officials necessary for the planning permits he needed, he remained on the periphery, never gaining the full acceptance he so desperately wanted.

The day his petition to join the Freemasons was rejected, despite the recommendation by her father, he punched Juliet in the stomach and she lost their third child. He didn't admit the real reason for his rage; he never needed to, for the reasons were always so clear to her. Instead, he would pick a row with her about domestic trivia, or take offence at something she'd said, needling and digging at her until she shouted back, at which point the violence would erupt.

"You just won't shut up, will you?" he'd say. "You can see I'm having a bad day, and you start having a go at me! You're just like my mother, nag, nag, nag, it never bloody stops!"

Wham! And there she'd be, on the floor. When she miscarried, he said he was glad. He'd been angry when she became pregnant.

"You mean I've got to go through nine more bloody months of you whining about how tired you are, then eighteen more of sleepless nights? And years and years of expense?"

She was at fault because she'd tricked him, forgotten to take her pills accidentally on purpose. She couldn't blame him for being cross, but when her hopes for a daughter trickled away into a pool of blood on the bathroom floor, her grief was a physical pain, her sobs silent, from deep inside. *Wracking* sobs, she thought; she hadn't known what that term meant before.

She'd wanted a daughter so badly, a female ally in her male-dominated world.

Her mother had died only the year before, and Lara was not around at that time, far out of reach.

After the miscarriage Paul said there would be no more children, and had a vasectomy.

One day she woke up and thought, *I am a victim of domestic abuse. I am one of the statistics people read about.*

Once she'd said those words to herself, she cried, often. She couldn't leave; she'd been out of the workplace for too long to earn a proper salary, and Paul would never let her take the boys. Her parents had left her money in the form of a bond, but once that was gone, she would have nothing.

Over the years she became the arch diplomat, able to detect her husband's moods even from his back view, the set of his shoulders, careful that her words would never set him off.

After a while she cared less that she didn't know where he went at night; she liked it better when he wasn't there. The less she asked, the less he told her.

Their sex life had all but petered out, and she wondered if his needs were being met elsewhere. That hurt, but not as much as it might have done at the beginning of their marriage.

Her jealousy stemmed only from the fact that another woman might be treated to the Paul she'd once known, the one with whom she'd fallen in love.

When she thought about that, she plunged back into the pit of gloom, wondering what it was about her that brought out the worst in him.

She stared at the television screen. The news programme had finished, moved on to some late-night chat show, but still she sat.

Abused when young.

Bullied or ridiculed by peers.

A need to control.

A lack of remorse.

The news stations were giving out a number for people who might have information about the murders, and she wrote it down. Not that she would dream of ringing it up. You couldn't bother these people on a silly hunch. They would think she was ridiculous.

She *was* ridiculous.

Lara was right; she spent too much time inside her own head.

And she knew exactly who would suffer if the police came to the door wanting to interview Paul.

Sometimes, when he was being particularly vindictive, he told her she was 'a mental case'. Maybe the police would think she was, too.

The heating went off at eleven, as it always did, but she didn't get up; she pulled the shawl collar of her dressing gown closer round her neck, tucked her legs underneath her. The television flickered; a huge basketball player flashed white teeth at a skinny Hollywood actress she vaguely recognised, while the chat show host played sycophant. Presently, the door banged, and the sound of Sam and Max's laughter filled the house. One set of feet running up the stairs, the other walking into the kitchen. The sound of the fridge opening, the *kwishhh* of a can being opened. Sam, nicking one of Paul's lagers.

Juliet got up and wandered into the kitchen; Sam slurped from the can and grinned at her.

"Yes, I'm a bit drunk, and yes, I'm nicking Dad's beer." Behind the cheerful smile lurked that cocky air of challenge. "If you're going to have a nag-fest, can you do it quickly? Because Max is setting up FIFA 15, and I need to go upstairs and whop his arse!"

He winked at her to show—*pretend*—that he was only teasing. How well his father had taught him.

Juliet managed a smile. "Do what you want, you usually do."

She turned back into the living room, shutting the door behind her. As she sat back down on the sofa, she surprised herself by thinking, *I'm surrounded by rude oafs who have no respect for me.*

If only she'd had a daughter.

Max wasn't so bad, he was softer than Sam, holding back, in his elder brother's shadow, but even he had his moments.

Tonight felt so strange, as if she was slightly drunk herself, though she'd only drunk two glasses of red wine.

What the hell? The other three members of her household would be the worse for drink that night, so why shouldn't she be the same? A large glass of brandy, that was what she needed.

She stretched out on the sofa, glass in hand, gazing at the ceiling, and allowed herself a fantasy. Two men appearing at the door and taking Paul away. Her home, peaceful without him. Her sons needing her, instead of treating her like a housekeeper. The three of them, pulling together.

Would it be so bad?

She turned over, burying her face into the cushion, thinking hard, pulling something out of her memory bank that she'd read about Sonia Sutcliffe, wife of the Yorkshire Ripper, who suffered terrible harassment because people thought she must have known. Max and Sam's lives would be hell. *What does your dad do? Oh, he's the Lyndford Strangler, haven't you heard? It's okay, though, I take after my mum.*

No, no, for goodness sake, it would be a nightmare.

And of course, Paul wasn't a murderer. He was an arrogant bully with a dangerous chip on his shoulder who kept secrets and lied to her, but this didn't mean he was capable of murdering three young women.

Then again, it didn't mean he wasn't.

Chapter Two

Steve: The Friend

Lyndford, South Lincolnshire

Eleven days later: Tuesday, 17th February 2015

Tuesday night was Sports Night, even if there was no big match on, and the lads cheered when it was Steve's turn to host, because he had Sky Sports premium package and an eighty-four-inch TV screen with 4K resolution and surround sound. Best of all, he lived alone.

Steve was sure his turn came round more than once every five weeks, but sometimes Woodsy cancelled if his girlfriend was having 'one of her turns'. None of them were quite sure what these turns actually entailed, but Woodsy assured them he was better off out of the house when she was 'on one', let alone inviting four mates round to drink beer and get rowdy.

Dan lived alone, too, but he only had one three-seater settee and no armchairs, so two of them had to sit on the floor. Then there was Dan's elder brother, Noel, who spent weeks away at a time, working on construction contracts around the country, and lived with their dad when he came home.

"Fuck the rota, let's just have it at Steve-o's every week!" said AJ, plonking his arse onto the black leather recliner and taking a swig from his bottle of Bud, whooping as he made the most of the chair's swivel action.

Bloody cheek. The recliner was perfectly positioned for optimum televisual enjoyment, with its stand-alone ashtray and small table, coasters at the ready; it was Steve's chair, where he sat every night to watch his favourite crime and investigation programmes or documentaries on the history channels. He didn't watch sport when alone; Dan had persuaded him to get Sky premium 'for the lads'.

Annoyed though he was, Steve didn't try to stop AJ sitting in his chair.

AJ was the boss.

His house was the second favourite Tuesday Sports Night venue, but Steve hated going there. AJ lived in a brand new, detached bungalow out at Waterton, bought with the proceeds from his scrapyards (one on the outskirts of the village and the main one in Lyndford, down Crow Lane, near the industrial estate). When Steve was at AJ's house, he felt like a commoner allowed into the king's palace to sup at his table. Didn't care for his wife, either. Hard-edged chav called Roxy, with so much Botox that she had only one facial expression, permanently set at wide-eyed suspicion.

Neither did Steve like AJ.

Trouble was, these were the only friends he had.

He was only a member of AJ's inner circle because of Dan.

AJ thought Dan was *focking mint*, and Steve and Dan's friendship began when they were children; they were closer than Dan and Noel had ever been. Thus, the free pass into King AJ's lair.

Steve didn't make friends easily; some people just didn't, did they? Not everyone could be madly bloody gregarious, and he had a need for solitude and privacy that, he knew, came from growing up in foster care. Didn't take a degree in psychology to work that one out.

His flat was his castle and, most of the time, he liked to pull up the drawbridge and forget the outside world.

He enjoyed his job tinkering in the peaceful workshop at Lyndford Computer Solutions, and he had everything in his flat that he needed (except a girlfriend), but now and again everybody wanted to go out, have a bit of a chat and a laugh.

Used to be it was just Steve and Dan and whoever else they bumped into, but in the past couple of years Dan had started hanging out with his brother again, and hanging out with Noel meant hanging out with AJ.

Since Dan became AJ's second-in-command, Friday's lads' night out had progressed from a leisurely crawl round the same old pubs they'd been using since before they could legally drink, bumping into people they knew, to a whistle-stop tour of the trendy bars Steve hated, sometimes culminating in a visit to Rockerfellas, the lap dancing club on the new Meadowfields Leisure Complex on the edge of town.

Meadowfields, indeed.

The building of the complex had decimated the abandoned fields where Steve and Dan had enjoyed so many childhood adventures. The leafy lanes along which they'd dawdled on summer afternoons were now ghosts beneath the hum of traffic on the entrance roads, the babbling brooks and shimmering streams forever quiet. Made him feel sad.

If left to choose his own entertainment venues, Steve would rather spend the evening tied to a chair in a darkened room than hit Meadowfields.

The leisure complex comprised an over-priced cinema with five screens, a 'fun house' for the under tens, a bowling alley, and a family-friendly pub where they served food all day long, so kids could gobble microwaved E numbers while Dad had a pint after an afternoon's bowling. Then there were the fast food chains, and Feed The World, an all-you-can-eat buffet with 'delicious multi-national cuisine'. Steve had been there once, and none of it was delicious enough to make him want to continue eating once his most basic hunger pangs were satisfied, but, come noon every Sunday, discount sportswear-clad, pasty-faced families queued to stuff themselves to bursting point for twelve pounds a head. At night, Cinderella's night club and Rockerfellas lap dancing club opened for business.

The others thought Meadowfields was brilliant.

Steve wouldn't have minded going bowling, which seemed like a much better way to meet girls than playing eye-meets in pubs, but Dan and AJ said it was for students, families and nerds.

Sometimes he wished he had the confidence to make new friends, but Dan was his brother in all but blood. He'd been the stability in his life since they were seated together on their first day at school. Dan was just *there*. Woodsy was a decent enough bloke, but Steve had never warmed to Noel, a strong, silent type who he suspected had secrets of the unsavoury kind. Noel had always been there, too. He'd protected him and Dan when they were kids, leaving them in no doubt about who was boss. Yeah, he could live with Noel. It was just fucking AJ.

Aside from not liking the bloke, Steve suspected that not all his activities were strictly legal. How much scrap metal did you have to trade to buy a pad like his detached sprawl at Waterton? Dan had more to splash around since he'd been hanging out with him, too.

AJ brought out the worst in Dan, for sure. Dan hero-worshipped the dickhead, and, alas, emulated some of his worst characteristics. Before, Steve had never noticed what a complete tit his best friend could be. A bit racist. A lot sexist. Bigoted tendencies had long been a part of his nature, which Steve either took the piss out of or ignored, but nowadays they were fast taking over from his more likeable traits. Like, before, you might have said, 'Dan? Oh yeah, sound bloke. Bit of an ape sometimes, but he's alright.' Now, though, if you didn't feel for him the sort of affection that stemmed from lifelong friendship, you'd more likely say, 'Dan Thewlis? Hmm. Take away the offensive shit that comes out of his mouth, and he's okay. Trouble is, most of what comes out of his mouth is offensive shit.'

Steve felt silly for thinking so, but it was like AJ had opened a door into the dark side of Dan's mind. He could pinpoint the moment Dan changed into someone he'd cross the road to avoid, down to the night he said, "Let's swing past the Boar, Noel's going to be in there." And there Noel was, with his pal AJ.

If the concept didn't sound even sillier, he'd think Dan had sold his soul to the devil.

On that particular Tuesday Sports Night, the boxing was in full swing. Steve didn't know who the contestants were and didn't care (he preferred snowboarding or ice climbing feats if he had to watch sport at all, not two AJ types punching the crap out of each other), so he watched the others watching, instead.

AJ, leaning forward, can in hand, fist clenched, saying stuff like, "*Goo* on, my son!"

Dan at the end of the three-seater settee nearest King AJ, mirroring his mentor's gestures and sentiments.

Noel at the other end concentrating on the screen with a keen eye, long legs stretched out in front of him, Woodsy in the middle guzzling Stella and stuffing nuts into his mouth.

The match came to an end and AJ and Dan flopped back, exhausted, as if they'd been fighting the match themselves. Dan opened fresh cans and they raised them in celebration; presumably their boy had triumphed.

Noel lifted the bowl of mixed nuts from the table to reach the local paper, below.

He turned a few pages, stopped at one, and sniffed. "See they've found another body."

From where he sat, perched on his high-backed computer chair, Steve could see photos of the crime scene. "What, a new one?"

"Yeah." Noel frowned, and his eyes travelled down the page. "Early yes'day morning. Dog walker saw a head sticking out of the river, down near Monk's Park."

Woodsy laughed. "Cor, imagine that bastard! Y' walking along, minding your own business, waiting for y' dog to have its shite, and you see a pair of dead eyes staring at you, out the water. *Fuck*!"

"Another one near Monk's Park?" AJ nodded. "That'll be another prozzie, then, won't it?"

Noel was still reading. "Don't say. They've not identified her yet."

"Yeah, but it will be, though, won't it? If it's up there. Same as the others."

"They reckon it's the same bloke, then?" Dan asked. "What's it say?" He put his hand out. "Give it here."

Dan leant over and snatched the paper from Noel. He stared first at the headline ('*Fourth Body Found: Lyndford Strangler Strikes Again?*'), then turned the page and laughed.

"Make for amusing reading, does it, Danny Boy?" Steve asked.

Dan didn't look up. "I'm just laughing at how they make it obvious she's a *hoo-er*, without saying so in as many words. Like, 'the victim was pulled from the River Lynden, close to Monk's Park Trading Estate, where sex workers are known to ply their trade after dark'." He tossed the paper back onto the table, and picked up his can. "Don't know why it's front page news. I mean, it's only a load of tarts getting bumped off."

Woodsy looked up, frowning. "Fucking hell, Dan. Behave."

Dan wiped his mouth. "Well, what do they expect? Getting into cars with complete strangers. Every time they do that, they're risking their lives, and all for a bit of smack."

"S'right," said AJ, picking up the TV remote control and flicking through the channels. "What d'you fancy next, lads?"

"It's not always because of drugs, though, is it?" Steve said. "I mean, they're not all smack heads, necessarily. I've read that some students do it to supplement their student loans. And single mums. There are the ones who are forced into it, by human traffickers, too. I saw a documentary about that the other night."

"Yeah, that's well sad," said Woodsy.

Dan sat back, and waved his hand as if to dismiss what they'd said. "Yeah, yeah, yeah. You know what I mean, though, don't you? They ain't, like, *normal* people. It's not like if it was a decent girl. Say what you like, but it just ain't so shocking when it's a proz. I mean, they mess with danger every day, don't they? And they let any pervy old stranger do all sorts to them."

AJ nodded. "Yeah, he's only saying what everyone else thinks, even if they don't admit it."

"Too right. The dregs of any society will come a cropper. Way of the world." He and AJ clinked cans together.

Steve shut his eyes for a moment. Would it matter, would it really, really matter, in the grand scheme of his life, if he told the two of them to get the fuck out of his house and take their moronic opinions with them? Probably not, but he wasn't quite brave enough to do it.

"That's not untrue, but no one deserves to die like that," he said, so quietly that he doubted anyone even heard him. AJ had found a football match he wanted to watch, and the noise of vuvuzelas from the South American stadium filled the room.

"I'll tell you what I read the other day," Dan continued. He lit a cigarette. "Some pro who reckoned she'd been raped." He laughed, and shook his head. "You're having a laugh, aren't you? How can you rape a prostitute?"

"If she didn't agree to the transaction, i.e. her services for the punter's money, then it's rape," Steve said.

"Correct," said Noel.

"Bit of a grey area, though," Woodsy said.

"I don't see how she can prove it," said Dan. "I reckon what happened is that he didn't pay up 'cause she didn't do what she said she'd do, so she started bleating." He took a drag from his cigarette and blew a smoke ring. "That's what I reckon."

Steve shook his head in disbelief. "What about lap dancers? Those ones you pay to do private dances down Rockerfellas; would they deserve it, as well? Even if they don't go the whole hog, it's still a sex-for-money trade-off. Would they be fair game, too, huh?"

Dan looked at him, bewildered for a moment, then laughed. "What're you on about? You're not going all women's lib on me, are you, Turner?"

"He'll be burning his bra next!" said AJ. "Crying rape when it's what you do for a living, Steve, mate—it'd be like you going into your computer shop and kicking up because your boss tells you you've gotta take the back off a laptop, wouldn't it?"

Steve joined in with the laughter this comment provoked (and he supposed it was quite funny, really), even though their fuckwittery was crossing all boundaries of ignorance.

Dan didn't laugh quite so much in the Boar and Dragon, two nights later, when Joe the landlord turned the TV on just as the news started.

The victim from earlier in the week was still not officially named, the body not claimed, but one of the girls from Monk's Park had come forward to say she'd seen her there on the night she was killed; they'd argued because the dead girl had strolled onto her 'patch'. Later, she'd seen her laughing and chatting to some bloke before she got into his car.

The girl had supplied information about the man's appearance to the police, and the facial composite filled the TV screen.

Was he the last person to see her alive?

"Bloody hell, Dan, it's you!"

AJ's bellow filled the room as he jabbed his finger at the TV screen then turned to Dan, pointing at them, back and forth. "Mate, what you been up to?"

Steve was not the only person whose head jerked up, studying first the composite then comparing it with the face of Dan, at the bar. His eyes flicked back to the screen and back to his friend, several times.

Despite the strange quality of such composites, all present could see that, yes, the software-produced image did indeed feature the same square jaw, the same deep-set eyes and slightly brutish face as Dan Thewlis, even down to the dark wavy hair that needed cutting, the shadow that appeared around his chin if he didn't bother to shave for a second time before going out in the evening, as he didn't when, on nights like tonight, he was not out to get laid.

Wasn't a spitting image, but it was enough like him to make you look twice.

Over the past twenty-five years Steve had seen Dan talk his way out of a thousand and one scrapes, from nicking sweets from the corner shop, to having no homework to hand in, to placating furious girls, demanding to know why he hadn't turned up for their date the night before. Again, his presence of mind saved the day. He looked around the room, and laughed.

"It's a fair cop, guvnor!" he said, and raised his glass to his audience. "Suppose I'd better take meself down the cop shop and 'fess up!"

Laughter carried around the room; Dan turned back to the bar, grin still in place, and punched AJ in the arm.

"You wanker!" he said. "Thanks a bunch!" Steve watched them laughing, slapping each other on the back, ordering more drinks. Thus, the evening's entertainment.

"How sad would you have to be to pay for it off one of them dirt boxes up Monk's Park?" AJ said, as the face of the unnamed girl appeared on the television screen.

Never had Steve felt more like thumping Dan's new friend. She wasn't a *dirt box*, whatever that was supposed to mean. She was a poor, frightened girl whose life had been snuffed out in one tragic, pointless moment.

"Too right, mate." Dan nodded at the barman and gestured with his finger to Woodsy and Steve's empty glasses. "The day I need to pay for it is the day I chop me old man off." He winked at a girl on the other side of the bar, who smiled back, clearly pleased by his attention.

Pity Dan was such a good-looking bastard. Made him think he could get away with all the shit he did and said. Problem was, he mostly could.

"So, Dan," said Woodsy, leaning in to join the fun. "You ain't told us yet. Where were you Sunday night when this girl got wasted?"

Dan took a sip of his pint, the foam leaving a small white moustache on his upper lip, and grinned. "Why, are you thinking of dobbing me in? I was round my gran's, if you must know, and I stayed the night 'cause I'd had a nip of Scotch too many and couldn't be arsed to get a taxi home. Alright?"

Woodsy folded his arms and stuck out his bottom lip. "Coulda sneaked out and done it. In the middle of the night when your old dear was asleep."

Dan stood up, pulling his shoulders back, and slapped Woodsy on the shoulder. "Yeah, but I *didn't*, did I?" He handed Woodsy his fresh pint. "You can go down and have a chat with the rozzers if you want, mate. I won't hold it against you."

They all laughed, Dan and AJ, Woodsy, the landlord, the barman, and Steve chortled along with them.

But he remembered Dan's dad asking him if it was true that he'd been stealing chocolate from the corner shop, and that split second of panic on Dan's face before he came out with his alibi.

He remembered noticing that same look before Dan spun some yarn to his teacher about not having finished his project because he'd had to visit his gran in hospital. He'd seen it many times, more recently, before he conjured up the slick charm with which he appeased the girls who'd waited at home for the lover who never arrived.

He was the only one in the room, he was sure, who knew Dan well enough to see that same shadow darken Dan's face the moment AJ said *bloody hell, Dan, it's you!*

Shit. Surely not.

Steve shut his eyes. He'd seen so many programmes about serial killers on the Crime and Investigation channel that he could probably enter it as his specialist subject on *Mastermind*. He'd seen interviews with ordinary people from Cromwell Street who couldn't believe that genial odd job man Fred West tortured young girls in his cellar, and patients who'd been treated by and trusted Dr Harold Shipman for years.

Didn't Peter Sutcliffe's brother actually joke with him how close a resemblance the official photofit was?

Pack it in, he told himself. *Stop it. How much have you had to drink? Dan's your mate, you've known him since childhood.*

Anyway, didn't serial killers start their careers by torturing animals when they were children? Dan had never done that. Ian Brady threw cats off balconies. And who was that one who dissected live frogs and toads? Steve knew all about such monsters. In fact, he'd go as far to say he had an almost unhealthy interest in them; if anything, he fitted the public's idea of a multiple murderer more closely than Dan. A bit of a loner, a fascination with murder and the psychology behind it.

Only difference was that he cared about people. Psychopaths and sociopaths, though, the sort of people who became serial or spree killers, they didn't.

Did Dan? Steve sipped his beer and thought about it. Yes, his friend was a great one for beer-fuelled declarations of eternal male comradeship, and he visited his gran on a fairly regular basis, but did he have much in the way of empathy, generally?

Not as far as women were concerned. Dan had only one lasting relationship under his belt; his first long-term girlfriend had left him, a decade ago, when he was twenty-four. Thinking back, that was when the old Dan started to become the new Dan, even before AJ. Once he'd finished drowning his sorrows, Dan scythed his way through the available female population of Lyndford like a rutting stag in mating season. Even the few who lasted longer than one night received their marching orders once they started talking commitment. Occasionally they dumped him, after listing his shortcomings, but he never cared.

"Apparently I'm an emotional cripple," he announced, cheerfully, after the exit of the last one.

Steve felt sorry for the girls Dan hurt. Sometimes he'd try to comfort them; one had even become his girlfriend for a while. Sort of. At least, she used to meet him for a drink a couple of times a week, and sleep with him now and again, but more often than not she ended up talking about Dan. Steve knew he was that cliché, the less attractive friend with the listening ear. He couldn't count the times his friend's cast-offs had told him, *you're so much nicer than Dan. I reckon I fell in love with the wrong one!*

Mostly, such comments came out after he'd bought them a few glasses of wine and listened to their troubles for three hours. He wasn't stupid, he knew how easy it was for a girl to kid herself she fancied that average looking guy with the gentle eyes who'd been nice to her, when she was a bit pissed and a bit lonely.

Steve looked around the pub. Nearly everyone had returned to their conversations, their drinking, their flirting with the opposite sex—apart from two girls in the corner, busy studying something on an iPad. They kept looking up at Dan, then down at the screen.

Probably wanted it to be him, so they could tell all their friends they were the first ones to spot the Lyndford Strangler.

"Nah, thin the face down a bit, and it's Noel," he heard Dan say, and indeed he was right. Those e-fit pictures could look like anyone if you wanted them to.

On Sunday night Dan had been asleep at his grandmother's house, knocked out by too many glasses of whisky.

Most importantly, Dan was his friend, not a murderer. And this wasn't like the people of Cromwell Street who used to wave to Fred West every morning. He *knew* Dan, inside and out.

And Dan was no killer.

Because if he was, that would mean that he, Steve, was pretty stupid, wouldn't it? After all the programmes he'd watched, to not recognise a serial killer standing in his own backyard.

Alone in bed that night, though, that look of panic on Dan's face kept playing on his mind, over and over.

Chapter Three

Angelika

Friday, 20th February

DCI John Reddick and DI Cara Nolan stood before the pictures of four girls, pasted up on the whiteboard.

Jodie Walker, Leanne Marsh, Kayla Graham, and 'Angelika'.

"I still say it's not the same perp," said DI Nolan, tapping her finger on the photo of the most recent victim, identity unconfirmed apart from a tiny tattoo on her shoulder: a dove, and a name they'd presumed, in the absence of any other information, to be hers. "The calling card is half the bloody point, isn't it? Our man wants us to know it's him."

"Mm-mm. We can't make assumptions, though. He could have been disturbed, not had time for his usual handiwork." Reddick folded his arms. "But, yes, you're probably right." He glanced at his colleague. "You'll make absolutely certain the press don't find out, of course. About the signature, I mean."

Cara Nolan elected not to honour this instruction with verbal assurance; his implication that she might not have already done so was insulting. Reddick should be the one to ensure its secrecy anyway, as solving the case could depend on it; the responsibility was above her pay grade.

"An illegal, then," she said.

"Yep. Well, possibly. Tina says the dental work looks Eastern European. No specific DNA, either; reckon the killer must have been wearing a hazmat suit."

Cara reached out and touched the photo again, running her hand down Angelika's long, fair hair. She'd been pretty. She felt a rush of fury. "Poor kid. Who are you, eh? Who did this to you?"

Reddick's mouth set in a grim line. "Mr Nobody, that's who. We've not got so much as a fingerprint match. No likely lads on any of the girls' social media sites. Tell me, how can some bloke who's never been in trouble with the law come out of nowhere to do all this?"

Chapter Four

Tamsin: The Colleague

Monday, 23rd February 2015

"Have you seen this man?

Wanted in connection with several murders in the area.

Lyndford police are seeking a Caucasian male aged between 35 and 50, with thick, dark brown wavy hair, dark eyes and a square jawline. Could have been seen around the Monk's Park Industrial Estate or the Riverside Walk/Spencer Road area of Lyndford on Tuesday 3rd February or Sunday 15th February 2015."

The Lyndford Echo

At ten to nine that morning, Tamsin Verden was possibly the only person at the *Lyndford Echo* who wasn't joining in one of the conversations buzzing around the building about the latest gruesome discovery.

Tamsin had much more salubrious things on her mind. On Friday night she'd finally got it together with Jake Fallon, after months of anticipation.

Workplace attractions were so difficult; people worried about gossip, about management disapproval but, just when she'd begun to despair, he'd broken through his 'work and love don't mix' barrier (for he'd confirmed this as the reason for his reticence), and accompanied her home after the Friday night office drinking session in the King's Head.

Everyone at the *Echo* had been exhausted by five o'clock on that particular Friday afternoon. The e-fit picture of the Lyndford Strangler had been published for the first time the night before, and, despite the article bearing the police hotline number, the paper was inundated with calls.

It seemed every person in the county wanted to be the one to catch him, and Helen Morse, Editor in Chief, was no exception.

"Wouldn't it put us on the map if a call generated by one of our articles led to his capture? Come on, chaps, let's make it happen—all hands on deck!"

Every department had helped with the influx of calls, from Tamsin and her colleagues in Human Resources, to Jake's IT office in the basement, where he worked with just one assistant.

A voluntary skeleton staff remained behind after five, to man the phones until midnight. Not the 'in crowd', though, for whom Friday night in the King's Head was a standard. Sadly, no one in the Human Resources department boasted membership of this elite group, which consisted of newsroom staff and management, along with the chosen few who had friends in those departments. Tamsin had tried walking through the newsroom late in the afternoon, chatting to people, in the hope that someone would say, 'hey, we're all going for a drink, d'you fancy coming?', but it was such a bloody *clique* that no one ever did.

Jake was always asked along. Every Friday, she hoped he might ask her. Every Friday she was disappointed, but of course it wasn't his place to do so. His own invitation came from the Queen Bee herself: Rachel, a snarky bitch who strode around with pencils stuck in her super messy half-up, half-down hairdo (how much of a pose was that?). Then there was her sidekick: flashy, handsome Sanjay. They sat at the top of the office social hierarchy, deciding who was 'in' and who was 'out'. That was how it seemed to Tamsin, anyway.

The reason for Jake's open invitation was obvious—Rachel was after him. She was so blatant it was pathetic. Every time Tamsin looked through the window of the newsroom, she could see Jake bent over her desk. Silly cow must keep summoning him to her side. Still, who cared now, eh? It wasn't Rachel he'd gone home with on Friday night!

Tamsin had been at the *Echo* for about four weeks before her eyes met Jake's across a crowded room. Until that day she'd had her head down, learning her job, too busy to suss out the talent. But when he arrived in HR to fix someone else's problem, their eyes met, and that was that. That magic connection. Twice more, she'd looked up and caught him checking her out, and he stopped to look back at her, with that gorgeous half smile, when he left the room.

After that, she made it her business to seek him out. Luckily, she was pretty damn useless when it came to technology, so she had cause to nip down to IT several times a week. Every time, the *frisson* between them grew stronger; it was there in the way they looked at each other, in the way he took such care with her queries, making sure that she understood exactly what he was telling her, never getting impatient when she admitted her lack of technical prowess; if anything, it became a bit of a joke between them.

"Tear-your-hair-out alert!" she'd say, as she entered the IT room. Or, "Yoo-hoo, it's your favourite Luddite!"

"What, again?" Jake would say, laughing. "What wrong buttons have you pressed this time, eh? I'm surprised your computer doesn't blow up!"

She'd gaze around at all the screens and keyboards in the little room where Jake worked, so far away from the chaotic glamour of the newsroom, and say something like, "You've done well, Jake—got yourself your very own man-cave!", or "Do you mastermind future moon landings from here?"

Jake loved her quips. Okay, so she practiced them at home. Nothing wrong with that.

At Christmas time she gave him a special card, i.e., not one out of the Morrisons box of fifty that she bought for everyone else. Inside she wrote, *Thanks for all your help, and sorry for being such a klutz! Tamsin x*

She gave him an expensive pen in a velvet-lined gift box, engraved with his name. *Some people still write in longhand! Your favourite Luddite x*

The next day she came to work to find a box of Ferrero Rocher on her desk. The card said, *Thanks for the pen, and I'm happy to help! Jake x*

He hadn't bought anyone else in HR a present. Tamsin ate one chocolate every night, and thought of him buying them, thinking of her, while she did so. She treasured that one kiss after his name, most of all.

Jake was a favourite in the office. His easy manner was a hit with everyone, but whenever he had cause to come up to HR, he talked to her more than anyone else.

Her colleagues noticed it, too.

"I think someone likes you!" the supervisor, Kim, would say, with a wink.

Every day she waited for him to say something, anything that would push their relationship up a notch. *To ask her out.* They chatted when they saw each other in the corridor, she sent him funny cartoons and memes via email, which he said really brightened up his day.

She grew so tired of waiting for something to happen. In despair, she sought the male point of view from Brandon, the young psychology graduate who she'd befriended as the 'new boy' in her department; she cornered him by the filing cabinets while everyone else was at lunch.

When she said, "Can I ask you for the male point of view on something?" he shrank back and looked around, as if hoping the question wasn't aimed at him.

She laughed. "Don't look so scared!"

"I don't know anything about clothes," he said, immediately, "and please don't ask me if you look fat; my girlfriend's always doing that."

"Oh dear!" Tamsin said, smiling to put him at his ease.

He relaxed. "Yeah, the thing is, if I tell her she doesn't she says I'm lying, and if I tell her she does she bursts into tears and refuses to go out of the house."

"Well, don't worry, it's nothing like that." Tamsin gave him a brief outline of her problem. "The thing is, I know he likes me," she said, leaning against a desk and folding her arms. "You don't get that wrong, do you?"

"Yeah, I've seen you chatting."

"Mm, everyone keeps mentioning it." She smiled. "So why won't he ask me out?"

Brandon opened a drawer and leafed through the manila folders inside. "Perhaps he's got a rule about not getting involved with workmates. Lots of people feel like that, I think—and Kim told me that it's actually frowned upon, unofficially."

Tamsin groaned. "Oh, no! It's such a waste, though, isn't it, if you've met someone you really like. What can I do? Brandon, help me!" She laughed, trying not to sound too desperate. "You're a guy, what would make you take the plunge?"

That worked; he smiled, and she felt he was really giving the question some thought. "You could catch him outside work. When he's had a few drinks. Women don't realise—it's nerve-wracking making the first move. Hey—they all go to the King's Head after work on Friday, don't they? Sanjay asked me down once, but I was already going out."

How come Brandon got invited but she didn't? He'd only worked there two months! "But I haven't got anyone to go with; I can't just turn up. Would you come with me?"

He shut the drawer and laughed. "Well, that wouldn't help, would it? It might look like we're together, then he definitely wouldn't make a move."

Although Tamsin assured him that male and female colleagues went out for drinks together all the time, Brandon couldn't be persuaded.

Still, faint heart never won fair IT manager. She would stride in like she had a right to be there, because she did, even if no one had invited her; it was just a pub, wasn't it? So what if she wasn't part of the clique?

At first, she felt ridiculous, sure everyone was staring at her, Billie No-Mates who'd arrived uninvited. She ordered a glass of wine and stood at the bar checking her watch every few minutes, looking at the door, as if she was waiting for someone. To her enormous relief, one of the delivery men came up to the bar and started chatting to her, then invited her to sit down at his table (seeing as her friend had let her down!), after which his crew started buying her drinks.

That night, everyone seemed anxious to imbibe as much as they could in as little time as possible, and Tamsin joined in. Events became hazy, fast; she remembered Rachel and Sanjay and some of the other trendies coming over, and then, *then*, there was Jake, just when she thought she'd engineered the opportunity for nothing.

He wandered through the door with the top button of his white shirt undone and his jacket slung over his shoulder. His eyes looked as though he hadn't slept for a week, his gorgeous thick, dark hair tousled, as though he'd been running his fingers through it in despair all afternoon.

He looked like a harassed news reporter from a 1950s film, not an IT brainbox. She wanted him so, so badly.

"Jakey!" called out Rachel. "Over here! We've got you a pint in!"

Jake looked over, distractedly, wearily, until his eyes fell on his friends. He raised his arm in acknowledgement and, as he did so, he noticed Tamsin sitting there.

She put her hand to her cheek, ashamed of how hot and flushed she felt after four Bacardi and Cokes. No matter; Jake's face broke into a smile as he saw her, his gorgeous eyes crinkling up, as though laughing at a private joke.

Their private joke. *Yes*, her eyes said to him. *I'm here.*

The joy she felt on waking was better than anything Tamsin had ever felt, in all her thirty-two years.

She snuggled into that warm cocoon of contentment and let her eyes open gradually. Everything was perfect; she didn't even have to make the morning dash to empty her bladder, because she'd awoken at five o'clock to nip to the loo. She'd taken two paracetamol and drunk more water to stave off the hangover while he slept peacefully on, not stirring as she moved around him. How she'd longed to kiss him as he lay there, with his head on her pillow, but she'd resisted the temptation; just looking at him, knowing he was there, at last, was enough. She'd climbed back into bed, carefully, and curled back into her normal sleeping position, facing away from him. Just in case she snored in her sleep. Ever since an ex had told her, years ago, that she sometimes did, Tamsin was paranoid about doing so in the presence of a new lover.

Now, as the few minutes of netherworld between sleep and wakefulness seeped away, she cupped her hand over her mouth and breathed into it to make sure she didn't need to clean her teeth again before she woke him; no, it was okay. A good gargle with the Listerine after cleaning them at five a.m. had worked its magic.

She reached for her phone on the bedside table. Nine-thirty. Not too early.

Tamsin turned over.

The loving smile froze on her face.

The sight of the empty pillow beside her was like a kick in the stomach.

She sat up and looked around the room, frantically; his clothes were gone! As she bounded out of bed—yes, yes, surely he must be in the shower, or downstairs making coffee; never mind, they could always go back to bed again later—she saw the note propped up on her dressing table.

Got text from my dad at 7.30 reminding me that him & Mum are visiting for weekend, had to get home to tidy flat! Didn't like to wake you. Sorry to rush off! CU Monday. J x

Tamsin sank back onto the edge of the bed with a thump, the note still in her hand. So the fantasies she'd weaved in the early hours of them spending Saturday and Sunday together, walking in the park, talking about their lives, making glorious love over and over, cementing their relationship, would not become reality this weekend.

Disappointment flooded over her.

There had been too many, over the past ten years.

No, stop it, she told herself. He had a perfectly good reason for leaving. The note was sweet, kind, and it had a kiss at the end. Everything was okay. Last night had been more than wonderful. It wasn't just the way he'd responded to her in the pub (and she wished she could remember more about that; they'd both been pretty hammered). It wasn't even the fabulous, wild sex, it was the between times, when they lay in each other's arms, at perfect peace.

She lay back and hugged his pillow to her face, enjoying the faint scent of him, and smiled to herself, letting out a little moan or two when she thought of the way he'd taken her, roughly, urgently; no, he hadn't been the gentle lover she'd imagined, but she wasn't disappointed. The build-up of passion between them over the past few months was such that there was no need for wooing and long drawn out foreplay. The first time was quick, sudden, up against the wall as soon as they walked into her flat. Then they'd wandered into her bedroom, stripped off, and fallen on to the bed. He'd kissed her so hard that she was sure she must have bite marks over her body, then he'd clasped both of her tiny, fragile wrists above her head in his one, strong hand, so tightly that she couldn't do anything but surrender to him, and she'd loved every minute, lying back and letting the sensations overwhelm her.

The frenzy of their coming together left them both exhausted. Breathless.

"You didn't ask me my 'safe word'!" she said, running her fingers up his chest.

"Eh?"

"The way you held my hands above my head." She giggled. "Like, I suddenly shout 'cheesecake!' or something, and you let me go!"

He laughed. "I don't know anything about all that. You could have wriggled out if you wanted to, anyway."

As if she would ever want to wriggle away from Jake.

"I was only kidding," she'd said, as she wrapped her arm around him, stroking his back. She looked up at him. "At last. I was starting to wonder if this would ever happen."

He'd kissed her on the nose. "Well, I think it was pretty much on the cards that it would at some point!"

That made her so happy. "You felt it too," she said, nestling her head against his chest. "That connection between us. Sometimes you just know, don't you?"

He stroked her head. "You do."

"You wonder, though, don't you?" she said. "You wonder if it's your imagination. But I knew there was something between us."

He didn't speak, just carried on stroking her hair. He didn't *need* to speak. Their bodies had communicated in so many more ways than mere words.

Everything felt so *right*. She was tempted to talk more, to discuss every single time they'd chatted at work, tell him how she'd felt, hear him tell her, too, but she could tell he was sleepy, and of course men didn't feel the urge to talk about their feelings in the way that women did.

Didn't want to put him off. Men hated women who prattled on. That he was there at all said everything.

Even though he hadn't stayed.

By eleven-thirty she'd showered, washed her hair, eaten breakfast and tidied the flat. The time was right. Not too early, not too desperate, but not too late, as if she didn't care (or, worse, as if she was the sort of slob who slept in until mid-afternoon).

She picked up her phone to text.

Hey you... hope you're having a great time with your folks (smiley face) *Still coming down from last night* (kissy face) *Drop me a text or give me a ring when you have a moment xx*

Exactly the right tone. She was pleased with herself.

Then she panicked. He'd never given her his phone number. She'd nicked it from the HR records. Oh well—

The reply came just a few minutes later.

Gd morning! Out shopping w M & D. Last night gr8. CU Mon, J (smiley face).

She was a little disappointed that the text was not more personal, but never mind; he was unlikely to write something sexy or romantic with his mum peeping over his shoulder. She wondered what they'd be doing all weekend; she knew so little about him. But there was plenty of time to find that out, to find out everything.

He hadn't questioned her having his number, anyway.

And now she had more than just hopes and fantasies to sustain her until Monday morning.

Jake wasn't in his man cave; Dev, his assistant, thought he'd nipped up to the newsroom.

Tamsin's heart was beating faster as she entered the lift. When the lift doors opened, though, she saw that various people from all departments were in there, talking about the latest grisly murder, discussing any information gleaned from the Friday phone calls. Angelika, they'd called the girl; they'd been talking about it in HR. Tamsin closed her eyes. Yes, it was tragic, but she didn't want to think about bad things this morning. She just wanted to see Jake.

And there he was, at the end of the room, chatting away with Rachel. Jealousy stabbed at her heart; why hadn't he come down to see her, or rung her or texted her, first thing? Instead, he was talking to Rachel.

(He could have texted her this morning, on the way to work. To say he was looking forward to seeing her, anything.)

(Or last night, after his parents left. Was he really too tired even to send a text?)

Bloody show-off Rachel. What was that sticking out of her stupid hairdo this morning, a cocktail stirrer? Looked like it. Was she flirting with him?

Stop it. Don't be silly. Du-uh—she's probably got an IT problem!

Tamsin put on her best smile and walked the length of the long room, willing him to look up and notice her.

When she was about ten yards away, he did so. He smiled, and the sun came out.

"Hey, you," she said, as she approached them.

Rachel looked up, too. "Hi, Tamsin; you after the latest on Angelika, like everyone else?" She shook her head. "It's all I can think about today, it's such a shock, that poor girl, and so soon after Kayla." She pushed a picture over the desk. "I hope they find that bastard soon, and skin him alive."

"Oh—yes, it's awful, isn't it?" Tamsin's eyes swivelled to Jake. He was no longer looking at her, his eyes fixed firmly on Rachel's computer screen. "Can I have a word, Jake?"

"Sure!" He grinned. "What have you done this time, eh? Don't tell me, you've accidentally deleted the last ten years' HR files, right?"

"No!" She laughed, looking into his eyes, trying desperately to convey that she wanted to talk to him alone.

"Good! Is it urgent?" She noticed him glance at his watch; that lovely, strong forearm covered in dark hair, those hands that had roved over her body so expertly, that hand holding her wrists so tightly, as if he wanted to *possess* her—

"Tamsin?"

Loud laughter across the room jolted her back into the moment.

"Oh—no!" She smiled at him. "I do need to see you, though."

He frowned and grimaced. "Ouch! Honey, I'm snowed six feet under already this morning; do you want to send me an email with a brief outline? I'm trying to get to everyone this morning but it'll help if I know what it is; I might be able to email you back the answer."

(*You can come up to help Rachel but I have to email?*)

"Oka-*aay*." For a moment she despaired, but then she understood. Of course. Now, even more than before, he wanted to make sure no one knew about them. Cocking her head to one side, she gave him a subtle, sexy (she hoped) wink. "I'll go back to my desk and email you now."

She teetered back off down the room, hoping he was enjoying the sight; her black trousers and high-heeled boots did wonders for her rear view.

Carefully, she composed her email:

Good morning, Gorgeous! Totally understand why you did the 'just colleagues' bit just now, don't worry—makes it more fun, doesn't it? Love a bit of secrecy and intrigue! Anyway, are you free for lunch? We could meet somewhere NOT the KH; I'll be wearing a pink carnation and carrying a copy of the Lyndford Echo!

Half an hour later, he replied:

Can I take a rain check on that? I'm up against it for the next few days like you wouldn't believe, doubt I'll be taking any lunch breaks this week. I'll be staying until at least six tonight as it is! (face with downturned mouth)

Not quite the reply she was hoping for. She tried again.

Oh, poor you! So did you have a fun weekend with your folks?

Yeah, it was good (smiley face).

She replied immediately:

Great stuff! Okay, then, how about you come round to mine one night for dinner? I could cook, we can watch a film and chill. Sound good?

She waited another half hour for a reply.

It does sound very tempting, but to be honest I'm busy all week, and the thought of it is already making me feel exhausted. I've only got one night with nothing arranged; I'll need to catch up on my sleep. Sorry!

This time, Tamsin didn't tell herself it was okay. Was the bastard brushing her off?

A rush of tears flooded into her eyes, blurring them. All around her the HR department was going about its usual business, keyboards tapping, phones ringing, while she sat at her desk in her private hell.

Fuck it, she thought. *No more playing it cool.*

Jake, has something happened? I thought you loved Friday night as much as I did. You said you knew we would get together eventually. Well, we have; so what's happened between then and now? Is it because we work together? If so, I can be really discreet. No one will ever know.

Twenty minutes went by.

It's not that. Yes, Friday night was great.

So what is it?

Look, we spent a great night together. This week I'm very, very busy. That's all.

Okay, so how about the weekend? Next week?

Tamsin, I've got a hell of a lot on my plate this morning. I really can't do this now.

Why was this all going so wrong?

Do what?

Half an hour she waited. Nothing. She tried again

What's going on? I thought you meant everything you said.

Everything what?

That I was so gorgeous, that you were so pleased we'd come together at last, that you'd fancied me for ages.

You are gorgeous, Tamsin, I had fancied you for ages, and yes, I was pleased that it happened.

So?

So what?

So why are you giving me the fucking brush off?

During the twenty minutes Tamsin waited for a reply she wished, a hundred times, that she hadn't used the 'F' word.

I'm not giving you any brush off.

Okay, so when shall we get together?

Twenty minutes.

Tamsin, please understand. You're an amazing girl. We were attracted to each other, we spent a fantastic night together. I thought you were cool about it.

Slowly, the reality dawned on her.

I am. I just thought it was the beginning of something that would be great for both of us. I thought that if you fancied someone and you had real chemistry between you, it meant more than just some sordid one night stand.

This time she didn't get a reply until the afternoon. At lunchtime she walked past the King's Head, where she saw him deep in conversation with Sanjay, over pints and sandwiches.

So snowed under with work that he wasn't taking lunch breaks, then.

When Tamsin got back to her desk after lunch she couldn't concentrate on work, and just sat, staring at the meaningless, unimportant *nothing* on her computer screen, willing herself not to cry.

At two-fifteen another email appeared.

It was entitled *Forgive Me*, and her heart leapt. Sanjay was always nice to her; perhaps he'd told Jake he was acting like an idiot. It was all going to be okay.

She opened up the email.

I'm sorry, Tamsin. I read the signals wrong. Yes, I find you attractive, yes I like you, yes, I've enjoyed our little flirtation over the last few months. But I'm not looking for a relationship right now. Sorry if I've hurt your feelings. Still friends, right? Jake x

She didn't reply. She didn't trust herself to do so. The pain and disappointment were too great; she wanted to scream and cry and shout obscenities, email all those obscenities to him, too, tell him she'd thought of nothing but him for months and how dare he, how *dare* he play with her feelings like this? But most of all she wanted to turn the clock back and make Friday night not have happened, so that she would still be travelling in glorious anticipation, instead of reaching her destination and finding nothing but a shitty, empty hole in the ground.

And *what* a brush-off. What a crappy, insulting, *cliché* of a brush-off. Anyone born earlier than two hours ago knew that 'I'm not looking for a relationship right now' was a euphemism for 'I was only after a shag'.

She stood up. "I'm feeling really sick and ill," she announced. "Kim, is it okay if I go home?"

Kim looked up, surprised. "Oh—yes, yes, of course, love. You get yourself off, and we'll see you tomorrow; phone me if it gets any worse, won't you?"

When she got home, she wept until her eyes were red, swollen and sore. Her heart was broken. How could she bear to go into work every day, knowing it had finished, run its course, knowing she would see him but he would no longer be sending her those little messages with his eyes?

Because there was no reason to flirt with someone you'd already slept with and didn't want to sleep with again.

Been there, done that, game over.

The more she thought about it as the night wore on, the more confused she felt. How could someone who'd seemed so warm, so friendly, such a thoroughly nice guy, use her like this for his own ends? That person who'd emailed her—that wasn't the cute, funny Jake she'd laughed and joked with. That was a hard-hearted brute who didn't care about her feelings; thinking back, she realised that the final email was probably a result of his conversation with Sanjay, who was a bit of a 'player'. Sanjay had probably given him a half hour masterclass in how to let a girl down gently without her making a fuss and slagging you off to her friends.

The kiss-off email was the only one that had ended with his name, and an 'x'.

It was almost like he was two people. The one who'd charmed her for all these months, then Mr Ice Man.

He'd deceived her, utterly and completely.

All that, just for a shag? For an ego boost? Or did he enjoy building someone up only to break them down?

She thought about their one night together. The sex had been almost *rough*. At the time she'd found it exciting, evidence of his passion for her, and thought more tenderness might come with time, but as a one-off it made her feel like an *object*.

And had he really been so sweet afterwards? When she replayed the whole night in her mind, she forced herself to admit that it was she who'd said all the romantic stuff. All he'd done was agree.

He'd *used* her, so cleverly.

Now she began to wonder exactly who the real Jake Fallon was.

Chapter Five

Ellie

Fagin's Club, Spencer Road, Lyndford

Friday, 17th April

The graffiti-covered door of the lavatory cubicle creaked loudly as Ellie Kane wrenched it open, stopping to peel off a sheet of toilet paper that had attached itself to the platform sole of her shoe. She staggered out, pulling her dress down over her hips, and squinted at her reflection in the dirty, rust-stained mirror.

Bloody hell, she looked slaughtered.

"State of me!" she said, out loud, and giggled.

The strip lights not only made her skin look like *cack*, but also showed Fagin's ladies' toilet facilities in all their grubby glory, and she wondered, for a moment, what the hell she was doing there.

Friday night, that was what. Her favourite night of the week, when anything could happen.

Lurching towards the basins she dropped her bag into one of them. Yuck, hadn't noticed it was all wet. Never mind. She rifled through the bag, looking for her make-up. Cover stick, yeah, there it was. Kohl pencil. Bollocks, couldn't find her lipstick. Or her hairbrush.

The outer door opened and slammed shut.

"Have you got a hairbrush I can borrow?" she asked the girl who'd just walked in, but the words came out all wrong, slurred, and the girl just gave her a weird look and banged into one of the cubicles. Stupid question anyway. She had a platinum blonde mohawk, spiked up with hairspray. Like she would use a hairbrush.

Did your mum get raped by a cockatoo?

Ellie giggled again, fluffed up her long, dark hair with her fingers, and teetered out of the toilets into a dimly lit corridor. Red walls. More graffiti. Lots of doors. So how did she get back to the bar? She didn't know this place, hadn't been there before. Full of punks, emos, goths and the odd biker, not her scene at all. Couldn't even remember getting there. She'd started the night in the Crown and Cushion with the girls but it soon turned into one of *those* evenings, when they bumped into *everyone* they knew, and she'd ended up veering off to the King's Head with Shaun who she knew from college (and who was kind of hot), and a couple of his mates whom she didn't know, then they'd gone to another pub she'd never been to before. She'd done a couple of lines with Shaun in the toilet and shared a spliff outside, then they wandered up to Fagin's.

Wouldn't be seen dead in there if she was sober.

She wasn't dressed right, stood out like a little girl who'd fallen down the wrong rabbit hole in her clubbing dress and heels. Bloody cold, too; somewhere along the way she'd lost her jacket.

She tried a couple of doors but they were locked, then stumbled into the gents; the stink of urine, the male laughter and shouts of 'Come in, don't be shy!' sent her reeling back into the corridor. Ah, noise, up at the far end; yes, that must be it. She pushed open the door. Oh. Not sure. It was a bar, but was it the one she'd been in before? It seemed bigger. Perhaps she'd just entered from the wrong side. Couldn't see Shaun and his mates. Hmmm.

Some old Prodigy song blasted out. The room smelled of old beer and patchouli oil. Sticky floor. No seats, but never mind, she could lean on the bar, have another drink while she waited for Shaun. He was bound to come up to get a drink sooner or later, he'd been necking the Jäger Bombs all night. Never known anyone drink so quick. 'Cept her, maybe! Ellie giggled to herself, and looked up at the blackboard behind the bar. *Ooh* look, double vodkas for one pound forty a throw. *Fucking A!*

She ordered one, with a shot of lemonade (fifty pence extra and no bloody ice), and drank it as she scanned the room through the darkness. She wandered around, bag over her arm, drink in hand, but couldn't find him. Lots of people, but not partying, just drinking and talking. Mind you, who could dance to this music? Hmm, were there two bars? Must be; she couldn't see Shaun's mates, either, but, then again, she couldn't remember exactly what they looked like.

She opened her purse. *Fuck.* Only a tenner left and she needed that for a taxi. Where was bloody Shaun? He said he'd see her alright if she ran out of cash.

Best to stay at the bar, then they'd spot her.

A guy with dreads was getting a drink. Combat jacket and patterned trousers. Probably skint, looked a right dirty old New Age traveller type. Worth a try, though.

She edged up to him, and smiled.

He smiled back. Yeah, definitely worth a try.

"You wouldn't buy a drink for a hard-up student, would you?"

Unfortunately, she fell off one of her heels whilst making this request, burped loudly, clutched onto his arm for support, and some of his beer slopped down his jacket. He looked at her with distaste.

"Hard-up student, yeah. Wankered chav, no."

Oh, well.

His voice was really posh; funny, that, when he was so scruffy.

Ellie looked around; not so many people there as earlier, she was sure. Must be getting late. What to do? She looked at her empty glass. No one to talk to and no money left. Might as well go home, then.

Ellie staggered out, found herself in another dark corridor and pushed the bar on a fire exit. The cold night air hit her. Eh? Where the fuck was she? She'd stepped out onto an unlit, empty side street, not one she recognised. Backs of buildings, wheelie bins. She stood on the narrow pavement, feeling through her bag for cigarettes. Now, where was Fagin's, exactly? Far end of Spencer Road, wasn't it? So, was she round the back or at the side?

Lighting her cigarette took a couple of attempts, and she heard her bag plummet to the ground just as she managed to draw the much-needed nicotine into her lungs. *Bugger it!* The strap had snapped undone and half the contents spilled onto the pavement: make-up, tissues, Tampax, perfume. Hoisting the shoestring strap of her dress back onto her shoulder, she crouched to pick her things up, shoving them back into her bag with the hand that wasn't holding the cigarette, swaying on her heels as she stood up.

God, it was bloody cold! Ellie wrapped her arms around herself, and shivered. Quiet for a Friday, too; must be later than she thought. Usually the streets were noisy until at least midnight. But there weren't so many pubs and takeaways down this end of Spencer Road, were there? *Takeaways.* Oh, for some chips—wow, she was *starving!*

Hadn't had any dinner before she came out, and the appetite-suppressing effects of the Charlie she'd snorted earlier had completely worn off now. Home, pyjamas on, cheese on toast under the grill. Bliss! Or her mum might have left some dinner out for her.

Gotta get home. Start walking. The thought of being warm, at home, sitting in bed, watching telly while she ate her supper, spurred her on. She rounded the corner, quickening her pace.

Another side street. More bins and backs of buildings. This time, though, she could see a main road at the end. Street lights and traffic. *Phew.* Must be Spencer Road. Right. Call a cab. She teetered along, fumbling in her bag, cigarette in mouth.

Shit. *No, no, please no!* Where the hell was her phone? Don't say she'd lost that, too! Oh no, no, *no!* Her whole LIFE was in that phone!

She rounded the corner onto the main road and crouched down on the pavement, scrabbling frantically through her belongings, drawing deeply on her cigarette. It had to be there somewhere; how many times had she been unable to find something when she was pissed, and then in the morning found it exactly where she thought it wasn't? *Right.* She emptied the bag out on the pavement, kneeling under the street light. Checked all the inside compartments. No. It wasn't there. It really fucking wasn't there.

Ellie piled her belongings back into her bag, dragged herself over to a wall and began to cry. She was miles from home, freezing cold and she'd lost her phone. She couldn't walk all the way, she'd get hypothermia or something, her shoes were killing her already and it was dangerous, too, her mum would go mad. *Think. Think.* She could go into a kebab shop and ask to ring from there. If she could remember the cab numbers; damn, she hadn't got a clue what they were, they were programmed into her phone. There would be a number on the wall in a kebab shop. But they might not let her use their phone if she wasn't spending, and she only had enough money for the taxi. Time and a half after midnight. They might take pity on her, but those Greek or Turkish guys (or whatever bloody nationality they were) were so flippin' lecherous. Just 'cause their women went around in veils and all that, they thought English girls were fair game.

Anyway, she couldn't see any kebab shops. Just a couple of restaurants, and she was too pissed to go in and ask.

Phone box. She could find a phone box. There were cab numbers in phone boxes, weren't there? But what if there wasn't one for miles?

Ellie felt suddenly very, very vulnerable indeed, out there alone in the cold, dark night. If only she was wearing a jacket, she'd feel better; her pale blue dress was skin tight, short and low cut. Her shoes were bright red. What if someone saw her walking along and thought she was a prostitute? For the first time, she understood what her mother meant about going out dressed in her underwear. She hugged herself, rubbing her hands up and down her arms to create a little warmth.

Footsteps. A man turned the corner, out of the side street she'd just walked down. She froze. What if he was a mad rapist, or something? Or a nutter? As he drew nearer, his feet the only sound apart from the occasional car whizzing past, she dared herself to glance up. He looked okay. Older. Well, not *old*, but not like Shaun and the guys she hung out with. He looked smart. Normal. Decent. Probably just some bloke walking home after a night out with a mate, going home to his wife and kids.

"'Scuse me," she called out as he walked past. "Have you got a phone I could use? I need to call a cab to get home, and I've lost mine!"

He stopped and turned back, smiled at her. "Sure." He reached into his pocket. "Dial-A-Cab okay? Do you want me to ring for you?"

"Oh, yes please!" Ellie smiled with relief. Brilliant! She'd be home within twenty minutes, with luck. Home, and safe, and *warm*.

"Okay. Now, where to?"

"Cranston Avenue."

"Right." He tapped a few keys and raised the phone to his year. "Hi, can I have a cab from Spencer Road, by the alleyway that runs down the side of Fagin's club, please? Yeah, that's the one. Straight away, yeah. Smith. Cheers, that's great, thanks."

He clicked his phone off and put it back in his pocket. "I always say 'Smith' when they ask me my name, it's easier, isn't it? It'll be here in five minutes, anyway, love."

"Oh, thanks *ever so* much," Ellie said, weak with relief. "I was beginning to think I'd never get home."

"Happy to help a damsel in distress!"

Ellie laughed. "My knight in shining armour!" Stupid thing to say. Sounded like a come-on. After tonight she was never getting this pissed ever again, she really wasn't.

He took a step closer. "What are you doing out here on your own, at this time of the night—sorry, morning?"

"Oh, I mislaid my mates! You know how it is."

He laughed. He seemed really nice. "Good night, then? Had a few sherbets?"

"Yeah! I don't know how many; that's bad, isn't it?"

"Ah, you're only young once." He glanced up and down the road. "Do you want me to wait with you? Doesn't seem a very good idea, you standing out here like this on your own."

"Would you? That'd be great." Ellie shivered again. "I feel a bit scared, to be honest."

"Not a problem; bit of luck the taxi shouldn't be too long. Hey, you're shivering—sorry, where are my manners?" He shrugged off his jacket and handed it to her. "Here."

As she draped it round her shoulders Ellie sighed with relief. Everything felt better now that she was warm (and covered up). "Thanks *so* much. I was bloody freezing!"

He stuck his hands in the pockets of his jeans, and grinned. "Well, you girls, you will go out in your underwear, won't you?"

"That's what my mum says!"

They both laughed, and the Lyndford Strangler moved closer, smiling at her under the dim glow of the street lamp.

There would be no taxi; he'd only pretended to make the call.

"Your mum's right," he said, as he edged his arm along the wall behind her. "You can't be too careful, out here all alone, can you? Especially not these days."

Chapter Six

Dorothy: The Mother

Clovis Court, Lyndford

Friday, 17th April

Dorothy Beck had suffered a shock that afternoon, and she still wasn't at all sure what to do about it.

All evening she'd been trying to settle into her book, a soothing piece of nostalgia set in a Suffolk village during the Second World War, but she kept turning a page only to discover that she hadn't taken in any of the words on the previous one.

She knew why not. Orlando had told her he was going out for his Friday night drink with Colin, but she wasn't sure he was telling her the truth.

Until that afternoon, she'd never doubted anything he told her.

The previous evening he'd set off to his metal detecting club. Every Thursday night, without fail, Orlando attended the club meetings in an upstairs room at the Swan pub, out on the other side of Lyndford town centre. Or so she'd thought.

He'd arrived home later than normal, saying he'd been for a pint with the other members. At the time she'd hardly looked up from her television programme—but that afternoon she'd bumped into club chairman Ray Goosey when she was out shopping, and he'd asked her why Orlando didn't go to the meetings any more.

"Haven't seen him for over three months," Ray said, sadly. "Shame, he was always one of our most enthusiastic members. Hope he hasn't got bored with us!"

The conversation with Ray Goosey brought to the fore something that had troubled her for the past few months.

She suspected her son was hiding something from her.

His 'pint or two' on a Friday night lasted much longer than it used to. Until about six months ago he'd returned by ten at the very latest, often with chips, a naughty treat; there was something rather fun about eating them straight from the polystyrene trays. Not as good as the newspaper of her youth, but never mind. Her parents, dead for over ten years now, would have been shocked by such slovenly behaviour, which made it even more appealing.

He hadn't brought chips home for months now. She was always in bed by the time he got home, anyway.

Now there was his attendance at the metal detecting club, or lack thereof. Last night he'd set off at six thirty-five precisely, with his equipment and the diary in which he itemised when and where he found his various artefacts.

Orlando always set off at six thirty-five because (he said) it took ten minutes to drive to the Swan, and he liked to get there exactly fifteen minutes before the meeting started to park the car, make a cup of coffee from the tray provided, and lay claim to his favourite seat in the room.

Dorothy and her son both had a 'thing' about sitting in their favourite seats, wherever they went; it was a mutual idiosyncrasy and one of their private jokes.

"Sorry, Mum, gotta go; if I get there one minute later, Monsieur Von Tedium with the Fisher F4 will have already plonked his vast and terrifying behind on my chair!"

It was all lies, though. She knew Monsieur Von Tedium existed because she'd met him at the club's open day last summer, but, unless Ray Goosey had been lying, he'd been free to use Orlando's chair for months.

Dorothy had always thought that complete honesty with each other (they called it *transparency* these days, Oliver told her, with a twinkle in his eye) was the cornerstone of their life together. That, and adherence to their routines.

They didn't stick to routine for the sake of it, because that way lay dullness and possible insanity. Modifications were accepted into their daily regimes when necessary, though life had altered little in the twenty-six years since Orlando started his job at the DSS, now the Department of Work and Pensions (as a behind the scenes man; he never dealt with the public). The job meant flexi-time, but he liked to keep the same hours each day: eight-thirty to four-thirty, with half an hour for lunch.

Orlando had risen through the ranks slowly to become an Executive Officer and supervisor of his section, but he supervised in a mild, 'now, what do we all think about this?' way only, and didn't want to progress any higher. Too much responsibility, and he didn't need the money.

Dorothy teased Orlando about the boring image of the lifetime Civil Service employee, and he played it up to amuse her, talking in a monotone about paperclips. They prided themselves on their lively minds. She'd had a stab at learning Italian, just for the hell of it, and for a while Orlando went to car mechanics evening classes, not only for practical reasons (to save money on garage costs), but because he found the subject interesting. Dorothy had wondered if he might meet a nice girl there; didn't girls join such courses in order to meet men? Or was that just a silly bit of advice from 1960s women's magazines? She feared, however, that her son was too shy around women to make a move. He was a nice-looking young man, tall and dark, but he let his hair grow too thick and unruly and didn't know how to carry himself; he walked and sat as though his long, lanky limbs had sprouted overnight and he had not yet learned what to do with them. She wasn't sure if she was disappointed or relieved about his apparent invisibility to the opposite sex; she wanted him to have a full life, but dreaded the prospect of him leaving her. Not that Orlando had ever shown signs of wanting to move out. Why would he? There wasn't anything he wanted to do that he couldn't do in their home, or so she'd always thought.

Perhaps there was now, though. Whatever it was he did on Thursday nights, and maybe on Fridays, too.

Dorothy abandoned her book, got up from her chair and went to the sideboard. A nice glass of sherry, perhaps. Yes, why not? She took her glass back to the sofa, stopping on the way to turn the fire on. That was better. Nice and cosy. If only she wasn't so worried about Orlando, she'd feel perfectly content.

What was he hiding?

Orlando didn't lead the sort of life that necessitated secrets.

She remembered something he'd said on the way home from church a few Sundays before, that had made her laugh and laugh at the time.

"I really must break out and do something dreadful soon. Angela Wykes and Mrs Gibson are starting to smile at me when they bring round the collection plate."

Angela Wykes and Mrs Gibson (Christian name unknown) were the two pursed-lipped, flower-arranging stalwarts at St Peter's. To gain their approval, Orlando said, one must lead a life so respectable that one might as well be dead.

"I suppose you could always ask for a second sip of the communion wine," Dorothy suggested.

"No, serious measures are called for, before I get press-ganged into making crosses for Palm Sunday. I think I'll spray paint some rude words in the vestry."

Was he already breaking out and doing dreadful things?

Dorothy couldn't imagine what they might be. Orlando's favourite pastime was fishing; he liked the peace, he said. He caught eels at a place near Peterborough, on occasion, or bream and tench in Norfolk. A solitary pursuit, but he chatted to other anglers now and again, and showed her photos of him holding his catch. She enthused, even though she felt sorry for the fish.

If anyone thought it odd that a man of forty-three still lived with his mother, neither of them cared.

She'd realised a while back that she could remove from the back of her mind the niggling worry about *when Orlando moves out.* His few nervous forays into the world of romance had not come to much, and what would be the point of them both paying a mortgage? Shortly after his thirty-fifth birthday he announced he was having his bedroom redecorated; he chose some devilishly expensive, deep indigo carpet and watered silk wallpaper, and she understood this meant he was going nowhere, and had no intention of ever doing so. His home was there, with her, in the cosy two-bed semi at the bottom of the cul-de-sac in Clovis Court she bought when he was just twenty. Her father had advised her that prices were at all time low, and she should get a foot on the property ladder. He even gave her the deposit.

Buying the house in Clovis Court was the best decision she'd ever made. Security equalled happiness.

Dorothy had observed people who lived scattered lives, and any happiness they gained seemed only fleeting.

Bernard Townsend, Orlando's father, had led a scattered life. Divorces, affairs. Kisses, whispers and lies, bedsit living and temporary jobs.

In 1971 Dorothy was a quietly pretty, and desperately introverted, twenty-year-old (going on fourteen, she once heard her mother say to her father), working as a typist in a small insurance firm. Potter Insurance had looked the same for two decades, with its large wooden desks, big old clunky typewriters and a jangling bell on the front door. Mr Potter himself hadn't revised his behavioural code for two decades, either, and didn't realise that women no longer had to put up with personal comments about their figures and the occasional pat on the bottom.

His friend, door-to-door insurance salesman Bernard Townsend, often popped in for a cup of tea, or a little nip of something stronger. Bernard was equally free with his words, but the other girls in the office said this was a different kettle of fish because he was so handsome, and they grew most excited when he came in. Dorothy thought he was very handsome, too, a bit like Pete Duel from *Alias Smith and Jones*.

One day Bernard Townsend stopped by her desk on his way out, and asked her if she'd like to go for a drink. Dorothy was terrified. She was flattered, and of course his chiselled jawline and practiced smile made her feel quite weak, but she'd never been on a proper date.

"Oh, you lucky, lucky thing!" moaned Janet, who typed at the big table nearest the door and sported the most amazing eye make-up. She and Rosalyn gave her lots of tips on what to wear, what to do, and what to say.

When Bernard Townsend picked her up, she was still more terrified than excited, but he was so smooth, so charming, that her fears melted along with the ice in her first Dubonnet and lemonade.

After the third drink, just when she was beginning to relax and maybe even respond a little to his courting technique, he picked up his cigarettes, wallet and car keys and said he'd better be getting her home, because he didn't want her parents to worry about her.

"If I get you home on time your dad won't mind me taking you out again!" Bernard reassured her, and gave her thigh a quick squeeze that sent little shock waves rushing through her. He smiled at the look of disappointment on her face, and took her chin in his hand, drawing her face close to his for a light kiss on the lips. "I'm serious about you, Dorothy," he said, "and I want to do it right."

He took her out again the following week, to see a film and eat a Chinese meal, but when he picked her up for the third date he asked if she would mind if he entertained her at his flat.

"I'd love to take you somewhere special, but I'm waiting for an important phone call from a big customer—a huge commission, darling." He took her hand. "Which will mean more money to spend on *you*!"

She laughed, feeling gloriously carefree, loved, a real woman at last. "I don't mind where we go," she said, and she meant it.

She didn't notice at first that his 'flat' was actually a bedsit; it was only when she looked around, puzzled, for a door to the bathroom, that he told her that he shared one down the landing, and explained the sofa on which they were sitting was the type that opened up into a bed. His 'kitchen' was nothing more than a kettle on top of a fridge and a little appliance with two electric rings.

"I'm sorry it's a bit bleak," he said, passing her a drink. "That's why I need to make sure I don't miss out on lucrative accounts, so I can move on."

The drink was whisky this time, mixed with ginger ale, and no ice, and it was stronger than she might have liked; after her first sip he laughed at her shocked face and poured in a little more ginger ale. It was still far too strong, but she didn't like to ask for more.

As he cuddled up to her on the hard, uncomfortable sofa (that you could pull out into a bed), he spoke to her of how badly he'd been treated by the wife who divorced him, how she employed a clever lawyer who took his house away, leaving him able to afford only this bedsit.

"That's so awful," she said.

"The only way is up!" He smiled and refilled her glass, and this time he didn't add the extra ginger ale. "All I need is a few top-class customers who'll recommend me to others, a bit of money behind me, then I can rent a flat, or even look around for somewhere else to buy."

"I'm sure you'll do it," she said, gazing into his beautiful, sincere, dark brown eyes. "I should think anyone would want to buy insurance from you." She giggled, surprised at herself; the whisky made her garrulous. "My dad says you have to think positively, then you get what you want!"

"Absolutely!" Bernard Townsend liked that, and clinked his glass against hers. He lounged back, arm snaking along the sofa behind her, his face moving nearer to hers. "If you cut me in half, you'd see 'winner' written all the way through, like a piece of Blackpool rock."

She breathed in his aftershave, and laughed, gaily.

"Have you been to Blackpool?" he asked. "No? Good, bloody awful place! Tell you what, though, the countryside in the North West of England is beautiful. I'll have to take you away to the Lake District for a weekend some time, how do you fancy that?"

Dorothy fancied that a great deal, and Bernard poured her another drink, urging her to enjoy it, relax, while he scoured his bookshelf and boxes for that brochure about hotels in the Lakes. He knew just the place, he said. If she squared it with her parents, he'd book for two months hence, in June, when the weather was better, what did she think?

Dorothy glowed as he outlined this plan. Two months hence—that meant he really was serious. It meant—did it? Oh, did it? —that Bernard was her boyfriend. There had never been anyone she could refer to as *her boyfriend* before; how she'd envied Janet and Rosalyn when they talked about Dave this and Chris that; even at school there'd been girls who were going steady, who said the words 'my boyfriend' twenty times a day and were admired by the quiet ones, like her, who didn't know how to flirt and couldn't imagine a boy ever liking them enough to cast them in the role of girlfriend.

Bernard was not just some boy, though. He was a handsome, experienced, thirty-two–year-old.

"Bernard, I've never had a real boyfriend before, it's lovely." Her silly mouth again, turning her thoughts into words. Bernard turned around from his position crouched over his box of unpacked books, with an amused expression on his face, and laughed.

"Not as lovely as it is to have you as my girlfriend!" He abandoned the search and moved back to the sofa, taking her in his arms. "You're the sweetest thing. Dorothy, will you think I'm crazy if I say that I'm falling in love with you already?"

"I'm falling in love with you, too," she whispered, as he kissed her neck and unbuttoned her blouse.

"You're different from all the other girls," he told her. "They're silly and giggly, but you've got so much more about you. You're a deep thinker, aren't you? I think that's what attracted me to you." He looked up, as if in deep concentration, and clicked his fingers. "Then I realised what it was. We're soul mates; I felt it every time I looked into your eyes. Even before we first talked, isn't that weird?"

"Really?" Dorothy couldn't imagine how he could have known such a thing but the joy she felt in hearing him say so made her want to float up to the ceiling. She slid into his arms in euphoria and joined him in gently shedding their clothes as he whispered how lucky he was to have found her, how they were going to be so, so happy together. When she realised that this was it, that *it* was really going to happen, she stopped for a moment, concerned, her whisky-befuddled mind thinking back, calculating; it was okay, she should be safe, and anyway you couldn't get pregnant the first time, everyone knew that. Nevertheless, she would go to the doctor on Monday to go on the pill. No longer worried, she surrendered to the joy of Bernard's love.

It was only much, much later, as her taxi sped home through the quiet, rain-splattered streets, that she realised Bernard had never received his phone call, the one he'd needed so badly. Oh dear, she did hope it would come tomorrow; she felt humbled, too, that he'd been so caught up in making love to her that he hadn't wanted to spoil the moment by revealing his disappointment.

Twice more, in the following week, she went up to Bernard's bedsit. Each time they had sex on his hard, uncomfortable sofa bed, and each time, blissful in his arms, she fell more deeply in love. On the Friday, though, he had bad news for her.

"I've got to go up to Scotland for three weeks, on business," he told her. "But I'll phone you to let you know where I'm staying, you can write to me and I'll try my hardest to reply; I'm not very good at letter writing!" He paused, laughing in that way she found so irresistible. "Tell you what, I'll take you out somewhere wonderful for dinner for a proper celebration when I get back—I've got some great leads, so this should be a profitable trip!" He held her hand and gazed into her eyes. "I've got something to work for, now."

She was terribly disappointed but made the most of their night together and went home smiling, warming herself with his final words.

"What are three weeks, when we have the rest of our lives together?"

Alas, Bernard never did phone, or write. Three weeks later (dreadful, horrible weeks, when she'd cried into her pillow every night) Dorothy could no longer ignore the fact that she was pregnant. Still, the hope remained that some emergency had occurred and he'd been unable to get a message to her; she couldn't imagine *what*, exactly, but surely no one could make all those promises if they didn't mean them.

Every minute of every day was torture to get through. Once she was sure that she did indeed have their child growing inside her, she steeled herself to go into Mr Potter's office and ask if he knew where Bernard was.

"Sorry, love, I never know when I'll see him from one week to the next! Always been a bit of a fly-by-night." Mr Potter smiled, kindly, but she could see that look of amusement in his eye, and it told her everything.

She turned to walk out of the room, but he called her back.

"Has he been making his daft promises to you, love?" He shook his head. "Oh dear, oh dear. I did tell him to leave my girls alone; he ought to carry a government health warning, that one. Tell you what, I'll give Turnbulls a ring, see if we can locate him, how about that?"

Dorothy looked at him, not understanding. "Turnbulls?"

"Yeah. Firm he works for." Mr Potter sat down and picked up the phone.

She'd been so swept away by Bernard's declarations of love that she hadn't even thought to find out such a detail.

Alas, Turnbulls were of no help; Bernard Townsend had handed in his notice a few weeks before, forwarding address unknown. Gone to live in Scotland, they thought; he had a woman up there.

Her mother was furious and called her a silly little tart, and much worse.

Her father didn't say anything, just hid behind his newspaper. They were ashamed of and disgusted by her, said her mother.

Theirs was not a sociable family and they had little to do with the other people in the village, so it was easy for her mother to make up a story about a fiancé in the army who'd died in Northern Ireland; she even made Dorothy wear a pretend engagement ring and talk about this mythical boyfriend down at the village shop, to add weight to the story of his unfortunate demise which she announced as soon as Dorothy's stomach started to protrude.

Enquiries were made as to the whereabouts of Bernard Townsend, with no results.

"Men like him just melt back into the ether when the going gets tough," Dorothy's mother said, with a sniff or two.

Dorothy didn't want to see him. Ever. She knew she wouldn't be able to bear it.

She was scared she would still feel the same way about him.

Her parents rented a flat in Lyndford for her and the child; Dorothy felt cast out, like a fallen woman in Victorian times, but her mother told her they couldn't deal with a screaming baby in the house, not at their age.

"Especially not the offspring of some dodgy jack-the-lad," said her father. "Bad genes will out. Probably turn out to be a criminal. Or a communist."

"Or a hippie," her mother said, with a shudder.

Later, she wondered how she'd survived that time. Lonely, pregnant, heartbroken, she walked around in a daze, but the memory of Bernard's empty words of love faded, in time, and she was surprised to find how determined she felt; all that mattered was the instinct to care for her unborn child.

She called her baby Orlando because she thought it a beautiful, romantic name, and she wanted him to have a wonderful life. Her parents visited her while she was in hospital, but once she was home, she relied mostly on the health workers and her own common sense.

Her relationship with her mother and father, always distant, became increasingly strained over the years. They were pleasant to Orlando when she took him to visit, but they didn't treat him with real warmth, not like grandparents should treat their only grandson. Instead of love, they gave her money.

As soon as Orlando started school, Dorothy found a part-time typing job, wanting to be independent.

At least once a week she found herself telling him *it's just you and me, against the world*, even before he was old enough to know what the words meant, but, later, she wondered if they'd sunk in, somehow.

For all those years, it had just been her and Orlando. They had such a close relationship, barely a cross word, and they held no secrets from each other.

Until now.

What on earth had changed?

She couldn't pinpoint any one moment.

For the last few years their routine had scarcely varied. On Monday nights they went, together, to their book club, something they looked forward to. They both liked to expand their outlook by reading 'outside their comfort zone', and made some interesting friends.

Orlando's subtle sending up of the more pretentious members of the group gave them much fodder for private merriment.

"I don't understand what you mean by the 'passive voice'?" he would say, frowning in an exaggerated manner. "I thought Richard seemed quite aggressive. 'Specially when he punched Étienne."

Tuesday night was spent at home, then on Wednesdays they both enjoyed an art class; watercolours, at Lyndford College. Sometimes Orlando joined the other students for a pint in the pub afterwards. Thursday was metal detecting club (allegedly!), and Friday night was pub night, while she stayed at home. Weekends were spent in quiet, non-demanding companionship: shopping, gardening, doing odd jobs around the house, watching television, reading. Church on Sunday, but their attendance was more social than devout. Orlando took his occasional fishing trips to Norfolk, or went down to that spot in Kirton, where the river widened out, with David from the metal detecting club.

So tonight was pub night, but she was sure there would be no chips. Last week he hadn't returned until after midnight. He said he'd got involved in a backgammon tournament, but—oh, there was just something about the way he didn't quite look her in the eye when he said it.

She wondered if he had a girlfriend, and didn't like to tell her. Or a boyfriend, even; well, she was okay with that. If Orlando had developed a relationship of any sort, she would welcome his friend into their home.

He was quite friendly with Colin White from the art class; there had been some mention of Colin being *that way*, and he was one of the people with whom Orlando went for a drink after the class.

She didn't know how to broach the subject, though; a wall had grown between them, an invisible one, an awareness of words unsaid.

Orlando had a secret; she knew he did.

Dorothy searched back through her memories of him for any signs, any private problems he might have had over the years. He'd never even rebelled as an adolescent. When he was old enough, she told him the truth about his parentage. As soon as he started school he'd begun to ask why he didn't have a father; at first, she said Bernard had gone away and left them, but when he was about twelve he wanted to know more, to seek out this father who'd left them all alone, which was when she made the difficult decision to tell him the truth.

"Did he divorce you?" he asked. "Were you even married?"

Orlando knew about sex by then, of course, and the gaps in the biology lessons had no doubt been filled in by the boys in the playground. Telling him a carefully worded truth about her naiveté had been so hard, but Orlando reacted in a mature fashion. He put his arms around her, saying that he was so sorry that a man had been so horrible to her.

A couple of years later, when some of his friends were starting to have girlfriends, he began to ask her about it again, wanting to know more about why a woman would *do that* with a man she hardly knew. He seemed angry, agitated, every time he brought it up. He knew how the boys in his class talked about girls who were 'easy'.

"Girls who go with boys they're not properly going out with, they're slags," he said. "People write about them in the toilets. 'Melanie York is a slut', stuff like that." Hearing those expressions coming out of his mouth hurt, badly; memories of her mother using similar words to describe her came flooding back, and she felt he wanted to hurt her, too. She explained as best she could that sometimes boys could lead a girl on with promises; the girl's only fault might be gullibility. Sometimes, a boy pretended he wanted to go steady with a girl so she would do what he wanted.

"It's hard for me to discuss this with you, darling. I don't want to embarrass you."

After a while he said he understood, calmed down, and they never spoke of it again.

She hadn't thought of all that until now; it was so far in the past, but now she wondered if he was hiding something *of a sexual nature.*

It was a part of life that didn't concern either of them; Orlando had never seemed bothered one way or another, which was odd in itself, now she thought about it. If a television drama headed towards the risqué, they'd laugh and say, "Oh, here we go again!" talking over it until the scene had ended. Her experience with Bernard Townsend had put her off men. She'd had a few male friendships over the years but only one had grown a little closer, and Orlando teased his junior school teacher about being 'Mum's boyfriend'; she hadn't led a completely nun-like existence, but she could never trust anyone enough to let them into her heart. Orlando was the centre of her world.

She suspected she might find her answer if she went through his room, but that was one thing she promised herself she would never do. They respected each other's privacy, always had done.

It would all come out in the wash, one way or another. She wouldn't push it. Orlando would tell her what he was up to in his own good time.

She pulled her cardigan round herself more closely, and looked at the clock.

The time was fifteen minutes past midnight, and he still wasn't home.

Chapter Seven

After Ellie

Sunday, 19th April

Michelle Brand

Lita Gomez

Jodie Walker

Leanne Marsh

Kayla Graham

Angelika

Ellie Kane

"Her phone's going straight to voicemail and she *always* answers it, even when she's in the bath, or at work," Ellie Kane's mother told them the afternoon before. "You know what girls her age are like, they do all that binge-drinking, she gets so drunk she doesn't know what she's doing—I feel sick every Friday night when I see her skipping out of the door in a dress that looks more like underwear, and I don't relax 'til she's home. I've been up all night, I started ringing her friends at eight. Dani and Natalie, they said it was a funny night, they met up with all sorts of people and split up, and Anna said she thought Ellie went off with Shaun, this lad she knows from college, and I found out where he lives, I've been round to his flat but he said she went to the toilet and never came back, so he thought she must've gone home. I know, I know, she's probably crashed out round someone's house, or ended up with some fella. Don't raise your eyebrows at me like that, she's a grown woman, isn't she? I was married at her age, her love life's her own affair. She'll probably come back at tea time, moaning about her hangover and asking for cheese on toast, like she normally does."

The face of Ellie Kane, identified by her poor, destroyed mother, tore at DCI John Reddick's heartstrings more than the others. Not because Ellie was an 'ordinary' girl, a student; he was well known for railing against the attitude (thankfully, less prevalent now than during his early days in uniform) that a prostitute, a junkie or a down-and-out's life was worth less than that of an upstanding citizen. Funny how you didn't notice the shift in thought, didn't see the tiny seeds of change floating in the wind, until one day you looked back and said, *did people really think like that?* However archaic that point of view seemed now, he knew, even though few dared voice it—not to him, at least—that it still existed in some corners of the Force.

Ellie.

Jodie Walker from 2014 had cut him up, too (lovely girl by all accounts, who'd taken every wrong turn in life that a person could) but she hadn't sent him spiralling into this weird pit of what felt almost like personal grief. It was just something about Ellie Kane's face, in those pictures her mother brought in. She looked so *bright*. Around the Christmas tree, playing with her younger siblings, holding up her brand-new empty folders before she went off for her first day at college. The wife she would have been, the mother, the friend. The older woman, accomplished, wiser; the grandmother. A whole life never to be lived, just so that some insane toe-rag could satisfy the fucked-up shit inside his head.

Ellie.

Nineteen. Racketing around a bit, perhaps going off with men she didn't know, now and again, but what young girl didn't occasionally put herself in a situation that would be considered, at best, unwise?

Difference was that most of them didn't turn up on a slab, strangled and raped. With the word 'slut' carved into her body. The location of the killer's calling card was different each time, and sometimes hard to find. Ellie's was just below her left buttock. This detail had not been released to the press, but the lack of it on Angelika's body was the reason some thought she should not be considered one of the Lyndford Strangler's victims. Reddick kept an open mind; the others all had mid to dark brown hair, whereas Angelika was fairer of skin, with hair the shade they used to call mousy brown, or light brown, but was now described as dark blonde. Could be seen as darker at night, though, under dim light.

He reached out and touched Ellie's face, on her photo.

Jodie, Kayla and Angelika had been prostitutes, Ellie and Leanne weren't. Lita was, Michelle wasn't.

Where was the connection?

Ellie and Michelle were abducted on nights out, the worse for drink and wearing party or 'clubbing' clothes.

Leanne was last seen leaving work.

None of their personal effects, their bags or phones, had ever been found. No calls had been made to indicate they might be in trouble. No signal could be traced from their phones, so it was assumed they had been destroyed.

"I'll tell you something about them all, sir."

Cara Nolan's voice snapped him out of his thoughts.

"What?"

She coughed. "They're all well-endowed in the chest area. I noticed it with a couple of the actual bodies, and others from their photos."

"Hmm. Might be just coincidence. If they were wearing jackets or coats, he probably wouldn't notice, anyway."

"Unless he'd been watching them. Chose them."

"Mm-mm. Could be."

Who are you, arsehole? Reddick had leapt at the information about Ellie's friend Shaun, but knew he was on a hiding to nothing as soon as the lad opened the door to the beer can-strewn chaos he called home. Shaun was only twenty years old, had platinum blond hair and an alibi for the rest of the evening; he'd been screwing one of the Fagin's barmaids in the cellar.

Hopes had been raised when the two girls from the Boar and Dragon said they thought they'd seen the man from the e-fit picture, but they hadn't been able to add anything except that, yes, it looked like him, and he'd been larking around with his friends at the bar. Was he a local? They didn't know; they'd never been in the pub before. The landlord had been questioned but said the picture looked a bit like hundreds of blokes he knew, but not that much like any of them. Two locals said it looked a bit like a bloke called Dan Thewlis but, when questioned, Thewlis had alibis for the nights of the murders (albeit not all completely watertight).

"It's not him," Cara Nolan said. "If he was in Norwich the night Kayla Graham was killed it's highly unlikely he did the others."

"It's still possible he did it. Not all the hours were accounted for. Or there could be two of 'em. Working together. One of 'em might be more careful than the other."

Nolan gave him one of her 'looks'. "I doubt it. And his alibis for Brand and Gomez are sound, as far as I can see."

There was something about Thewlis that Reddick didn't like, though. He was too cocky. Wouldn't let them take any samples, and his brief assured him they weren't anywhere near a stage in the investigation where he was obliged to do so.

Bloody Philip Landers. The lowlife's best friend.

Shame you couldn't keep a bloke in a cell just for being an obnoxious dickhead, really.

Chapter Eight

Maisie: The Teenager

Kirton and Lyndford, South Lincolnshire

Sunday, 19th April

"Zack! What the hell—what are you doing—come down from there, *now*! Now! That water's *deep*—Maisie, hold this—*Zack*! Stop, get down!"

Maisie Todd caught the picnic holdall as Gary flung it in her general direction, and watched him bound over the bridge. He reached her little brother in four desperate leaps before hauling him away from the bridge's low wall where he'd been sitting, quite happily, dangling his legs over the side, throwing stones into the water and singing quietly in the weak spring sunshine.

Maisie shook her head, turning to her mother. "What his problem? Zack's only playing."

Pru Todd sniffed. "Oh, you know. His sister."

"Oh. Yeah." Maisie kicked at a stone. "Zack's not going to drown. He's a good swimmer, for a start off, and, anyway, we don't see him when he's out playing on his own, do we?" She laughed. "He could be sitting a hundred feet up on dangerous bridges every day, for all you know."

"I know, I know. I'm just saying, that's why Gary gets paranoid when he sees kids mucking about near water. Cut him some slack? For me?"

Maisie wrinkled her nose. "Okay, but he hasn't got the right to tell us what to do."

"Well, no, strictly speaking he hasn't," Pru said, "but as he's an adult and you're children, I think we can allow him a little authority if the situation calls for it, don't you?"

"I'm fifteen." She flicked her hair over her shoulder. "There aren't any situations that call for him having authority over *me*."

Pru put her arm around her daughter's shoulder, and laughed. "You'll get used to him."

Maisie felt irritated by both her touch and her amusement, and shrugged off the offending arm. So bloody patronising.

"I don't think so." She wanted to go home, or round to Bethany's. Anything would be better than playing happy families with her mum's new boyfriend, just because it was the first day when it wasn't totally bloody freezing cold. Why did grown-ups want to go on stupid walks? It wasn't like there was an end destination, and they couldn't even go to the café up on Kirton Hill to get burgers and some of that fabulous salted caramel ice cream with the huge bits of gooey toffee, because muppet Gary had lost his job.

"Well, why can't you pay?" Maisie asked her mother earlier that morning, when she saw Pru packing up a picnic of cheese rolls, millionaire's shortbread and bottles of Oasis. This would be just as much fun as going to the Hilltop Café, Pru declared; she'd always loved picnics, hadn't she?

"Yes, when I was a little kid. I don't want to sit in my coat eating cheese rolls out of a Tupperware box in a windy flipping field. Please, Mum, let's go up to the café." No reaction. Plan B, then. "I'll let you have my biggest gooey toffee bit out of the ice cream!"

"No, and *ssh*," Pru hissed. "Don't make Gary feel bad; you know he likes to pay, and if he buys us all burgers and chips and ice creams—and Zack will want one of those chocolate milkshakes, too—it's going to cost him half his dole money."

"So we have to suffer because of his stupid pride."

"You're not exactly suffering. We're going out for a lovely, brisk walk in the spring sunshine, and having a nice picnic." Pru raised an eyebrow. "My heart bleeds for you."

In fact, the rolls were gorgeous, not boring old cheddar but applewood smoked cheese on tiger bread and brie on poppy seed, with thin slices of vine tomato and fresh basil leaves; Pru managed a small local deli, the fringe benefits of which were worth the long hours, she said.

Even that made Maisie cross. Running that deli was bloody hard work. Pru left for work at seven in the morning, five days a week, and came home at six, flaked out. Shouldn't she be able to enjoy the money she earned in the way she wanted? But there they were, food eaten on a wooden picnic bench amongst a load of other families pretending to be having a good time, though Maisie had to admit it wasn't quite as cold as she'd anticipated (okay, and the daffodils along the bank and the narrowboats on the river looked lush, and sitting in the sunshine was kind of nice, really).

She watched as Zack zoomed down the bridge towards them, arms outstretched like an aeroplane, laughing, followed by Gary, who strutted along like some kind of brave hero who'd just averted disaster.

"My two gorgeous goldilocks!" he said, as he approached. "I'm such a lucky guy!"

Maisie leant over behind her mother's back and made loud vomiting noises.

"Maisie, stop it!"

She sat up. "I'm not his anything. And your hair's mid brown with ash blonde highlights, hardly bloody goldilocks." Happily, Gary was distracted by some kid flying a kite, and didn't sit back down with them. "Can we go home now? I mean, we've had the picnic and the walk. We've, like, done the family bit."

Pru gave her another of those tolerant smiles that irritated the hell out of her. "Yes, okay. Give him a chance, though, huh?"

"I have. I do."

"I know." Pru touched her shoulder again. "He's a good man, Maisie. D'you think I'd have let him come to live with us if I wasn't sure?"

Maisie didn't answer that. Her mum was madly in love; for the first few weeks she'd acted even more retarded than Bethany did when she started going out with Conor. Sighing and secret smiles. Maisie was pretty sure she'd have let Gary move in anyway, whether he was a 'good man' or not. The day her mum announced the move she'd had this lame expression on her face, like it was the best day of her whole life.

But then she hadn't had a boyfriend for ages, at least, not one who wanted to stick around.

Maisie talked to her friends about it; Bethany and Saffron were in the same boat, having to put up with strange blokes around the house. They understood.

Maisie wasn't a kid and she knew that her mum wasn't exactly *old*; at thirty-eight, she still wanted a life. Boyfriends, too. *Beyond gross*—some nights Maisie heard her and Gary *doing it*. Thank God for iPods.

Even more embarrassing, Saffron's mum worked at the Jobcentre and signed Gary on for his benefits every fortnight. Seemed like Gary brought them nothing but bloody embarrassment.

On the drive home Maisie gazed out of the window, earbuds in place, watching her mum and Gary chatting away in the front, and, out of the blue, she felt a wave of loneliness. What must it be like, to have a proper family? Like, your mum and dad together and happy? She shut her eyes. She wasn't totally dense; she knew her mum was trying to give them that very thing. Gary was better than the last boyfriend, who'd told Pru he 'couldn't do the whole kids thing', and definitely better than the one before, who drank too much and couldn't aim right when he took a piss.

The bathroom used to *stink*.

Maisie thought her mum must be one of those weak women who needed a man to give her life meaning, like Ms Brownlow, her history teacher, talked about. Ms Brownlow often sidestepped onto this subject during lessons about how World War One changed the social structure of the country, or the founding of the Suffragettes movement. She'd stress that women these days didn't know how lucky they were because they could do a whole bunch of stuff on their own, not like in olden times when they were hardly allowed to do anything. Her job, she said, was not just to educate them about history, but to show how it related to their lives now, as women of the 21st century.

"Sadly, even with all the opportunities open to us nowadays, some women still feel incomplete without a man in their lives," Ms Brownlow would say. Maisie liked it when she digressed from the history lesson and talked about *important feminist issues*. She was going to be like Ms Brownlow when she grew up. She would forge ahead and do what she wanted, and not have a load of kids unless she could support them on her own. Pru was a lovely mum, but she was weak. Kind of dreamy. She was good at getting her and Zack to paint and read, creative things, but when she had boyfriends, she always put them first. That was how it seemed to Maisie, anyway.

"It's been called the Cinderella Complex," Ms Brownlow told them. "Women waiting for Prince Charming to make their lives whole. This is, of course, perpetuated by the men who run the film, TV and publishing industry, because we can't help but be influenced by what we watch and read. They give air time and column space to Barbie doll role models, keep women fed on a diet of romcoms, give them the subtle message that if they buy their frocks, get their boob jobs and wear ridiculous shoes that stop them running away, they'll attract an alpha male to look after them." She always got really warmed up at this point. "This is how so many men in positions of power want it, because it keeps us in our place. Never mind building up your own social and career support network, just muddle through and wait for your prince to sweep you off your Jimmy Choos and install you in his castle, where you'll live happily ever after. Or so you reckon, until one day you wake up with four kids and a husband who hits you, is unfaithful or simply spends all his time down the pub. But you can't escape, because you've got no money, no skills, and no confidence in yourself."

Maisie suspected that Ms Brownlow wasn't supposed to be telling them this sort of thing when she was teaching history, but she liked hearing it. They all did (apart from Bethany, who worshipped at the altar of the Kardashians).

It made Maisie feel pumped up, determined and raring to go.

If her mother was more like Ms Brownlow, she would have boyfriends to take her out now and again, but still put her and Zack first. She wouldn't let men move in with them and lay down the law, like they always did. Maisie could tell that Pru was 'fulfilled' (a Ms Brownlow word) now she had a man about the house once more. She smiled a lot and cooked proper dinners with puddings, and kept talking about doing stuff *as a family*.

Gary wasn't family, though. Chris Todd was their dad, even though he'd buggered off when Zack was a baby. Maisie didn't even know why they still had his stupid surname. Wasn't like he gave a shit about any of them. He sent money on a regular basis, but forgot their birthdays more often than not, and didn't send proper Christmas presents, just money for Pru to get them something. He had a new life, with a new woman.

Maisie didn't care. She wasn't just kidding herself about it, either; she really didn't. Once, she'd talked to Ms Brownlow about it, who understood. Maisie had 'innate strength' that would see her through, she said.

She also said that Maisie could call her Kate, and talk to her whenever she wanted. Maisie didn't want to get too friendly with her, though, because

Bethany and Saff thought she was a lesbian, so if she became friends with her, they'd probably tease her about being a lesbian, too, especially Bethany, who loved to stir stuff up.

Pru told her that being homophobic was as bad as being racist, and Maisie didn't think she was either, but she still didn't want anyone thinking she was a lesbian. Pru called them 'same sex couples', but Gary said 'rug munchers', and much worse things about the men, things that made Zack laugh, and Pru never told *him* off for it.

Maybe, Maisie thought, she was just the little tiny bit of homophobic that made you glad you weren't one.

Up in her room, Maisie switched off her music and lay back on the bed. She could hear much movement downstairs; Gary must be cleaning again. The house had never been so spotless.

"What can I say? I'm a self-confessed clean freak!"

Puke. Maisie, Bethany and Saff agreed that anyone who said they were a 'self-confessed' anything was a total douche.

Maisie thought he had OCD, actually. She'd read about it. He was always washing his hands, and reminding them all to wash theirs. Like they never knew they had to wash their hands after they'd been to the toilet until he moved in, right? He was forever cleaning the bathroom, and had a thing about wearing clean clothes every day, all of them, even jeans; he and Pru argued about the fact that the washing machine was constantly on. He showered every morning and every night, too. Pru complained that their electricity bills were going to be sky high; she was particularly worried now that Gary had lost his job.

"Not to mention the water rates," Pru said to her the other day, in hushed tones. "Can you and Zack shower at school, after PE, when you can? I don't like to tell Gary he can't have one, it seems a bit—well, you know, a bit picky. Mean."

That pissed Maisie off. Seemed Gary had to be wrapped up in cotton wool because he was *unemployed*, like it was an illness.

He'd come home in a state of high agitation the day he was laid off from the warehouse, a job he'd complained about from the word 'go' anyway, because it was beneath him; previously, he'd worked in sales.

"Okay, so I packed the wrong parts for a very important customer who needed them for a rush job," he said, flopping down on the sofa and holding his hand out for the can of lager Pru offered, ignoring the glass in her other hand, "and Wes, you know, that idiot of a floor manager, he said that because this so-called very important customer got the wrong parts he didn't get the rush job done on time, so he lost his own client. Apparently, I'm to blame." He drank the lager down practically in one go, then crushed the can in his hand (as if it was the floor manager's neck he wanted to crush, Maisie thought).

Pru sat on the arm of the chair, massaging his shoulders; Gary appeared not to notice she was doing so.

"So did you pack up the wrong parts, then, or what?" Maisie asked.

"Maybe I did. If so, I hold my hands up. But they're passed to me by these two lads, the pickers, who select the parts as per the works instruction from the sales office. Okay, so I have my copy of the works instruction and they didn't correspond with what I packed, but those bimbos in the office have been known to write it down wrong, so I presume that the pickers have done their checks and given me the correct item. I mean, in a place with over ten thousand different products, mistakes happen. At the end of the day I was given the wrong products to pack. Yet I'm the one who gets the old heave-ho."

"You can appeal, can't you?" said Pru, in a soothing voice.

He leant forward, elbows on knees, away from Pru's hands. "No point. I reckon they wanted an excuse to fire me. That Wes, he didn't want to listen to my side at all, so I told the arsehole what I thought of him—"

"Can you not swear in front of Maisie and Zack, please, honey?"

He looked up at her. "Oh yeah—sorry. But, yeah, 'cause I didn't exactly mince my words, I've kind of burnt my bridges."

"That job was beneath you anyway." *Rub, rub*, went Pru's work-worn hands. "You'll find something else, soon. Something in sales, more suited to your capabilities. Perhaps this was meant to be."

Maisie wondered if Pru's soothing voice got on Gary's nerves, too.

"Sure I will. But I'm not holding my breath, 'cause when they ask my former employer why I left he'll say I was sacked for incompetence."

"One mistake—"

"That Wes, he never liked me, not from the moment I started there. And I reckon those lads, the pickers, they fucked things up for me on purpose so I'd get the boot." Gary flopped back, and took hold of Pru's hand; he didn't notice her wince at his choice of language. "So, you'll have to put up with me around the house a bit more, I'm afraid, gang. Until I find something else."

That something else hadn't materialised yet, though.

Pru said being unemployed could be very demoralising for a man, so they should make allowances. Maisie and Zack would understand once they were out in the working world, trying to compete in a busy market.

So they made the required allowances, even down to missing out on salted caramel ice cream.

"It's so messed up," Maisie said to Bethany, later that evening, "It isn't his house, he's not our family, and right now he's not even giving Mum anything towards the bills, but we all have to tiptoe round him. Like, he has to come first. We have to be quiet in the morning so's not to wake him, 'cause he doesn't sleep well. And he goes out at night, but he's supposed to be broke. Friday night he was out with some bloke he used to work with, and he didn't get in until gone one. How come he can go out boozing until one in the morning if he hasn't got any money?"

Bethany giggled. "Perhaps he wasn't out boozing. Perhaps he really *is* the Lyndford Strangler!"

A couple of months before, after the body of a girl called Angelika was discovered, Bethany had pointed out that the e-fit photo in the paper looked like Gary. It did, too; if it hadn't been for the fact that they'd all been at home together, watching DVDs, on the night they thought the girl was murdered, Maisie might have been seriously worried.

Now, though, she found herself almost wishing it *was* him, so the police would catch him and he'd go away.

"You could sell your story to the paper if it is him!" Bethany went on. "That picture did look like him, didn't it?"

"It looked like a lot of people." She laughed. "It wasn't as ugly as Gazza!"

"He's not ugly. He's quite hot, for an old guy."

"*Ugh,* don't even! You don't fancy him, do you?"

"I'm just saying. He's not ugly." Another pause. "And he's not that bad. Not really. Not like some of the losers my mum's brought home."

Maisie sighed to herself. "I know. I still think he's a tit, though."

"Zack likes him, doesn't he?"

"Yeah. And Gran and Grandad do. I dunno. There's something weird about him."

Bethany laughed. "Must be all that strangling he does in his spare time!"

"*Maisie!*" Zack's voice from halfway up the stairs. "Mum says tea's ready!"

"Gotta go," Maisie said, and clicked Skype off. She didn't go straight downstairs, but lay back on her bed.

Maybe Gary would get bored soon, and leave. Only problem was, he'd have to find some other sucker to take him in, wouldn't he? Something told

Maisie that, despite her mother's insistence that he hated being out of work, Gary wasn't making a great effort to find anything.

Six months, he'd lived with them.

What did they actually know about him? Not a lot. He was forty-two, he came from London originally, he'd worked mostly in sales, his parents lived in some cottage on the west coast of Ireland. He'd said maybe they could all go over there this summer, but how, if he wasn't working? Would her mum have to fork out for it?

He'd moved to Lyndford from Norfolk eighteen months ago when his firm relocated, he said, but how could he just up and move like that? He'd been in a bedsit when she met him; how come he didn't have his own house? Her mum had met him at a singles night; perhaps he was one of those weirdos who preyed on lonely single women, the ones you read about.

Or perhaps he was just a lonely guy looking for a new start in life. Maisie rolled over onto her front. Either way, she wished he hadn't picked on her mum.

In the meantime, her pasta and Bolognese sauce would be getting cold.

When she got downstairs, though, the serving dishes sat on the kitchen table with their lids on, untouched. Maisie wandered into the living room, to find her mother and Gary standing in front of the television. Even Zack was looking at the screen.

"Brrrrr!" Her mother shuddered, and snuggled up to Gary. She turned her head as Maisie walked into the room. "Guess what? They've found another body, down by the river, right near where we were this afternoon. She's been there for a couple of days, they said. Ugh—doesn't it send a chill down your spine?"

Zack looked up. "Yeah, if we hadn't come home when we did, we'd have been there when they found it! It might have been floating under the bridge while I was sitting there!" Typical ten-year-old boy; he looked more excited than appalled by this.

Maisie remembered the haste with which Gary had pulled Zack away from the river. Oh yeah, it was because he was scared of him drowning, wasn't it?

Or perhaps he didn't want Zack to see his dead victim beneath those murky waters, a soul in torment calling out from *the other side*, to a rescuer who would never appear!

Scary!

She looked at Gary. His reaction to the news item was as normal as normal could be. He studied the TV screen with a concerned and horrified look on his face, his arm around Pru's shoulders in a kind, protective sort of way.

He kissed the top of her head. "Well," he said, looking round at Zack and Maisie and smiling, "I hope this hasn't put anyone off their tea? The Bolognese sauce tastes great, even if I do say so myself!"

Oh yeah. He cooked, too. A guy who did housework, and cooked. No wonder her mum thought she'd hit the jackpot.

It was only as she was sprinkling parmesan on her pasta that Maisie thought about Gary getting in so late on Friday night. It was definitely in the early hours; she knew, because she'd woken up to go to the loo and heard the front door opening and closing. As she was dropping off, she heard Gary's tread, soft on the landing, as he went into the bathroom, and then the sound of the shower going on.

But he always showered last thing at night.

Or was this a routine he'd established, to cover up his Lyndford Strangler activities?

"Why were you in so late on Friday night, Gary?" she asked. *Might as well come straight out with it.*

He didn't even flinch. "Yeah, I'm a dirty stop-out, I know! No, seriously, I just went for a couple of beers with Jimbo and Ken, then we were playing cards round Ken's." He pulled a silly face at Pru. "I didn't lose any money, honest!"

Maisie stirred her pasta round with her fork. "You shouldn't be gambling at all if you're broke, should you?"

Her mother put a hand on her lover's leg. "Sweetheart, they only play for fifty pees. I don't mind that." Maisie could see the warning in her eyes. *Let's not make this an issue, eh?*

Okay, Maisie thought. *As long as he really was playing cards—*

Chapter Nine

Juliet: The Wife

May ~ June 2015

Even as the words fell from her mouth, she knew she would suffer for them later.

She said them halfway through the evening, so from that moment the whole dinner party was spoilt, every second edging closer to the moment when she would be alone with Paul. Her face ached with smiling and chatting about things domestic and parental, stuff that normal, happy wives and mothers talked about, her whole body stiff with the pretence that she was just like them.

She'd been looking forward to the evening. Fiona, the wife of Oliver, Paul's bank manager and friend, was a wonderful cook, and Juliet had met the other guests on a few occasions over the years: headmistress Eve and her college lecturer husband Keith, architect Rob and his gorgeous wife, Aurelia, who dabbled in painting.

These were the people with whom Juliet felt at home. No one in this group would make her feel useless for being a stay-at-home wife and mother; why work, when she didn't have to? Eve loved her career, and Aurelia was arty and fascinating, but Fiona, like Juliet, was a dedicated housewife. Never 'homemaker', which was a ghastly, lower middle-class Americanism, Fiona said.

"We're wives and mothers, and proud of it!"

These were the people with whom Paul longed to feel at ease; he, too, had been looking forward to the evening.

Last year he'd bought some large, shabby industrial premises out on Crow Lane, a two-mile long road on the south westerly edge of Lyndford, separated from Monk's Park industrial estate by waste ground, and skirting the fields towards Kirton. Long ago a thoroughfare used by the inhabitants of smallholdings and a now deserted hamlet, Crow Lane comprised shabby auto repair and car parts businesses, ancient industrial units in various states of disrepair, the local scrapyard and even a few Victorian residential buildings, rundown places that were surely due for demolition. Paul's premises were currently rented out to a couple of Eastern European men (who Paul suspected might be a bit 'dodgy', but money was money). At the moment they were used as garages for repairs and MOTs, with vast rooms upstairs empty or used for storage, he was told.

"Probably housing twenty Ukrainian families, for all I know; I'm saying nothing! Not my worry, as long as they pay the rent."

The buildings were old red brick places with dangerous looking fire escapes, a health and safety nightmare, Paul said; they would need major renovation. When the tenants' lease was up, in a year's time, Paul wanted to employ Rob's architectural services, his intention to turn it into smart commercial units. Long-term plans were afoot for the whole area and Paul had been clever enough to make his purchase while it was still viewed as a white elephant. In the meantime, he wished to 'cultivate' Rob, he said, so he'd get a good price when the time came.

He'd been nervous before they went out; as Juliet fixed his tie she felt a rare rush of affection for him, wanting to say, *calm down, they're just like me, they're not nobility*, though she knew ease in social situations was a matter of familiarity, and, despite his outward show of confidence, her husband felt as awkward around the professional classes as she would if she walked into one of the rough pubs down Spencer Road.

Ever the accomplished hostess, Fiona had seated them around the table with no guest placed near their own spouse, and female alternating with male. When they started dessert, however, she tapped a teaspoon on her glass. "Chaps, this is daft. I'm trying to talk to Juliet over Keith's head, and Paul is trying to talk to Rob over Eve's—how about we swap places so that we women can sit down here and talk about what really matters, and you men can do all your my-car's-bigger-than-your-car stuff at the other end of the table?"

So, amid much jollity, they changed places, and the wives' topic of conversation turned to that dinner party mainstay: education. Led by headmistress Eve, who listened to the other wives' comments with great interest, they'd moved onto the expectations of parents, and teenagers not understanding how lucky they were to have the advantages given them simply by the good fortune of their birth.

"Alexander's constantly chewing my ear off about having to go to St Stephen's," Fiona said. "That's the trouble, isn't it, with all these bloody village schools closing; we haven't got any choice but to send him to Hartford Road. Now he's attained Olympic level in sulking because he wants to go to Lyndford Comp with all his horrible little friends called Shane and Duane, or whatever the hell their names are!"

All the women laughed.

"Lyndford Comp's a perfectly decent school," Eve said, eyebrows raised. "It's actually got a slightly better GCSE pass rate than St Stephen's."

"I dare say, but my concerns are not just about his academic future." Fiona pushed a piece of aubergine around her plate. "Evie, I know you think I'm a silly snob, but I don't want him spending his lunch hours learning how to deal crack cocaine." More laughter. "Still, he's going to St Stephen's and that's that, however many tantrums we have to deal with."

Aurelia gave a dramatic sigh. "I wish Lucas *cared* where he went to school; that would be a start. He's so bloody lazy! He thinks a place in the business will fall into his lap, and refuses to understand that qualifying as an architect takes years of hard work. He's under the impression he'll be allowed to take shortcuts because Rob's his dad." She fiddled with her earring. "I don't know, maybe the best thing would be for him to look for a rich woman, instead."

"I don't envy today's young adults; there are so many distractions for them," said Eve, "not to mention that sense of entitlement that seems to have become a part of the teenage psyche over the past twenty years or so. Not only do they think it's their right to go to university, but also to spend a gap year getting drunk on beaches in Southeast Asia." She smiled at Juliet, who stiffened with the realisation that she was about to be brought into the conversation. "Do you have the same trouble with Sam and Max, Juliet?"

She took a deep breath. "Oh, for sure. Sam's already saying things like 'I'm not going to study for three more years like some geek, or be a nine-to-five stooge working for 'the man', I'm going to buy and flog houses like Dad'. He's adopted phrases like 'making a fast buck'; I don't know where they come from."

The other women enjoyed this, and Juliet warmed with the feeling of others listening to her, being amused by her. They liked her, they didn't think she was stupid or irritating, not like her husband did.

Fiona nodded. "Paul did it all himself, didn't he, from scratch? I so admire that."

"Oh yes. He didn't have the advantages Sam and Max have."

Aurelia rested her pretty, pointed chin on her hand. "Pulled himself up by his bootstraps, eh?"

They were all looking at her, interested. Juliet smiled. "Yes, he certainly did that. I'm so proud of him. He didn't have any help from anyone, but he'd already bought and sold several properties by the time he was—ooh, about twenty-four, I think."

"Bloody hell, really? I can't imagine Lucas even knowing where to start. I'm sure he doesn't even know what a mortgage is; I reckon he thinks houses are things you just *have*, automatically, like the ironed clothes in his wardrobe and the food in the fridge!" Aurelia reached across the table and squeezed Juliet's hand. "Come on, give me an inspiring story I can tell him, to shame him into getting off his backside!"

Juliet laughed. "Oh well, Paul started with nothing at all—less than nothing, really. I think that was what spurred him on. He was terrified of ending up like his father." Something told her she'd already said too much, but she was so enjoying their attention.

"Sounds interesting; tell all!" Aurelia leant forward, anxious for juicy gossip.

"What do you mean by 'like his father'?" asked Fiona, with a frown. "I thought his pa managed a shoe factory." She smiled. "Not the most glamorous of jobs, but there's nothing wrong with it."

Juliet glanced up; should she? The men chatted away, enjoying an anecdote related by Oliver; she was safe, they weren't listening to the women's conversation.

"Perhaps I shouldn't say anything," she said.

"Go on," Aurelia whispered, touching her hand again. "They're not listening to us!"

The tiny voice in the back of Juliet's head said, *silly bitch. Bored and privileged, just after a bit of gossip at your husband's expense. At your expense, too, if you're not careful.*

Oh, what the hell? Being centre stage for once felt so good.

The other women mirrored her movement as she leant in, closer to them.

She took a sip of her wine.

"Just between us, okay? Well, Paul's dad worked in a shoe factory, yes, but he certainly wasn't the manager—I don't know where that came from, Fiona—and he drank away his wages every week. Handy with his fists, too. Paul used to get home from school and find his mother passed out on the sofa, drunk." She lowered her voice. "I gather where they lived was quite *squalid*. Like something from one of those documentaries you see about life on sink estates. Yes, Paul's done amazing things, considering his start in life."

Alas, as Juliet began this speech, she failed to notice that the men's conversation had just been punctuated by one of those momentary lulls that come after the telling of a hilarious anecdote, when the laughter dies down. This lull may have lasted only a second or two, had the words 'handy with his fists' and 'squalid' not provoked shocked gasps amongst the other women.

Wine had blunted Juliet's senses and she didn't notice, until she stopped talking, that her hushed, conspiratorial tones were not quite as hushed as she thought, or that all ears were directed her way.

Wine made her brave, too, and her first thought, as she saw her husband's face, was, *oh, for crying out loud. It's nothing to be ashamed of. Triumphing over a ghastly upbringing is fashionable, and class stopped mattering decades ago—look at Alan Sugar!*

But it mattered to Paul, who'd worked hard not only to attain the way of life he wanted so badly, but to rid his voice of working class vowel sounds, to eat the food and speak the language of the middle classes, to hold his knife and fork the way they did (not like a pencil, as his mum had), to behave as if he *belonged*.

Poor Paul. So insecure he'd actually told lies about his background.

The other three couples looked at Paul's angry face, then back at Juliet, taking in her discomfort.

"Bloody good for you, Paul!" Aurelia's loud drawl rang out around the room. "And I'm going to tell that tale to Lucas every night as a bed time story, I don't care if he *is* seventeen!"

Everyone laughed and raised their glasses to Paul, the sticky moment danced over with the skill of the socially adept.

And he smiled back at all of them, except Juliet.

The tiny voice in the back of her head congratulated her. She'd paid him back for all she'd suffered at his hands.

There. Serves you right.

Should she go the whole hog, hurl more wine down her neck, turn to the other women and laugh, hysterically, announcing that she was in trouble now, that she'd get *the shit kicked out of her* when she got home, just like Paul had by his dad? Should she point out that his worst nightmare had actually come true because, give or take a few bob in the bank and a smart house, he was exactly, *exactly* like his violent thug of a father?

But Juliet did neither of these things. She sat in her chair, winding her napkin around her hands in her lap, willing her burning face to cool down, and the moment passed; Fiona changed the subject so smoothly that any remaining awkwardness floated out of the open window into the warm evening air; a moment later the guests were sharing memories about their favourite dinner party disasters.

Juliet's private discomfort would last much longer.

Paul prolonged her agony by making sure they were the last to leave, and this alone increased her fear that her punishment would be worse than usual.

Sadistic bastard. He knew exactly what he was doing.

Even after the other guests had gone, and Juliet could see that Oliver and Fiona wanted to get off to bed, Paul accepted a final glass of port. This embarrassed her, as she knew it was offered only out of politeness; Fiona had allowed herself a couple of none too subtle yawns, and turned off the garden lights. Usually, Juliet would never be bold enough to suggest making a move while Paul's glass was still half full, but he'd had far too much to drink and she feared that if they didn't leave soon, they wouldn't be asked back—for which she would also be blamed.

It was after one when she put her front door key in the lock, Paul standing behind her, his silence loud and heavy in the night air, as it had been during the taxi ride home. The house was quiet; no, she could hear the buzz of cars round a virtual track from one of the boys' bedrooms upstairs.

Paul heard it too.

"Kitchen."

She followed him in and sat down at the table, taking off her uncomfortable high heeled shoes and massaging the balls of her feet while she waited for him to pour himself another drink.

He didn't look too thunderous. Had the alcohol taken the edge off? Perhaps, even now, she could deflect his attention.

"That went well, didn't it? I saw you chatting away to Rob; Aurelia said how fascinated he is by what you do." She'd said no such thing, and the false brightness of her voice made her cringe.

"Did she?"

She smiled at him. "Oh, yes! She said we must go over for a barbecue, maybe bring the boys too, once the school holidays start." That was a lie, too, but never mind. "Hers are the same age, I'm sure Lucas would get on with them, if we can persuade them!" She was babbling now, but she couldn't stop. "Perhaps you could bring up Crow Lane then? Tonight went so well, and—"

"Yes, it did, didn't it?" Paul put his glass down on the table. Precisely, evenly.

Her heart beat hard in her chest. "I'm sure Rob would love to get involved, and I *do* like Aurelia, she's such good company, and—"

"It would have gone even better, of course, if you hadn't broadcast my private business to the whole of the table."

Oh God. It had started.

You're a rational adult, talk to him as an equal. Stand up for yourself.

"Paul. Listen. I'm so, so sorry, I shouldn't have said it, and you're right, it's private. I'm truly sorry, I made a mistake, but no one cares about stuff like that these days, I'm sure they won't even remember, it won't matter at all—"

"It matters to me."

"Yes, I understand, but I don't know why, it's something to be proud of, that you've got this far from nothing. You should talk about it openly; people would admire you for it." She couldn't stop the words coming out of her mouth; sometimes, her fear made her stupidly brave. Or bravely stupid. She was going to get clobbered anyway, so she might as well defend herself rather than just take it.

He laughed. "You've got no idea, have you? Until tonight, they all thought I was in their shitty little private, privileged club. You know Oliver and Rob went to minor public schools? They thought I was one of them, and that matters, in business."

"But they don't care about all that," she said. "It's not like when you were at school; this 'club' thing, it's in your head. People are judged on what they *do*, once they're past the age of eighteen, not where they come from. That's one of the great things about life post-Thatcher's Britain; I saw a programme about it the other day. Anyone can do anything; we've become a classless society." But her voice was less confident this time. She heard it shaking, felt her heart thumping.

He moved nearer.

"Shut up, you stupid cow. I don't give a shit what you've seen on that box in the living room that rules your life, it's not your fucking business to tell a pack of strangers about my past. You're my wife, you're supposed to support me, not do your best to show me up."

He was right. Of course he was right, she should never have said what she did.

She began to cry. "I'm sorry, Paul, I really am. You're right. I'm really sorry, I shouldn't have said it." Her whole face quivered as she looked up at him, silently pleading with him not to do what she feared he would. "Oh my God, I feel terrible, Paul. Please, please don't be too cross with me. I know I did wrong. Please—"

Too late.

"Stupid, useless bitch."

She yelled out as his fist collided with her skull, throwing her head back against the wall. Some deep part of her, the one that made her say what she said at the dinner party, thought, *you bastard, how dare you do this to me*, but that part was very small, and she knew she was in the wrong, that although she didn't deserve to be hurt like this she deserved some sort of punishment, but all these thoughts were mixed up in her head and she just wanted it to be over. So she took the punches—four of them, two to each side of her head—and didn't even scream, because she mustn't let the boys hear, and then she just slid down to the floor and sobbed, quietly, thankful at least that he'd finished.

She sat there for some time.

Silence reigned, apart from the background whirr of the virtual racing cars. At first, she thought he'd gone out again, but no, even in his current frame of mind he wouldn't be crazy enough to drive around at this hour with all that alcohol in his system. She looked out into the dark garden; a shaft of light across the lawn told her he was in his office, at the back of the house.

That meant he'd be drinking and doing whatever else he did in there, for some time. He kept the room locked. To keep the boys out, he said.

Bloody men. I hate bloody men.

She rested her head on her knees, and her thoughts drifted to all those poor, murdered girls. How they'd felt must be like this, a hundred times over.

At least she knew it wasn't him. Paul always stopped himself when he'd reached a certain point. He never crossed the line.

Or was that just with her? Did he take his frustrations with her out on others?

If he did, it would be her fault.

She wept.

Her head hurt, and she felt bruised and cold all over. She ached for someone to put their arms around her, comfort her, but there was never anyone to do that, so she went upstairs as quietly as she could, got into her nightie and sank into the welcoming, soft arms of her bed.

After the storm came the period of calm.

Sometimes, when the Tully family chatted over breakfast, on normal days when everything was good, she pretended life was always like that.

She didn't let herself remember the night of the dinner party.

Didn't want to think about those horrible murders.

She'd stopped reading the articles. Turned the page of the paper if she saw them mentioned. So what if one or two of the murders coincided with Paul's mysterious nights out? Wasn't her life difficult enough, without driving herself mad with groundless suspicions?

But did hiding from her own thoughts mean she was an optimist, or a coward?

If we could understand our own motives, God wouldn't have invented therapists.

She laughed when she thought of that; it was quite clever. Years ago, she used to have a fine sense of humour. Lara always told her how witty she was. She couldn't imagine, now, being thought of as anything but useless and dull.

I'm depressed, she thought. Recently, she forgot all sorts of things, little domestic chores she'd meant to do, items that should have been purchased on her weekly supermarket shop, plots of films she'd only just watched.

(Murders in the newspaper.)

Confusion could be a sign of anxiety and depression; Juliet knew all about this. And a side effect of those wretched pills she took, which she didn't think made her any happier. Looking up symptoms of illnesses was something she'd been doing since the boys were young—and hypochondria itself was a symptom of anxiety and depression. Or was it a result of those things? Was symptom obsession itself a psychological disorder with its own symptoms? Oh, God!

One thing she found hard to forget, however, was that list of psychological traits of serial killers. She may be ignoring the articles in the newspaper, changing channels when something came on the television, but she'd looked up the list of characteristics common to psychopaths and multiple killers several times, since seeing that programme.

Abused as a child

Bullied by his peers

Lack of remorse

Sadistic tendencies

Paul hadn't hit her since the night of the dinner party, but that meant nothing.

His outbursts were rare enough to maintain the appearance of a normal marriage to everyone else, yet frequent enough to keep her fearful.

Accidental, or a planned campaign?

She hadn't meant to talk to Lara about the dinner party, but she couldn't help it.

"What you said isn't so bad. He shouldn't be so touchy." Lara always made her feel better. "Some successful people would boast about it—that they'd done so well after such a rubbish start in life."

"I know," Juliet said, "but Paul isn't one of them, and I should have respected that; it's up to him whether or not he's touchy about it. I had no right to blurt out his private history to a group of people who don't know him that well—or to anyone at all, really."

"Fair enough. I do see what you mean. But people don't care; they probably won't even remember. Mostly, people only think about themselves, and it's not that much of a shocker, anyway. You said sorry, right?"

"Of course I did. I felt terrible."

"Well, stop beating yourself up about it, then. You made a mistake that's not likely to have far-reaching consequences, and you apologised. However pissed off he is, whoever was in the right or wrong, it's done."

Thinking about it brought back the shame and hopelessness of that night, when she'd needed someone to comfort her and there was no one to do so.

"You're going to forgive yourself, aren't you?"

"Yes."

"Are you sure?"

"Paul was furious."

"How furious?"

Juliet shut her eyes. "Very." The physical injuries mattered little, compared with the pain of knowing that someone she loved, a man whose children she'd borne, could do this to her.

Lara knew. "He hits you, doesn't he?"

She closed her eyes. "Yes."

"How badly? I mean, it's all bad, whether he hit you fifty times, or just once, you have to understand that, it's *always* bad—"

"Four times. Two punches to each side of the head."

"Did you see a doctor?"

Juliet laughed. "No, no! That wouldn't have occurred to me; it only hurt a bit, I just had a bump for a couple of days, that's all."

"He 'only' bashed you around the head so bad that you 'just' had a lump on your head—listen, you don't have to put up with this, not for one minute longer. Leave him, take the boys—you need to get out of there."

"I couldn't do that! One, they don't know about it, two, they wouldn't come anyway, and three, I'm not going to disrupt our whole family life just because of a tiff that got a bit out of hand."

"Can you hear yourself? This isn't *a tiff that got out of hand*! People aren't supposed to physically assault each other; this isn't acceptable under any circumstances."

"I know. It's just that there's more at stake here than how I feel about it."

Lara was not placated. "Look, you absolutely do not have to put up with this. You could be in real danger. Did you know that two women die as a result of domestic violence *every week*?"

"What I said was unforgiveable."

Lara laughed. "Classic battered wife's reaction, Juliet. Thinking you deserved it."

Juliet's confusion, her helplessness and frustration swirled together in her head until she thought it might burst. "I am not a classic battered wife, I'm *me*," she wailed. "I don't think I deserved to be hit, but I do think Paul had reason to be angry. Situations aren't black and white."

"Sometimes they are."

"I can handle it. I'm not as weak as you think I am."

Paul was rarely around when Lara showed up. On the occasions they did come face to face, he made scathing remarks about 'mouthy' women or 'ballbreakers'.

Lara said what he actually meant was that he couldn't handle women who didn't echo his opinions about absolutely everything.

Juliet played over the conversation in her mind for a few days after that.

There was so much stuff whooshing round her head, each thought, each feeling shoving the others out of the way, that she couldn't think straight about any of it.

She bought a book from Waterstones and read about Fred and Rose West, Ted Bundy, Jeffrey Dahmer, John Haigh, Ed Gein (that one really turned her stomach), Peter Sutcliffe. They were all so different, from the companionable, suave Bundy to the demonic Richard Ramirez.

They all seemed considerably more insane than Paul Tully, respectable property developer from Kirton, South Lincolnshire.

She hid the book under the cushion on her side of the settee in the living room, but Max discovered it.

"Cool book, Mum; makes a change! Can I have a read?"

That was the last she saw of it, but she looked up Ted Bundy and the others on the internet. They seemed so terrifying, so obviously evil, that she decided her fear must be a symptom of her own psychological problems; Paul told her she was 'mental', didn't he?

When she read in the papers that another recent murder and two from 2014 were being attributed to this Lyndford Strangler, she turned the page to read an article about a soap opera star getting divorced from one of the dancers on *Strictly*.

She was used to her own emotional and behavioural cycles as well as Paul's. After he'd hit her, she felt depressed for a few weeks until his renewed attention pulled her out of it. Six weeks later, she was more or less back to normal. He was genuinely sorry. This was the high point. They would pull through it. There was hope for the future.

She'd just entered this happy stage one dull, damp, chilly lunchtime in June.

Friday the nineteenth, to be precise.

The boys were at school, Paul was at work, and Juliet had eaten her sandwich and Petits Filous whilst watching *Bargain Hunt*. She'd cut up an apple and was slowly crunching each of the quarters when the national news began. Boring, boring. Politics and countries far away. Juliet looked out of the window and pondered over the phrase 'flaming June'; more often, these days, the weather in this first official month of summer was more like April or October.

Then the screen switched to the local news studio.

They'd fished another body from the river, this time out near Waterton. Early reports suggested that death had occurred only the night before; police were yet to confirm that it was linked to the string of murders attributed to the so-called 'Lyndford Strangler'.

Last night, Paul had not come home until just after two a.m.

He'd been to an Architects' Association awards dinner with Oliver and Rob, he said. A big night, because one of Rob's employees was to receive an award for work on the restoration of some local historic edifice.

She wouldn't have minded going herself, but Paul said Aurelia was unwell and would not be attending.

"So it's going to be a bit of a lads' night, I'm afraid!" He smiled; he looked genuinely sorry that she couldn't go.

He woke her up when he came in, even though he tried not to, but she never slept well when he was out.

"You know how these things can drag on," he said. "Especially when you're not drinking! But Oliver was and I'd agreed to drive him home."

"He kept you out until this time, just for a lift home? That's ridiculous, he could have got a taxi."

Paul laughed. "Tell me about it! I know, I know, but I'd said I'd drive him." He sat down on the side of the bed to undo his shoelaces. "It was okay; I made some good contacts, I think. I hope."

"Did Rob stay out this late?"

"No, he got a cab about eleven-thirty. Wanted to get home to Aurelia."

"Well, why couldn't Oliver have got in it, too? They live near each other, don't they?"

He sighed; she knew she was pushing it. Trying his patience. "I don't know, Juliet. Perhaps he didn't want to go home that early. I told Oliver I'd drive him, so I did. Shall we just leave it at that, eh?"

He undressed quickly, put on boxer shorts and a t-shirt, and got into bed beside her. A definite smell emanated from his body: the scent of the outdoors. A musty smell, too, of a damp summer night. Not the smell of someone who'd been eating and drinking in a nice restaurant for hours. She moved closer and threw an arm around him, not out of affection but to investigate further.

He was cold. Cold, as though he'd been outside. Surely if he'd been in the restaurant's function room, and then straight into his car, his body would be warm.

She nestled closer to him, and slipped her hand up the back of his shorts. His skin felt icy cold.

"Not now," Paul said, reaching back and pushing her hand away. "I'm tired."

She wanted to laugh; did he actually think she wanted sex?

He thumped her round the head, and he thought she'd want to have sex with him?

Paul showed little interest in her, not even when he was trying to be nice; they only had sex a handful of times a year, nowadays, and there was something awkward about it when they did. At first, she'd felt hurt, unattractive and rejected; now, because his touch represented fear, she was glad.

The tiny voice in the back of her head told her that making her feel unattractive and unloved was one of his ways of controlling her.

She said, "You're freezing."

"Yeah. It was cold in that restaurant. Let me sleep, now."

She didn't believe him.

She lay awake for a long time, listening to him snore.

Now, apple quarter in hand, she stared at the television screen. The cordoned-off area by the river, people walking around in those big white space suits.

The nightmare was back.

Chapter Ten

Maisie: The Teenager

Late June 2015

"Hey, you know that body they found last week?" Bethany leant against the railings and held her face up to the sun. "The one they reckon is the latest Lyndford Strangle?"

Maisie shrugged off her school backpack and took off her sweatshirt; the afternoon was warm, and she wished she was wearing a skirt, like Bethany, instead of her black trousers. "Yeah. What about it?"

"It's Alisha Pope. My cousin knew her." Bethany seemed excited by this information, and eager to impart more. "Jo said she, like, went really off the rails and went to live with this druggie bloke who sent her out to *sell her ass*!" She said the 'sell her ass' bit in an American accent, jerking her head from side to side and grinning as she did so. "God, can you imagine that? Being with someone who makes you be a prostitute? I mean, why didn't she just leave him?"

Maisie hoisted her bag back onto her back, and they walked on. "Bloody hell, really? Why would you love someone who'd make you do that? I hope they arrest him, too. What an arsehole."

"It's gross, isn't it? Jo said she was really clever at school, and dead pretty, all the boys fancied her, but she was a bit, you know, *wild*, always going off with the bad guys and drinking and all that. Then she turns up dead in the river."

Maisie felt tears spring to her eyes; she didn't know why. She hadn't known Alisha Pope; she was nothing to her. "That's well sad."

"I know!" Bethany still sounded more excited than anything else. "She used to be on Facebook but she hasn't used it for a while. I'll send you the link so you can see what she looked like."

Later, Maisie studied the pictures of the dead girl, and other ones on a page called 'RIP Alisha', set up by her friends. Bethany was right, she was so pretty, playing it up with the usual selfie duck faces and cute dresses. Nude lipstick, eyebrow tattoos and hair extensions. She looked like Michelle Keegan. Maisie knew her mum would call her trashy, but that was just the look these days, for girls who were into clubbing and dance music. She was always harping on about how in her day girls went out wearing *clothes*, ha ha ha. Preferring jeggings, opaques and DMs to chav gear (unlike Bethany, who did the whole TOWIE thing when she went out), Maisie quite liked her Mum's 1990s grunge look, even if her mum didn't know that was what it was.

She scrolled through Alisha's pictures again. How could a girl like that end up as a prostitute? Shagging strangers for money. Putting herself in such danger, every night. How scared she must have been. Who could have done that to her? Raped her, strangled her, cut her life off like that?

She felt *rage*, not only against the Strangler, but against the arsehole who sent her out there (perhaps they were one and the same?), against her parents and friends for not dragging her away from the situation she was in. Maisie was sure that if Bethany ever got herself in with the wrong crowd (and with Beth that was always likely), she would yell and yell at her until she came to her senses.

She felt angry with Alisha, too, for letting herself end up like that. This was what Ms Brownlow talked about, wasn't it?

Wafts of something that smelled like spaghetti Bolognese called her downstairs, where she found Zack flicking through TV channels, and her mum reading the paper.

"Isn't it awful about this girl?" Pru Todd said. "Her poor parents."

Maisie shut her eyes. "Her poor parents should have looked after her better, then it wouldn't have happened."

Pru looked up at her, with her sad smile, the one that said *you don't understand. You're just a kid.* "She was nineteen. She made her own decisions. Parents have to respect their children's independence, once they're no longer children."

Grrr! Why was everything irritating her today? "*Mu*-um! She was a *prostitute*! Never mind respecting her decisions; if I was doing that, however old I was, I hope you'd say, er, Maisie, this may not be, like, such a great idea, right?"

God, her mum was such a fucking hippie!

Zack chucked the TV remote control down beside him. "Is dinner ready yet? I'm starved."

Pru put down the paper and got up. "Okay, gutso, I'll just go and drain the spag."

"Where's Gary?" Maisie asked, as they sat down; only three places were laid.

"Yeah, where is he?" said Zack. "I wanted him to play Forza with me."

Her mother's face went all closed, the way it did when she was hiding stuff she knew would piss them off. "He's gone to stay with some friends in Great Yarmouth, for a few days. You know, love, he goes over there sometimes." She laughed, a bit too brightly. "He did have a life before he came to live with us, you know!"

She changed the subject after that, but Maisie knew she wasn't happy about wherever Gary was.

As soon as they'd finished eating Zack zipped upstairs to 'do his homework' (play GTA5, in other words; he'd sneaked in a copy from a friend because it was on Pru's list of banned games).

"Who are the friends Gary stays with?" Maisie asked, as soon as she heard his bedroom door shut.

Pru didn't answer her at first; she went out into the kitchen and came back with a small bottle of elderflower cordial, a bottle of white wine and two large glasses.

"You're too old for me to lie to, aren't you?" she said, handing Maisie the cordial and filling her wine glass almost to the brim.

"Yes." She opened the bottle. "Who are they, Mum? You always seem dead sad every time he goes."

Pru closed her eyes and leant her elbow on the table, rubbing her forehead. "It's his ex."

Maisie's mouth dropped open. "*What*? He goes to stay with his ex, and you let him? Mu-um! Why on earth—"

"Stop, stop, stop." Pru reached across the table and patted Maisie's hand. "It's not like you think. He was with this woman, Charlotte, for about five years, and she's got kids—he was like a second dad to them, they miss him. I think they're only about Zack's age, so they kind of grew up with him."

Maisie frowned. "Okay. So why does he have to stay there? Why can't he just visit them, and come back here in the evening?"

"That was what I said at first, but he explained and I get it now." She didn't look entirely convinced. "He wants to give them some stability, be there when they get home from school sometimes, stuff like that."

"And you're happy with that?"

"No, not really, but I understand it."

Maisie felt that irritation on the rise again. Never mind all this fairyland shit she came out with, where everyone was super reasonable, why was her mother such a sap? "Mum, where does he sleep when he stays there?"

Pru laughed. "On the settee, of course!"

"How do you know?"

She stopped smiling. "Because he's told me so and I believe him."

A thought occurred to Maisie. "Did he leave her or did she chuck him out?"

"Why? What difference does it make?"

"A lot. I know you'll say we're only kids so it's not the same, but it is. When Bethany's ex left her for someone else, she used to get him to come round to see her, pretending she needed him to help with her maths homework or something with her computer, I don't know, but it was really just so she could see him. And she'd sit really close to him, and get him to kiss her."

Pru looked out of the window. "It was mutual. They just decided to split up."

"Mum—"

"I wish I hadn't told you."

"I'm glad you did. It sounds well dodgy to me."

"It's not. You'd understand if you were a mother."

"Yeah, but it's not like he's their dad, is it? And we've managed just fine without one."

"Perhaps he wants to see them, too." Pru took a sip of wine. "I'm not totally happy with it, sweetheart, but I'm trying to be fair and not give him any hassle. He doesn't need it right now."

Maisie pulled a face. "Yeah, yeah, yeah. Mustn't upset poor little Gary, 'cause he can't find a job. But when he's away enjoying himself by the seaside with his ex, he could be looking for one, couldn't he? You're sitting here, doing his laundry and worrying about paying the bills, and he's larking about at the beach with his ex-girlfriend. It's not right, Mum."

"It's not like that."

"Seems like it to me. You ought to put your foot down."

Pru gave a long, loud sigh and pushed herself away from the table. "I will. Just not right now. We haven't been together long enough for me to make demands on him."

"What do you mean? He lives *in our house*!"

"I know, I know. I just don't want to rock the boat at the moment, okay?" She stood up and walked over to the window, wine glass in hand.

"Are you scared he'll go back to her if you make a fuss?"

No answer.

"You are, aren't you? Mum, if you're scared about that, should he be here at all? You don't have to put up with any old crap, just so he'll stay!"

Pru turned around and smiled. She looked sad. "I used to be like you, darling. So sure of what I would put up with and what I wouldn't. It's easy to make rules in theory, but life only gets more complicated the older you get. It's not easy, being nearly forty, with two kids and not very much money." She laughed. "And a saggy tummy and cellulite thighs! I'm not much of a catch."

Maisie folded her arms. "Yeah, well, nor's he. And forty's still young, you look great for your age, you're still pretty and you haven't got a saggy tummy at all."

Pru did the sad smile again. "Do you mind if we stop talking about this now?"

"Yes, I do. I want to know why we all have to tiptoe round the great god Gary."

"He's not had an easy life, darling."

"Nor's anyone. What's so different about him?"

Pru looked down. "You know. I told you. About his sister. She drowned when she was only thirteen. He was the same age, it's a really sensitive time in a young lad's development—"

"They were the same age? What, were they twins?"

"No. She was his step-sister. His mother married again a little while before."

Maisie's mouth dropped open. "Hang on a minute. So she wasn't even his real sister? What you're telling me is that thirty years ago he knew some girl who drowned, so we all have to feel sorry for him and allow him to do whatever he likes?"

"They were very close; Gary loved her like a real sister. Then, afterwards, her father's grief was so great that he couldn't deal with it, he just upped and left, so Gary had to be a pillar of strength for his mother, too. It's a lot to put on the shoulders of a thirteen-year-old boy, a huge trauma. He still gets upset when he talks about it."

"I thought his parents lived in a cottage in Ireland?"

"His mother married for a third time a couple of years later. So, another stepfather. More change."

Maisie said nothing. She felt a niggling mixture of impatience, pity and love when she looked at her mother's kind, sad eyes. When she was little, she'd seen her mother as the Great Protector who would always make everything okay for their little family, all by herself, whatever happened—but now she could see that she was far from invincible. She was *weak*. Even her boss took the piss, making her work all those long hours.

The Cinderella Complex. *Waiting for your handsome prince to rescue you and make your life complete.*

Gary Dunlop. Some Prince Charming, right?

Zack thought he was great, but that was only because Gary liked the Xbox. Then again, he did take time with him, showed a real interest in stuff he did. Her mum's friends thought she'd got herself a good 'un (stupid Wendy down the road said "you've got yourself a good 'un there" every time she came round, it even got on Pru's nerves), though maybe they didn't know about him nipping off to stay with his ex. Even Bethany thought he was okay, as stepdads went.

Except that he wasn't her stepdad. Thank God.

"Perhaps he's got a double life, and he's really married to this Charlotte!" said Bethany, on Skype, later. "And to relieve his frustration about this double life, he takes it out on prostitutes! Maisie, he really *could* be the Strangler! How cool would that be? Hey, we could go on talk shows, or write a best seller about it!"

Bethany's game didn't amuse Maisie as much as it usually did. She couldn't stop thinking about Alisha Pope, and her mum's pathetic face, scared to complain about her boyfriend going to stay with his ex-girlfriend in case he didn't come back. Sometimes Beth could be so fucking childish, it was like talking to Zack.

"Um, *why* would having two families turn him into a murderer? It doesn't make sense." She could hear the annoyance in her voice. *Everything* was so bloody irritating at the moment.

"Because he feels guilty!"

"Yeah, right. That makes zero sense."

Bethany sighed, disappointed. "So, what do you think? D'you reckon he's still shagging the ex-girlfriend?"

Ugh. "Wouldn't be surprised."

"Ask him," Bethany said. "Why not? If your mum won't, perhaps you should."

"*Be*-eth! I couldn't."

Bethany laughed. "I don't mean come out with it and say, *are you shagging your ex?* I meant, say something like … um … *did you have a good time in*

Yarmouth? and he'll say, *yes thank you,* and you could say, *I think it's a bit weird that you go and stay overnight with your ex, I hope you're not taking the piss out of my mum.*"

Maisie thought about it. "That's not a bad idea, actually."

"Do it. I would."

"Yeah, I know you would."

"Oh, Christ, yes, of course, I can see exactly how it looks, to you. Oh, bloody hell." Gary Dunlop held his hands up. "Sorry, sorry, I didn't mean to swear in front of you, don't tell your mum—honestly, it never occurred to me for a moment that it could be perceived like that. Your mum's totally cool with it, but yes—now you point it out I can see what it looks like. My bad, right?"

Vom. He really said that. He really just said 'my bad'. Bethany would hear about this later, that'd put her off him.

She'd caught him downstairs while her mother was in the bath, and dived straight in. "I just thought that you might be doing that thing you hear about men doing, you know, when they secretly have two families."

That wasn't exactly what she meant, but it was a good point to make. Just in case.

Gary huffed and puffed a bit, running big hands through his hair; Maisie tried to view him as her mother would and decided that yes, he was probably quite good looking if you liked that sort of thing. Hardly Jared Leto, but not bad for an old bloke.

Eventually Gary said: "I swear to you that there is nothing between Charlotte and me but friendship; if it wasn't for the kids we wouldn't even be in touch."

He looked sincere. She believed him. There was something else, though, that she had to ask him.

"Okay. But just one more thing."

He smiled. Nice, friendly, warm (still a bit snaky, though). "Anything. Shoot. And then I'm going to go upstairs and tell your mum she's got absolutely nothing to worry about. Christ, I hate to think I've hurt her."

"Okay." She had to know this, just in case Bethany started saying her stupid shit to people about Gary being the Lyndford Strangler. Murdering poor Alisha Pope. Yes, she would only be kidding around, but she always managed to take everything too far and some people wanted to believe any gossip. "The Thursday before last," she said. "Where were you? You went out and didn't come back until after two in the morning—I know, because you woke me up when you came in. I asked Mum, and she did that thing she does, you know, when she doesn't want to tell you something so she pretends she hasn't heard the question."

As soon as the last sentence was out of her mouth, Maisie wished she hadn't said it. She didn't want to discuss her mother's quirks with Gary. She felt disloyal but, worse, as though she'd welcomed Gary into her thoughts, her life, the family-only, private jokes, when she'd meant to keep the barrier firmly in place, always.

(*I don't want you here, I don't care how nice you are, or how much Mum loves you, I just don't want you here*—)

Gary winked and said, "Yeah, I know that one," and Maisie recoiled from him.

Then he smiled, looking a little sad. "It's okay. She probably didn't want to tell you. I went over to Yarmouth that night, too, because Charlotte's oldest—Bobby, he's a great kid—he's being bullied at school, and I went over to help him through it, to have a really good sit down with him and Charlie so we could work out what to do. Which was pretty damn exhausting, and when Bobby went to bed Charlie got us something to eat, and we talked some more, then I started off home; it's a good drive from Yarmouth to Lyndford, love."

Don't call me 'love'. "Oh. Yeah. Of course."

Gary held his hands up and accompanied the gesture with a stupid fake grin that made her want to throw his coffee in his face. "Tell you what, you can ask her yourself if you want further confirmation." He got his phone out of his pocket. "I've got her phone number right here!"

Retard. As if she'd ring up a total stranger with a dumb question like that. "No, it's okay. I believe you."

"Good, because your mum was fine with it, honest, love." That fake smile again. "I wouldn't have gone if she wasn't. Your mum—all of you—you come first, now. It's just that—well, you can finish a relationship with a woman, but your relationship with a child who's been in your care never ends, and it never should."

Maisie nodded, with reluctance. "Yeah. I get that."

The next day was Saturday and she got up to find Gary whistling as he put the washing on, emptying the dishwasher, putting the rubbish out and boiling the kettle to make Pru her coffee in bed. He turned to see her standing in the doorway watching him, and grinned.

"Hey, Mais, fancy some toast? I'm just putting some in."

"No, it's okay." She slunk back into the living room and switched on the TV, idly flicking through the music channels and wishing she had the courage to say what she meant.

When you leave Mum, don't feel you have to come back to visit me and Zack, will you? 'Cause we'll be glad to see the back of you.

Chapter Eleven

Hat

Wednesday, 24th June 2015

LYNDFORD STRANGLER KILLINGS
LINKED TO 2013 EAST ANGLIA MURDERS?

Could the brutal murders of Michelle Brand and Lita Gomez, in Norfolk during the summer of 2013, have been committed by the killer known as the Lyndford Strangler?

...the image below is a likeness of the last person to be seen with Alisha Pope, whose body was found at Waterton last Sunday.

The latest e-fit picture in the *Lyndford Echo* was not unlike the one put together by the girl who'd seen Angelika's last punter; the same prominent cheekbones, dark eyes, dark hair. This time, though, the face wore a close fitting, pull-on, black hat. The details had been supplied by a girl who had been chatting to Alisha Pope the minute before she was picked up and driven away, presumably to her death.

Juliet Tully gave a huge sigh of relief. Paul didn't own a hat like that.

Steve Turner thought he was going to be sick. This image looked so much like Dan, too. He wore one of those hats often, if it was raining; he was vain, and the damp made his hair curl. Said it made him look a twat. Steve thought back; it hadn't rained on Thursday night when the girl was killed, he was sure. Didn't stop the picture looking just like him, though.

Tamsin Verden stared at the picture for a long time, and all the vague thoughts and suspicions whirling around in her mind made sense.

Bethany showed the picture to Maisie on her iPad, at break time. "Bad news—I don't reckon the Lyndford Strangler is Gary after all," she said, shoving the screen in front of Maisie's face. "I mean, Gaz is quite hot, and this guy looks more like—well, a serial killer, doesn't he?"

Maisie looked at her disappointed face, and wanted to slap her. "Never mind. When him and Mum split up, I'll make sure she chooses someone more interesting. I'll get her to find a nice paedo next, shall I? Will that be enough for you to gossip about?"

She stalked off, leaving Bethany wondering what on earth she'd said wrong.

Chapter Twelve

Dorothy: The Mother

Thursday, 25th June 2015

Dorothy saw the newspaper in the library, where she enjoyed coffee and biscuits every Thursday morning. The library provided this refreshment on Tuesdays and Thursdays, and Dorothy always went on Thursday before doing her light shop, as opposed to the big shop on Monday.

Library day was part of her weekday routine that she enjoyed most.

Dorothy didn't feel very happy this morning, though. She hadn't been able to find her door keys that morning (goodness knows why they weren't on the hook!), so she'd missed the ten-fifteen bus, which made her arrive at the library twenty minutes later than usual. Her chair by the window was occupied by a stranger. Worse still, there were no ginger creams left, just boring old bourbons and rich teas, and those nasty ones with gluey jam in the middle that stuck in her teeth.

The stranger had taken her favourite *Daily Express*, too. She closed her eyes, and breathed deeply. Getting upset about things like this was silly and small-minded. It didn't really matter. Orlando often told her she ought to try the *Guardian*, and, for goodness sake, she could buy some ginger creams when she went to Asda, and eat the whole wretched packet herself when she got home, if she wanted.

She smiled at the other regulars: the old gentleman who read the *Daily Telegraph*, and the down-at-heel, shy looking young man she suspected was unemployed, who had his nose in the *National Geographic*. He ate more than his share of the biscuits, looking round to see if he dared take another one. Poor chap, perhaps he was hungry; she'd wondered, more than once, if he'd be offended if she offered him some money, or some groceries, maybe. She'd read that the dole was impossible to live on, these days. Perhaps she could start up a conversation with him, find out; she and Orlando had known lean times in the past so she was aware how depressing it was to be hard up.

A couple of other old gentlemen came in to drink their coffee and exchange comments about the weather and the ill-advised development of the town since the 1960s, while a lady of around her own age would thumb through the latest books from the New Release shelves.

Now there was the stranger, too, with her *Daily Express*—and, no doubt, her ginger creams lining his stomach.

Ah, well. No biscuits could only be good for her waistline. Dorothy sat down with her coffee and picked up the *Lyndford Echo*. Oh, delightful. Spread across the front page was more news about those horrible murders. Shocking, awful, terrible business, but Dorothy didn't feel like reading about it. She'd reached a stage in her life where she didn't want to know about terrorists and neo-Nazis, sex offenders and drug pushers. Wanting to live in blissful ignorance wasn't a sin, was it? She endured enough of her own troubles, and the grim reality of the dark side of human nature was too distressing. As far as crime went, *Midsomer Murders* was enough for her, nothing too gory in a nice village setting, and Jim Bergerac nailing the culprit.

She didn't want to read about prostitutes being strangled.

She flicked through the rest of the paper, but her eyes kept being drawn back to the front page.

Six girls they'd found now, and the murders might be linked to two others, in East Anglia, in 2013.

It wasn't just the article, though. She couldn't stop looking at the picture, one of those weird-looking computer images, cobbled together from various descriptions of the man who may or may not be the perpetrator of these horrors.

If she'd had a friend there, she might have shown it to them and laughed. Jollied herself out of the shock. As it was, she just sat and stared at it.

A dark eyed man with dark wavy hair, wearing a black pull-on hat.

It looked just like Orlando when he went off on his fishing trips.

In fact, it couldn't have looked more like him if someone had sat down in front of him and produced his portrait.

It looked so like him that she heard herself say, "Oh my goodness, that's Orlando," out loud, without realising she'd done so until she looked up and saw her fellow coffee drinkers staring at her.

Dorothy went into the newsagent when she got off the bus, and picked up a copy of the *Lyndford Echo*. As she paid for it, her hands shook.

She'd tried her best to laugh off her outburst in the library, and the rest of the group had either laughed along with her or sidled out a couple of moments later.

"Just the paper today, is it, Dorothy?" The nice Indian man smiled at her. They knew about customer service, these Indians, whatever people said about them taking over all the small shops. Or used to say; no one mentioned it now, it was just accepted that few paper shops or corner grocery stores were owned by English people any more. Every day she was confronted by another reminder of how different the world was now, compared to the one in which she'd grown up. Sometimes, though, the changes were for the good.

"I got some of your liquorice bonbons in," said the shopkeeper. She didn't even know his name, although he knew hers; that was bad, wasn't it? Rude. "I got them from the cash and carry especially for you!"

So of course Dorothy felt obliged to buy some, even though she was trying not to eat so many sweet things because they made her teeth hurt, and she'd seen something on television about how eating too much sugar could lead to type II diabetes, *and* because she felt so churned up since seeing that picture in the paper that she didn't feel like eating anything. It was getting on for lunchtime, but she couldn't imagine wanting any.

Home, shoes off, raincoat hanging over the kitchen door, Dorothy felt weak. Probably the energy-sapping weather; the sky and the rain made the June day feel more like autumn, despite the temperature. Always like this, nowadays. Every year she heard people saying 'we haven't really had a summer'; why were they surprised, why did they even bother to mention it, when sunny, dry summers were clearly a thing of the past? And they *had* been better, they *had*, those summers weren't just a rose-tinted memory of the over-forties. There were proper seasons, fifty or sixty years ago. When she was a child her mother would pack her winter clothes away in early May and get them out again in late September, when her summer dresses went back into boxes. For the last twenty-five years or so, she'd needed the same clothes pretty much all year round. Thin layers, that was the trick.

Without even unpacking her shopping, she sat down to study the paper once more.

The picture (*the man in the hat who looked exactly like her son*) was on the front, but the main feature was inside, spread over two pages. All those poor girls, and the dates they'd been found, the dates they'd been killed.

She read it all, every word, and then closed the paper and just sat.

Dorothy had always been a practical woman; when you were on your own with a child you had to be. She closed her eyes and imagined going about her daily chores, (Thursday afternoon: ironing) and thinking about dinner, perhaps reading a chapter or two of the current book club choice if there was time. Oh dear, oh dear, she wasn't in the right frame of mind at all, couldn't see herself enjoying the television whilst doing the ironing, as she normally did. She spun the task out to last longer if she found a particularly interesting programme, ironing items that didn't need it.

Orlando would see the pile of ironed socks and underpants on his bed, and say, "Aha, I see there was a good film on this afternoon!"

Couldn't imagine that happening today.

Not with this silly rubbish in her mind.

It was so silly it wasn't even worth thinking about.

Orlando had been staying out late and lying about his whereabouts, and he appeared to be the man the police were looking for in connection with a series of grisly murders.

Oh dear.

Of course it wasn't him. What rubbish!

Well, she would just deal with it, once and for all, and then she could get on.

In the kitchen, by the fridge, and the phone that Orlando had attached to the wall (a phone in every room, just in case anything 'happened' while he was out), was the calendar. Every year she bought a large one, with plenty of space to note appointments. She was meticulous about this. Orlando called it their 'life organiser'.

"If it isn't on the calendar, it won't happen!"

Dorothy took it off the wall.

In the dining room, she placed it next to the article in the paper.

Do it, she told herself, eyes closed. *Just do it. Stop all these silly thoughts, prove yourself wrong, then you can put it to bed.*

Hmm. If she was going to do this properly, she would need the previous years' calendars, too. These were stored away underneath the photograph albums, in the sideboard. She didn't know why she kept them, except that they were proof of her and Orlando's lives, in the same way that the photographs were. She had no siblings, and she doubted whether Orlando would have children now, so there would be only remote cousins to remember the two of them had ever existed.

From under the stack of albums she pulled out the 2013 calendar.

Back at the dining room table, she consulted the newspaper. Two summers ago, two girls had been found strangled, raped and dumped in rivers.

Michelle Brand: Costessey Pits, near Norwich, on 14th May 2013; they thought she'd been dead for around ten days.

Lita Gomez: The River Bure near Shearsby, on the day after August Bank Holiday.

Dorothy felt nauseous as she flipped the calendar over.

The weekend of the 4th and 5th of May, 2013, when Michelle had probably been killed, had been blocked out by Orlando, and marked with the words 'Fish. Burgh'. This, she knew, meant that he'd been on a weekend's fishing to Burgh Castle, near Great Yarmouth. The Monday was the May Day Bank Holiday, and he often made the most of the bank holidays to go on his trips.

She breathed out, long and loud. Burgh Castle, not Costessey. Miles away. Why would anyone kill someone then drive miles and miles to dump the body? That would be plain silly. She smiled, proud of herself for putting two and two together. Jim Bergerac would have spotted that straight away, too.

The smile faded from her face and she burst into tears.

What on earth was she doing?

She was sitting at her dining table, where she and her son ate every day, deciding whether or not he was a cold-blooded murderer, and pondering on methods of corpse transportation. What sort of person was she?

Oh dear, oh dear.

She had to carry on, though, now she'd started this awful process. Had to, or it would gnaw away at her.

She had to be brave, face it.

Through her tears, her hands shaking, she turned the pages of the calendar over to August.

August Bank Holiday, 2013. This time, two days were blocked out with the word 'Fish'. There! She had no way of knowing if he'd been anywhere near the River Bure in Shearsby. In fact, she had never heard of either the River Bure or Shearsby, which must mean that Orlando had never been there.

Oh, the relief!

All the same, she tore off the pages for May and August, ripped them into tiny pieces and threw them in the bin.

No, no, no. She began to cry again. Panic was making her act foolishly; why would anyone keep a calendar but tear out two months? That looked like an indication of guilt. She ripped the whole calendar to pieces, sobbing as she did so, crumpling all the pieces up, not even knowing why. If Orlando had anything to do with this, the fact that she'd thrown away a calendar wouldn't help him or anyone else, would it?

Silly, silly, silly. Silly old woman.

Dorothy looked at the picture again, and it made her cry even more.

If Orlando had anything to do with this, she couldn't help him, she wouldn't be able to live with the knowledge, so why was she bothering?

She sat down, closed her eyes, and tried to be calm. Anyone who knew Orlando would laugh at her. He was good, he was kind, funny, gentle.

But just occasionally, late at night when she was in bed, she wondered why he'd never shown any interest in getting married. Or in a love life of any sort. Had their close relationship damaged him in some way?

Damaged him badly? Like Norman Bates and his mother in *Psycho*?

She'd watched that film as a teenager, and it had terrified her.

Just do it, she told herself. *Do it, face it, look at the dates, then it'll be all over.*

Right.

Jodie Walker and Leanne Marsh. Found in September and October 2014, but the bodies were at more advanced stages of decomposition and an exact date of death couldn't be ascertained.

Dorothy shuddered, and read on.

Kayla Graham. Found on 6th February this year, possibly killed on the Tuesday 3rd.

The calendar showed nothing. Orlando must have been at home, but she couldn't remember one way or another. He rarely went out on a Tuesday, but she couldn't swear that he'd been at home.

Angelika. No surname, identified by a tattoo. Found on 16th February, killed the day before. Oh, thank goodness. The 15th was a Sunday, and Orlando *never* went out on a Sunday night. *Ever.*

Thank goodness, thank goodness.

There must be hundreds of men, all over the east of England, who looked like that picture. There were perfectly reasonable explanations for where he'd been on the dates when the girls had been killed.

She realised how hungry she was; a glance at the clock told her it was past lunchtime.

She would stop worrying about this now, go and make herself something to eat, and read a chapter of her novel before starting the ironing.

Before that, though, she'd have a quick look at the other dates, then this whole silly business would be done and dusted.

The photo of Ellie Kane was particularly heart-rending. Such a lovely looking young girl, standing in the garden with her little sister, who must be in pieces, now.

Poor Ellie had met her death on Friday, 17th April.

Another night that Orlando was out with Colin, so she could tick that one off, too. Good!

Alisha Pope (silly names girls had these days!) was found on Thursday 11th June, out at Waterton. Well, that was easy, she didn't even have to look. Thursday night was metal detecting night.

Oh. Yes.

Not according to Ray Goosey.

As Dorothy sliced tomatoes and cucumber, she told herself that, aside from this, there was not one date, not one single one of those dates, for which Orlando's movements could not be explained.

But the bad feeling wouldn't go away, no matter how many tea towels and pillow slips she ironed, no matter how hard she concentrated on giving Orlando's shirts the sharp edges he liked, no matter that *Deal or No Deal* was particularly riveting that day, with the nice young mother due to win either ten pounds or a hundred thousand.

It was because he was lying to her; that was why the bad feeling was still there.

In forty-three years, Orlando had never lied to her. So whatever he was covering up must be something pretty serious, mustn't it?

The nice young mother opened the wrong box, and Dorothy turned off the television.

Chapter Thirteen

Tamsin: The Colleague

Late July 2015

Her colleagues used their lunch breaks as a chance to sun themselves in the back yard for an hour; the countdown to the weekend had begun, and everyone was looking forward to two days off, or fortnight-long holidays for the lucky few.

Tamsin ate her lunch at her desk, unable to join in the trivial chatter of her workmates.

How could she, when she bore a burden she could share with no one?

Back in February, when Jake Fallon rejected her so cruelly, the intensity of her heartbreak had frightened her. Like many single women in their mid-thirties she was no stranger to romantic disappointment, but this was something different. This wasn't like meeting a guy in a bar, hooking up a few times and wondering if (hoping) it would become more than just a casual fling. This time, the steps had taken place in the right order. She'd got to know him as a *person* before they became intimate, and that familiarity had made sleeping with him so much more meaningful. She'd truly believed this was 'it'. The big one.

This time, she'd fallen in love.

Real, true love, not a passing crush based on physical attraction.

After that awful Monday she'd dragged herself into work each day, steeling herself for the pain that stabbed her in the gut every time she saw him. He was still pleasant, friendly, but he kept his distance.

She knew he was being careful not to give her any hint of renewed interest, and that hurt so badly.

Four years before, in the throes of a lesser, now forgotten heartbreak, Tamsin had discovered her bible: a self-help book called *Heal Your Heart*. Step one of the relationship break-up process was *shock*, and after *shock* came *grief*, which could last anything from a fortnight to several years.

Grief was the worst stage, by far. In *grief*, you felt powerless.

The book told her that *anger* came next—and, a few weeks after Jake had rejected her, Tamsin got angry.

Self-preservation kicked in, and with her anger came a cold, detached eye.

So he still wanted to be *friends*, did he? But he'd made her miserable; what sort of person would do that to a *friend*? He must have known how she felt, and he'd lied to her. *Used* her, to boost his ego. That was just plain *evil*.

Was he schizophrenic? Jekyll and Hyde. Mr Nice Guy, sweet, helpful, warm and considerate, who turned into a callous bastard the moment he got what he wanted?

Heal Your Heart told her that after *anger* came *resolution*, when your feelings levelled out and you were able to look at the situation without prejudice.

Resolution was good. Tamsin was surprised how quickly she'd reached this stage. Now that she was no longer in love with him and her rose-tinted spectacles had shattered underfoot, she could see Jake for who he truly was.

The way in which he could turn his charm on and off for his own gratification was alarming.

Tamsin began to think, a lot, about the evil men did to women. Before, her head had been saturated with Jake to the extent that there was room for nothing else, but now she opened her eyes.

And the Lyndford Strangler was everywhere, especially when you worked on the local paper.

She'd taken only an idle interest before, hardly giving the e-fit image of the killer a second glance, but now, along with her colleagues, she joined in with the jesting about who it looked like.

"It's Simon in the warehouse, I reckon."

"No, much too good looking! More like Mike in Telesales."

"Ooh, yes, could be, could be; he's a bit of a loner, too, isn't he? Just the type."

"It's the spitting image of my landlord," said Sophie, the junior assistant. "Paul Tully. I don't think I'd better report him to the police, though—he might put the rent up."

Brandon laughed. "I don't know, maybe you should, if you think it's him."

"Shit, yeah," said Sophie, posing in a theatrical fashion with hand to brow. "Might be me next!"

Kim, the team leader, ran her finger down the page. "I reckon it looks a bit like Jake from IT." She glanced up at Tamsin, and winked. "What d'you reckon?"

Tamsin felt her face and neck flush red.

This very idea had occurred to her only that morning.

Versions of the picture had been displayed since February, in the paper, all over the television, everywhere, until it was part of the wallpaper and she no longer saw it—until she found herself staring at the picture on the noticeboard in the staff tea room, while she was waiting for the water to boil for her coffee.

Her spoonful of Kenco Gold spilled onto the worktop. *It was him.*

The sudden clarity of vision felt so peculiar, as if the idea had been sent to her head by some outside force.

OMG.

Jake Fallon was the Lyndford Strangler.

Didn't she know his face better than any of them?

"What d'you think, then, Tam?"

Kim grinned, waiting for an answer.

Tamsin held up her hands. "I'm saying nothing!"

"Ooh, Tamsy, just think, you might have shagged the Lyndford Strangler!" squealed Denise, behind her back.

What?

Her head whipped round, just quick enough to see Sophie trying to shut Denise up. How the hell did she know about her and Jake?

Tamsin felt like hitting the silly bitch, but she could feel all eyes upon her. Waiting to see what she would do? They were *all* silly bitches. She fixed a smile onto her face. "Well, if I have, I'm certainly not going to be the one to call it in!"

Yet.

She'd searched her memory. Yes, oh yes, now she recalled Brandon's shocked expression when, back in April, he told her that on the night of Ellie Kane's murder he'd been drinking in Fagin's with Sanjay and Jake. The three of them had been all around the town, he said, with Fagin's as the last port of call.

"We might have even seen her," he said, at the time, clearly upset by the thought.

She chose her moment to quiz Brandon further, under cover of idle musing over whether he might have seen Ellie's killer; everyone at the *Echo* talked about the murders, so bringing up the subject once more would not look odd.

"I don't know, I wish I could remember the night properly, but Sanj and me, we were pretty wasted—he was trying to cop off with this girl with jet black lipstick, and I was trying to do the same with her friend, except that we were both too drunk to talk." He laughed. "I reckon they were winding us up. Must have thought we were a right pair of idiots."

She laughed too, willing her voice to sound casual. "And Jake? Was he trying to pull a Goth as well?"

Brandon looked at her with doubt, the smile fading from his face.

"It's okay," she said, patting him on the shoulder. "I'm over all that now!"

Brandon relaxed. "Oh, well, I seem to remember Jake wimped out before us and went home; said if he drank any more, he thought his stomach might evacuate his entire digestive system."

Jake had been out in the night, alone, in the same place and at the same time as Ellie had been abducted.

The psychiatrist's profile of the man they were searching for said that he might seem to be a completely normal member of society, but underneath there could lurk issues about relationships with the opposite sex; he might be unable to form and maintain satisfactory relationships.

It said lots of other things too, but that trait jumped out at her.

Tamsin collated every piece of information she could find about the murders. At home, she pored over it; somewhere, there had to be a clue.

Two months after Ellie, Alisha Pope had been dragged out of the river near Waterton. Vague physical description had been added by the girl who'd seen Alisha's last punter; white, aged anything between mid-thirties and fifty, with dark hair and dark eyes. He wore a black pull-on hat, and drove a smallish black or very dark green car, make unknown. Quite good looking, she thought.

An extra CCTV camera had been installed since Angelika was found, but this had resulted only in trade being conducted over a wider area, as the girls and their clientele slipped down the side alleys to do business.

Jake drove a black Fiat Bravo.

Alisha was murdered on Thursday, 18th June. Other than asking him directly, which she had no intention of doing, Tamsin had no way of finding out where Jake was that night, but her access to the HR records told her that on the Friday after he'd rung in sick.

Up all night, Jake?

Could someone for whom she'd felt real, genuine deep *love* be capable of such monstrosity? Wasn't she a pretty good judge of character? But she'd been wrong about him, for all those months. Thought he'd cared for her when all he'd wanted was to walk down the road from her flat the next morning, smiling that smug smile and drawing a satisfied tick in the air. Still, she mustn't be too hard on herself. Murderers often had wives, families, didn't they? Innocent people who had no idea they were living with ultimate evil. Jake had fooled her into thinking that he was worthy of her love, so couldn't he be fooling everyone else, too?

Every day since Alisha's death Tamsin had waited for someone else to notice, but Kim's joke was forgotten by everyone as soon as she'd made it.

She enlarged photos of Jake from Christmas in the office, enlarged the e-fit picture, printed them off and studied the two together at home, side by side, comparing the arrangement of features in minute detail.

A magnifying glass helped. She quite enjoyed it, sitting at home, quietly, carefully collecting all her evidence together, knowing that he was strutting around in blissful ignorance.

She watched him, all the time, whenever she could. He was really quite *cocky*; she hadn't noticed that, when she was in love with him.

Cocky about not having been caught, perhaps?

Now it was nearly August, five weeks since Alisha, and the police were no nearer to catching their man, or if they were, they certainly weren't telling anyone. 'Following many different lines of enquiry'; that meant they'd drawn a complete blank, didn't it? Tamsin studied the victims, too; they were all dark, pretty, with long hair. Like hers. She didn't look unlike a (slightly) older version of a couple of the girls.

Had she had a lucky escape?

It was Friday night; would he be out and about, later on?

Was the Strangler biding his time, making sure nobody suspected him, before striking again?

She was so involved in her thoughts and the items on her screen that she hadn't noticed that lunch was over and everyone was back at their desks, or that she'd forgotten to eat her second sandwich, until the door opened and Sophie called out, "Hi, Jake, over here! I think I've gone and deleted a whole spreadsheet!"

Jake Fallon, arriving to save the day. He turned his head to smile at Tamsin, giving a brief, cheery wave. She smiled back, thinly, and looked back down at her screen where her former lover's eyes looked up at her, revealing his true self.

Jake Fallon, bending over Sophie's desk, so helpful, so patient when the girl didn't understand his explanations.

Sophie was a pretty girl, with long, chestnut coloured hair; she could be Ellie Kane's sister.

Jake's deep, dark eyes twinkled and flirted.

The Lyndford Strangler had deep, dark eyes that watched those poor girls die in agony and terror.

Were they the same eyes?

The more Tamsin studied them, the more sure she was.

Chapter Fourteen

Steve: The Friend

Monday, 9th August 2015

Beads of sweat glistened on Dan's forehead and upper lip, and his hand shook as AJ filled his glass with Glenfiddich.

Steve had never seen him in such a state before. He'd been relatively calm on the drive out to Waterton, but AJ's presence and generous helpings of Scotch brought forth the new Dan, who Steve scarcely recognised.

"That evil slag," Dan ranted, yet again. "Screwed up, vindictive, psycho *bitch*."

"Chill, mate, chill." AJ patted him on the shoulder. "Look, we'll sort this fucker out. Philip's on the case, and I promise you, bro, you won't get a better defence. Listen, we'll *sort it*, okay?"

Warm summer rain splashed the windows of the conservatory at the back of AJ's luxury pad, trees danced in the wind below an ominous looking cluster of dark clouds. Thunder inside and out. This was absolutely the last place Steve wanted to be this Monday night, any Monday night, any bloody night of any bloody week at all, but Dan had phoned in a state so agitated that Steve had agreed to drive him over.

"I'm going to need a serious drink when I get there, and I can't drive right now, anyway, I'd crash the bloody thing. C'mon, mate, I don't want to have to ring Noel, I want you with me. I don't need an earful from big brother, you know?"

During the twelve-mile journey, Steve listened with growing concern to Dan's garbled account of events.

On Friday night they'd been in the Crown and Cushion, usually a one-drink pit-stop on the end of the week bar crawl, but they'd met up with a group of girls that AJ and Dan knew, and stayed put. Steve couldn't remember all their names, but he'd got chatting to the quietest of the group (as she would, no doubt, describe him, too). *Nina.* The only one not punctuating every sentence with pouts and suggestive looks and, thus, passed over by the other three; Woodsy was as bad as AJ and Dan for basing his choices on a woman's apparent availability.

Not that his Friday night flirtations ever went any further; his girlfriend might be something of a handful but Steve was pretty sure he was faithful. AJ, maybe not.

He and Dan were busy chucking banter back and forth with the two heavily spray-tanned blondes; shots were tossed back, saucy innuendoes flowed thick and fast. The blondes went to the ladies' to apply another layer of warpaint, Dan declared that he was about to score a hole in one, *no problemo,* and Woodsy tried his luck with the brunette with the not-quite-so convincing hair extensions, who was more interested in licking her lips at Dan over his shoulder, leaving Steve to talk to the one they'd all ignored.

Nina.

His lucky day. She was by far the most appealing. Although she wore the same uniform of short dress and daft shoes, her sun tan was the uneven, pale pinky gold of garden sunbathing as opposed to spray-tan booth caramel, she wore less make-up and, best of all, she didn't screech.

"I didn't want to come out tonight, but I work with this lot, and they made me," she told him. "I don't really like big, noisy pubs. I'd rather go for a walk in the country then go home and read a book." Steve liked her even more. She was like him. The reluctant tagger-on.

Pity there wasn't a club for people like them, so they could meet like-minded souls with ease, instead of having to ferret each other out in the partying throng.

Except that he wouldn't go to such a thing if it existed. The endless paradox: when you were lonely but anti-social, how the hell did you get to meet people?

Steve and Nina paid little attention to anyone else as they got to know each other. She was so easy to talk to; she liked history and the countryside, books and films. Hated dance music, loved rock and blues. Enjoyed her job at Della's beauty salon, but wanted something more; trouble was, she hadn't decided what, but when she had she would go for it. He'd never wanted to carry on talking to anyone so much; usually, he became bored after about twenty minutes, around the time he detected them losing interest, too.

Where had she been all his life?

He received the odd nod or a thumbs up from the other guys, or, as the night wore on, lewd gestures from Dan, but aside from that he scarcely looked up to see how the mating rituals of the others were progressing.

Nina didn't want to stay out late; she had to go to work the next day, and she hated to go in with a hangover.

"I'm the receptionist, so it doesn't do for me to be sitting at the front desk stinking of drink and whining about my headache, does it?"

Her friends were less conscientious. So Steve and Nina left at eleven, saying a quick goodbye to the others, both pleased to be away from the crowds. Took a slow dawdle home, weaving in and out of the late-night revellers. At her front door they kissed, and arranged to meet the following Tuesday night.

"I'll be knackered after work tomorrow 'cause we're fully booked all day and we stay open till six, and I'm crap company when I'm tired. Sunday I've got to go see my gran in Market Harborough with Mum and Dad," Nina told him, but Steve didn't feel he was being held at arm's length. He knew they were reasons, not excuses.

He spent the rest of the weekend at home, peacefully, accepting Nina's friend request on Facebook, putting his dislike of social networking sites aside for the sake of what might be the beginning of something special. They texted, he watched several hours of stuff on the Crime and Investigation channel and the whole of the first series of *The Wire*, over again.

These were the weekends he liked best. Perhaps in weeks to come he could share them with Nina, incorporating the walks in the country she loved. He would like that too; he felt silly and aimless going for a walk on his own.

Dan texted to enquire about his success and, no doubt, to boast about his own, but Steve replied evasively, and ignored further queries. He didn't want the intrusion into his own thoughts.

This was the happiest he'd felt in ages.

The good feeling stayed with him all day at work on Monday, as he began the countdown to seeing her again. Thirty-two hours to go. Twenty-nine hours to go. Twenty-seven and a half, twenty-six.

Which was when he got the phone call from Dan.

"Thanks for this, mate," Dan said, as he got into the car. "Where you been all weekend, anyway? With that bird from Friday? I could've done with talking to you."

"Sorry. I just felt a bit incommunicado. You know how I get, sometimes. So what's up?"

"I tell you, I don't know where to start," Dan said, pulling the seat belt round him. He was shaking, badly, unshaven, and he stank of cigarettes.

Steve turned to look at him properly for the first time. He'd never seen him so jittery. "What's been going on, then?"

Dan wound down the window and lit a cigarette. "D'you mind, just this once, mate? I need it."

Steve did mind, but he let it go. "Okay."

Dan took a long, deep drag, and hung his arm out of the window. "It was that bitch from Friday night. I'm fucking gobsmacked. I mean, it was *Cassie*. She *knows* me. I thought she was sound. I reckon she was egged on by her mates, you know how birds get when they're all together."

"Egged on to do what?"

"Oh, nothing much. She only went and reported me to the Old Bill for attempted rape, didn't she?"

Shit. "You what?" Steve seriously didn't need this. He eased out onto the main road, every instinct urging him to turn around and drive home again.

"I kid you not, me ole fruit. C'mon, you know Cassie, don't you? She used to go out with old whatsisface, you know, geezer who worked at the gym. Mr Muscle. Fancied himself." Dan clicked his fingers. "What's his fucking name?"

"Oh yeah, yeah. I thought I knew her face. You mean Mitch Haddon, right?"

"Yeah, that's him. Anyway, she was with him for years, that's how I know her."

"So she's not with him anymore?"

"No, hasn't been for ages. But, y'know, I always knew she had the hots for me. Used to give me the old come-on, you know how they do."

"Right." Dual carriageway coming up; he'd need to concentrate. "Yep, I know who Cassie is. So are you going to tell me what happened?"

Dan chucked his cigarette out and wound down the window, slinking down in the seat. "Well, the usual. Or so I thought. I fancied her, she fancied me, that's how it goes; I thought it was one of those things when two people who've got a bit of the old chemistry between them finally get it on. Like, get it out their systems. Job done." Another click of the fingers. "So I'm talking to her all night, we're getting closer and closer, the odd bit of touchy feely as the night goes on. You know, she puts her hand on my waist and kind of pulls me to her like she wants it, doesn't moan too much when I touch her on the arse. I mean, you saw how she was dressed, didn't you? She was flashing her kecks every time she got off the bar stool, for fuck's sake."

Steve glanced at the darkening sky; not for the first time, he wondered if he'd be friends with Dan at all if they didn't have that history of a hundred imaginary battles fought, solar systems explored, dens made in secret places to hide from the bigger boys. If they hadn't sniggered together over their first dirty mags, lied to the teachers to save the other from detention.

When you had no real family, your friends filled the gap.

Thinking about it, he forced what little there was of his 'laddish' side out when he was with Dan, and Dan tempered his, both of them maintaining the bond formed when they were kids.

But maybe such bonds weren't made to last forever.

"Cut to the chase, Dan."

He laughed. "The chase! That's a laugh in itself, there weren't much of one. As I said, I wanted her, she wanted me, it was game on. So we get a taxi home together and I ask if I can come in. She says no at first, but what I did, I shoved a tenner at the taxi driver and hopped out after her so she had no choice!" He laughed again as if he was the very fellow, for executing such a stylish move. "It was only an 'alf hour walk back to mine anyway, and I reckoned she was just playing. I was right, as it happened, 'cause when I said, 'go on, let me come in, just one drink and I'll go', she gave me that *look* and said, 'okay then'."

"So you were going along with the traditional male belief that an invitation for a drink means a shag, right?"

Dan laughed. "No, no, not necessarily, I ain't a fucking Neanderthal! But, you know, she had that glint in her eye, and the sparks were flying—it was going to happen."

"But it didn't."

"Too bloody right it didn't." Dan set his mouth in a grim line. "So, she pours us both a glass of wine and she puts some music on, and we're sitting on the couch, bit of banter, and then we start to kiss. Like, a lot, she was seriously eating my face off." He sighed. "You know, bro; there are kisses that mean you have to ask for her phone number before you get anywhere, and there are pre-shag kisses, aren't there?"

Steve grinned, thinking back to the one he'd shared with Nina, which was neither of those things, and so much more. "Yeah. Yeah, I guess so."

"So I go down to first base," Dan went on, "just over her top, and she doesn't mind that, she's stroking my back, and—well, there's me, with Iron Man in my pants—"

"Too much information, mate."

"Believe me, I've had to give the police every fucking gory detail, and not mince my words, either. So, anyway, there we are, she's breathing pretty heavy, and I'm kinda like, time for left hand down a bit, I think." He laughed, to himself. "Even then it was still all hunky dory, both of us definitely up for it. Or so I thought." He wound the window down and lit another cigarette. "So I put my hand on her leg and start to slide it up. And that's when it all went crazy."

The sky overhead looked dark, menacing. "What sort of crazy?"

He shook his head. "I couldn't believe it. She pushed my hand away. So I tried again, and she pushed me away again."

Steve badly, badly didn't want to be in his car listening to this. "So what did you do?"

Dan frowned, as if he was recollecting the exact sequence of events. "Well, I got hold of her wrist and held her hand down by her side, then, before she could muck about any more, I zoomed straight in for the promised land, and I didn't bother with all that slow stroking bollocks first. I reckoned she was just playing about, you see, sort of teasing me. Like it was a game; she was pretending not to let me but we both knew she wanted me to go for it. So I did."

Is that what you thought? Really? "Went for it how?"

"Thought you didn't want any gory details? Well, I had another go and she tried to push me back, like, by my shoulders, and told me to pack it in."

"So why didn't you?"

Dan turned and looked at him as if he'd just said something stupid. Dan often did that. "Well, I didn't think she meant it, did I? She's like that, Cassie; she flirts and teases, you know? I said, 'come on, babe, look at the state you've got me in', and I whipped down my zip and grabbed her hand, put it on my dick, but it was still, like, light-hearted, right? All, y'know, part of the game. But she pulled her hand away, and I started to feel a bit pissed off then, 'cause she was taking it too far, so I pulled at her kecks, but they sort of ripped. I wasn't being rough; it was only a little bit of lacy stuff, hardly even a proper item of clothing. Well, I mean, you can imagine the scene, we were lying on the couch and she's bare-arsed, she's been flirting and leading me on all night, and I just thought—well, I wasn't pleased."

They didn't speak for several seconds, as Steve negotiated his way off the dual carriageway and round the roundabout that led to Waterton. Then he said, "But she didn't choose to be *bare-arsed*, did she? And it sounds like she wanted to stop the minute it got past a bit of a snog."

Dan gave him that look again. "Hey, man, whose side are you on?"

"No one's. I'm just looking at it from both sides. You're a big, strong bloke, that's all."

"Bollocks. She'd been half-naked from the moment she got dressed to go out that night. You saw her. I mean, she was wearing that tiny short dress, and her knickers—well, if you can call 'em knickers—"

Steve chose not to comment. Dan's mood was as taut as a bowstring, and he didn't want to be on the receiving end if he suddenly flipped.

"I mean, they dress up with it all on show, it's obviously they're going out to get laid, same as we are, nothing wrong with that." Dan put his hand up. "And no, I *don't* mean they're asking to be raped. Like I said, I'm not a fucking Neanderthal. What I'm saying is, I've seen hookers more respectably dressed, and Cassie, she's been giving me the come-on all night, and then she suddenly decides to act the fucking virgin."

"You stopped, then, right?"

Dan was silent for a moment. "Yeah, course I did." He sounded weary. "But she says I didn't. She says I pinned her down, forced her legs open, smacked her around a bit and tried to fuck her, but it's not bloody true."

"What did happen, then?"

He pulled on his cigarette. "Well, I stopped. Rolled off, did up my pants, said I was sorry I'd read the signals wrong, and went home. End of story, I thought, but then on Saturday night I'd just got in from Brafield—I'd been down with Woodsy since first thing, for the banger racing—when the Old Bill knocks on my door and arrests me for attempted rape. Seems she'd been there all day, sitting there in one of them gowns getting photographed and examined."

Steve frowned. "Photographed and examined for what? You said nothing happened."

"Scratches, bruises, bumps, you know. Telling her pack of lies to some do-gooder. So then I'm questioned and asked how I got the scratch on my neck, and they're showing me photos of bruises up her legs, and all that jazz. I didn't get out until late Sunday afternoon and I was so shattered I just slept right through. Didn't even go to work today. Couldn't face a day of bloody nagging housewives and blocked sinks. I rang AJ, though, while I was there, and he got our brief down, Sunday afternoon. Philip Landers. Good bloke. Stopped me having to be prodded about."

In silence, they entered the village of Waterton and drove through the rows of neat cottages, past the village green and small row of shops. Out to an estate built on the end of the village, past a field, until finally they reached AJ's lair.

Looked more like the house of an architect, or a wealthy lawyer, Steve thought, than some yobbo who owned a couple of scrapyards. Was there really that much money to be made in the game?

Within minutes they were sitting in the conservatory, where AJ wound a whisky-fuelled Dan up to a state of misogynistic ranting.

"Fucking women, who can work out what goes on in their twisted minds, eh, Dan, mate?" He shook his round, shiny head. "It's like, what's their motive? I reckon it's to get attention, so all their mates'll say, *oh, you poor love, men are such animals.* They love that sympathy bit, women, don't they? I mean, Roxy, she's a good girl, one of the best, but she does it, 'n' all. Half the time when she's in a mood with me I don't know what I've supposed to have done wrong, but you can bet your arse all her mates and her mum do. Then I get her to tell me, and it's nothing, just something I said or forgot to do, and I'm fucking Public Enemy Number One all of a sudden. Her mates and her mum, they wind her up so she gets even madder about whatever my so-called misdemeanour is, but if she'd just come to me and told me, straight out, we could've got it sorted."

Dan helped himself to more whisky. "Too right. My ex, she was just the same. They all gather round like some witches' coven, and suddenly you're frigging Satan, not just some bloke who forgot to admire their new frock."

He and AJ loved this, clinking glasses and laughing.

"Them beauty salons they go to, they've probably got cauldrons out the back where they cast their evil spells." AJ threw his head back and chortled at the picture he'd created. "Fucking nutcases, the lot of 'em. Pity we have to fuck 'em, or we could just get a housekeeper and a cook and do without them completely."

Steve laughed, too, but only because AJ and Dan were behaving in exactly the same way as the women they described. Happily, they took his merriment as appreciation of their humour, and AJ rewarded him with another alcohol-free lager.

"Shame you're driving, mate," he said. "Hey, you was getting on well with that other one, weren't you, on Friday night? What was her name? So, what's going down there, then?"

"She's called Nina. Yeah, I'm seeing her again."

"Well, I hope you fare a bit better than our pal here." AJ slapped Dan on the shoulder. "She's one crazy bitch, mate, and it's only her word against yours. I tell you, she ain't got a leg to stand on. All them mad lesbo do-gooders will try an' make her think she's got a case, but she ain't." He laughed. "Hey, pity you're not black. Or a Muslim. Then they wouldn't have dared bring charges against you in case you started crying racism."

Dan sighed, deeply and loudly. "Yeah, but I ain't, am I? Noel went ape when I told him. I said he's not to tell Dad." He turned to Steve, and the worried look on his face, coupled with his concern for his father, pierced the part of Steve's brain that still felt affection for his old friend.

"I didn't do it, Steve. I really fucking didn't. You do believe me, don't you?"

Until then Steve hadn't. But there was something about the look in his eyes, and he cursed his own bigotry. Was he so against the new Dan that he was ready to condemn him without even considering his side of the argument?

"Course I believe you, if you say it's true," Steve said, even though he wasn't a hundred per cent sure of anything, now.

"Good. I couldn't hack that, if either of you two or Noel thought I was guilty."

AJ handed him a cigarette. "As if! We know what these nutty birds are like, don't we?"

"Too bloody right. And I don't want Dad knowing, 'cause I'm fed up with being the black sheep, as it is."

Concern for himself rather than his father, then.

"No worries, mate, we're with you all the way, and I promise you, Philip will run rings around these arseholes! I tell you, what we need is a night down Rockerfellas. You know where you are with a lap dance tart, don't you?"

That's the last thing he needs. Steve wanted, so badly, to get away from the two of them and the world they inhabited. He remembered feeling the same, twenty-five years before, when Dan had tried to make him steal from the corner shop. Steve liked Mr and Mrs Hayes who ran it, he didn't want to steal from them. The sensation had been the same then; he'd wanted to run outside, far away from Dan, and breathe clean air.

The events of the evening stayed with him all the next day, as he beavered away in the workshop of Lyndford Computers; for the first time, he wished he had a job that offered more interaction with others. The only people he saw all day were the guys from the shop front, when they brought in a couple of malfunctioning printers for him to inspect; mostly, they were too busy flogging cut-price DVD packs and printing ink to have time to chat. Not that he wanted to chat, particularly. What did he want? Just not to be thinking about Dan.

At lunchtime he dragged a chair out to the back yard to sit in the sunshine while he ate his sandwich and crisps. The yard was a tiny ten feet square space filled with weeds forcing themselves through the broken paving slabs, bursting bin bags and large pieces of polystyrene packaging waiting to be broken up, but just being out in the warm summer air made him feel better.

Steve stretched his legs out, flicked a bit of stray tomato off his t-shirt, looked up at the white clouds floating across the blue sky and lit a cigarette. *Nina Night*, at last. Nina was clean and good, and would erase the shadow of the evening before. No, he mustn't jump ahead, but if they got on as well as they had on Friday, and it became *something*, maybe he could distance himself from his old life.

The thought of walking through an imaginary door and closing it behind him felt so good.

Shouldn't be relying on one person I've only just met to make that happen, though. But didn't everyone do that? Meeting a new person with whom you hoped to have a relationship heralded that added bonus, the prospect of a new phase in your life.

Anything was possible when you were two.

He shut his eyes, thinking of her gorgeous, soft green eyes, and the way she flicked back her hair from her forehead, constantly; when she did so it fell back over her face within seconds, in a sexy, loose wave. He'd watched her doing it all night on Friday. After a while she gave up and shoved it behind her ear, which was kind of cute, too.

Steve leant forward, elbows on knees.

Shame she was friends with the girl his best mate had (allegedly) attempted to rape. Not the most auspicious of starts.

"Oh yeah, we were there for her, all weekend. Well, it's what you do when your friends are going through it, isn't it?"

Nina stirred the ice cubes around in her long vodka and lemonade; they glinted in the last remnants of the evening sunshine.

"Yeah. Course it is."

He'd known they would have to either agree not to talk about it or dissect the ins and outs in great detail, but either way the subject had to be broached. It couldn't sit there, like an elephant enjoying a pint of Stella in a corner of the pub garden, without being mentioned by either of them.

He swirled his beer round in its glass. Seeing Nina walk into the pub to meet him had been such a thrill; veteran of many dates though he wasn't, he remembered that apprehension, wondering if the person he'd fancied a few nights ago, in the haze of darkness and alcohol, would seem so attractive in the cold sobriety of early evening. Worse, would she be disappointed by *him*? And did having little faith in his own appeal give him less of it? He was sure it must do. Dan's finger-snapping confidence worked every time; even if girls pretended to be annoyed by him at first, more often than not he won them round by the end of the evening. Then again, Steve didn't want to appeal to the sort of girls who fancied Dan.

He'd placed himself at the bar to wait for Nina, facing the door, so she'd see him immediately; her face lit up as soon as their eyes met, and he knew, instantly, that everything was going to be okay.

Drinks bought, they made their way out to the beer garden that wasn't much bigger than the back yard of Lyndford Computers, just a rectangle with four benches, a couple of tubs of late summer flowers and hanging baskets. Better than sitting inside, though, and he needed a cigarette.

Nina grinned, and put her unpainted lips around the straw, looking up at him from under long, thick lashes as she did so; Steve found the view enchanting.

"I bet you've been hearing all about it from his side, have you?"

He grimaced. "Yeah. I don't take much notice, though."

"Oh, come on, how can you not? Your best mate gets accused of attempted rape; you must have an opinion about it."

"I have, but it's not fully formed yet." They both laughed. "Do you think it's as bad as she says, then?"

Nina frowned. "Well, yeah, kinda. I mean, she tried to push him off, and he tried to force her. How much worse does it have to be?"

"I wasn't belittling her claims. I just wondered if you thought—well, if you think it's absolutely as she says, that's all. When he told us about it—AJ and me—he admitted he went a bit too far, but he said that when she made it really clear he just, you know, zipped himself up and got out of there."

Nina gave a short, harsh laugh. "Yeah, right. That's after he'd torn off her knickers—I mean, *ripped them off*—pinned her down and forced her legs apart with his knees. Steve, she's got bruises up the insides of her legs, at the top. He actually put his hand around her throat to hold her down when he was trying to force his way in; she's got little red marks on her neck to prove it. I didn't see her that night, or on Saturday; she only phoned Della. But we all went round when she got home, and she was in a right state. You don't make that sort of thing up, and Cassie's not like that, anyway."

"No." Steve thought about Dan's earnest eyes, insisting he hadn't done all of which he was accused.

"I mean, she doesn't have any motive to lie. She never had any beef with Dan, she liked him."

"Yeah, I see what you mean."

"Cassie's not the over-emotional type, or an attention seeker," Nina went on. "She's, you know, a happy person. After she split with Mitch she just got on with her life. She helps Della run the salon, and she's doing these courses in skin care and all that, 'cause she wants to help Della expand, become a partner; that's what she's into. You know, she's a hard worker who likes to go out at the weekends and have some fun, that's all. She's got no reason to make up something like this."

Sitting here talking about it in the sunshine, everything seemed clear.

Dan had every reason in the world to lie, Cassie didn't.

Nina made her sound fairly level-headed, whereas Dan's whole personality was a swirling miasma of prejudices, complexes and falsehoods.

"How did she get him to stop, then? I mean, he's a pretty strong bloke."

Nina laughed. "How do you think? She used the one weapon we girls have—she kneed him in the balls. So he's groaning his head off, and she pushes him off and runs upstairs and locks herself in the bathroom. He just left then, thank God. Perhaps he came to his senses."

"You reckon he did it, then, a hundred per cent?"

"Totally. Only problem is, she said, that 'cause she does kick boxing and judo, his defence is likely to say that she could have got the bruises doing that." She pulled a face. "Just a shame she'd been to judo on Thursday night and kick boxing on Wednesday!"

"So it could end up being her word against his."

"S'right."

Nina's glass was nearly empty.

"Do you want another one of those?" Steve gestured towards her glass.

"Sure do!"

Her smile softened his heart into a big, quivery marshmallow. He stood up. "Shan't be a minute. Do you fancy going for something to eat in a bit?"

"Love to, I'm starving!" She laughed. "On one condition: that we keep discussion about Cassie and Dan to no more than ten per cent of the evening's conversation."

Steve smiled with relief. "Works for me."

Whether Cassie or Dan were telling the truth, though, neither of them ever found out for sure, because a few days later Cassie withdrew her complaint.

According to Nina she was gutted but said she'd been advised by her solicitor that the CPS would say there was not enough evidence, and that even if it went to court it was unlikely that anyone would judge Dan guilty without reasonable doubt. Cassie refused to talk about it any more, to any of them.

"She just wants to forget all about it," Nina told Steve.

Dan and AJ were jubilant, insisting on a lads' night out to celebrate.

"Told you justice would win through!" AJ said, and joined Dan in yet another 'high five'. "Philip knows his stuff, don't he?"

Glasses were raised, backs were slapped and drinks drunk, but Steve was sure he saw a knowing glance flit between Dan and AJ.

Had she been threatened? AJ fitted the gangster stereotype so well, the sort of brute who would have no qualms about scaring the life out of someone to keep them quiet.

Or perhaps he'd just been watching too many programmes on the Crime and Investigation channel.

Chapter Fifteen

Tamsin: The Colleague

Lyndford Echo: Friday, 2nd October

THE LYNDFORD STRANGLER: IS HE RUNNING SCARED?

Every day that passes gives us hope that the multiple murderer known as the Lyndford Strangler has struck his last blow.

No victims have been found since the body of Alisha Pope was pulled from the River Lynden at Waterton ten weeks ago, and, significantly, no more young women have been reported missing in the area. The bodies of Ellie Kane, 'Angelika' and Kayla Graham were discovered this year, and Leanne Marsh and Jodie Walker in autumn 2014. Police have not confirmed that the 2014 Norfolk murders of Lita Gomez and Michelle Brand are attributed to the same killer, but it is generally thought that the similarities between the cases are too great for this to be ruled out.

Has the publicity around the case and the distribution of the e-fit images of the killer got him running scared? We pray that this is the case. In the meantime, if you have any information that may help the police, please call the hotline number at the end of this article.

Have you seen this man?

He is assumed to be living in or around Lyndford, and may have been spotted around the Monk's Park area, or Riverside Walk/Spencer Road. Police are also interested in talking to anyone who was in Fagin's Nightclub in Spencer Road during the early hours of Saturday, 18th April, who may have seen any incident they regarded as suspicious.

South Lincolnshire Police confirm that all information will be treated with complete confidentiality.

"Well, that's an invitation for every nutter from Notts to Norfolk to ring up the hotline and report their neighbour as a homicidal maniac, ain't it?" said Sanjay. "'Cause they know they won't be found out for grassing them up, I mean!"

Laughter rippled around the room, and Editor Helen Morse arched an eyebrow. "There is that risk, yes, but assuring complete confidentiality means that if anyone suspects the identity of the real killer, they won't be scared to come forward." She smiled. "Isn't a few busy days on the phones worth the possibility of catching the killer before he strikes again?"

The laughter mellowed to a hum of agreement. Helen clapped her hands. "Come on, chaps. I know we'll get an increase in calls to the paper however many times we reiterate that the hotline is the number to ring, but let's do our civic duty without complaining, shall we?"

"I reckon we get the worst of the crackpots calling us," Brandon said, slouching over the desk, "'cause they're the ones who aren't even sharp enough to read the bit about calling the hotline number."

Tamsin laughed. The calls from reception had been routed to HR, as their work did not suffer the deadlines of other departments. They'd been instructed to keep the calls brief and, as they had no police training, to engage in no conversation apart from giving out the hotline number, but it wasn't always so easy when someone had plucked up the courage to phone up and was eager to impart all they knew. Brandon, who'd volunteered to man the extension for the afternoon, had received six calls confessing to the murders, a few deliberately time-wasting pranks, and at least two who insisted the Lyndford Strangler was hiding in their attic.

Laughing with Brandon made Tamsin feel less tormented by her thoughts.

"Coffee? You look as though you need it!"

"Thanks, yeah. With a Valium top."

As she emerged from the kitchen five minutes later, she saw Jake sauntering down the corridor.

Her heart began to thump, as ever. Would it always be this way?

She wished she had never known him, never been attracted to him. His constant invasion of her thoughts made her weary; if only she could just go to work, enjoy her job, moan about it a bit and go home again in the evening, like everyone else, without all this *stuff* whirling round and round in her head all the time.

"Hiya!" he sang out, as he swerved to saunter past. "TFI Friday, eh?"

"Too right." Aha, an opportunity. She moved in front of him so that he had to stop, too. "What are you doing this weekend, anything nice?"

His smile became guarded. "Oh, this and that. Couple of drinks with the lads. Footy. Maybe go for a run." He stretched his arms up and yawned. "Could do with one tonight, might wake me up a bit." He smiled with his mouth, not with his eyes. The eyes were dark, unfathomable.

"The life of a single guy, eh? Where do you run?"

The smile was still in place, but his eyes grew even more wary. "Nowhere regular. Down along the river, mostly. Or I drive out to Kirton, there's a good stretch there."

She wanted to laugh out loud. Of course, the classic double bluff! *Why would I tell people I went running down by the river where the bodies are found, if I murdered them?*

His eyes challenged her, his face bore that cocky look she hated, the one that made her wonder why she'd fallen in love with him.

I don't love you now. I hate you.

"Have fun." She brushed past him, the familiar smell of his skin, his cologne affecting her senses, still. Infuriating. How could you feel attracted to a man you detested?

She hated him for doing this to her.

Got to keep my head straight. She stopped in her tracks, coffee from one of the cups splashing onto the carpet. The enormity of her suspicions swamped her. How could she deal with something this huge?

It was too much, far too much. All day people had been wasting Brandon's time, wasting *police time*, when the cops should be out catching the real killer, when, *oh God*, the real killer might just have passed her in the corridor.

She needed help. She couldn't bear this burden alone.

Back in the kitchen she poured the coffee down the sink, then marched back to HR.

"Brandon, it's almost five—sod the coffee, how about I take you for a drink?"

Brandon lifted his pint to his lips, clearly unsure what to say.

He was her friend, yes, but should she have trusted him with this?

She smiled, nervously. "I know, I know, it's a lot to get your head round, isn't it? But what if I'm right? Not only does he look exactly like the photofit—and believe me, I haven't just glanced at it, I've examined each facial feature in minute detail—but he fits the profile, too. He's single, he's got a strong personality, he's intelligent, confident, he has problems forming relationships with women." She shrugged her shoulders. "Think about it. If you didn't know him, you'd say, yeah, it just could be."

Okay, so she'd modified and embellished the standard serial killer profile to emphasise her argument, and but surely this was permissible in the light of so much other evidence. "He left Fagin's around the time Ellie Kane was killed—not only does he look exactly like the man the police are looking for, but he was actually on the spot at the time of one of the murders."

Brandon took a large gulp of lager, wiped his mouth with his hand, and looked out of the window.

"Well?"

He looked back at her, his face expressionless, and, finally, shook his head. "Tamsin, you can't do this."

"Why not?" She held up her hands. "It's confidential, and I think I've got a pretty strong case."

"No, I mean you *really* can't do this." He sat back. "Come on. We're mates, you can talk to me. What's going on, eh?"

"What do you mean, what's going on? You heard me. It's all there."

He looked down for a moment. When his eyes met hers again, he looked sad. "Please don't get annoyed with me, but this is all about him ditching you, isn't it?"

Oh dear, oh dear, oh dear. She should have known, shouldn't she? She managed a smile. "Come on, Brandon, I thought you were better than that. Of course it isn't. I'm over that, I have been for ages." She laughed, and held her hands up. "Hey, I'd be some sort of weirdo masochist if I was still hankering after someone who could do those terrible things, wouldn't I?"

"But that's the point, Tam, he hasn't done any terrible things. I know him, he's just an ordinary bloke."

"Ah. You see, that's what happens." She shook her head. "Everyone thinks that. That's why these monsters never get caught. But even if it wasn't Jake—and I'm just saying 'if'—the Lyndford Strangler is still someone's son, or someone's colleague or husband, isn't he? There could be someone else sitting at home right now thinking, oh, it can't be good old Bob, he's just a normal bloke. But just look at the evidence."

"Evidence? What evidence?" Brandon's tone grew more impatient. "He looks a bit like the facial composite, yes, but so do hundreds of other guys."

"I've examined all the features, in minute detail."

He frowned. "Have you? Really?"

"Yes, and what about that night at Fagin's?"

"What about it? Hundreds would have gone through the place on a Friday night, and the police don't even know it was someone from there; they only mentioned it because that was the last place Ellie Kane was seen. She could have been picked up miles away; she lived out on Cranston Fields."

"Okay, well, what about the two in 2013? In Norfolk? I remember him telling me that he often goes down for weekends in the summer, because he's got some friends who live by the coast."

"Thousands of people go to Norfolk in the summer. Hundreds of thousands."

Tamsin stared into her vodka and lemonade. This wasn't going as she'd imagined, at all. "It's not just that. It's his Jekyll and Hyde personality."

Brandon laughed out loud. "What Jekyll and Hyde personality? C'mon, get real. Okay, he acted as though he was into you then he shut you out; well, that happens to hundreds of people all over the world, every day. Doesn't mean the person they fancy is a serial killer. As for those other characteristics you mentioned, well, if you take a cross section of the public and ask them if they think a certain group of personality traits apply to them, or their next-door neighbour, they'll probably hum and ha, then agree that most of them do. It's easy enough to distort a suggestion so it concurs with the outcome you want. People do it with astrological traits all the time, for a start off."

She folded her arms. "Very clever, Mr Psychology Degree."

"Listen." Brandon reached over the table and took her hand. "You're not thinking straight. You're demonising Jake because he didn't want a relationship with you, that's all."

She whipped her hand away. "No, that's exactly what I'm *not* doing! Can't you see? It's all there!" She reached into her bag and slammed down two pictures, the e-fit of the Lyndford Strangler, and an enlarged photo of Jake. "Look! It's the same bloody person!"

"It's not unlike him, but these pictures are never exact likenesses, anyway." He looked around the pub, nervously. "You've got to stop this."

"Why? Do you think I should wait until another girl gets killed?"

Brandon picked up the photos and handed them back. "You're not seriously thinking of going to the police, are you? Do you realise what will happen if you do? He'll be taken down for questioning, people will get to hear about it, and you know how gossip gets around. If that happens, he'll be furious, and justifiably so."

"So what?"

"So don't you think he might guess it's you?"

She laughed. "Why on earth would he? We're just colleagues, I behave no differently towards him than I do anyone else."

Brandon shut his eyes. "Sorry, mate, but you do."

"What do you mean?"

Silence.

"Come on, tell, me, what do you mean?"

"Oh, I dunno; you seem kind of on edge when he's around, I suppose. Nervous. Jumpy."

"Yeah, nervous and jumpy because I'm scared of what he can do!" This was a blow; it was of prime importance that Jake didn't know she was onto him.

"Probably no one else would notice, but it's my 'thing', isn't it?" Brandon looked sad.

"Does he notice?" She shut her eyes.

"I don't know, maybe not now, but before—"

"Before, what?"

He bit his lip, clearly working out what to say. Or whether to say it. "Look, I wouldn't have dreamt of telling you this before, but I think you should know, now, if only so that you see how this will look if you do anything stupid. Before—well, you know, before you and Jake got together, Dev used to call you his stalker. And, um, Jake did sometimes, too."

Tamsin's eyes welled up with tears. His *stalker*? But they'd been friends, good friends, he'd liked her. They'd had a *connection*. She swallowed hard, willing those tears not to fall. "Well, doesn't that underline everything I said about his split personality, doesn't it? Shows what a nasty piece of work he is. I wasn't stalking him. We got on brilliantly, we were so in tune—"

"I'm sorry." He reached for her hand again. "I won't say anything to anyone, but please, please, don't tell anyone else what you've told me. You'd probably lose your job, apart from anything else."

She grabbed hold of her bag and stood up, so hurt that her words struggled to get past the lump in her throat. "What about friends? Would I lose my *friends*, too? Would you still speak to me? What about if I'm right? You'll be coming round and thanking me then, won't you? I'll be the hero, the person who put the Lyndford Strangler behind bars!" She picked up her drink and swallowed the last of it down. "Think on that!" *Don't cry. Don't cry.*

"Tamsin, please, stop it—"

"It's okay, I get it! I'm on my own."

She managed to get out of the pub and into her car before the tears began to fall.

She pulled herself up, sharply. Sometimes, doing the right thing meant you were alienated from those around you. But if you didn't have the courage to do what you knew was right, you were nothing, weren't you?

So, she was on her own. She could deal with that.

As she drove home, she allowed herself a fantasy; her picture on the front of the *Lyndford Echo.*

The woman who caught the Lyndford Strangler.

Stalker, eh? Bastards.

She'd show them. All of them.

PART TWO

Closing In

October 2015

Chapter Sixteen

Sarah

Friday, 2nd October

Sarah Craske had been telling herself the same thing for weeks now. Just one more night, a good one, and she'd quit. Then she'd take up that place in the clinic (Mick said he couldn't get them to keep it open forever), and turn her life around.

The ever-present 'Catch 22' situation, though, was that to face doing what she had to do to earn money, she needed The Precious, and to get The Precious she needed money. Only other alternative was going back to Caleb, 'cause he'd keep her fixed up, but the price was too high. Being out there on your own was hellish, but it was better than being owned by an evil shit like him.

This time, she meant it. This time, she really would quit.

Putting on her make-up in the dingy, cluttered bedsit she called home, Sarah contemplated how life might be, if she was clean. She knew from a couple of stints in rehab that it was horrendous at first, then just frustrating and boring, but there had been little snatches of happiness, too. Of feeling good about herself. Of *knowing* herself, trusting her emotions, her reactions, because they weren't befuddled with chemical highs and comedowns.

As for before, the years before she'd got into it in the first place, that was too long ago to be relevant. A different life. So long ago, now. She cursed the day she'd bought her first little wrap of whizz off Mel. Sexy Mel. He left her, of course. Got her hooked, then fucked off. Came back when she got out of rehab the first time, then fucked off again when she couldn't kick it. After that came the downward spiral, to this. This *shit*. Escort work of the semi-respectable kind, then the less respectable. Then Caleb.

By that time, she needed him.

Back in the early days she'd thought it fun to call it her Precious, like Smeagol in *The Lord of the Rings*, because it was her delicious, naughty secret tucked away in her Marc Jacobs handbag that made her sparkle and kept her thin, but now the comparison was all too real. Without it, she was Gollum in torment. And of course, the product description of The Precious had changed, over time.

She used to be pretty. Pretty damn gorgeous, actually. Happy, envied. She still looked good when she got dolled up, did her hair right, but she could never tell if what she was, what she did, was written all over her face. She was too thin. Her boobs had survived, but her skin looked thin, dull and parched. She was thirty-three years old; this couldn't go on much longer.

She wanted a *life* again.

Not this life. This life was shit.

More or less satisfied with her face and hair, she sighed heavily and reached for her working gear, strewn over the armchair. Fishnets and a short denim skirt. Over-the-knee boots; at least they offered a bit of warmth. She used to wear good clothes, classy ones. A lifetime ago, before Mel, even, she'd had a boyfriend with his own recruitment agency. Martin. Her life was one of expensive restaurants, new cars, holidays, a lovely house. But she'd longed to be thin, so she'd sought the easy route. Started on diet pills off the internet, then came the hard stuff. Eighteen months later she was as skinny as a supermodel—and an addict. *Be careful what you wish for.* Now her wardrobe consisted of variations on her whore's uniform, jogging suits for home, and, hanging up in her tiny wardrobe, a couple of dresses for the twice-yearly visit to her parents.

Best not to think of them.

Sarah clattered down the stairs and out through the front door of the crappy old rundown house where she lived. Three storeys, divided into bedsits. No man's land, for labourers passing through, illegal immigrants, and her. In Victorian times they were smart houses for the moneyed middle classes who wanted to live away from the hubbub of town, surrounded by fields; she'd read an article about it in the paper. By the 1950s the houses had been divided up to house those who worked in nearby factories or on the land. The house in which Sarah lived was one of only a few left in Crow Lane; most were knocked down in the 1970s, with cheap industrial units thrown up in their place.

The bedsit would do for now. It was dirt cheap, and situated ten minutes from Monk's Park. Convenient for work. She laughed to herself. The landlord could advertise it as such, couldn't he? *Accommodation for single 'working' women, close proximity to*—oh, fuck, it wasn't really funny, was it? It was tragic. Lyndford was an affluent town, a smart place to live, which meant a good stream of punters after dark out here on the eastern side, the scruffy bit, where the people who knew how to get stuff on the cheap went to get their cars fixed, in the day time. Only people like her actually *lived* there.

She rounded the corner onto the industrial estate. Some girls were already out, more these days. Some had gone to ground earlier in the year, when Alisha and Kayla got done in. And that Angelika, but no one knew her, she wasn't a regular. The girls all watched each other's backs, even Alisha, who'd been a right bitch, but you wouldn't wish what happened to her on your worst enemy.

The girls were huddled in groups, smoking, taking the odd swig from bottles of cheap spirits, but Sarah stood apart.

Perhaps I ought to tell them it's my last night, she thought. *Perhaps they'd have a whip round, get me a leaving card and a present, then we could go down to the pub to get drunk. Pile into an Indian restaurant afterwards.* Oh no, that was what normal people did. Normal people, like in the life she used to have.

The life she would have again.

It was around eleven when the car drew up. Sarah had been thinking of calling it a night; the hidden pocket she'd sewn into her handbag was bulging with notes. She'd smoked a rock earlier (she and Mandy, crouched by the skips behind the packaging warehouse), had the odd snort to keep herself going, and drunk about a quarter of a bottle of vodka, so she felt fairly anaesthetised. One more couldn't hurt, and she liked his car. Once upon a time she would have known what make it was. The driver cruised along, surveying all the girls before making his choice, ignoring those who tried to attract his attention.

He wound down his window. Quite a nice looking fella, as far as she could see in the dim light of the street lamps. Dark. She liked his face. Wearing a hat; well, it was a cold night.

Some vague memory of that serial killer in his hat floated into the back of her mind, but the rest of her was floating, too, nicely apart from reality, and it only danced into her head for a moment before wafting away again.

She approached the window. The smile came easily; she felt good. "Hi, darling, what you after?"

"Just straight."

She quoted a price and he nodded; damn, perhaps she could've got more, seeing as this was her last punter, ever. "I've got a place round the corner."

"Let's go, then."

She sighed with relief as she sank back into the warmth and comfort of the car.

"Nice?" He smiled at her.

"Very." She closed her eyes; the gear and vodka had mixed together just right, to bring on the good feeling. A straightforward fuck; this one should be pretty painless, then she could kick him out, go to sleep, and never do this ever, ever again. "Crow Lane, number five. There's some houses near where you turn into the road, before you get to the garages."

"I know it."

Sarah looked out of the window into the night. When she came out of the clinic she was never coming back here, even if she had to go into a YWCA hostel for a while before she got on her feet. Then she'd go back to Norfolk, where she used to live. Mick would help her, surely.

"Here," she said, as they approached the turn off for Crow Lane.

But the Lyndford Strangler drove straight past.

Sarah sat up, staring back out of the window. "Hey, what are you doing?" She shut her eyes, panic rising in her chest.

Hang on—

The picture in the paper.

The fuzz in her brain cleared.

The picture. *The picture.*

Oh

God

No

No, no, please God, please don't let this be happening, please, please, not me, don't let this be happening to me—

She turned her head to face him, in terror.

What she'd thought was one of those thermal, pull-on hats was a fucking balaclava, which now covered his face.

He wore black leather gloves, too, and a polo neck jumper. The only part of his body she could see were his dark, dark eyes.

Sarah began to cry, wildly, desperately, tugging at the door handle.

"It's locked," he said. "Save your energy."

"Please, please let me out," she cried, "I promise I won't tell anyone, just let me go!"

Nothing. He just kept driving, picking up speed.

"You fucking arsehole, let me out!"

She pulled at his arm, tried to grab the steering wheel, until he threw off her hand, forcing her back into her seat, and *wham!* —

The world inside her head went black.

Chapter Seventeen

Juliet: The Wife

Monday, 5th October ~ Wednesday, 7th October 2015

Paul Tully was not the Lyndford Strangler.

Juliet had stopped worrying back in June, when she saw the e-fit image of the man thought to have murdered Alisha Pope.

It was the hat; Paul didn't possess any such garment. Juliet was a hundred per cent sure of this because she bought, laundered and kept track of his entire wardrobe—she knew how many shirts were in the ironing basket, how many clean pairs his sock drawer held, at any one time. If there was one thing for which she could give herself a pat on the back it was domestic efficiency, and she had certainly never purchased a hat like the one in the picture, which was the sort of item labourers wore on building sites. She'd seen them, in the winter, working on Paul's houses. *Thinsulate.* A cheap make. She took a look at them in a shop that sold camping gear, just to reassure herself (yes, they cost just two-ninety-nine), and to make absolutely certain she rummaged through his wardrobe, through all his drawers, feeling like a lunatic as she did so, but she must have no room for doubt.

The only hats her husband owned sat in a neat pile on the top shelf of his wardrobe, next to the fleecy tops and jogging bottoms from a good quality men's outfitter that he wore for country rambles or hiking with the boys. The hat collection consisted of an olive green, soft leather one with a woolly lining and ear flaps (for the winter hikes), one dark red bobble hat that she'd bought him on a skiing holiday, long ago, and a black, furry Cossack style affair that looked so good with his charcoal grey winter coat, but he'd only worn it once or twice; the winter was rarely cold enough. Oh yes, and a silly, gaudy baseball cap that Sam had insisted he buy, about ten years ago, during a boating holiday on The Broads.

That was all. Paul *never* did his own clothes shopping; he probably wouldn't know how! And the Lyndford Strangler was unlikely to go out and buy a special hat to kill women in, was he?

After she'd been through his drawers she sat down on the floor and laughed.

She'd been so silly! But she mustn't blame herself, because she knew that physical abuse within a marriage brought with it all sorts of mental aberrations, and it was highly likely that her overwrought state of mind had induced her fears.

She could mend the problems within her marriage. All on her own.

The summer had been good, all thoughts of serial murders forgotten. Juliet took Lara's advice to work on her self-esteem, and read an internet blog article called *Ten Ways To Reclaim Your Life*. Its words inspired her.

Be proud of and utilise your talents.

Congratulate yourself on your achievements, however small they seem.

Be kind to yourself; take time to do something you enjoy.

She invited Rob, Aurelia, Oliver and Fiona round for a barbecue, and the evening was enjoyed by all; the lamb marinated in lime and coriander went down particularly well. Paul had scarcely raised his voice at her since that awful night of the dinner party. They'd crept around each other for a few days and the atmosphere had affected the whole household, but after a few days he'd slipped into attentive mode. The weird thing was that he'd remained there. She kept waiting for him to start being offhand with her, flying off the handle, but it didn't happen.

Juliet didn't look too deeply into the possible reasons for this; perhaps it was simply that he'd decided to be happy. He couldn't *want* to be in a marriage fraught with violent arguments, could he? Men with anger problems could change. The blog article said that whether or not you were happy was within your control, and nothing to do with your circumstances. Maybe Paul had realised it was time to reclaim his life, too.

Juliet smiled all through summer, especially during the August fortnight in France, which was such a success that the word 'idyllic' ran through her mind as one to use when she told their friends about it. Paul's mood remained buoyant almost throughout; he only became just a little bit angry with her three times, and on two of those occasions she'd deserved it—forgetting to pack the wine on a picnic, locking them out of the *gîte* so they had to knock up the farmer at ten o'clock at night.

The other time didn't count, because he'd been drinking. He'd made a *mistake*; anyone could do something they later regretted when they'd had too much to drink; well, look what she'd done on the night of Fiona's dinner party! Paul had apologised to her and said he didn't want it to ruin their holiday, and, really, it hadn't hurt that much. It was just a little push, that was all. Nothing serious. It wasn't like he'd hit her, not like before.

Juliet carried on smiling as she waved Sam and Max off to start their new terms in September, Sam to do a one-year business course at Lyndford College, Max to begin his final 'A' Level year. Paul's business was flourishing, and Rob was keen to look at Crow Lane once notice was given to the current leaseholders. September felt more like the new year than January, her life having revolved around new schools and school terms for the past fourteen years. The only slight blot on the landscape had been a little trouble with a girlfriend of Sam's; she claimed he'd been violent towards her during an argument, and her parents had been making all sorts of threats, but Sam had sworn that the girl was lying. Juliet and Paul believed him, and Paul smoothed the whole nasty business over.

Sam did take liberties with the truth, but only about silly things; he would never lie about something as important as this, she was sure.

As late summer faded into autumn, Juliet began to think about her own role within the family. Sam would be out in the working world soon, and Max off to university, no longer dependent on her; soon there would only be Paul to look after. She didn't want to become like her mother, whose every day had centred around her father coming home from work.

"It's hard to make stimulating conversation over the dining table when all you've done for the last nine hours is make casseroles, hoover carpets and watch the clock ticking round," she'd said, more than once.

Enlivened by the upswing of the past months, she obtained a brochure about short courses starting at Lyndford College in January. Should she try her hand at life drawing? Or jewellery making? She enjoyed crafting, was good with her hands; she might possess a real skill waiting to be unearthed, and now she had the time to find out. The more she mulled over the possibilities, the more she fancied making jewellery. Max had told her about an online shop called Etsy where you could sell things you made. Paul might actually be proud of her!

'My wife, yes, she runs a flourishing jewellery business. Uh-huh, makes it all herself, she's really tapped into the market, quite the entrepreneur!'

Lara thought it was a great idea, of course. "Hey, you might become renowned for your designs and earn a ton of money," she said. "Financially independent, even!"

"Stop it!" Juliet went quite pink. "Let's not get ahead of ourselves, I haven't even enrolled on the course yet."

A nine-week beginner's course looked to be the way forward. Reasonably priced, students to supply own materials. Just the thing.

On Monday 5th October she settled down, after lunch, to fill out the application form. When she nipped out to the hall to get her bank card out of her handbag, she smiled at her reflection in the hall mirror. She loved the boost that the summer sunshine had given her looks, even though her hairdresser and the girls at Just Beauty in Lyndford told her she ought to cover up with sunhats and sun-blocks. Her sleek blonde bob was bleached almost white in some places, a remnant of the *idyllic* fortnight. The texture was a little straw-like, but she liked the effect. She blushed; it was almost sexy. She hadn't felt sexy in years, if indeed she ever had. Her face, neck and chest still bore their light tan, but—oh dear, were they age spots? Early July had seen her forty-ninth birthday, so perhaps she shouldn't complain.

Juliet put one side of her hair behind her ear, pouted, and laughed at herself; did she look like a jewellery designer? Pity about the sagging jowls. And the knowledge that, at some point during all that summer barbecuing and Pimm's drinking, her body had edged out of size fourteen and up to size sixteen. Never mind, that could be remedied.

Or accepted, Lara would say. *Liked, even. There's nothing wrong with being a size sixteen. Who says you have to adhere to the magazine image of perfection?* But Lara wasn't married to Paul.

It was only when she began to write her card details on the submission form that she noticed it had expired the day before. Damn! Where was her new one? Paul opened all the letters from the banks; he must have forgotten to give it to her. Goodness knows where it was. Oh dear, this was the only account in her name only; Paul went through the joint account and credit card statements online, several times a week (she always dreaded the inquests into why she spent so much at the supermarket), and she didn't want him to know about the course until she'd plucked up the courage to tell him about it.

The home atmosphere had improved, yes, but if someone at work had put him in a bad mood, he might still belittle her idea, and she wasn't strong enough to withstand that yet.

Never mind, she could pay for it the old-fashioned way, with a cheque. Their cheque books, rarely used, were all in Paul's office.

Juliet never felt comfortable entering that room, not even when she went in to clean, which was silly, because Paul wasn't hiding anything, though she suspected that not all of his business dealings were totally above board. Not that she'd know where to look even if she wanted to find such things out. It was just that—well, Paul's office was his private space, and she respected that. Just as her domain would be Sam's bedroom, when he moved out; she'd already earmarked it for her sewing room (or her jewellery studio!).

She knew where the cheque books were: in his desk, the second drawer down. As she rummaged in his desk-tidy for the key, though, she spotted something that made her stomach lurch.

A letter from the police.

It was the logo that caught her eye first, and she couldn't stop herself picking it up. Probably a speeding fine. That would be why he hadn't said anything; her anxiety over his driving habits got on his nerves.

But the letter wasn't about a speeding fine.

It was a short, polite request, dated the week before, for Paul to present himself at the station in order that he might be eliminated from an ongoing enquiry.

His car had been identified by CCTV cameras as having been seen around the Monk's Park Industrial Estate between eight p.m. and two a.m. on several occasions that year.

He was advised to report to DI Cara Nolan within the next fourteen days so that the matter could be cleared up as quickly as possible.

Juliet sank down onto Paul's high-backed leather chair, the letter still in her hand, all thoughts of jewellery courses forgotten.

The idyllic summer might never have happened.

Exactly how often did you have to drive around Monk's Park late at night in order to get one of these letters?

On several occasions.

How many did 'several' mean? Three? Thirteen? Thirty-three?

The serial killer list crept out of its hiding place in the filing cabinet of her mind, and floated in front of her eyes.

A need to control.

Appears to the rest of the world to be quite normal—charming, even.

The mask of sanity.

And even if it wasn't as she feared, what was he doing driving around Monk's Park late at night?

"Getting a cheeseburger," he said, and laughed. He was making a cup of coffee when she plucked up the courage to confront him, and carried on with what he was doing as if they were chatting about something normal.

As if the police wanting to interview him about a series of murders was all in a day's work.

Can believe self to be untouchable.

"What do you mean?"

"A cheeseburger? It's a small amount of minced, grilled beef formed into a round, flat shape, fried, then placed in a bun, with a slice of cheese on top."

Round and round he stirred the coffee. "I'm surprised you've never come across one before."

"Don't be silly, this is serious," she said. "What I meant was, where and why would you buy one on Monk's Park Industrial Estate late at night?"

"There's a van at the truck stop out towards the dual carriageway. Chuck's Snack Wagon, I believe it's called. Best burgers I've ever eaten. Bacon sandwiches aren't much cop, but the cheeseburgers: mwah!"

"You drive all the way out there for junk food, when you've either had or can have dinner at home?"

"Not often. But sometimes if I've been working late, or if I've been out for a drink, or whatever, I drive through the industrial estate and out the other side to the truck stop. I wouldn't mind one now, actually." He laughed. "Good and well done, proper beef burned round the edges, a shit load of fried onions. Oh, and a slice of that lovely plasticky processed cheese you won't have in the house. Two, if I ask nicely." He chucked the teaspoon into the sink and smiled at her, nastily. "Shows my working-class roots, I suppose. Sometimes I don't want beef *en*-fucking-*croute*, I just want a burger."

"And you'll drive all that way to get one?"

He shrugged his shoulders. "Yeah, sometimes. 'Specially if I've been out at Crow Lane."

"Why would you be there?"

"Oh, for God's sake, Juliet. I've got premises there; you know I have."

"Yes, but you're not working on them. It's rented out, isn't it?"

"Yes," he said slowly, as if talking to a particularly dim child, "which means I have tenants, and sometimes I have stuff to discuss with them. Or I want to assess necessary repairs. Or I'll get an idea I need to discuss with Rob, for their renovation. For crying out loud, do you want a list?"

She looked at the letter, still in her hand. "This is about the murders, though, isn't it?"

"Yes."

"So what did they ask? Did they make you take a DNA test, or be in an identity parade, or what?"

He folded his arms. "Don't be stupid. I was just being eliminated from routine enquiries. They asked me where I was on certain nights, and I told them I'd check my diary and get back to them. Which I will. I don't reckon they can insist on anything else unless I'm being charged, or am a genuine suspect, which I can't be, because I haven't murdered anyone, at least not as far as I can remember."

"But you'd give samples if they asked for them."

"No, I most certainly would not."

She felt sick. "Why not? What's the harm, just so you can be on your way and not get any more letters like this?"

"Because I don't want my DNA on any bloody database. On principle."

"What principle?"

"Because they don't need it. Any more than they need my email address or my fingerprints, or details of my whereabouts, but unfortunately I do have to provide those."

"Have you told Graham about it?"

"No, why should I? I don't need a lawyer. Not unless they want further information, in which case I shall consult him first."

Juliet caught her breath. "I still can't see the harm. Why wouldn't you say yes? You've got nothing to fear, if you haven't done anything."

She'd done it again. As soon as the last five words were out of her mouth, she could have pulled her tongue out.

His smile faded.

The atmosphere, already teetering on the edge, grew darker, her words echoing around the silent room.

He took a sip of his coffee, and looked at her over the top of the mug. "What do you mean, *if* I haven't done anything?"

"I didn't mean it like that, it was just a turn of phrase—"

He held his finger up, shaking it from side to side. "Uh-uh. No, no, no. You just quizzed me, like a cop would, about why I would mind giving a DNA sample if I have nothing to hide. You asked me to justify my reasons for saying no." He put his mug down, without care; coffee spilled onto the worktop, and Juliet checked her automatic reaction to sprint over, cloth in hand. "Now, how do you think that makes me feel?"

"Paul, I didn't mean it like that, honestly, I didn't think what I was saying—"

"Precisely; you said exactly what was on your mind, without thinking about it, just like you always do. Only this time, the thing on your mind was, ooh dear, might my husband be a serial killer?"

Her face grew hot. "No! I didn't think that!"

He wasn't listening. "Can you imagine if Rob had got one of these letters? I bet your great mate Aurelia, who you think is so marvellous, would just laugh about it, along with him. Or if Oliver had got one—do you think Fiona would have doubted, even for a nanosecond, that there was anything other than a perfectly reasonable explanation? But oh no, not you. You think the worst. I tell you what, I wish I had a supportive wife who believed in me, too, but oh, no—I was stupid enough to marry Miss Juliet Russell who thinks she was born with a fucking silver spoon in her mouth, tells all our friends what a scumbag I used to be before I married her, and now thinks I might be the Lyndford Strangler, to boot! Lucky old me, eh?"

He picked up his coffee and drank, then he just stared at her. Juliet stood, still as a statue, dreading what might come next, willing herself not to flinch in advance as he lowered the mug. Was he going to throw it at her?

They stood like that for some seconds, as if challenging each other, then Paul shook his head, and emptied the rest of the coffee down the sink.

"Stupid bitch," he muttered, and pushed past her out of the room.

Her body went limp and she collapsed into a chair, weak with despair, as he slammed the door behind him.

The progress made through summer was erased, as if it had never been.

On Tuesday morning Paul left for work early, without speaking to her; she heard his car drive off as she walked downstairs. He didn't come home until late, and on Wednesday morning he managed to sit through a whole family breakfast without actually addressing one word to her.

That lunchtime found her in front of *Bargain Hunt* with her sandwich, her pot of Petits Filous and her apple. *As usual,* she thought. *Sitting here, lonely and depressed, wondering if I'm going mad.*

Tim Wonnacott congratulated the Blue Team on winning thirty-four pounds, and the credits rolled; as she'd only just taken the lid off her fromage frais, Juliet decided to leave the television on for the news.

"*Lunchtime today: is she the one that got away? Suspected to be the latest victim of the so-called 'Lyndford Strangler', Sarah Craske may have invaluable evidence that will help police to catch the south Lincolnshire serial killer.*"

Juliet stopped, the spoon halfway to her mouth.

A picture of a girl in a hospital bed filled the screen, her long, dark hair spread out on the pillow, her face covered in bruises, a soft brace around her neck.

An on-the-spot reporter at the hospital said that Miss Craske had been attacked a short while before midnight on Friday night, after being picked up by a stranger in the Monk's Park area of Lyndford and driven out into the countryside where her abductor dragged her out of the car and assaulted her. After a horrific struggle, she escaped by stabbing him in the groin area with the heel of her boot, then running for her life. She managed to hide down a grassy bank, up to her ankles in a muddy stream, and waited there, crouched and shivering, too terrified to move in case he was searching for her, until dawn. She then made her way across fields and alerted the occupants of a nearby farm.

Back to the newsroom:

"*Miss Craske suffered from hypothermia, cuts, bruises and severe blows to the head, attempted strangulation, cracked ribs and sexual assault. She has only just recovered enough to talk to the police and give details about her attacker, whose face she saw, briefly, when he picked her up, although as soon as she was in the car, he pulled down a balaclava to hide his features. Police say that the man in question might have bruises on his upper body, though she was unable to remove the balaclava during the struggle. They have issued this e-fit image, which they hope is the most accurate likeness so far.*"

Juliet dropped the pot onto the table, fromage frais splashing everywhere.

They'd said between mid-thirties and fifty. Before. Paul was fifty-two, so it couldn't be him, could it?

But he was no gone-to-seed fifty-year-old; he was still in shape, still attractive, and the picture looked so like him that she felt as though icy water was trickling down her back. Her whole body shook. Friday night, they said. Friday night. *Think, think*. Was Paul out on Friday night? *Think!*

She dashed out to the kitchen to look at the calendar; no, Friday 2nd of October was blank. But—yes, yes, of course, he'd rung her at around five to say that when he finished at the office, he was going down to Crow Lane with

Rob, then he would take him for a drink afterwards. He hadn't come home until after midnight.

She'd feigned sleep, her head turned away from him.

Oh no. No, no, no.

Think, think.

All she had to do was to ring Aurelia to find out what time Rob had got home, but she couldn't summon up a convincing reason for doing so, knew that the fear in her voice would give her away.

She'd been kidding herself, all because of that stupid hat.

She clamped a hand over her mouth, taking great, breathy sobs; she ran upstairs, wailing, straight into the bedroom, rifled through Paul's wardrobe looking for anything, she didn't know what, anything that would give her a clue, but there was nothing, nothing amongst the rail of neatly pressed shirts and suits—she pulled out his shoes, everything from the shelves beneath the clothes, emptied his drawers, not having a clue what she might hope to find, finding nothing. Weeping, her chest rising and falling in panic, she staggered into the bathroom and emptied the laundry basket, but, oh no, she'd done a wash since then—down into the utility room, but there was nothing anywhere, no piece of clothing with blood on it, nothing torn, no shoes with mud on, not like before—oh, but he would have cleaned them, wouldn't he, after that time she'd asked him about it? In the garage she searched for rags with mud on, something that would show evidence of a hasty clean up, anything, the hat, *the balaclava*—nothing.

She remembered reading in that book, before Max nicked it, about the Yorkshire Ripper having been questioned and let go, before they realised it was him—oh, and the stupid excuse about the cheeseburgers, Paul's insistence that he would not give a DNA sample—he was clever, so clever; he'd hidden everything. He was way ahead of them all.

Juliet sat on the concrete floor of the garage and sobbed.

She needed help, someone to talk to—

—*please, please, someone help me*—

Slowly, gradually, her panic simmered down; she despaired. Her legs felt leaden, but she dragged herself back into the house, pausing outside the office, knowing that she couldn't face rifling through it, not with Paul the way he was at the moment; if she left one thing out of place, which she was bound to do in the state she was in, no matter how careful she was, he would find out, and he'd be *furious*—if he knew that she knew, she might be next, an accident, everyone knew how stupid, how *dithery* she could be, after all—Sam always told her she was dozy—these things *did* happen in ordinary, normal families, and everyone was surprised when the secrets came out, shocked, because they'd never suspected what was going on behind those respectable, closed doors—

Holding onto the bannister she pulled herself up the stairs, back into the bedroom where she sat down on the bed and surveyed the mess she'd made. All those neatly folded jumpers strewn across the floor.

She thought, *I'm going mad.*

If only she could examine him for bruises, marks, but there was such distance between them these days, he turned away from her when he dressed, she didn't even enter the bathroom when he was taking a shower, she'd feel embarrassed, invading his privacy—overnight, they'd become antagonistic strangers once more.

The little voice of reason in her head told her that this was no way to live, tiptoeing about, being pathetically grateful for the periods during which he was actually nice to her. Weren't husbands supposed to be nice to their wives, generally?

Lara. She needed Lara.

Lara would never let it go, though. Lara wouldn't stop to listen to any case for Paul's innocence. Lara would make her go straight to the police.

"Better to know, once and for all," Lara would say. "If you're right, you might be saving another girl from the ordeal Sarah Craske went through, or worse."

Oh, and that was the point, wasn't it? Not only to see justice served.

Okay. Right. She would put all those clothes away, go downstairs (clear up that spilt fromage frais, too), and have a nice, soothing cup of camomile tea. Or a gin and tonic, a large one, to calm herself. Then she would talk to Lara.

No, she would close her eyes and let Lara do all the talking.

Lara would make the right decision. She always did.

Chapter Eighteen

Maisie: The Teenager

Thursday, 8th October 2015

Saffron caught up with her as she ambled through the school gates at the end of another long day.

"Hiya, you walking home?"

Maisie turned and smiled. "Yeah; your mum not picking you up?" Bethany had gone into town; she was pleased to have someone to walk with.

"No, she's working late."

"Bummer."

"Yeah." They pushed through the crowds at the gate, then Saffron stopped.

"Maisie, can I talk to you about something?"

Maisie smiled, put her arm through her friend's, and they walked on. "'Course. What?"

"It's a bit weird."

"I like weird."

"Okay." Saffron pulled her arm away, pulled out some chewing gum and fiddled with the wrapper.

"Go on then. Hit me with it!"

"It's about Gary." She popped the piece in her mouth and chewed for a while before replying. "It's, like, a bit intense."

Maisie felt her smile fade away. "Yeah? What about him?"

No reply.

"What? C'mon, then, tell us."

Saffron looked at her feet. "Mais, my mum—look, she probably didn't mean it, I might have heard it wrong—"

"What does she think?" Maisie hadn't known her heart could beat that fast.

"Well, she, um—" Saffron bit her lip and gazed up at the sky. "She thinks he, er, might be—um, well, you know—look, it's just silly, but—"

"*What?*"

She stared straight at her. "Um, she thinks that Gary—well, that he might, like, be the Lyndford Strangler." Then she laughed. "I know, it's crazy, isn't it? Messed up, or what?"

A gust of wind blew Maisie's hair across her face and she closed her eyes for a moment. The scents of early autumn floated into her nostrils; rotting leaves, a crispness, a smoky feel to the air. Everything seemed to stop.

"Why does she think that?"

Saffron turned round to carry on walking, and Maisie grabbed at her arm.

"Hey! You can't say something like that then just walk off."

Saffron pushed her arm off. "Get off, Mais, don't be arsey with me, I'm just saying, 'cause I thought I should. It's not easy, is it, telling your mate something like that. I didn't have to."

She hoisted her bag further onto her shoulder and set off down the road; Maisie hurried to fall into step beside her.

"Sorry. Tell me why she thinks it, then. Please."

Saffron kept her eyes on the ground as they walked. "I heard her in the kitchen. She was talking to Brian. You know Mum works at the Jobcentre? Well, she signs Gary on—"

"Yeah, yeah, I know that."

"Okay, well, she, like, she signed him on, on Tuesday. The staff in the Jobcentre are given all those e-fit pictures of the suspects, like, as soon as they come out, and she had the new one up on her screen—you know, like, minimised—and when she was talking to him she kept flicking back to it, with her screen turned away so he couldn't see what she was doing, and she said it looks just like him. That's what she was telling Brian, anyway, after it was on the telly. I'm sorry, I just thought I'd better tell you, just in case she does something about it, 'cause you might want to tell your mum, or something, I dunno."

"Yeah." They walked on.

"I don't want to make trouble, and Mum would go mad if she thought I'd said anything."

Maisie buried her hands in her pockets. "Did she say she was going to go to the police?"

"Dunno. I just heard her and Brian talking and Mum was like, *it's Gary*. Then Bri noticed I was listening, and he shut the kitchen door. I didn't hear nothing else."

"Shit."

"Yeah, but if she'd gone to them, they'd have come to arrest him by now, wouldn't they?"

"I don't know. I don't know how it works."

"No, nor do I."

They walked on.

"Then it was on the telly again last night, about that girl who got away," Saffron said. "Mum didn't say anything but she gave Brian one of those *looks*, you know how they do." She laughed. "Like they think we're still little kids who don't notice anything."

Maisie felt sick inside. If Saff's mum thought this, how many other people did? Had she told anyone else at the Jobcentre? "Do you know if she's told anyone else?"

"No. I mean, I don't know if she has or not. I'm just telling you, you know, so that you can warn your mum, or something. I dunno."

"Mmm." She wouldn't do that. Couldn't. If Saff's mum didn't say anything she'd be worrying her for nothing.

"Have you seen it on the telly?" Saffron asked.

"No. Well, yeah, bits. I've not taken much notice." She'd been more worried about other stuff lately. Like how pissed off her mum was about Gary going to Yarmouth to see Charlotte.

"Well, I'll tell you what else it said. It said that he would have bruises on him, 'cause of the girl fighting him off." Saffron turned to her. "You could look, couldn't you? Like, if you see him coming out of the bathroom, or something."

Maisie gave a grunt. "*Ew.* I try not to; he gives me the creeps. Anyway, it was a week ago now; they'd be gone, wouldn't they?"

"Oh. Yeah."

Mum might have seen them, though. "Saff, tell us if your mum says anything else, will you?"

"Course I will."

"Like, if she says she's going to the police or anything." She thought about her mother, opening the door to the police, and it made her want to cry. "Will you promise me you won't tell anyone about this? Really fucking promise, I mean, don't just say yes and then go and tell half the school." She drew her breath in. "'Specially don't tell Beth. You know what a blabbermouth she can be."

Saffron laughed. "Yeah, like, total gossip whore! Course I won't. Mum would kill me if she knew I'd said anything, anyway."

"I know, but it's not just 'cause of that. This is serious. It's not just, like, a bit of gossip. It's my *mum*."

"Yeah, no problem, I get it. Honest, I promise I won't. Hey, I just thought."

"What?"

"Like, du-uh! Was he out last Friday night? You know, when the girl was attacked?"

Out of nowhere, Maisie was hit by a lightning bolt of anger. She wanted to shout at her friend to keep her nose out of her life, and tell Saff's mum to keep her crap to herself, too. "No. He wasn't. He was home with my mum watching telly. So there. And you can tell *your* mum that from me, okay?"

She walked off, quickening her step, leaving her friend standing there.

"Maisie! What's up? Where you going? Wait for me!"

She turned around. "You tell anyone about this and I'll—just don't, alright?"

Saffron held up her hands. "I promise. I said so, didn't I? What's the matter with you?"

Maisie turned her back and crossed the road, into the traffic, hardly noticing when a car narrowly missed her; a horn tooted.

"*Stupid idiot!*"

She gave him the finger and leapt over to the pavement, nearly knocking a cyclist off his bike in the process.

"Maisie! Come back!"

She turned her back and stared into a shop window. Shit, now she was on the wrong side of the road, and she'd have to wait until Saffron had walked on before she crossed back again or she'd look a right muppet.

She'd lied, of course. Gary had not only been out on Friday night; he hadn't come home until halfway through Saturday morning. Pru said he'd had to go over and see Charlotte again, because of the kid having a bad time at school. She'd been pissed off, hitting the wine. Said she respected Gary because he was making sure little Bobby was okay, but her actions made rubbish out of her words. Later on, Maisie heard her crying.

Fuck it, she thought. She was going to get to the bottom of this. She'd bloody well get Charlotte's number out of Gary's phone, and ring her to find out if Gary really was there, and while she was at it, she'd have a bloody good go at her, and tell her to leave Gary alone, 'cause he was with her mum, now.

Not that she wanted him to be, in fact she'd clap her hands if the lazy tosser went back to live with Charlotte tomorrow, but she couldn't bear seeing her mum made a fool of any more.

"Hello?" Girly, sing-song voice. Sounded like a right stupid cow.

"Is this Charlotte?"

"Who wants to know?"

Here we go, then. "My name's Maisie. I'm ringing about Gary Dunlop. He lives here, with my mum and me. And my little brother."

She heard Charlotte's sharp intake of breath. "Yes, I know. What about him?" Not hostile; cautious, curious.

Oh dear. What did she say now? Why hadn't she worked out a script? "Well, I just want to know if he was with you last Friday night."

"Yes. Why d'you ask?"

The relief Maisie felt was so great that she almost forgot about the main purpose of her mission.

"You still there? I said, why d'you ask?"

Gulp. What now? "Well, I just wondered why you keep getting him to go over to see you, 'cause he's not, like, with you any more, is he?"

Charlotte laughed. "If he wants to come over and see me an' the kids, he's always welcome."

"Yeah, but it's not 'cause he wants to, is it? You ring him up to get him over whenever you've got a problem, don't you?" Maisie felt herself floundering. "You know he hasn't got a job? That petrol money he spends to get to Yarmouth, he should be giving that to my mum."

"Yeah, well, that's his choice, isn't it?"

Grrr! "Yes, but he wouldn't have to make the choice if you didn't keep relying on him. Can't you get your own boyfriend?"

Stupid cow laughed again. "That's not what it's about. Gary lived with me and my kids for a long time. He's like a dad to them."

"Yes, but that's not fair on my mum."

"That's for them to sort out, isn't it?" There was a pause. "Listen, whatever problems your mum's got with Gary not paying his rent, or whatever, it's got nothing to do with me."

"It's not just about him not paying his rent—anyway, he doesn't pay rent, he's not a lodger; he lives here."

"She lets him live there for nothing?" Laughter again. "Bloody hell, I thought *I* was a soft touch!"

Maisie could feel her cheeks flushing with anger, and the words fell out of her mouth before she could stop them. "Why don't you stay out of his life? He's my mum's boyfriend now, not yours!"

"If you say so." Another pause. "Does she know you're ringing me up? Did she get you to do it for her?"

"No. Course not. She wouldn't lower herself."

Another laugh. "But you would, right? Tell you what, pet, why don't you leave it for the grown-ups to sort out?"

What did she think she was, eight years old? "Why don't you piss off?"

"Hey, hey, that's enough, pack it in. I don't need some kid giving me earache down the phone. Listen. If Gary still wants to come over and see us, it's not me your mum's got a problem with, it's Gary."

Oh dear, this wasn't going the way she'd intended it to at all. She'd thought she was going to sound all strong and adult and hard, so the silly bitch would cower and slink away. "You shouldn't be letting another woman's boyfriend stay overnight with you!"

"Yeah, well, like I said, perhaps you ought to ask him whose boyfriend he thinks he is. And if he chooses to have a drink when he's here, so he can't drive back, I can't stop him, can I?"

"Is that what happened on Friday?"

Charlotte was silent for a moment; Maisie heard her breathe in.

"I already said so, didn't I?" Pause. "Look, I've got to go. Don't ring me again."

She hung up.

Maisie dropped her phone and curled up on her bed. She felt cold; the evenings were getting chilly, but Pru hadn't put the heating on yet. Probably to save money 'cause of the amount Gary wasted.

What did Charlotte mean, 'ask him whose boyfriend he thinks he is'?

Pru, Gary and Zack were downstairs, clearing up after tea, larking about, all the normal early evening stuff.

A wave of depression crept over her and she slid under the duvet, pulling it round her even though she was still fully dressed, in her school shirt, sweatshirt and trousers. Life seemed even more unstable than usual these days, shifting around on crumbling foundations, liable to collapse at any moment.

Don't fucking cry. She had to be strong for her mum, who was not strong at all. What if Gary left her, and went back to Charlotte? She'd go to pieces.

But what if he stayed, and the police came round to arrest him? They didn't know for definite that it was the Strangler who attacked that girl. Could've been someone different. Her mum would crack up. What about her gran and grandad, too? They were old, and her grandad had a dodgy heart. This might finish him off! And the trolling mob would be out in force, she and Zack would go through unbelievable shit at school; she'd seen what Jade Morris went through, in Year 9, when her dad went to prison for attacking some girl. It'd be like living in *hell*. She could take it, just, but Zack was only a kid. They might have to move house! Move away from all her friends!

Maisie pulled the duvet over her head and let the tears flow.

"What am I going to do?" she whispered out loud, and it made her feel a little bit better, as if somebody might hear her.

Bethany was too silly; she couldn't tell her. And she couldn't absolutely, definitely trust her. She'd likely as not 'just' tell one person, who'd 'just' tell someone else, and before you knew it, it'd be all over Snapchat and Twitter, all round the school. *Maisie Todd's stepdad is the Lyndford Strangler!* She trusted Saffron, but once you opened up to a mate about how scared you were about something, you'd let your guard down, hadn't you? All you had to do was piss them off and they could use it against you. Saffy was sound, a proper good mate, but—no, it wasn't worth the risk.

Why did bloody Gary have to be in their house at all, ever? Everything was alright, they were happy before he showed up!

Maisie clutched the edge of the duvet to her chest, staring up at the ceiling. She'd never felt more alone and lonely in her life.

That was when she remembered. Ms Brownlow. Kate. She could talk to her. She was exactly the right person to talk to about this—and, right now, Maisie didn't care if she slept with men, women or giraffes. Kate Brownlow would understand.

All she had to do was get through the weekend, and on Monday she would get some help.

When Zack came up at eight o'clock to say they were all going to watch a film, he found her fast asleep.

"I can't even work out which bit I'm most worried about, it's just everything."

Maisie was crying by now, blowing her nose and wiping her eyes with the man-size tissues Ms Brownlow passed to her. She'd allowed her fears to flow, unchecked, while the teacher sat silently, just listening and giving the occasional prompt, looking in turn sympathetic, sad in an exasperated sort of way (about the Charlotte situation), then horrified (about the bit Saffy's mum said). Talking your problems through was like being sick, Maisie decided; scary beforehand, total crap while you were doing it, but afterwards you felt so, so much better.

The more she talked the easier it became, all about how much she disliked Gary but was so mixed up because if he went, her mum would be heartbroken, about the fear that he might be *that monster*, about Charlotte, and the prospect of her and Zack being tormented if what Saff's mum thought was true.

Best of all, Ms Brownlow didn't say anything stupid like 'let it all out', or 'it's alright, it's alright', when it clearly *wasn't*, Maisie wanted to scream at people when they said dumb stuff like that.

"Okay," said Ms Brownlow—she really must try to call her Kate—at the end. "This is a hell of a lot to process, so let's take these things one by one."

She smiled. "It's easier if you break problems down, that way they don't overwhelm you. First of all, I know it's a real worry for young people these days, but let's put the possibility of internet bullying thing to one side, because there is nothing happening at the moment, and Saffron has promised you can trust her."

Maisie tore at the crumpled tissue in her hand. "I hope so."

"Yes, well, she's always seemed like a fairly sensible and sensitive girl to me. Do you use the social networking sites a great deal?"

"No. I mean, I do, but I'm not addicted like some people, I don't live on them." She grinned. "I'm not always posting selfies and checking how many 'likes' I've got every five minutes."

Kate Brownlow laughed. "I'm delighted to hear it! Well, perhaps wind it down even more for now. Just as a precaution. If you're not on them, you won't be there to bait; internet trolls want a reaction, that's why they do it. If there isn't one, they move on to someone else. What about Zack?"

"He's not allowed yet. Mum does that parental locking stuff on the social networking sites. He's not even allowed a smartphone till he's twelve."

"Good. As for your mother and her relationship with Gary, I know it's so frustrating when a loved one is engaged in what you perceive as an ill-advised relationship, but unfortunately you have to let people make their own decisions."

"He's such a tool, though."

Kate Brownlow laughed. "Yes, but, alas, those we care about fall in love with the most unsuitable people. I did; my mother used to despair over my choice of men! I'm more sensible now, thank goodness."

Not a lesbian, then. Not that it would have mattered in the slightest, after all, Maisie realised. She smiled, then frowned. "What about the other thing? You know, the police."

When she'd told her about Saffron's mum, Kate kept saying, "Oh my goodness, oh dear. Oh dear, oh dear", and stuff like that. Now she sat back, clasping her hands around her knee. "I'm going to have to give that one some thought, is that okay? You've given me some shocking information to process, and I need some time to mull it over."

"It's confidential. If you go to the police and say you think you know who it is, I mean. It says so on the adverts for the hotline."

"Yes, but you can't initiate a course of events that could get a man taken in for questioning about something as serious as this, without having all the facts and giving them proper consideration."

Maisie stared down at the varnished floorboards of the school counsellor's office, where they sat now. Pru had always wanted to get the floors done like that in their house. Said it would be much easier than hoovering. "Yeah. I get it."

"Whether or not Saffron's mum will spread her suspicions around, we don't know."

"Do you think I should talk to her?"

Kate screwed up her nose. "Not sure; it might be bad for Saffron." She blew a stream of air out through her mouth, loudly. "Not as bad as it would be if the Lyndford Strangler strikes again, admittedly, but—let me have a think, Maisie."

"Okay." She bit her lip. "I keep thinking about when I talked to Charlotte, though. When I asked her, the second time, if he really was with her on that Friday night—I dunno. I didn't notice at the time so much 'cause I was so angry, but when I thought about it again, she didn't sound like she was that sure. Like, she wanted to get me off the phone 'cause she was lying."

"Really?"

"Yes, I think so. But why would she lie, though?"

"Who knows? People do so for all sorts of reasons, usually ones we know nothing about."

"Do you think he might not have gone to see her, then? Like, be up to something else?"

"I don't know, I don't know him!" Kate laughed. "I couldn't possibly comment."

Maisie frowned. "Something just didn't ring true about it."

"Are you sure? I'm not questioning your judgement, Maisie, but sometimes we can see things that aren't really there, if we've already demonised someone in our thoughts."

"I'm sure. More so now I think back to how she said it. I'm not just making it up, honest."

"Okay."

Maisie wasn't sure what that 'okay' meant. "I don't see how I can find out."

Kate looked out of the window. "I remember, years ago, having a boyfriend I didn't trust." She laughed. "I used to check the mileage on his car!"

"Did you?"

"Mm." She smiled. "Gave me a starting point, anyway."

Maisie swallowed, hard. "If I wanted to do that, how would I?"

The older woman put her head on one side. "What sort of car has he got?"

"Um—it's a Golf, I think. Is that a make? Him and Mum, they say things like, shall we go in the Golf?"

"A new one?"

"Dunno. He bought it second-hand while he was working. It's new*ish*, I think."

Kate narrowed her eyes. "Hmm; my friend's got a Golf. I think you can see the mileage even when the engine's off."

Maisie was unconvinced. "I don't know anything about cars. Where do I look?"

"Should be a little display on the dashboard, behind the steering wheel, it won't be hard to find. Oh dear, I'm really not sure I should be suggesting this to you."

"You're not. You just mentioned something that you did once. I remembered you talking about it, and it gave me the idea."

They both laughed.

"Okay," Kate said. "What you do is find out the exact distance between your house and wherever Charlotte lives, make a note of the mileage before he leaves, and again when he gets back. If it doesn't show anything like the necessary amount of miles, then you know."

Maisie frowned. "Okay, I can do that, but—well, I still can't see why she would lie."

"To give him an alibi, perhaps, for something about which we know nothing," Kate said. "She won't be the first woman to do that for a man she loves." She shrugged her shoulders. "It's possible."

"At least I could say to Mum that I he's lying, then," Maisie said, slowly. "She'd hate it, but it would be better that she knows."

Kate Brownlow nodded her head. "Exactly. It won't prove anything else, but it would be a start, wouldn't it?"

Maisie felt herself shaking, with excitement, fear, relief, all mixed up together. "This is serious shit, isn't it?"

Kate smiled, sadly. "Yes. I couldn't have put it better myself. It is, indeed, very serious shit." She dusted her hands together. "Right, first things first. Do you know how to look up distances between towns on the internet?"

Maisie gave her a withering look.

"Sorry! I forget; girls your age have forgotten more about the internet than I've ever known." She laughed, but it faded, quickly. "And this may sound odd, but I hope he did go to Yarmouth."

"So do I." Maisie bit her thumbnail. "I don't think I've ever hoped for anything so much."

She began to cry all over again.

Chapter Nineteen

Dorothy: The Mother

Tuesday, 14th October 2015

Flicking through the photographs of happy times gone by, held in place on the black pages by photo corners (did anyone else still do this, these days?), Dorothy pondered how much less *immediate* your problems seemed when you were older—which was odd, really, considering that you had so much less time left.

When you were young, with all the time in the world, every emotion was reacted to, each thought expressed as soon as it came into your head; it all seemed so very *urgent*. When you reached the autumn of your life, though, you could mull stuff over for days, weeks, months, even, without actually doing anything. Or just wait to see if things changed of their own accord.

The autumn of your life. Dorothy liked that expression. Some days, though, that autumn was not the mellow golden glow of early October, but the dank gloom of late November, with winter peeping around the corner.

Maybe it was just the wisdom that came with years. Despite having fewer years available (ten? Fifteen? Twenty-five?) in which to rectify problems, age and experience meant you considered the bigger picture before making a move.

Or maybe it was just because you had less energy. Less inclination to do something that might induce upheaval.

Orlando's behaviour remained odd. He still came in late with no explanation given unless she asked for one; could be simply that, at the age of forty-three, he was finally spreading his adult wings. Wanting to live his own life. She had to respect that, and indeed would be happy to do so if it wasn't for that strange invisible barrier between them.

Orlando was a part of her, she knew when there was something wrong. And try as she might to ignore it, the dark shadow was always at the back of her mind. The computer-produced images looked so much like her son that she had to stop herself clutching her stomach in pain and shock, every time she saw one on the front of a newspaper in the supermarket, or in the library. Had others noticed? Their friends at art class? Ray Goosey and the other metal detector fanatics (even though they hadn't seen Orlando for weeks)?

His colleagues?

Dorothy sipped her coffee and continued looking through her photograph album, lost in the past. Orlando as a small child, at the funfair, the seaside. Playing with a neighbour's children; all of them, together, a picnic in the back garden. That coach trip they'd taken to Whitby, fifteen years ago. Lovely place. She smiled. They'd been the youngest on the coach, by far, and the long weekend had been orientated towards the needs of pensioners, with stop-offs for tea and cakes every hour, or what felt like every hour. Orlando had said *never again*, but they'd both enjoyed it.

Time was getting on; she needed to think about starting dinner, never mind wallowing in memories of times gone by, pleasant though it was.

Dorothy got up, and picked up the BHS bag from the table. New socks for Orlando, the plain black ones he'd requested. She'd take them up and put them in his room, change out of her smart skirt and into comfortable clothes. Her petrol blue, light cotton, drawstring-waisted trousers were actually called 'leisure trousers' in the catalogue, but they had a nice matching top (called a 'shell top', for some reason), so they didn't look too sloppy.

"Think of them as 'lounging pyjamas'," Orlando said, "then they sound positively glamorous!"

Up in his room she opened his sock drawer to put away the new items and rearrange the mess, generally; her son was a devil for putting away socks with holes in, instead of giving them to her for mending, or throwing them out.

Which was when she saw it.

A box, tucked away at the back of the drawer, behind the thick woollen socks he wore when he went fishing in the winter.

It was dark wood, about eight inches by six.

It was locked.

Dorothy stared at it for a long time.

If the box was locked, it meant it was private. Never mind who a box belonged to; she was a decent human being who wouldn't dream of rifling through someone's personal belongings. The respect for another's privacy was all. Just as Orlando had never made enquiries about her occasional boyfriends in the past, she had never asked him for details about the few times he'd taken girls out, always cottoned on quickly if he seemed not to want to talk about something, never pried into his thoughts.

She wouldn't consider so much as picking it up, if only she didn't think he was actively hiding something from her. *Lying to her.*

If only she hadn't seen those horrible computer images that she tried not to think about, every hour of every day.

Dorothy cried so rarely that some detached part of her mind was struck by how unfamiliar it felt when she began to do so.

If the box was locked, it meant it was private.

Or *secret*. Was there a difference between the two words?

Oh dear. Oh dear.

She put her hand over her mouth, clutching her face, trying to stop crumpling into the full despairing weep, but tears seeped out of her eyes and over her fingers.

I've got to, she thought. *I've got to put my mind at rest, or I'll end up asking him, and that would never do, that wouldn't do at all—*

No, she couldn't. It was wrong. She shut the drawer and went downstairs.

Five minutes later, she went back up again.

Please, God, forgive me.

She thought she knew where the key was likely to be, and there it was, in the little tin he'd bought in Sheringham, as a child. The battered lid showed a faded picture of Happisburgh lighthouse.

That must be it, a tiny thing, amongst a pile of other bits and bobs. Tickets from concerts, unusual stamps, all sorts of odds and sods that would mean nothing to anyone except the person to whom they were precious.

The little key fitted perfectly into the lock of the box.

The sensation of suspense as she lifted the lid reminded her of watching a hundred and one murder or thriller or gangster films with Orlando, in which the main character took delivery of a package and took his time opening it, to keep the audience on the edges of their seats. Safe on the settee in their house in Clovis Court, she and Orlando would hold their breath. What would it be? Something covered in blood?

"A dead crow!"

"A finger!"

"Sawn-off genitalia!"

"Orlando, *really!*"

In his little box, though, there was no deceased bird or severed body part.

But the contents were hardly less disturbing.

Orlando Beck's secret collection, hidden away in a locked box, consisted of a partially used lipstick, two pairs of earrings, a necklace of turquoise stones, two pairs of tights, a hair comb with a peacock design, a ring, a little mirror with an enamelled back (the type girls keep in their make-up bags), black mascara and a palette of eyeshadow (partially used).

The jewellery was rather gaudy, the make-up from cheap brands.

The sort young women with not much money might own.

The sort with which street walkers might adorn themselves (she imagined).

The box fell from her hands, back onto the cushion of neatly arranged socks. Breathing slowly, slowly, she took two steps backwards and collapsed back down onto the bed.

She could still feel the box in her hands.

One word swirled round and round her mind.

Trophies.

Her stomach churned, tightened; she clutched it and it heaved; for a moment she thought she was going to be sick, but no, that was silly, it was only on television that people threw up whenever they had a shock.

Instead, she looked down at her slippered feet on Orlando's deep indigo carpet, and she wept.

Trophies.

She'd read about that somewhere, how serial killers took things from the victims. Mementos of their handiwork.

There was no other explanation for that bizarre collection.

A little cry of pain escaped from her lips.

They could have belonged to former girlfriends, or one she knew nothing about—

But why would he keep them? Even that was a bit—well, *creepy.*

Better a creep than a monster, though.

She could deal with it, show him the error of his ways, make him understand such behaviour was a little odd. If women thought he was creepy, it might explain why he'd never had much luck with them.

She fell back, dragging herself up the bed towards the pillows, sobbing.

No, no, no. She heard herself whispering as she curled up in a ball and let the tears wash down her face, dampening the pillow slip.

Somewhere downstairs the landline rang, then her mobile, but she couldn't heave her body off the bed.

The sky darkened as she lay there.

She knew it must be past the time Orlando normally came home from work, but she couldn't move.

She slept.

When she awoke, Orlando's bedside lamp was on, and he was sitting beside her, shaking her shoulder.

"Mum? Mum! Oh, thank goodness, you're awake! Why are you in here? What's the matter? Are you ill?"

Slowly, he came into focus and she smiled at him.

"I'm fine. I was just putting some socks away, and I sat down on the bed—I felt tired." She shook her head, as if to wake herself up. "Silly me. I must have dropped off."

"I was worried sick." He bustled about, shutting the curtains, taking off his tie. "I rang you because a couple of bigwigs from Head Office were down and wanted to take me for a pint; I couldn't really say no, and I didn't know what you were making for dinner, I was worried it might be something that wouldn't keep, and when I couldn't get hold of you I just thought, oh, she's got the radio on in the kitchen, but you know me, I couldn't stop worrying, so I came home as soon as I could."

"I'm fine." She looked up at him. "There's no dinner."

"That's okay." He squeezed her shoulder and smiled. "Sloping off for a kip in the middle of the afternoon, indeed; you'll be drinking pink gins and entertaining gentlemen callers in your housecoat, next! Now, how about I go out and get us some lovely fish and chips?"

"Yes. Yes, that would be good." Even though she wouldn't be able to eat a thing.

"Double curry sauce?" He always smothered his chips in the stuff; she found it quite disgusting.

She managed a weak smile. "Very funny."

"Right, I'll just nip out, okay? Oh; I might pop in to see Colin on the way, I've got some DVDs for him."

"I'll put the plates in to heat up in half an hour, then, shall I?"

"Give me an hour. Or a bit longer if we get chatting! Tell you what, I'll call you when I'm on my way home."

She pulled herself into a sitting position and watched him walk out of the room, whistling.

His sock drawer was shut. As soon as she heard him close the front door, she opened it. His secret box was locked again, the key returned to the Happisburgh lighthouse tin.

He must know she'd been prying, then.

How could he possibly explain it?

How could they both live with the knowledge that she knew about it?

If she tried very, very hard, perhaps she could pretend she'd never seen inside it.

Slowly taking the steps downstairs, she looked out of the window. The sky was black, the night looked cold, and Orlando pulled his collar up. He was smiling.

He would see Colin the next night at art class; why didn't he wait until then to give him the DVDs?

She watched him reach into his pocket and pull out his black hat.

Chapter Twenty

Steve: The Friend

Thursday, 15th October, 2015

"You coming out, then? Eight o'clock in the Boar."

Steve shut his eyes. "I dunno."

"C'mon on, man. You haven't been out with us for weeks, and it's Woodsy's birthday." Dan laughed. "You can get a pass for the night, can't you? Or has she got her feet under the table already? Hey, I notice she's already put an end to Sports Night."

"That's nothing to do with Nina. I just haven't felt like it."

"So get the night off."

Night off. He'd tell Nina that one; she'd think it was funny, too. "I'll see."

"No, come on, say yes now. We're going down town, then we thought we'd go up to Rockerfellas, what d'you reckon? Noel's coming, too. C'mon, let's make a night of it!"

That sealed it. AJ and the Thewlis brothers at a lap dancing club.

He'd rather stick pins in his eyes.

"Nah, sorry, mate, I just don't fancy it, not tonight."

Dan laughed. "Don't worry, I get it. Her Indoors says no to lap dancing and strip clubs, right? You can always say we're going to the casino instead."

"It's okay. I'll give it a miss."

"Suit yourself. Just don't forget who your mates are, right? You might need us a few months down the line when you're bored shitless and getting nagged to fuck."

Although Dan's words annoyed the hell out of him, the mood of the conversation was reasonably light, and Steve smiled. "I'll risk it."

"Well, I hope she's worth it, buddy."

Steve laughed. "So do I!"

Nina was more than worth it; he already knew that.

In the two short months since she'd entered his life, everything had changed. They talked about getting a place together, and this made Steve think about moving on career-wise, too; his computer skills far outweighed the challenges of his job. He liked the idea of building a good life for the two of them, maybe having children if the relationship grew stronger. That was what you did in your mid-thirties, wasn't it? You made decisions about which way your life was going, starting building for your later years. Sounded boring, but it wasn't. They could travel, have new experiences. Together.

Steve loved her. She said she loved him too. He'd never been happier in his life; being loved was a whole new experience.

The wonderful relief about finding your right person was that you no longer had to do the stuff you hated in order to find someone with whom to live it.

The thought of going on a lads' night out made him want to hide under the bedclothes and never come out. Loud, packed hell-holes blaring out music he hated, drunk girls careering about, groups of lads acting hard or stupid. The cattle market. He hated Rockerfellas. Hated how all that female flesh turned the guys into some kind of weird cross between dirty raincoat pervs and eager schoolboys.

Pitiful.

AJ nudging Woodsy on the arm, pointing at a dancer who was targeting him, and saying, "she likes you, mate!"

Then Woodsy would grin and pull back his shoulders, puff out his chest, though surely they must know that the women didn't like *any* of them, that they were just a means to the rent, or whatever, and the smiles and pouts went to the suckers who put their hands in their pockets the most often, encouraging them to keep tucking those notes in their knickers.

When one of the girls offered a private dance, they kidded themselves it was because the girl fancied them.

"Where's AJ?"

"Oh, he's pulled!"

Horrible.

"I wouldn't be with you if you were the sort of person who wanted to go to those places," Nina said.

He'd met the gang down the pub a couple of times since he and Nina started, but the outings had been token gestures. Once he'd had a pint and caught up with what his friends were doing, endured all the jokes about his new status as a pussy-whipped softie, he wanted to go home. And there was no way he was going through the tedium of Tuesday Sports Night, ever again.

"You've moved on, that's all," Nina said, later that night as they lounged in front of the TV, Steve lying with his head on her lap. "People change; their friends don't necessarily change with them. From what you say I reckon the gap between you and Dan started widening a long time ago."

"Yeah," said Steve. "I know this sounds a bit weird, but it's like AJ's got some sort of *power* over him. He used to be okay, most of the time. It's like he's turning into AJ, now, though."

"It happens. The side of him that you don't like now must have always been there; maybe AJ just brought out the bits that were simmering underneath."

"You mean like Myra Hindley."

She laughed. "*What?*"

"I don't mean exactly like her." He pulled himself up into a sitting position and grabbed the remote, flicking through the channels. "But according to many she was a fairly normal person until Ian Brady got hold of her. I'd say the sadistic monster must have always been inside her, though."

Nina shuddered. "Don't. That's too horrendous to think about. *Ugh!* Even her name makes me shiver. But yeah, that's what I mean. Kind of like a volcano, with all that red-hot lava waiting to burst out. Could be Dan just kept it well hidden."

Steve put his arm around her, still flicking at the channels until a programme caught his eye. "That looks good. *American Psychopaths.* Fancy it?"

Nina looked up at him. "Aren't you glad I'm not the sort of bird who wants to watch romcoms?"

"Same as what you said to me about lap dancing clubs."

"What?"

"I wouldn't be with you if you were."

"D'you know what I think? I reckon you like watching all these programmes about psychopaths because it makes Dan not seem such an arse in comparison."

Steve laughed. "If there weren't thousands of weirdos like me, there wouldn't be so many of these programmes. But, yeah, I think you're right about Dan. What AJ's brought out is probably here to stay, now the genie's out the bottle."

She snuggled into his shoulder and looked up at him. "Well, stay in touch, but you shouldn't feel obliged to go pub crawling with him if you don't want to."

"No." Steve stared ahead. He'd never mentioned the other thing to Nina.

The Lyndford Strangler thing. The picture. Which looked less like Dan some of the time, more like him at others.

Even Dan made jokes about it now. "I see I'm on the front page again!"

Steve tried to shut all the bad stuff out as he leant his face onto the shampoo-smelling softness of Nina's hair. They were cosy, together, and life was good. More than good. He didn't need to think about shit like that. Dan was a twat, but surely his best mate couldn't be capable of brutal murder? If he was, what did it say about him, Steve, that he'd been lifelong friends with him?

He wanted so badly to forget the fears, but that fleeting look of panic on Dan's face, that first night, was always in his head.

As he stared at the screen in the warm, lamp-lit glow of the cosy room, listening to the catalogue of horrors perpetrated by America's most prolific serial killers, terrorists and drug lords, he felt an urge to flick over to a nice wildlife documentary, anything clean and normal.

The look on the face of 'Night Stalker' Richard Ramirez reminded him of his friend. Ted Bundy's eyes were just like Dan's.

Good looking men. Lady killers.

All at once, Steve knew he had to discuss it with Nina. Even if she thought he was stupid, even if she said he ought to talk to the police, he couldn't keep it to himself any longer.

He picked up the remote control and flicked the TV off.

"Hey, I was enjoying that!" Nina sat up. "What're you doing?" She laughed. "Oh, I know. Don't tell me, you want to put on *My Best Friend's Wedding* instead, don't you?"

Steve smiled. "I wish it was only that." He took her hand and held it tightly. "Nina, there's something I need to talk to you about."

Chapter Twenty-One

Montana

Lyndford Police Station

2.30 am, Friday 16th October, 2015

Montana Smith was tall, with waist-length, dark brown hair (hair extensions, DI Nolan informed him), and sexy, full lips. Fabulous looking girl, a product of so many mixed races that he was glad he didn't have to make a decision on her IC classification. Exotic, slanted eyes, light brown skin, limbs strong and sinewy. Not a woman to mess with, for sure. DI Nolan nicknamed her 'Michonne', after some character in *The Walking Dead*, she informed him. Not a programme he'd ever seen.

Montana's face was still painted in heavy make-up, and she wore a fuchsia pink tracksuit that did little to disguise the fake boobs, tiny waist and long, finely muscled legs: the tools of her trade.

Despite her ordeal, DCI Reddick noticed, she seemed relaxed, confident—pleased with herself, even.

"See, I knew not to have a shower, 'cause you need to look for evidence, don't you?" She smiled proudly, and held up her hands, waggling her fingers around. Ridiculously long, fuchsia pink talons with gold tips. "I didn't even wash my hands, though God knows I'm dying to! But there's sometimes bits of 'em under the fingernails, isn't there?"

"That's appreciated, makes our job easier." Reddick couldn't work out if he liked her or not. Not that it mattered. "In your own time, Montana."

She sat back, relaxed, and crossed one leg over the other. "Well, I was just heading for my car, wasn't I? I was parked in the Bella Pasta car park 'cause me and a couple of the girls, we'd had a bite to eat there before work. You need a bit of sustenance to do what we do!" Her laugh was harsh, and she was less beautiful now that she'd opened her mouth; the East Midlands accent had a cruel effect. "I just had a small pasta dish, 'cause it fills you up, but not too much 'cause you don't want a bloated stomach, do you? Not when you're dancing."

"And you left the club around one a.m?"

"Yeah. I was having an early night, 'cause I'd done two really late ones. Loads of private dances, and I can only do so many of them before I feel like I'm not really giving the guy his money's worth, you know? So, yeah, it was completely dark, there was no one around, and this fella, he just comes up behind me and grabs me round the neck and the waist, like, with both his arms"—here she stood, to demonstrate the action—"like, with one hand over my mouth, and he dragged me off onto the bit of wasteland by the car park, you know, where it's all just grass and that. Pity I'd had a couple of voddys, or I'd have reacted quicker! Oh—I weren't over the limit, honest, officer!" That shrill laugh again. "But, anyway, he obviously thought I was going to go down without a fight, but the big galoot reckoned without me being the star pupil in my aikido club." She sat down and laughed, loudly, folding her arms and nodding her head. "That showed him! D'you know aikido?"

"I'm not familiar with it, no," said Reddick. "It's a martial art?"

"Yeah! Well, I got my act together once he tried to pull my drawers off, I'll tell you that for nothing." She grinned, widely. "Bit of a kick to put it all into practice for real!"

"Did you harm him?" asked DI Nolan. "Scratch him, pull out his hair, punch him?"

"Didn't need to." Montana Smith flicked a long lock over her shoulder. "Aikido *redirects the momentum* of the attack; it's not a fight." She changed her pose, hands clasped around one knee. "The principle of aikido is that both the attacker and the opponent remain unharmed."

"*Great*," muttered Reddick. No DNA traces—no evidence.

"So," said DI Nolan, "basically, you were attacked by a man dressed in black, including black gloves and a black balaclava covering his face, you fought him off and he got away without a scratch?" The frustration in her voice was evident.

"That's right!" Montana shone with pride. "It was so *empowering*, you know? It might sound weird but I actually got a bit of a rush from it; I thought, now's my chance to prove what I'm made of! It's bloody good, aikido, you ought to get your officers on it!" She jutted out her bottom lip, then giggled. "I just wish I'd got the chance to do a leg throw!"

"His height? Body type?"

"Tall-ish. I'd say five eleven, maybe six foot. Kind of normal, you know? And slim, but not thin. Fit, but not OTT. Just a normal bloke, yeah?"

"His hair colour? Face shape?"

She rolled her eyes. "Well, I didn't see that, did I?" She lifted her arms and made inverted commas in the air with her long, shiny fingertips. "Like, *duh*—he had a balaclava on, remember?"

DI Nolan closed her eyes. "I hoped it might have slipped at some point."

"No, sorry, love! Aikido's not aggressive, y'see."

"Is there anything else you can tell us?" Reddick leant forward. "Anything at all? You didn't see his skin, even the colour of his eyes?"

Montana pondered. "Brown, I think." She giggled. "His eyes, I mean, not his skin; he was definitely white. But his eyes were dark. Uh-uh, yeah, dark brown. I looked into them when he, like, had me pinned down, before I, y'know, got my act together."

"From what you saw, did you recognise him as anyone who might have been in the club that night? One of the regulars? Anyone who was being belligerent towards you?"

"Well, I only saw his eyes, didn't I? That was when I was trying to work out which of my throws to use; it needs to be second nature, that's the problem. I tried a *nikyō* first; that's the 'second technique'." She stared at the floor for a moment, then executed a few arm movements. "Damn it, I wish I could have another go!"

When Montana Smith breezed into the interview room announcing that she thought she'd been attacked by 'that serial killer', Reddick's heart rate had quickened in anticipation; had he but known the real reason for her excitement—

"There really is nothing else you can tell us?" DS Nolan asked. "Did he speak to you? Call you by name?"

"No, but I definitely know it was one of the punters from the club."

"How?"

"Well, 'cause of what he said."

Reddick hardly dared glance at Nolan. "He *spoke* to you?"

"Oh, yeah. Yeah, he did, yeah."

DS Nolan folded her arms and leant forward onto the table. "Did you not think to mention this before? So, come on, what did he say?"

Montana Smith frowned. "It was when he had me on the ground. Like, with his arm across my chest, like, here, right?" She brought her arm up, just below her neck. "Hang on, let me think. Yeah, he said, 'I'm going to mark you, you fucking slut'. Something like that."

Reddick caught his breath. "You're sure he said 'slut'?"

"Yeah. Pretty sure, at any rate."

"Think. It's important."

"I am." She frowned again. "Don't hassle me, I'm tryin' to think, I was more bothered about how to get him off me than remembering his exact bloody words. Yeah, that was definitely what he said. 'I'm going to mark you, you fucking slut'. Then he kind of climbed onto me, and started to pull my trousers off, and he said 'I've been watching you, slut'. Then he said it a couple more times."

"Said what a couple more times?"

"Slut. He kept calling me 'slut', like the word got him going, you know?"

Reddick felt the muscles in his neck tense up. "And would you recognise his voice again?"

"Oh yeah, I reckon so. No worries."

He hardly dared look at DI Nolan, in case his excitement was obvious. *I've been watching you. Slut.*

In one moment, the search had narrowed right down. From half the male population of South Lincolnshire, to a group of men who'd visited Rockerfellas lap dancing club on the night of Thursday, 15th October. What, two or three hundred of them?

Nolan turned to him as Montana Smith sashayed out of the station. "The words 'I've been watching you' don't necessarily mean he was watching her that night, though, do they?"

He hated her for expressing the thought that had just occurred to him, too.

"No, but it's a good place to start. Okay. You know the drill. CCTV from the club, the signing in book, interviews with the staff, credit and debit cards, every bloody thing you can get." He rubbed his hands together. "We're going to get this bastard now."

Chapter Twenty-Two

Tamsin: The Colleague

Monday 19th October

"Have you seen the news?" Kim waved a copy of the *Lyndford Echo*'s lead article. "Another girl got picked up by a bloke they think is the Strangler, but she fought him off and got away, same as Sarah Craske! Must be losing his touch!"

Tamsin's colleagues crowded round, peering over Kim's shoulder.

Sophie laughed. "Says she does all that martial arts stuff; ha-ha, I bet he was pissed off when she started giving it large with the drop kicks."

"Maybe they'll be making an arrest soon, then," said Brandon. "I saw the area cordoned off with police tape on Sunday when I went up to go bowling on Sunday; wish I'd known what it was for."

Tamsin felt sick. Jake had been away all the last week, staying with friends in Cambridge. Or so he'd claimed. "How do they know it's the same guy who did the murders?" she asked.

Brandon looked at her, oddly.

"Dunno, they never say, do they?" said Kim. "I s'pose that's so the killer doesn't know exactly how much they've got on him."

Tamsin leant closer, elbowing Sophie out of the way so she could read more. The article made it sound as though the police were convinced that this Montana Smith's attacker was their man.

But what if it wasn't?

So many questions darted in and out of her mind.

What if some innocent man went to prison because she hadn't spoken up?

What if the next girl wasn't a martial arts expert, and got herself killed?

What if Jake hadn't really been in Cambridge?

"I'm going out, Kim." She picked up her bag and stood up. "I'm sorry, I have to, I won't be long."

Kim looked up from the paper. "Eh? Er, sorry, Tamsin, no, you're not." She frowned. "We don't do flexi-time here and even if we did, you can't just wander off in the middle of the morning. Can you tell me what's so urgent?"

Tamsin clutched her bag. "No. I can't."

"Well, unless it's a matter of life and death I'm going to have to say no." Those words left her with no option.

"It is. It's a matter of life and death, it truly is."

Kim got up and walked over to her, lowering her voice. "Tamsin, love, do you want to come and tell me what's going on, somewhere private?"

Everyone was looking at them.

"No. I'm sorry, I can't."

"Okay." Kim took her by the arm and led her over to the door. "Listen," she said, gently, "you're obviously distraught about something, but if you have to go out during office hours you do need to tell me why."

"I can't."

Kim's demeanour changed. "If you won't tell me, I can't give you permission. Whatever it is, you'll have to wait until lunchtime. I'm sorry."

Tamsin ignored her, reaching for her jacket on the coat stand. "I am, too." She concentrated only on what she was doing, but could feel her colleagues staring at her. No one spoke. Six pairs of eyes bored into her. "I've got to go. I really have." Her arms shook as she shoved them into the sleeves of her jacket. "I'm sorry, Kim. You'll just have to sack me, if that's what you need to do."

She was vaguely aware of someone asking her if she was okay as she fled out of the door, hurrying down the corridor, fingers shaking as she tried to do up the zip of her jacket, but she didn't turn back.

She didn't care. This was too important.

"Tamsin! Tamsin, wait!"

Brandon caught up with her, grabbing at her shoulder. "What are you doing? Where are you going?" But she knew that he knew; she could see it in his eyes. "Look, I know what you're doing, and you've got it all wrong."

She pushed his hand off, hoisting her bag over her shoulder, gripping the strap.

"I have to." Her whole face shook with emotion. "How can I not?"

"Because it's nuts. Because you'll lose your job. Because—look, please, just don't. Come on." He put his hand on her shoulder again. "Let's go and have a cup of tea and talk about it, I'll tell Kim you're a bit upset about something—"

"No!" She swiped his hand off once more. "For Christ's sake, Brandon! Some innocent guy could end up in prison, just because I was too scared to speak up! That's not right, is it?"

"That very rarely happens these days. Technology's much more advanced, it's more difficult to make those sort of mistakes—"

Her face felt hot; her temples throbbed. What was that phrase? "All it takes for evil to triumph is for good men to do nothing!" she said. Was that right?

"That isn't why you're doing this, though, is it? Slow down. Try to be honest with yourself."

"I am!" Her voice was getting louder. "It's the rest of you who aren't!"

"*It isn't Jake.*" He reached out to touch her arm, but she brushed it away. "Tamsin, listen! He was in Cambridge when that girl was attacked."

"You don't *know* that! He could be lying! It could be his alibi, can't you see?" She was yelling at him now; up the corridor people stopped and glanced back in their direction, she could sense their eyes on her, but it didn't matter. "How can you know? You don't!"

Brandon put his hand to his forehead. "Please stop this, you're going to regret it, it'll be really, really bad for you." Bloody idiot looked as though he was going to cry. Too scared to admit that his mate was a monster.

Oh yes, of course, of course.

She could see it all.

She knew exactly what would go down next. Brandon would warn his friend, and by the time she even reached the police station, Jake could be miles away. She closed her eyes for a moment. Had to stop that happening.

Be calm. She relaxed her shoulders and dropped her bag. "Christ, what am I doing?"

"Tamsin?" The boy looked so confused she wanted to laugh.

"You're right," she said, and patted his arm. "Of course you are. Oh, Brandon." She forced a laugh. "I just had a picture of me walking into the police station accusing Jake of—bloody hell. Talk about a reality check. God, what's the matter with me?"

Brandon narrowed his eyes. "Really? Well, thank goodness for that. You've really had me worried." He reached out for her hand, but he had a weird expression on his face. Not one she recognised. "Come on. Let's go and have that cup of tea, shall we? I'll tell Kim you're not feeling well, perhaps you can go home for the rest of the day."

"Would you?"

"I'll even ask if I can come with you, if you don't want to be alone."

He was so transparent. Her eyes welled up with tears, because of the inevitability of what she had to do, and she let them fall; they would serve their purpose. "I do want to go home. Look, I'm sorry." She brushed the tears away with her hand. "Oh, what's the matter with me? I think—I just want to go home now. Alone."

"Alright." Brandon's voice was soft, relieved, comforting. "I'll take care of Kim."

"Thank you."

He leant forward and hugged her. "Hey, don't worry about it. We all go a bit off our rocker sometimes."

She pulled out of his embrace. "Well, thank goodness there are people like you to put lunatics like me straight, eh?"

He smiled. "You promise you're okay?"

"Yeah. I am, really. I just need to take a bit of time, I think. Perhaps take a couple of days off."

"You're really not going to do anything silly?"

"No. I promise."

To her surprise, he leant forward and kissed her cheek. "Take care. Look, if you want to talk later, just give me a ring."

"Sure." She was anxious to get away, now. "I'll be okay. You go." Without looking at him again she turned around and carried on walking.

"I'll call you later!"

Brandon's words barely registered with her as she pushed open the main door and hurried out towards the car park.

All the way to the police station, she rehearsed what she would say when she got there.

"*I'd like to speak to the officer in charge of the Lyndford Strangler case. I believe I know his identity.*"

No, not enough impact.

"Bring me the person in charge. Tell him I can deliver the Lyndford Strangler."

Yes, that was better. Perfect.

Back in the offices of the *Lyndford Echo*, Brandon bypassed the HR department and dashed straight down to IT.

He'd stuck up for Tamsin over and over again during the last few months; people could be so unkind, when she was obviously having some sort of meltdown. Whether or not it was provoked by Jake's rejection of her he couldn't be sure, he hadn't known her long enough to tell, but if this got out it could send her over the edge. Rachel, in particular, was an acid-tongued bitch, and she had the hots for Jake; many had noticed Tamsin's peculiarities, generally, but it was Rachel who'd stirred up the whole stalker thing. Before, it had just been a mild joke between Jake and Dev, but she told everyone about the Christmas pen and Tamsin's delusions about her and Jake's 'special connection', and made Tamsin look an idiot. Mind you, Jake must have told her the details. Pillow talk, no doubt. Maybe Rachel's desire to get the best story for the paper spilled over into the rest of her life, too.

All the same, Jake needed to know, just in case the police took her seriously. Brandon had not been fooled by Tamsin's ridiculous, pretend change of heart, but he'd thought it best to go along with it; she seemed positively unhinged.

As he walked down the corridor, he passed the e-fit picture of the Lyndford Strangler, stuck up on a noticeboard.

She'd got one thing right, anyway. It did look a hell of a lot like Jake.

Chapter Twenty-Three

Maisie: The Teenager

Monday, 19th October 2015

Kate Brownlow's eyes were filled with sadness as she took Maisie's hand in both of hers.

"I think it's time, don't you?"

Maisie's lower lip just wouldn't stop quivering. Stupid thing. "I'm so scared."

"I know. But you can do it. We both can."

At around four on the previous Thursday afternoon, Maisie had arrived home to find her mother back early from work, arguing with Gary in the hall.

Raised voices could be heard as she walked up the driveway, but the minute she opened the door they fell quiet. A bad sign.

"Mum? What's up? Why are you home early?"

Pru Todd lifted her hands ceiling-wards. "Ask *him*. Why am I home early, Gary?"

Gary assumed the facsimile of sincerity that Maisie had come to know and loathe so well. "Love, love, I'm gutted you had to come home to this. I'm so sorry, but I really do have to go over to Yarmouth to see Bobby. The bullying—his mum's at her wits end." He shrugged, helpless. "What can I do? I'm stuck between a rock and a hard place, you know? I can't tell them to sort out their own problems, can I? Not when Bobby's coming home with not only bruises but his expensive phone stolen, and his mum's in tears on the phone 'cause she doesn't know what to do. It's just one night. I'll be home as soon as I've seen him off to school tomorrow; I want to go in and have a word with the headmaster, get it sorted once and for all, then I won't have to go over so much, will I?"

Maisie laughed. "You're kidding, right? Kids who grass, or get their parents up the school, they get picked on even worse."

"I know, I know, but this time it's an actual theft of property, isn't it?"

"Yes," said Pru, "it is. So Charlotte can go into the school herself. Is she so helpless she can't even do that, for her own child? Or hasn't she got any brothers, a father, a male friend?"

"She hasn't, no—"

Maisie put her school bag down. "Mum, I just thought. Why don't you go with Gary? You could help Charlotte. Give her another mum's point of view."

Pru folded her arms, challenging him. "That's not a bad idea. Yes, I can do that."

"*Whoa*, no, no, no!" Gary shook his head, and held his hand up. "I really don't think that would be a good idea. It would just fan the flames."

Pru's eyes narrowed, her face pink with anger. "Fan what flames?"

"Well, you know," Gary said. "It wasn't easy for either of them to accept it when I left, and—"

"The way you act there's no reason for her to accept it, is there?" Pru stormed off down the hall and into the kitchen, Gary following. Maisie watched them for a moment, her mother clutching the edge of the kitchen sink, looking out into the back garden, Gary next to her with his arm around her shoulders.

This was her chance.

She dug in her bag for a pen, opened the front door as quietly as she could, and dashed out to the road, where Gary's car was parked. Now, where was the mileage? She shaded her eyes with her hand as she peered through the window at the steering wheel. Oh—yes, that was it, between those two dial things. Heart beating fast, squinting, she copied the numbers down onto her hand, then stood for a moment and stared at them, checking back and forth with her hand to make sure she'd got them in the right order.

Whizzing back into the house, she couldn't help grinning to herself. If he got caught out because of this, it would be down to her! Maisie Todd, girl detective! She dashed straight upstairs to scribble the number down. Then she wrote it in two more places, in case she lost the first one, and put it into her phone, too. A few moments later, she heard the front door close, and Gary's car drive away.

Pru was still standing at the sink, looking out.

"Mum, are you alright?"

She didn't move. "No, of course I'm not."

"I just wondered—'cause, you know, you came home early. I thought might be something really serious, like, you know, not just Gary going to see Charlotte again."

Pru turned around. "Well, that's serious to me. When my partner phones me in the middle of the afternoon to tell me that, yet again, he's driving God knows how many miles to see his ex, *and* he's staying the night—yes, that's pretty *serious*." She clenched her fists against the edges of the draining board.

"But he's only staying over because he wants to go to Bobby's school in the morning."

"So he says. Anyway, I can't deal with going back to work. Which means I'll have to phone Tanya to get her to supervise clearing up, and cashing up, and she always forgets *something*." She sighed. "Last time she left the prawns in the chiller cabinet over the weekend, d'you remember? We couldn't open the shop until the afternoon because it smelt so bad."

Maisie smiled. "Yeah, I remember! It was disgusting."

"I can smell it even now. Oh, I don't know. I can't work out if I'm being unreasonable or not. About Charlotte and Bobby, I mean."

"I don't think you are. It's him who needs to tell her, though." She sat down at the table. "You ought to stand up for yourself more."

"I know."

Dare she say it? "Mum, do you always believe him? About where he goes, I mean. About him staying at Charlotte's overnight."

Her mother's face closed off. "Of course I do. Where else would he be going?" She turned back round to face the window. "Go and get out of your school clothes, and I'll get dinner started."

The conversation wasn't working out how she'd intended. *Mum, do you think Gary might be the Lyndford Strangler?* No, bad idea.

It seemed silly even to her when she said the words. Upstairs, she stripped off her school uniform and retrieved leggings and a crumpled t-shirt from the drawer into which she'd stuffed them the night before. If he wasn't going to stay with Charlotte, he was probably just involved in something else dodgy. When she thought about the Lyndford Strangler stuff it seemed possible, but when she was actually face to face with him it didn't. Gary was a slimy arsehole, but a murderer? He was too normal, that was stuff on telly, it wasn't their lives. They were just ordinary people, who nothing much happened to.

He was home when Maisie returned from school on Friday afternoon. He'd put on a washing load, tidied the living room.

"Hi, honey, had a good day? Don't make a mess if you're going for a shower," he called, as she went upstairs. "I've just cleaned the bathroom for your mum so she can have a good soak when she comes in!"

I'll make as much mess as I want, she thought. *It's my house, not yours.*

When she came down, she found him settled on a chair in the living room in front of the TV, with a clear view of the road outside, so Maisie couldn't see how she might get out to check the mileage on his car.

Pru came home at six, and Gary launched into an account of Bobby's state of mind and his interview with the headmaster that morning. Pru acted as though she wasn't even aware of him speaking, let alone interested, and he tailed off. Maisie enjoyed his awkwardness. *Bobby's not our family, we don't know him, what makes you think we care?*

"Tell you what," he piped up, eventually, "how about Chinese for tea tonight?"

Maisie glanced at her mother as he went through to the kitchen and rummaged in the drawer for a menu. Pru's face remained deadpan.

"My treat," he announced, coming back into the room and handing menus to both of them. "Have anything you want; I reckon I can stretch to it! Maisie, nip up and get Zack down so he can choose, too, then I'll give them a ring. It's free delivery over forty quid, so don't hold back!"

"Zack! Come down!" Maisie hollered, and thought quickly. "I'd rather have fish and chips, I think. I'll go with you, if everyone else wants some as well."

Gary frowned, with that put-on smile she hated so much. "Really? I thought you were the girl who'd do anything for a king prawn chow mein!"

Wanker. "You can get chow mein from the chip shop, and you get more prawns. And I know Zack would want chips; he doesn't like the Chinese ones."

"Fish and chips?" Zack clattered down the stairs and appeared at the door. "Yeah! Can I have a saveloy? And a pineapple fritter?"

Gary ruffled his hair, and Maisie wanted to hit him. *Double wanker.* Pretending to be all fatherly. Did he do that to Bobby, too?

"You can have anything you like, kidda! Can of Dr Pepper, too, I bet?"

"Mum? What do you want?"

Pru stood up. "Nothing. I'm not hungry."

Gary smiled at her. "You sure, sweetheart?"

"Yes. You can pick me up a bottle of wine, though, if you're flashing the money about. Pinot. Actually, no, make it two."

"Shall we go, then?" Maisie said. "Come on. I'm starving."

Gary held his hands up. "Can't keep a lady waiting! Come on then, Maisie-Daisy, let's go."

Maisie's stomach churned so much as they walked down to the car that she doubted she'd be able to eat anything at all, let alone a whole chow mein, but she had to take a look in that car.

"Buckle up!" Gary said, as he got in beside her.

She forced a smile, and took a quick look at the mileage as he switched the engine on. From the pocket of her jeans, she eased out her phone and scrolled down to find the number she'd tapped in the afternoon before.

56,491 minus 56,453.

Since yesterday afternoon, Gary had driven a total of thirty-eight miles.

Wherever he'd been for the last twenty-four hours, it certainly wasn't to Yarmouth and back.

Maisie texted Kate Brownlow with the information as soon as she'd forced down her dinner.

Oh dear, oh dear, Kate texted back. *I know what you're thinking, but he could be up to anything. Don't assume the worst. Come and find me on Monday, or give me a ring if you need to talk any time over the weekend, okay?*

Maisie loved how Kate used proper spelling and punctuation in her texts, it was cool. Hey, perhaps she could start a new trend! The very fact that she was on the end of a phone made Maisie feel stronger; she could wait until Monday.

Kate made her feel safe.

Bethany's complaints of boredom went unheeded all weekend; no, Maisie didn't want to go into town, or down the park, or sleep over. She just wanted to be alone, think, and escape into her boxed set of *Harry Potter*.

On Saturday night, Bethany sent her a message to say that she'd been into town on her own that afternoon, and bumped into Gary. He'd given her a lift, she said.

"There's deffo something sexy about him, isn't there? I tell you what, if I was ten years older I so *would*!"

That message made Maisie feel disgusted, but just a little bit better. If Gary was the Lyndford Strangler, wouldn't he have taken the opportunity to make off with Bethany?

Maybe she was too close to home.

Maisie was waiting. Quietly. For what, she wasn't quite sure, but like the last day of the school holidays, a curious air of *finality* hung over the whole weekend.

Kate Brownlow texted her on Sunday evening to say that she would see her after lessons had finished, the next day.

The first lesson after lunch was chemistry; she was in the lab, pretending to watch Bethany and Grace arsing around with a Bunsen burner, when she heard Kate's voice in the background.

"Maisie!" She turned around to see the chemistry teacher, Mrs Miller, smiling at her. "Could you just pop over here for a minute?"

The feeling of nausea had been with her all day; now, it intensified.

"Ms Brownlow needs to speak to you," Mrs Miller said. "A family matter, apparently." She looked at Kate enquiringly, clearly keen to be enlightened. Then she trilled, "it's okay, I'm sure it's nothing to worry about!"

Piss off, Maisie wanted to say. *Why are you sure? How the hell would you know whether it's anything to worry about or not?*

Without speaking, Kate led her down the corridor to a bench in an alcove by a window. It was sunny outside; the warmth through the glass made it feel like summer.

Kate said: "I'm sorry to drag you out of class, but this can't wait."

"What? What is it?" Nausea enveloped her. Her mother—had Gary hurt her mother? "Has something happened to Mum?"

"Oh no, no, sorry, Maisie, I didn't mean to scare you!" Kate took a deep breath, and took her hand. "Look, another girl was attacked late on Thursday night; I saw it on the lunchtime news." She bit her lip. "Late on Thursday night, when Gary said he was somewhere he clearly wasn't."

Maisie's mouth dropped open. "Shit, really?"

"I think it's time I went to the police." Kate looked kind of apologetic.

"Already? I thought you said we mustn't jump to conclusions, and we need to look for more evidence, first." Maisie put her other hand to her stomach, and felt her face crumple up. Panic overwhelmed her; her breath seemed to stick in her chest.

"No one's accusing anyone of anything," Kate said, "but I think I need to talk it over with someone at the police station."

"Just, like, a chat?" That sounded better.

"Yes, just a chat. That's all. The police know what they're doing, they'll be able to tell us if we're worrying for nothing."

"It's real, isn't it?" Maisie heard her voice, silly and shaky, like a child. "What we're doing, I mean. Do you think it really is him?" She began to cry. "What will Mum say if she finds out? She'll be so cross with me." The tears wouldn't stop coming, flowing out, down her cheeks and onto her clothes; all the emotion of the last few months spilled out. "I'm scared."

Kate put her hand on her shoulder. "I know how hard it is for you, but I promise I'll take responsibility for this; I could have just gone, but I thought I should tell you first. Your mum won't know. Anything I tell the police will be completely confidential, anyway, and don't forget, we're just talking it through, not making a citizen's arrest! Now look, I don't expect you to come with me, it might take hours; you can just go home, I'll speak to the Head, and—"

"No." Maisie wiped her eyes and sniffed. "I'll have to come with you. There's no way on earth I can go home and pretend nothing's happening."

"Are you sure?"

She nodded. "Yeah, I'll text Mum and say I'm going to Beth's after school, or something, but I've got to come. They'll need information from me, won't they? Like, all the times when he's been out on the nights the girls were murdered, and about him showering and washing his clothes all the time—"

"Maybe. Here." Kate handed her a tissue. "Yes; I suppose we'll have to mention all those things; I know, I know, it's seems so crazy, but every killer is someone's son, someone's husband, brother or boyfriend. We'll just have to hope we're wrong."

"I've just thought." Maisie wiped her eyes and blew her nose. "They'll have to search the house, won't they? Then Mum will know!"

"Yes, I would imagine so, but not unless they're pretty sure it's him. There won't be a SWAT team breaking the door down before you get home!" She frowned. "Has your mum got family? Parents?"

"Mm-mm. They live in Suffolk, though—I dunno, they're not—well, they're sort of old-fashioned. Mum's kind of the black sheep of the family. Her brother and sister are, like, dead normal, a bit snobby, they think Mum's a hippie. They'll go mad if they find out about this."

"Ah." Kate looked thoughtful. "Well, we'll cross that bridge when we come to it. *If* we come to it, we might not. Let's get the police over with, first."

Maisie wiped her eyes and blew her nose. "It's real, isn't it?" she said, again.

Kate exhaled, loudly. "'Fraid so. We've got to do it, though."

Then she said the words that made all Maisie's fears seem insignificant.

Kate said, "The thing is, Maisie, if that *was* him on Thursday night, another girl might not be so lucky. If we act now, it might save someone's life."

Chapter Twenty-Four

Juliet: The Wife

Tuesday, 20th October 2015

Lara said, "If you don't go, I will."

She had to talk to Lara about it, because there was no one else.

She had to talk to her to stop herself going insane, because after two weeks of surreptitiously watching Paul's every move, inspecting his clothes and analysing everything he said, she'd come up with nothing concrete, but so much circumstantial evidence that she was in a permanent state of nervous tension. She couldn't sleep, couldn't eat (for once, the weight loss brought her no joy), and was in danger of developing a drink problem.

Of course, Lara went on and on and *on*, nagging in her ear non-stop, asking her what she was so scared of. When Juliet floundered, unwilling to take the step that could never be untrodden, she played her trump card.

"Sarah Craske and Montana Smith fought him off. What if the next one isn't so strong? What if you're right, and it's him? If another girl gets killed it'll be *your fault*. *You* will be the cause of her death, of the pain her family will live through for the rest of their lives. *You*."

Juliet said nothing as Lara's voice rang in her ears, and wondered if she was as scared of her as she was of Paul, sometimes.

Easier to be a mouse, hiding in the shadows.

Lara always did what she knew was right, regardless of anyone else's opinion.

Justice was more important to Lara than any of Juliet's silly, cowed, pathetic arguments.

"If it's not him, no one would never know that you'd been to the police."

"I would know."

"Okay. But whether the worst is true or not, you need to ask yourself something very, very important."

"What's that?"

"If you truly think this man is capable of committing murder, what the hell are you doing still living with him?"

Chapter Twenty-Five

Steve: The Friend

Tuesday, 20th October, 2015

Sleeping (or rather, not sleeping) in his car during the early hours of Tuesday morning had been a most uncomfortable experience, and they'd ended up just driving along the coast, waiting for a café to open so they could get some much-needed coffee. That was the trouble with packing in a hurry; you didn't think to make up a flask. At least they were safe, now.

The dawn had been quite beautiful, so peaceful; if only the circumstances had been different.

Lying on the bed in a Travelodge on the outskirts of King's Lynn while Nina took a shower, Steve contemplated that the last few days had been the worst of his life so far, with the last twenty-four hours winning the prize for the most crap of all time.

The weekend had been bad enough. He'd ended up wishing he hadn't mentioned his fears to Nina because she wanted to dissect every tiny detail about the subject. By Sunday afternoon, he had to ask her to stop.

"But this is important, Steve. There isn't anything else right now that matters more." He sighed. "Yeah, I know, I know."

How could he make her understand? The difference was that Nina actually *wanted* it to be the truth (she hadn't said so, but he knew) whereas he dreaded that outcome.

Nina's opinion of Dan was as low as it could possibly be, because of Cassie. She wanted him to pay, and pay again.

"So what's your problem? Why aren't we on our way to the police station, instead of sitting here arguing about it?"

Vaguely, the thought occurred to him that yes, they were having their first row. No, their first heated discussion; Steve wouldn't let it degenerate into a row, not least of all because he couldn't explain himself to her in any way that seemed reasonable.

Yes, Dan was a complete dick, worse than a complete dick, and yes, if the truth was as Nina hoped then going to the police was the right, the *only* thing to do, but it just wasn't that simple. It should be, but it wasn't.

Dan was his friend. He'd been his friend for over twenty-five years.

"It's not like he's a member of your family, or a *real regular guy*," Nina went on. "He's a sexist, racist brute who got away with attempted rape, let alone anything else. Who knows what else he's done? That e-fit picture is the spitting image of him. You'd be doing a public service to get him locked up."

"You can't go to the police and accuse someone of multiple murders just because you think they're a bit of a wanker."

"For Christ's sake, Steve! Dan isn't just 'a bit of a wanker'! That he could do what he did to Cassie—and he bloody well did do it, whatever him and AJ's solicitor cooked up between them—if he could do that, it shows that he's not right in the head, doesn't it?"

"I know."

"You believe me about Cassie, don't you?"

"Yeah." Everything Nina said was right. "Yes, I do."

"And the police issue those images for a reason. They're not just there so that you can say, 'ha, ha, ha, it looks like my mate, isn't that funny?'"

"I know."

"Well, let's get ourselves down to the cop shop, then. Now." Her voice had calmed down about three notches, but she was already putting her shoes on, reaching for her jacket.

"Not yet."

She flopped back into the chair. "Steve, for fuck's sake! What are you waiting for? A little more detail in the next bloody photofit? Some other girl to get brutally murdered?"

Steve shut his eyes. Nina had a stronger personality than him, and he liked that; you couldn't have two procrastinating wimps in one relationship. How lucky he was that she loved him. She was good, and beautiful, and right about everything, especially when it came to making those life-changing decisions he found so terrifying.

"I try to make changes all the time," she'd said, when he told her he liked this quality. "I like to evaluate, see what's working and what's not; I can't help it, it's a bit of an obsession! Doesn't mean I don't make mistakes, but I'm so aware of how short life is. You have to go with your gut, and do what you know you should."

She was right, but this one had to be his way. "I need to do something about this when the time feels right. For me," he said, slowly. "Can you let me do that?" He ran his hands through his hair. "I don't want to argue you with you. I love you. But Dan and me—"

"Uh-huh. Dan and you." She stood up and walked over to the window, and he sensed that she was about to come out with another truth that would be too much for him to hear, right now.

Oh dear; the downside of assertive people was that they did tend to get on your case a bit too much. She wasn't going to let this one go.

"Nina." She turned around, and he smiled at her. "I think I need to be on my own for a day or so, is that okay?" Even as he said it, he knew that as soon as she'd gone, he'd wish he hadn't sent her away.

She smiled back. Just. "Sure. If that's what you want."

"It's not that I don't want you with me, it's just—"

"It's okay." She walked back over to where he sat, and kissed him. "I do understand, honest. But if you haven't done something about it soon, I'm going to."

And he might have carried on sticking his head in the sand, had he not seen an article on lyndfordecho.com, on Monday afternoon, about a lap dancer from Rockerfellas who'd been attacked, on the very night of Woodsy's birthday outing.

Steve sat and stared at the piece, reading it over and over, before he picked up his phone.

Even then, he sat for a long time before calling.

Dan hadn't been in long, himself, he said. *Good to hear from you, mate. Makes a change. Telly broken down, has it?*

Yeah, yeah, yeah. No, just thought I'd check in. You know (laugh). Well, okay, I've got twenty minutes to kill while my dinner's cooking.

Thought as much! So, did y' get up to much at the weekend?

Oh, this and that, not a lot, you know Nina and me, we're the dull old pipe and slippers couple.

Yeah, you're getting to be a right boring bastard, you know that?

Always have been, mate, always have been. So how did it go on Thursday night?

Thursday night?

Yeah, you went out for Woodsy's birthday. Did you get to Rockerfellas?

Yeah, we did, yeah.

Any good?

Not bad. Woodsy got wasted, anyway! (laugh)

So how long were you there?

I dunno, why?

No reason. Just wondered. If you made a night of it.

Yeah, we did, yeah.

Hangover next morning?

(laugh) Just a bit! I had a fucker of a blocked khazi to sort first thing, too. Smell makes me gag just thinking about it. Got to get a different job, I seriously have.

What about the others?

What?

I mean, did you all get hammered?

Yeah! We weren't as bad as Woodsy, though. He was a total mess.

(laugh) Did he get home all right?

What? Yeah, I guess so. AJ had to babysit him in the cab, or the driver wouldn't have taken him. Said he'd make sure he got him in the house without waking up Her Indoors.

Good shot! Did you all leave together?

'Bout the same time, yeah. Well, within half an hour or so, any road.

In the same cab?

(pause) No, 'cause that'd be twattish, wouldn't it? Seeing as AJ and Woodsy live in a different direction from me an' Noel.

Oh, yeah. So you and Noel got a taxi home together?

Nah, he suddenly stood up an' said he was leaving 'cause he had to get up early, y'know what Noel's like when he's got his mind set. I still had a full pint.

So what time did you leave?

I dunno, I didn't look at my fucking watch to check in. Hang on a minute—what's with the twenty questions, all of a sudden?

Pause.

"Are you fucking quizzing me, Stevie boy? You are, aren't you?"

"No! No, what would I be quizzing you about?"

"That's what I was wondering. Since when did you ring me to see if I had a good weekend? In fact, since when did you ring me at all? I can't remember seeing your number coming up on my phone once over the last couple of years."

"Hey, calm down. I was just at a loose end, thought I'd give you a call, that's all."

"No, you're fucking not. I know you, mate." He paused, and laughed. "Oh yeah, oh yeah, I know what it is. Your Mrs, she's read about the assault on that lap dancer, hasn't she? And she's got you to ring me up to see if it was me, which you're quite happy to do because a) you're a henpecked twat and b) you never believed me about that bitch Cassie, did you?"

"I—"

He'd never felt so useless, so transparent.

"Well, you can fuck right off," Dan snarled at him, and hung up.

Shit. Shit, shit, shit and shit.

Steve's brain hurt. Didn't want to know about it anymore. Didn't want to think about it.

He went upstairs and ran a bath (he'd been lying about the dinner in the oven). Lots of bubbles, some stuff Nina had bought him. He lay in it for ages, music playing. Steely Dan. The favourite band of his last foster dad. Only thing he remembered about him; when he left, he bought all the CDs.

He listened to *Can't Buy a Thrill* and *Pretzel Logic* all the way through, running the water out and pouring in more hot, more bubbles, until he thought he might fall asleep in there. Wished he'd been the age he was now in the 1970s, when it was okay (in fact, positively *de rigueur*) to be laid back. Becker and Fagen's nostalgic lyrics and mournful melodies made the perfect soundtrack to his fantasy of hiking along empty roads in Oregon. Or Iowa, or South Dakota. One of those nothingy sort of states. Alone, going nowhere in particular, with no one to bother him. Or heading up to Yukon Territory, near Alaska. That would be good. No, too cold. One of those dusty crossroads with nothing to see, anywhere on the horizon. Becker and *Fagen.*

Fagin's. Hadn't one of the Lyndford Strangler's victims spent her last night there?

Shit. Back on that again. Shit, shit, shit and shit.

He missed Nina, too. Badly. Didn't enjoy things in the same way, if she wasn't with him. Funny, that. Everything that, a few months ago, he was just fine doing on his own, now seemed wrong without her by his side.

Out of the bath, he wrapped himself in his shabby old towelling dressing gown (Nina was buying him a new one for Christmas), and sat on his bed, flicking through the channels. Landed on Crime and Investigation, as ever.

Perhaps he was so used to watching stuff about grisly murders that he'd become de-sensitised, which was why he didn't see the urgency that Nina saw.

Either way, he'd speak to her about it again, tomorrow. Perhaps go and talk to the police, informally. There, that would be a good compromise, wouldn't it?

Nina must have heard the news, too, about the girl from Rockerfellas.

He wondered how she'd reacted.

Why she hadn't called him.

Sometime around ten, he dozed off, the television still chattering away.

When he woke up, it was to the sound of his phone. The ringtone intertwined with a dream in which he was stuck out somewhere, miles away, with Dan and AJ and Noel, and he couldn't get back, couldn't remember Nina's number. His phone wouldn't work, he was desperate to ring her and say he was coming home before she lost faith in him—but, oh, thank God, that must be her, phoning him, except that his bedroom came into view and he wasn't in a club with the lads, but in his bed, alone, and his phone was ringing in the real world, but by the time he realised this it had gone to voicemail.

He turned over.

As soon as the voicemail alert ended, the ringtone started again.

Nina!

Steve reached out a sleepy arm and grabbed it from the bedside cabinet.

It wasn't Nina. The time was after midnight, and the caller was AJ.

Why would AJ be calling him after midnight on a Monday?

Why would AJ be calling him, full stop?

He felt sick.

"Hello."

"You fucking *cunt*," AJ snarled down the phone at him. He sounded drunk. "You fucking little rat. Call yourself a fucking mate? I tell you what, you're dead meat; when Dan gets out you are so fucking dead meat."

Steve tried to focus. "AJ—what's going on? What're you on about?"

"Yeah, like you don't fucking know. Like you don't know Dan's been hauled down the fucking nick. He *phoned* me, you cunt. He told me all about you ringing him up, giving him the fucking third degree 'bout what he was doing on Thursday night. If it ain't you, it's that fucking little cunt you're knocking off. The fucking mate of the slag who tried to fit him up. Fucking cunt."

A part of his consciousness listened to AJ's tirade with detachment and ached to comment on his limited choice of adjectives, but, alas, witty rejoinders had never featured amongst his verbal skills.

Instead, he said, "AJ, you've got it all wrong. I've been at home all night. I haven't talked to anyone since Dan."

He heard his accuser make a spluttering noise of disbelief down the phone, followed by the words, "You're dead fucking meat, mate. You and that cunt you're shagging. I ain't fucking joking. I'd tell you to watch your back, 'cept you won't see us coming. And that ain't a threat, it's a fucking promise. Know that, cunt. You're dead fucking meat."

And that was all. AJ hung up.

He stared at his phone. One unanswered message. Nina had texted him while he was asleep.

I need to talk to you. Please don't be cross, but I did it. When I heard about the girl who was attacked on Thursday night, I had to. Please call me. Doesn't matter what time.

The time was almost one a.m. He called her number.

"Steve? You got my text?" He could hear her relief. "When you didn't call straight back, I thought you were so angry with me, I didn't know what to do—"

"Yeah. I got it. It's okay, I'm not cross."

"Honestly?"

"Honestly. Um, I hate to sound dramatic, but I think you'd better pack a bag. We need to disappear. Now."

Chapter Twenty-six

Dorothy: The Mother

Wednesday 21st October, 2015

"Dorothy? Are you alright? Can I help?"

She opened her eyes to see the vicar smiling down at her. Nigel Green, who she'd known ever since she and Orlando moved to Clovis Court. They'd thought it great fun that they had a real, live Reverend Green at their church, like in the Cluedo game. Orlando still joked about it.

"Look! You can see the lead piping under his cassock!" he'd whisper, as Nigel climbed the steps of the pulpit to give his sermon. "He'll be sloping off to the conservatory soon, I'll be bound," or "Did you see the way he was looking at the candlestick? I'm sure he was weighing up its possibilities."

Dorothy struggled not to giggle out loud when he made such jokes; they'd probably make Nigel laugh if he heard them, too.

She wasn't laughing now, in the pew halfway down the aisle, her hands together in prayer. She hadn't knelt because she didn't want to draw attention to herself, not like Angela Wykes and Mrs Gibson who fell to their knees in the front pew and honoured the cross with a dramatic bow before and afterwards. Their performances were more exaggerated if there were visitors admiring the architecture.

Or people like Dorothy, who just needed a place of quiet.

Strangers with problems.

Maybe those strangers were like her, too, in that they weren't totally convinced by religion but thought they'd try a prayer, just in case there really was a place called Heaven with a big fatherly person looking down on them all, unlikely though it seemed.

"The bible isn't to be taken literally, I don't think," Nigel said, years ago, when a twenty-year-old Orlando said it sounded like a rather optimistic fairy story, "though we all take different meaning from it. To my mind it's symbolic, and more about God and the Devil within us all, though of course, yes, I believe in our Heavenly Father and the afterlife."

Dorothy wasn't even quite sure what she was praying for. *Please don't let it be true. Please don't let Orlando have done anything bad. Please take care of us.* She, who had always been so sure she didn't need anyone to look after her, now needed strength from elsewhere to hold her up.

Elsewhere, anywhere.

She smiled up at Nigel Green. "I'm not absolutely alright, no, but I can cope."

Nigel sat down beside her. "Are you sure?"

"I think so."

"Would you like to come up to the vicarage?" He smiled, so kindly. "We could have a cup of tea; Mrs Green was baking earlier today, so I'm sure there'll be sponge cake, or possibly some cinnamon buns, if we're lucky."

The prospect was so tempting, but Dorothy knew she couldn't burden him with the enormity of her fears.

"I'd love to, but I'm afraid I do have to be getting back. I made a casserole earlier, and I need to put it in the oven soon if it's going to be ready for when Orlando gets home." She felt guilty about the lie; she hadn't even thought about what to make for dinner.

"I understand." He took her hand in his, and the gesture was so comforting that she had to stop herself clinging to him. "If there's anything you need to talk about, though, you can always come to me."

"Thank you." Even those two short words had to struggle past the lump in her throat.

"Remember," said Nigel Green, "God never gives us a burden heavier than we can handle."

She found solace in his promise, even though she doubted it.

After the vicar had gone back to do whatever vicars did in the afternoons (lead piping in the conservatory aside), Dorothy picked up her shopping bag and wandered back out into the hubbub of the real world. If only she had a true belief, she thought, as she moved along the busy streets, then the church might seem like the 'real' world. She could understand the attraction. Nuns and monks who made the decision to lock themselves away from modern life, in safe, peaceful surroundings. She'd always felt, secretly, that devout religion was something of a crutch. Believing in a big, comforting figure who would make difficult decisions for you, and forgive you if you did anything wrong. All you had to do was declare that you believed in his existence, convince yourself of the fact, and you no longer had to take total responsibility for your life. Must be lovely.

She and Orlando had discussed this, many times; like her, he believed in the basic power of *good* within man, as opposed to the one of *evil*, and it was this that he liked to think about when he went to church. Nothing more than that; if some people needed to give this strength or energy (or whatever it was) a name, and make up tales about shepherds and people walking on water, then that was up to them.

Orlando was intelligent, not like those lunatics who believed that God made them kill prostitutes because they were evil. Orlando was *good*, she was sure he was.

Dorothy wandered into the pedestrianised area of the town centre, where the smarter shops were situated, and sat on a bench between two tubs of greenery. The day was chilly, but bright; perfect autumn. Leaves whisked along the ground in the brisk wind, people stuffed hands into coat pockets. She peered into her bag at the odd array of goods she'd bought, to see if there was anything from which she could make a meal. She'd shopped in a daze, without a list, taking down familiar items from the shelves without thinking.

She was stumbling around in fog.

The day after she'd found the trophy box—she couldn't think of it any other way, no matter how she tried—she went upstairs to take another look. It was missing. She'd peeped into a couple of his drawers but couldn't see it, and neither could she bring herself to rummage through any more of her son's belongings.

Then she read about the girl being attacked on the previous Thursday night.

Thursday night, when Orlando had (allegedly) gone to metal detecting club, and then for a drink with the other members, not returning until after midnight. He'd gone for a curry after the pub, he'd told her the next day.

Guidance, she thought. *I need guidance.* For the first time in her life, since Bernard Townsend had left her with his child in her womb, she felt so helpless. Could she ask for help from a god in whom she wasn't even sure she believed?

She stared again at the items in her shopping bag. Carrots, a tin of tomatoes, onions, potatoes, butter, a pound of cheese. No, not a pound. Some other silly weight she was too old to understand. Not that she was old. Sixty-five wasn't old, not these days, but her menopause had come early and she'd slipped happily into middle age when she was around forty-two. Breathed a sigh of relief when her fiftieth birthday arrived; it was the age she was born to be. She hadn't worn jeans since she was a girl, had never been comfortable in them. Always been happier in jumpers and skirts, tights and shoes. She'd never kept up with modern music and fashions; they didn't interest her. She still thought in pounds and ounces, feet and inches. Made pots of tea with leaves, not teabags in cups. She was born only six years after the Second World War ended, for goodness sake; when the twenty-first century came, with all its technological changes whizzing around her like a manic babble in languages she didn't understand, she'd felt the world galloping away from her.

She looked at the people walking past. Young men in those hooded sweatshirts that made them look like criminals. Young women who ought to be at school or college, pushing pushchairs. They weren't called pushchairs now, though, were they? *Buggies.* That was what they called them. Horrible word. Lots of people of different races, different skin colours. That could be such a good thing, but few had thought it through; man was a territorial beast and it would take more than thirty years of idealism, education and good intentions to change human nature. Still, you had to start somewhere, if only to rid new generations of the prejudices of her parents, who'd boycotted shops if they were run by foreigners, even those like Suresh Desai (she knew his name, now) who remembered what sweets she liked.

A group of smart young women emerged from a trendy clothes shops, squealing as they examined their purchases, diving into the one that sold all that gorgeous soap; Orlando had bought her some once, for Christmas. She liked that shop; you could smell it even yards away from the entrance. A beautiful blonde girl and a handsome young man left a wine bar, cuddling, stopping to kiss. What must their lives be like?

Dorothy sat on her bench and clutched her bag to her side, feeling more sad and alone than she had ever felt in her life, ever, even more than when her parents sent her away. Then, she had Orlando. She had *herself.*

Two girls sauntered past, arm in arm, chattering, laughing, dressed in short skirts, thick tights, high, clumpy shoes. Dorothy thought about the Lyndford Strangler, and wanted to shout out to them, *stay together! Keep safe!*

She peered up at the blue sky with its strange, muted light of approaching dusk. Out of the corner of her eye she could see the tower of the church.

Show me what to do, she thought. *Help me.*

God never gives us a burden heavier than we can handle.

She closed her eyes, and out of nowhere a sense of calm washed over her. She knew what she had to do. Once she saw the path in front of her, the solution was so clear that she actually felt her shoulders lift.

Whatever the outcome, she must face it. There was only one way forward.

Tamsin arrived at the station breathless, flustered, but resolute.

Maisie held Kate's hand as they walked in, surprised to find that she didn't feel silly doing so.

Lara knew what she had to do. Juliet was far too much of a wimp.

Steve was glad Nina had made the call; he would never have been able to.

Dorothy sat on the bus feeling as though she was going to her own funeral.

Chapter Twenty-seven

The Charge

Thursday, 22nd October 2015

In a stuffy, cluttered office, DCI Reddick stared at the four pieces of paper on his desk, and pushed one forward.

That was him, then.

All those hours, weeks and months of work had come down to just this. All those possible suspects discarded, hundreds of interviews, fingerprints, DNA samples, endless tedious hours trawling through CCTV footage, social media sites, phone records. Twenty-three men from Rockerfellas club the week before, narrowed down, other possibles via evidence from the public (and Reddick never failed to acknowledge how difficult it must be to come to terms with suspicion of a loved one, or even just a friend, or colleague), two of those crossing over with the list from Rockerfellas. Applications made to hold three for up to ninety-six hours, in case the providers of alibis could not be reached, but that time wasn't needed in the end.

DNA tests taken, fast-tracked to prove the indisputable truth.

Weariness on the faces of all who had been involved in the case, relief and anger on those of the innocent when told they were free to go.

Alisha Pope's friend and Sarah Craske had picked the prime suspect from the line-up and Montana Smith had identified his voice.

Now there was only one thing left to do.

"That's it, then. We've got him." DCI John Reddick exhaled, long and loud, and gave his colleagues a half smile. "Let's go and get it done."

They walked down the corridor in silence. Reddick experienced that sensation of déjà vu, though the mixed emotions of triumph, sadness, fury and bewilderment had never been as conflicted as they were at this particular moment.

Many cracked open the champagne in these circumstances, once the charge had been made, had a celebration in the office; he could see why such elation was common, but he could never feel it.

The satisfaction at having finally got his man was mixed with sad knowledge that the conclusion would be of scant comfort to the families of the victims (Ellie Kane would never get to live her life), and a strange, flat, emptiness. The bursts of adrenaline, the sleepless nights, the long hours, the frustration, the challenge, the exertion of brain power had come to an end. It was over. They'd got him.

They opened the door and walked into the room where he sat, attended by two officers.

"Stand up."

The suspect stood. Tall, good looking fella; Reddick pondered on the events in his life that had made him into what he was, coupled with that old, old question: was he made or born this way? Had the desire to cause death been mutating in that damning DNA from the moment he was born, skulking in the shadows for its trigger? For surely, he could not be sane; those dark brown eyes challenged him, eyes that might well inspire the prison groupies to start writing letters almost as soon as he began his sentence, but they showed no sorrow, no remorse, just resignation, maybe even a little pride.

Yes, he actually looked cocky. Still.

Reddick wondered if he would be so cocky when another type of justice was meted out by the inmates (and the screws) in the high security prison where this monster would live for the rest of his life.

He took a deep breath.

It was time.

"Gary Dunlop, I am charging you with the murders of Michelle Brand, Lita Gomez, Jodie Walker, Leanne Marsh, Kayla Graham, Ellie Kane and Alisha Pope, and the assaults of Sarah Craske and Montana Smith. You do not have to say anything, but it may harm your defence if you do not mention now, something which you later rely on in court. Anything you do say may be given in evidence.

Chapter Twenty-Eight

1986

He hadn't wanted to go down to the lake with his stepsister, but he didn't feel he had any choice.

"This holiday will be a late honeymoon for Derek and me," his mother had told him, "but with a difference, because you and Violet are coming along! But you're not kids, you can take yourselves off and find things to do, can't you? Give us a bit of time on our own?"

He heard that wheedling tone in her voice that he hated; she used it on Derek when she wanted something.

Gary still thought of Derek as *his mother's husband*. Not as his stepfather; well, he hardly knew the bloke, even though they'd been married two months now. Gary felt fairly neutral towards Derek Dunlop, aside from welcoming the change in surname. He'd been given the option to keep his own father's name, Cox, but jumped at the opportunity to get away from endless jokes at school. Silly quips about tyres were easier to deal with than the cock ones. No, he had no issues with his mother being married to Derek.

The problem was his daughter, Violet.

His new stepsister, and the sexiest girl that ever walked the earth.

Gary's feelings towards her were a swirling, torturous mix of contradictions. He desired her, feared her, hated her and loved her, all in one go, and each reaction stabbed him in the gut several times in the course of any given day.

"Girls mature earlier than boys," his mother told him, a little apprehensively, before the first time Violet came round for tea with Derek. He hadn't taken much notice of her words, but as soon as he met Violet he understood.

They were both thirteen. Gary was shooting up in height, but his body remained skinny, awkward, and his shoulders had yet to broaden. His smooth face was still that of a child, though he was training his hair into the Nik Kershaw hairstyle. All the girls liked Nik Kershaw. Alas, he still *felt* like a child, much of the time. He hadn't yet learned how to swagger and flirt, how to swear with aplomb. If a tougher kid threatened him, he lay awake at night worrying about it. His first cigarette made him sick, and he wasn't sure he was ever going to enjoy alcohol.

However, one part of him was embracing manhood with gusto. He woke up with embarrassing stains on the bedsheets most mornings, and the bloody thing made itself known practically every time he was within three feet of a pretty girl.

Especially Violet.

Violet was thirteen, too, but her birthday was in August, whereas his was in November, so she was a school year ahead of him. At the same school, worse luck. Violet was thirteen, but she was all woman.

When he was told that Derek had a daughter the same age as him, he thought, oh, *bor-ring*, some stupid girl who'll be chatting on the phone to her stupid friends about zits and dieting all day long (because although girls made his cock go hard, they were pretty bloody tedious).

Derek was portly, a homely sort of chap. Gary expected his daughter to be some shy, overweight blimp with frizzy hair and glasses. Braces on her teeth, perhaps.

He hadn't expected Violet.

His mother said she was 'quite mature for her age', which sounded even more boring; did that mean she'd be ticking him off all the time? Would it be like having two mothers in the house? But he'd missed his mum's anxious expression.

Violet Dunlop was a total sexpot.

She had thick, waist-length, deep chestnut brown hair that always looked as though it needed brushing, and sometimes washing, too; when it was dirty it exuded this weird animal scent that drove him *wild*. She twirled strands around her fingers, twisted it up into messy knots on top of her head when she was reading. Sometimes he watched, waiting for stray locks to tumble back down.

Violet had thickly lashed, sleepy eyes, and rubber (Dunlop) tyre lips that gave the impression of having just been licked or kissed; they made his groin ache every time he looked at them, and when he talked to her he only fixed his eyes on them to stop himself looking at her tits, which were huge, like two balloons, and looked all wrong jutting forth from her school blouse. She wasn't even particularly pretty; she was just so damn *sexy*.

Gary's mother was wary where Violet was concerned. He heard her talking to one of her friends on the phone, shortly before the Dunlops moved in with them.

"I'm going to have my work cut out with that young lady," Linda said, "she's a nice enough girl, very grown up, a bit *too* grown up, at times." Here she lowered her voice. "I have to be careful what I say to Derek, but sometimes she looks and acts like—well, a little *slut*, if I'm honest."

Even the word 'slut' gave Gary a hard-on; it made him think of how Violet had looked at him over the dinner table the night before, lingeringly, teasingly, biting her thumbnail in such a way that he could just see her cute pink tongue peeping out between those luscious lips of her.

Slut.

Delicious little *slut*.

From the moment she moved in, he was constantly, painfully aware of
her. If he was downstairs first, eating breakfast, he would tense as he heard
her footsteps on the stairs, waiting to see if she'd be dressed in her uniform
(the buttons on her school shirts strained across her chest), or wrapped up in
her big purple fluffy dressing gown (like a kid), or, sometimes, yawning and
stretching in the tight vest and matching shorts she wore for bed (tantalising;
Linda told her to go upstairs and get properly dressed when she appeared like
that).

She was an enigma, and he was on tenterhooks all day long. One evening
she might be friendly, chummy, like a real sister, larking around with him and
having fights over the TV remote control, then the next night she'd be aloof,
stomping upstairs to sit in her room all night, brushing off anything he said
with a scathing look.

Just occasionally, she'd be flirty. Those times drove him mental. She'd
snuggle up a bit too close to him on the settee, tickle his chin, play with his
hair, ask him if he'd kissed a girl yet, remind him that they weren't really
brother and sister.

He liked these times the best, but he hated them, too. His cock would
grow so hard he thought it might burst, and if he couldn't hide the lump in
his trousers he wanted to die with embarrassment; he knew she saw it
sometimes.

Of course, being grown up and totally obsessed with each other, Linda
and Derek noticed none of this. He didn't think they did, anyway. Hoped not.
They both treated him like a little boy, apart from when Derek attempted the
father-and-son bit, trying too hard to talk to him about stuff like football,
which he wasn't that interested in, anyway.

Linda came into his room once or twice, to ask him if he was happy, if
he was getting on with Violet.

"She's alright," he'd say. Then, to put his mother's mind at rest, he'd grin and say, "well, she's okay for a girl, anyway!"

That was the right move; all she wanted was confirmation that he was still her little boy. "I did worry about how you'd feel, having her in the house," she said, once.

"Why's that, Mum?" All innocence.

"Well, because you're both growing up, and I thought it might be a bit awkward, sharing a bathroom, and everything, when you don't know each other."

When she walks down the landing in her bra and knickers—

"It's alright, Mum," Gary told her. "I don't take much notice of her, really."

Once the bedroom light was off, though, his hormones told a different story. He'd discovered masturbation a couple of years before, and now, with Violet just a wall away from him, it had become an obsession. Afterwards, though, he felt so guilty. Grubby.

Didn't help that his mother had walked in on him doing it in the bath once, and he'd splashed around, praying he'd been successful in hiding what was going on under the bubbles, but Linda said something like 'I hope you're not doing anything dirty,' and slammed out, red-faced, then acted off with him for a couple of days.

Gary was mortified. All the boys at school talked about wanking, people made jokes about it and he'd even read that it was normal and healthy, but his mum was a bit funny about rude stuff.

He made sure the bathroom door was always locked after that, and soon discovered something that confused him: as soon as he'd ejaculated, he was no longer so desperate to touch Violet's tits. He'd feel ashamed that he'd let himself get carried away, yet again. Hated her for making his body react like that. Felt as though his mother knew what he was doing, even though she was downstairs watching the telly with Derek.

He was worried about the size of his penis, too. He didn't have a clue how long it was supposed to be, but it didn't seem very big, not even at its best.

Worst of all, all his schoolmates fancied Violet.

"Fucking hell, I wish *my* mum had married her dad!" said Darren.

"Look at the hooters on it!" said Lee. "Bet I get to see them first!" Lee was the best looking of his gang, by far; he strutted around, smoked, and his mum had let him have his hair permed like Jon Bon Jovi.

"There's no way she's a virgin," said Martin, as they watched Violet undulating across the playground.

That was what Gary thought, too. He'd seen her hanging out with some of the boys in the lower sixth; nothing raised a girl's status amongst her mates more than having an older boyfriend. He suspected she went off to meet them, when she told Derek and his mum she was seeing her friends. There was one called Garnett who fancied himself as a rapper, and another called Mack, who had a motorbike. Boys like that, aged sixteen or seventeen, they'd expect more than just a snog and muck around.

He was glad when school finished for the summer. Violet wore a tiny string bikini in the garden whenever his mother wasn't around to make disapproving remarks about covering herself up.

Now it was that dreamy, other worldly month of August, when the world took on a different hue, the long, mellow days stretched ahead, and the new family took off to a remote part of County Monaghan in Ireland for a whole ten days.

Out here, in the chalet near the lake, the world of school and noise seemed far away. Violet thought she was going to be bored, but Gary liked it.

The four of them spent idle days lazing in the sun, having barbecues, walking by the water, taking the odd trip into the nearest village for a potter around.

On the Friday afternoon they'd been shopping; when they got back, Derek produced an enormous lunch, with cold meats and cheeses, tomato salad and several bottles of wine. Gary and Violet were allowed to have some, watered down with fizzy water (a 'spritzer', Violet said it was called), and Gary liked how it made him feel. They ate in the garden, looking out onto the lake, relaxing in the warm sunshine; as the adults worked their way down two bottles of white wine, Violet winked at Gary and jerked her head over at their parents, making faces. By now, Derek and Linda were gazing at each other with secret smiles, holding hands, as if the teenagers weren't there.

"Tell you what," piped up Violet, "how about me and Gary go for a hike round the lake this afternoon, give you two a bit of time alone?"

This suggestion was greeted with enthusiasm, but Gary felt wary about the glint in Violet's eye; her face was flushed, and she seemed over-excited.

"I think I'll just go to my room and read," he said. They all laughed.

"Read in your room on a beautiful day like this?" his mother said. "What's the matter with you?"

Violet jumped up and put her hands on her hips; she wore a peach coloured cropped vest and white shorts, the gap at her midriff showing a trim, tanned waist. "Gary, I think Dad and Linda would like the house to themselves for a bit, you know?"

Linda and Derek looked at each other and then at their children and laughed, a little embarrassed, but alcohol made them bold.

"Yes, bugger off, the two of you, okay?" Derek grinned at Gary and squeezed Linda's hand.

"Wait for me, Gazza! I just want to pick up some provisions!" Violet darted into the kitchen, while Gary stayed there on the grass, trying not to look at the adults. His stomach churned round and round; he wanted to be alone with Violet but at the same time he didn't; he longed to touch her but felt the urge to run away from her, so he'd be safe.

"Well, we'll just go back inside," said Derek, holding out his hand to Linda.

"Okay." Gary didn't look up. He could feel the blood rushing round and round in his head.

Violet appeared five minutes later, slamming the front door behind her and running across the grass to where he sat. She dug into her small knapsack and brought out two litre bottles of Coke.

"Part Coke, part Bacardi!" she whispered, bringing her finger up to her lips. Her fingernails were long, and painted sugar pink. "*Ssh*! I poured some down the sink so I could put the booze in!"

"I've never tried Bacardi," Gary said. "What's it like?"

"Gorgeous! It tastes like being on a desert island!" She linked her arm through his. "Come on, let's go and have some *fun*!"

They walked down the lane and out onto the stony path by the water, further along until they could no longer be seen from the house. The lake was deserted, aside from a few people outside a cabin on the other side, so far away they were no bigger than stick figures in the distance, barely visible.

The sun beat down on them, the only sound the gentle movement of the water in the mild breeze, and the sounds of birds twittering in the trees above. Grey clouds edged in, far across the lake; Gary closed his eyes as they walked. He smelled earth, trees, clean air, with the promise of rain later, perhaps; it felt good.

Violet stopped, and took his hand. "Let's sit down here and have these drinks!" Gary opened his eyes and saw her gesture towards a patch of ground, partially hidden by vegetation and less stony than the rest of the bank; a sun trap. Leading to the water was a little wooden platform to dive from.

She fished into the knapsack again.

"Something to sit on—or lie on!" She winked, and he watched as she spread a plastic sheet on the ground.

"Thought we were going for a hike?"

"Don't be daft, I only said that 'cause I could tell they wanted us to leave them alone!" She giggled. "So they could shag!"

She sat down on the sheet, knees raised and apart; he could see white knickers up the legs of her shorts, and when he looked at her face she was smiling, watching him. "C'mon, then, let's get pissed!"

He took the bottle, not knowing how close he should sit to her. Oh no, it was happening again. It always happened when she was near. He bent his legs up like hers, so she wouldn't see, opened the bottle and sniffed.

Didn't smell like being on a desert island at all; he'd imagined a wonderful aroma of coconut and pineapples and sunshine, but it was nothing like that.

"It's a bit strong, but I wanted to make sure there was enough to get drunk! Go on, you'll love it." Violet leant back and raised her own bottle to her mouth, drinking it down as if it was just pop, then she sat up and laughed, wiping her mouth with her hand. "Whoo, that's got a kick! What you waiting for?"

Gary grinned at her, and did the same as she did. Bloody hell. He hadn't expected it to taste like that, either; he thought it would taste like rum and raisin ice cream, but it was like drinking nail varnish remover with a splash of Coke. "Christ," he muttered, spluttering.

Violet giggled, moving closer to him. "Good, isn't it? There must be at least eight measures in each bottle; I hope they don't notice it's gone!"

She threw her arm around his shoulder, casually, as if they were just mates, and suddenly the world seemed like a pretty fabulous place. There he was, Gary Dunlop, sitting by a lake in the sunshine with a gorgeous girl, drinking Bacardi and Coke; how jealous would Lee, Darren and Martin be?

Violet picked up some stones and threw them into the lake and he lay back, propping himself up on one arm as they laughed and chatted about which girls she hated at school, what she wanted to be when she grew up; afterwards he could hardly remember any of it. He swigged from his bottle as eagerly as she did from hers until nearly all of it was gone, and he was loving the sunshine, loving the sight of her long, untamed hair falling down her back, her tiny waist above the shorts, oh wow, and now she was kneeling up, bending forward and stretching, and her figure looked *fabulous*—

Oh dear.

He took off his t-shirt so he could place it over his lap.

She turned around. "Stripping off, are we?" With a grin, she pulled her top over her head to reveal a white, lacy bra. She stayed right where she was, kneeling in front of him, licking her lips in that way she did.

"Shall I?" she said. "Do you dare me?"

And then, oh God, then she unhooked her bra, and there they were, in all their glorious glory.

He thought his cock was going to burst. He couldn't take his eyes off them, wanted to shove his face in between them, squeeze them, bite them—

She leant towards him, pushing them together with her arms, running her tongue over those gorgeous lips, then she leant back, lifting her hair up and letting it fall down all over her shoulders.

She looked *fantastic*.

"You can touch them if you like."

"Vi—" He put his hand out, aching to touch her, wanting to, so badly, but he was scared, too; all of a sudden those two *things* of hers seemed too powerful, like they had complete control over him.

"What's wrong with you? We're not related, are we? There's nothing weird about it." She moved closer, pulled his t-shirt away from his lap, and leant over him so that her tits were just brushing against the skin on his (white, puny) chest.

Gary wondered if he might actually die, there and then. He couldn't speak. The world around him seemed hazy; this must be what being drunk was. It was good, but scary. He'd only ever got a little bit tiddly before, on half a glass of Derek's beer or watered-down wine, but this was something else.

Like being on a fairground ride, a seriously crazy one.

The blue sky, the warmth of the sun, and Violet's naked tits on his chest. He was in heaven.

Violet smiled down at him, her face shadowed by the sun behind her head, and she climbed astride him. The sun was behind her head, so he couldn't see any detail, just the shape of her.

He felt *drugged*.

Slowly, she undid his belt, and the zip on his trousers, smiling all the time, and then, *then*, she slipped her clever little fingers down into his underpants, not quite touching it but near, so near.

"Have you ever done it before?"

"No," Gary croaked, and she laughed.

"Like I didn't know that! I have, I've done it with Mack, you know, the one with the motorbike, and with Garnett; it's true what they say about black guys!" She giggled. "What do you think of that, huh? Mack's better at it, but Garnett's is *huge*!"

That worried him. What did you have to do to be good at it? What if he wasn't as good as Mack? He was already sure his wasn't as big as Garnett's.

The sun was in his eyes as she stood up, and the alcohol made his head pound as she pulled his trousers and pants off, then wiggled her hips, undoing her shorts, whipping them off, her knickers, too, before sitting back down on top of him. Hovering over his cock. Oh, God. Oh, the feel of her, the smell of her—

"Go on, then, do something. You have to do stuff to me, too." She took his hand and placed it on her breast, and he was overcome by the warmth and softness of her skin under his palm. *Oh, Jesus.* He squeezed it. Hard. He wanted to—oh, shit, he didn't know what he wanted to do, kiss it, dig his nails into it, chew great chunks out of it, it just felt *so damn good*—

"*Ouch*, not like that!" She sounded impatient. "You have to move your hand around a bit, you know, stroke them. Have you never touched a girl's tits before? Like this." She took him by the wrists and moved his hands across both of them, feeling her nipples grow stiff, and he felt as though his head was going to burst. She moaned her approval, and took his cock in her hand (how did she know how to do it?), and it felt wonderful, fantastic, much better than he'd ever thought anything could, ever, so good he didn't think he could bear it for another minute, not one more minute, surely nothing had ever felt like this—

—and then it was all over. The build-up of sensation, the explosion; he heard himself crying out and then he hurtled over the other side, came back down to earth, and lay back, panting, dizzy.

"Fucking hell, Gary!"

He opened his eyes. The sun had gone in, and Violet was staring down at her pretty little hand, with his mess all over it.

"Is that it?"

The sexy smiles were gone. She looked cross. Disbelieving, like his mum did when she told him off about something.

"I'm-I'm sorry," he muttered, struggling up on his elbows; he heard his stupid voice and knew he sounded a complete wimp.

"You useless twat. *Ugh!*" She wiped her hand on the plastic sheet, still astride him, naked, with that body, those huge tits that he'd longed to see for months (too big, scary big), and as for that *other part* of her that he'd fantasised about, all this time—there it was at last, waiting for him, waiting for his virgin dick that flopped there, spent, limp and useless.

"I'm sorry," he said again, "um, maybe if we wait a few minutes then start again, from the beginning—"

But he didn't know if it would get hard again, not now that she was so cross and he was shivering with sudden cold because the sun had disappeared. Oh God, and he was beginning to think he might be sick, too. Already she was climbing off him, reaching for her knickers.

"I thought we were going to fuck," she said, crossly. She really was *furious*. "Do you not know anything? Like, it's a two-way thing. You do stuff to me, but you hold yourself back, and you're supposed to put it inside, not shoot your load before it even gets there."

"I couldn't help it—"

She gestured at her private parts. "So, what am I supposed to do now?"

He didn't know what she meant, so he didn't say anything.

"I'm stuck here with nothing to do for ten days with you and your boring mum; I thought we could at least have a bit of fun, but you haven't got a clue, have you? You're just a kid, I should've known."

She glanced down at his pathetic excuse for a cock, now shrivelled back down to an all-time small, and then, to his intense shame, she knelt back down and picked it up between her thumb and forefinger, wiggling it about, as if it was a bit of soft plasticine.

"Should've known as soon as I saw this little tiddler that you wouldn't be any good." She waggled it back and forth, back and forth, laughing. "Tiddler, tiddler! Little baby chipolata!"

He pushed himself back, out of reach of her taunting hand. "Stop it!" Oh God, he wasn't going to cry, was he? He felt the tears welling up, knew his mouth was shaking.

"I probably wouldn't have been able to feel it anyway, Chipolata Boy!"

Still grinning all over her face that looked hard and scheming now, but still sexy, still so, so sexy, she jumped up and dragged her knickers up over her curvy thighs and hips, over *that place* that he'd never get to see again.

Gary stood and pulled up his pants and jeans, his face burning hot, the shame and disappointment mixed together with a lot of other stuff he didn't understand, anger and lust and disgust, all whirling around in his head along with the headache he didn't know came from the Bacardi and Coke, and the confusion at how this afternoon had moved, in an instant, from the best day in his life to the very, very worst.

Wasn't being drunk supposed to be brilliant fun? Wasn't that why people did it?

This wasn't fun, it was like his worst nightmare.

—which was about to get a whole lot worse—oh no—

No, no, no.

Don't let this happen, please don't let this happen—

It was coming, he couldn't stop it—oh no—*bluuuuurgh—*

Gary vomited what felt like the entire contents of his stomach, all those rich cheeses from earlier, mixed up with that foul-smelling alcohol. It shot out in a torrent, his guts heaving, and he clutched his stomach, moaning, falling to his knees.

"*Ugh!*" Violet's horrible, harsh voice. "I should have known; you can't even hold your drink!"

His stomach kept retching, his throat was on fire, and he crouched on hands and knees, willing it, *begging* for it to pass.

"Ugh, you stink!"

Why didn't she just piss off and leave him alone to die? It was horrendous, he was out of control, couldn't control his body or his mind or his mouth, anything.

He knelt on all fours, whimpering, praying the vomiting had stopped, while she stood behind him and laughed.

"Shut up!" he cried, but it came out like a mad hiccup as he vomited the very last of whatever was left inside his stomach.

Violet made noises of revulsion. "You'd better not have done any of that over my clothes!"

He couldn't stop the tears from falling. Angry tears, shameful tears.

"Fucking hell, I can't believe you're crying!" She was pointing at him, laughing. "You've only been sick, everyone pukes when they get drunk, sometimes! Do you want your mummy? Or are you crying 'cause you don't know how to fuck? Does icky Gary want mummykins to kiss it better?" She screeched with laughter, a horrible, wild, cackling sound. "I can't wait to tell the girls at school about you." She cocked her little finger in the air, wiggling it around. "*Tiddly widdly widdly*!" Dancing from side to side, she picked up her bottle of Bacardi and Coke and glugged back the last inch left in the bottom, then she took his and swallowed the tiny bit left in that, too. "Think I'll go for a swim, seeing as there's nothing else to do round here. See ya, Chipolata Boy!"

The sky was turning darker now, the sun all but disappeared behind the grey clouds.

She turned to walk off, but he couldn't bear to be left alone with his thoughts, his shame. He fell back onto the hard, stony ground. "Violet! Don't—come back! Violet—"

She whirled round, hair wrapping itself around her face in the wind. "What?"

"I'm—I'm sorry."

"Yeah." Big eyes, staring at him. "You said."

A terrible, awful fear tangled with the nausea in his gut. "You-you won't tell anyone, really, will you?"

She put her hands on her hips and laughed. "What, about the chipolata? I dunno yet! I might. If I'm bored and need a laugh. Your mate Lee, he wants to fuck me. I might let him, seeing as you can't. I'll say, I got Gary's pants off but he'd already come in them, and then he was sick all over me!"

To his horror, Gary felt his face pucker up, like a baby's. "Don't tell him," he wailed. "Vi, please don't tell him!"

She didn't say anything, she just laughed again, and ran over the stones down to the water's edge, onto the platform where she dived into the lake. *Splash!* The dark blue water lapped at the edge, and the sun peeped out, momentarily, shining on Violet as she emerged, hair stuck to her face, treading water.

Gary jumped up and ran to the edge of the platform, where he looked down at her grinning, wet face, just feet away. "Violet, don't tell Lee, please! *Please!*"

The tears were streaming down his face now, and he didn't care, he didn't care about anything as long as his mates didn't find out, but Violet just laughed.

"Depends!"

"Depends on what?"

"What you'll do for me. I want all your pocket money, every week, and you can get me money out of your mum's purse, too!"

"I can't do that!" he shouted back. "She'll know!"

"It's up to you! *Tiddly widdly widdly!*" She laughed again, and lay back in the water, kicking her legs up to keep afloat. "And I might still tell Lee, anyway! Yeah, fuck it, I will! It's too funny to keep to myself!"

His head throbbed and he shivered, he couldn't stop shivering; he wrapped his arms around his (skinny, white, childish) chest, but still he shook, all over, even his legs felt weak. "Violet, come back!" he called, but she'd turned onto her front and was swimming further out into the middle of the lake.

Gary stood on that platform, shivering and crying, watching her frolicking about in the water, hating her, hating himself for being so useless, wanting her, but hating her more than anything else, and more terrified than he'd ever felt in his life.

His life was *over.*

They were all going to laugh at him, everyone in the school would know.

She would tell Lee, and Lee would tell Martin and Darren, and they'd both tell everyone, and everyone in the whole school would know that Gary Dunlop couldn't fuck.

They'd tell people like that Mack and Garnett, and all the big boys would laugh at him, too.

The girls would point and titter at him in the corridor. Lee, Martin and Darren would be too embarrassed to have him as a friend. They wouldn't want to show themselves up by being friends with *Chipolata Boy.*

Oh shit, that would be his new name, wouldn't it? All the Cox jokes would start again, he'd have no friends, he'd never get a girlfriend—

He'd have to kill himself. Every day would be torture. Impossible to live through.

And every night she'd be there, taunting him by her very presence, in his home, the one place that should be safe.

Even if he locked himself in his room she'd be there, through that thin wall, or downstairs on the phone to her friends, laughing about him.

He didn't realise her scream was one of pain, not at first; he thought it was just another taunt.

"*Aaaaaah!* Gary—*oohhhhh!*"

He thought she was pretending to make having-sex noises, mocking everything he'd failed to do. "Fuck off!" he screamed at her.

"No—*aaahhh*! Gary, help! I've got cramp!"

She wasn't frolicking any more, she was floundering, her arms grabbing at something to hold onto, something to save her that wasn't there, her head disappearing under the water then appearing again to scream in terror.

"*Help me*!"

Gary's mouth fell open in shock, his lungs filling with air, and he tore off his jeans, ready to jump in and save her, despite everything, despite the fact that she was a *fucking evil cow* who was going to ruin his life—

—but then he just

didn't.

She waved her arms, yelling and screaming, and he just stood there.

"My leg! Help me! *Aaaahhh*!"

He watched her, and the day went quiet, as though he was observing the scene through a piece of glass.

Just like that, the mess in his head cleared, and the day turned from confusion to calm, from noise to silence.

The sky grew darker, and the sun disappeared completely.

Big, fat raindrops began to fall.

Violet threw up her arms, yelling, waving, *screeching*, but Gary carried on standing there, his jeans still around his ankles where he'd been about to throw them off to leap into the water and save the girl who would *destroy* him to provide herself with nothing more than a passing amusement.

Why should he?

Leave her.

If you don't save her, no one will ever know.

If he saved her, his shame would never leave him. Even if she didn't tell straight away, he would never be free, every minute of every day wondering when she was going to open her mouth.

But if she just wasn't there any more, it would all be over.

He stood, still as a statue, and watched her.

Her head went down, under the water, her shouts muffled as she bobbed and splashed up and down, *bubble, bubble, bubble.*

A glance told him that the people over on the other side of the lake were no longer there.

The rain fell, faster, now.

There was no one to hear her, or to see him standing there, watching her.

Watching Violet drown.

Her head surfaced once more, and he was damn sure he could see her big, brown eyes looking into his, pleading with him.

Knowing who'd won.

Not taunting me now, are you?

Slut. Slut who wasn't even fourteen until next week, but she'd already had sex with two boys, that he knew of.

As her head was swallowed up by the deep, dark water for the last time, he closed his eyes and opened his arms. Stretched them out. The raindrops soaked him, and it felt good.

The rain washed away his shame. And the puke.

She'd thought she held his life in the palm of her hand, but she was wrong. He held the power, not her.

He felt that familiar stirring, and looked down; his dick was hard again. *Tiddly widdly widdly*, eh? He smiled, undid his zip, and relieved himself into the water.

Now *that* felt good, out in the open air. He even thought about Violet's tits while he did it.

He was the last person to see them. Alive, anyway; others would see them when they fished her out, but they wouldn't be warm, living, sexy things any more, just slabs of cold, white, dead flesh.

Slowly, he walked back up to where they'd left their things.

Pitter patter went the rain.

There, they'd know she was a slut, now, just like his mum said; she'd gone swimming in just her knickers. They'd know she'd flashed her tits in front of him. Carefully, he packed all the stuff back up into the soaking wet knapsack, and—no.

Ah.

He'd have to rush back in a panic, wouldn't he? He'd say he was dozing on the bank, was awoken by her screams and the gathering storm, but was too late to save her, she'd swum too far out. He'd leave her clothes where they were, and the plastic sheet, and bottles, then they'd see what a *slut* she was for stripping off in front of him, what a *drunken slut* she was for stealing booze to drink before she shed her clothes.

That *slut* word excited him all over again, especially when he looked at her abandoned bra, but he forced himself not to think about it.

Gary pulled his soggy t-shirt over his head and looked out onto the lake, calm now, peaceful, the water dotted with falling raindrops. *Hmm.* Now he must run, so he'd return to the cottage out of breath.

The rain was good; he might get a bit muddy, then he'd look even more desperate.

He set off down the bank.

Although he'd enjoyed his secret for five years, until he was eighteen, he had no idea that he would become a killer. His career began when he was on holiday in Turkey with Lee and Darren, and he fell in love with a local girl with long, dark hair and a well-developed figure who wasn't anywhere near as sexy as Violet but reminded him of her. Unfortunately, Esra didn't feel the same way about him. One of her friends, a scrawny little thing who fancied him, told him that Esra giggled about him, and said she was only screwing him because he spent all his money on her.

She flaunted the latest necklace or scarf he'd bought her, and told them all what a besotted idiot he was. One of the necklaces she'd actually given to a boy she fancied, to give to his mother, the scrawny girl said.

Gary didn't reply. He just turned on his heel and walked away.

A couple of hours before he left to catch his morning flight home, he invited Esra for a last swim, promising an extra special goodbye present if she went with him.

It was the last swim of Esra's short life.

Afterwards he felt that same sensation, just like when he'd stood at the side of the lake watching Violet drown. Ultimate power. Show the bitches who was boss. Nothing gave him a bigger high, or a bigger hard-on. This time, though, he strangled her first; he wanted her to *see* that he was in charge.

He knew he was safe. She hadn't been interested enough in him to find out his surname or where he was staying, and he'd mentioned to no one that they were going for a midnight swim. In the days before mobile phones and mass use of the internet, people were much harder to trace; in the future he would learn to be much, much more careful, but this time he went home with neither worry nor backward glance.

Over the years he refined his art, learning how to time it just right so that he came inside the woman whilst she was in the throes of death.

Moving around helped.

He'd settled in Norfolk for some time, because Charlotte was besotted with him and let him get away with—*ha*! Yes, she let him get away with murder. Not that she knew.

Gary's victims were always Violet. Every time, he possessed Violet before he watched the life drain from her, before he saw in her eyes the knowledge that he was all powerful.

Not tiddly widdly at all.

The women he chose for relationships were fair, slender, acquiescent women who looked up to him, needed him. Like Charlotte, like Pru.

Charlotte got on his nerves after a while, and he needed to move away from Norfolk after Michelle and Lita. He liked the idea of being a part of Pru's family when he met her, even thought he might stop, but that little cow Maisie looked down on him, tried to make him feel small, and that made him angry all over again.

Made him hear Violet again.

Violet would always be in his head.

He loved her, missed her, hated her for making him do what he'd done, and what he must still do.

He kept Charlotte on just in case he needed to get away. She was such a pathetic sap that she even accepted him being in another relationship; she would give him an alibi whenever he wanted one, however outlandish the lies he told her, and never asked too many questions because she didn't want to know the truth.

Maisie, though, she'd been too sharp for her own good.

As for Bethany, with her sexy, curvaceous figure and soft, dark hair, he still fantasised about that time he'd offered her a lift home, when he bumped into her in town one Saturday afternoon. The little slut had *flirted* with him, as soon as she got into his car. Wound her hair around her finger, thrust her tits out and licked her lips. Just as the feelings within him were becoming uncontrollable, though, she spotted some friend of hers and decided not to go home after all. She'd jumped out of the car, thanking him, even blowing him a kiss, knowing nothing of the hair's breadth of circumstance that had kept her alive.

PART THREE

Afterwards

December

Chapter Twenty-Nine

Tamsin: The Colleague

Taken from lyndfordecho.com

HELL HATH NO FURY

by Rachel Wilkie

(Names have been changed throughout)

How does it feel to be unjustly accused of murder?

Back in February, IT consultant Jack Fallow, 34, had a one-night stand with a colleague. Had he been able to predict the consequences of that brief encounter, he would have gone home alone.

Jack slept with Tansy after a night out with workmates. Seven months later, he found himself sitting across a table from two detectives, arguing for his life.

"I first met Tansy just over a year ago, when she started with the company for which I still work," Jack told me. "She was chatty and friendly, and I soon realised she'd taken a shine to me. She'd come down to the IT department several times a week with problems she could have easily worked out by asking the person sitting next to her; my assistant would tease me about having a stalker. Almost every day, she'd email me those crass cartoons, hackneyed jokes and memes that do the rounds on social media. I did like her, though, and I found her physically attractive; if she hadn't been constantly in my face, I might have asked her out." He smiles. "A tip, ladies: men like to do at least some of the hunting!"

Jack felt he was being pushed into a corner. "She gave me a Christmas present, a very smart and expensive pen engraved with my name, as a thank you for all my help, she said. I found the gesture embarrassing; I was only doing my job, and I suspected she'd given me the present as an 'in'. Still, it was a sweet gesture, and I felt I ought to give her something back." He grins. "I picked up a five quid box of chocolates from the newsagent next door to our office, hoping that the modesty of my gift would convey that I was just being polite, but I think it only served to encourage her."

I couldn't help wondering if Jack allowed Tansy to read more into their relationship than there actually was, especially when, that night in February, they took their friendship to another level.

"It was a foolish move on my behalf, I know that now." He looks sad. "But I was young, free and single, and so was she; we were consenting adults. This is 2015; women chat men up because they want to sleep with them, just as men do with women. No harm done, or at least that was what I told myself at the time." He holds his hands out as if asking me, as a woman, to understand. "Look, I'd had too much to drink and I slept with a female friend with no intention of offering a lifetime commitment. So, shoot me!"

I asked Jack if Tansy thought the night meant more than casual sex.

"Yes. I realised she did, and I won't deny that I felt bad when I woke up. As if I'd led her on. I'm ashamed to say that I took the coward's way out and left while she was still asleep, leaving a note with some story about my parents coming to stay for the weekend. She kept texting and emailing me, suggesting dates, as if it was the beginning of something big. She presumed we were now a couple, and I thought, oh no, what have I done? I sent her an email to explain, but I can see now I should have done it in person, as we'd been friends for a while. Okay, I was cowardly. Like most men, I can't stand to see a woman cry."

Did he say anything, that night, to make her think he had feelings for her? Did he tell her he loved her, or imply this was so?

"No. Definitely not. But she twisted the things I did say, to make it sound as if I had. Then, later, I discovered that she'd been telling other colleagues about this 'special connection' she had with me; I think she'd convinced herself that we were 'meant to be', like something out of a romantic novel. But it was all in her head. I never felt any special connection with her. Now, looking back, I can see that every time I smiled at her or laughed at one of her weak jokes, she took it as an indication of what she wanted to see. Yes, I *flirted with her a bit. In offices, it happens. It's not serious. It's just something to make the day go round."*

Jack does not strike me as a 'notches on the bedpost' sort of man, and seems bewildered by the whole series of events. I expected him to tell me that she began the usual woman-scorned behaviour of sending persistent emails and texts, but he said she appeared to accept his decision.

"I could tell she was hurt, and that she still liked me, by the way she looked at me, but I thought she'd dealt with it, and moved on," Jake tells me. "I was pleased, thought it meant we could still be friends; I had no idea what was really going on in her distorted mind until the police arrived at my door to question me about the recent spate of murders in the area. The funny thing was—"

Jack stops for a moment, and puts his hand over his mouth, shaking his head. "I'm sorry, that sounds awful. Of course, it's not funny at all. Okay—the coincidental *thing was that I had already been questioned by the police as part of a routine check, because I visited Fagin's club on the night one of those poor girls was abducted; I'd used my debit card there and they tracked me down. Oh—questioned and dismissed, I hasten to add! I told no one about it, because it's not something you shout about, is it? When I was picked up again, I couldn't believe it, I was in a daze, it felt like some kind of weird prank, and when I asked why I'd become a person of interest they wouldn't tell me. It was a bloody harrowing night, though. I was interviewed under caution—well, you know the score. I was as helpful as I possibly could be, because I knew I hadn't done anything."*

Had he been scared that he might be convicted for something he didn't do?

"Well, yes, it did cross my mind," he said, "more than once, but I just had to keep calm and cling on to the fact that technology gives definitive answers. When I was left alone to think, in between interrogations, I did start wondering how they'd hit on me in the first place, and I have to say that Tansy crossed my mind. When I was released—and I tell you, that was one of the happiest moments of my life! —I went straight into work to see my boss. That was when I learned that Tansy had been on the warpath. She'd been talking to another colleague, Bradley, about her suspicions, and he'd intended to warn me, but he

couldn't reach me; I had the day off to install a new computer system for a guy I know,
which happened to be in a Portakabin in a scrapyard. You can imagine how noisy it was; I
never heard my phone all day. I knew nothing until I got home and found the police waiting
for me outside my flat.

Can you imagine how freaked out I was? Tansy had been watching me, gathering
what her twisted mind considered to be 'evidence'. Bradley had tried his best to dissuade her,
but she'd made up her mind. He hadn't said anything to me before because he didn't want
Tansy to lose her job, and he was confident that he could make her see reason, contain the
potential drama. Unfortunately, none of us understood how disturbed she truly was."

Jack looks sad. He seems genuinely astounded by all that has gone on. I wondered if
he blamed himself at all.

"Yes, a little. I shouldn't have slept with her, should never have given her cause to
hope that I'd fallen in love with her. But all I expected, at worst, was a few obscenity
riddled texts, or maybe a drink thrown over me in the pub!" He laughs, and I feel he is
doing so to lighten a situation that has affected him deeply. He doesn't blame the police.
"Goodness, no, they have to follow up all leads, however unlikely. It's a good thing they
take accusations seriously; if they hadn't, the perpetrator of the crimes wouldn't be behind
bars now."

Does he feel angry with Tansy? "I did, a little, but I don't now. I talked to my boss
about it, and to Bradley. He's our resident psychology buff, and he explained to me how
spurned love can turn into dangerous obsession. The rejected party wants to remain involved
with the object of their love, in any way possible. The thought of him or her living a happy
life in which they don't feature is unbearable, so they try to destroy that life, and justify to
themselves the methods by which this is done. I think Tansy convinced herself I'd done those
terrible things, to this end. I think she really believed it."

Jack is silent for a few moments, contemplating all that has happened. "Poor Tansy.
She's gone, now; she never returned to work—though of course she would have been let go, if
she had—and I hear she's living with her parents in another part of the country." He looks
sad. "I hope they can help her get her life back on track, that's all."

I asked him if this situation has put him off casual relationships with women.

"It's certainly made me think more carefully about how I behave, and it's made me more aware that we must not prey on the vulnerabilities of others for our own gratification. I've learned a lesson here, too." Then, just before I began to think he'd prepared the 'caring 21st century guy' script before he met me, the composed expression melted into a grin, and he gave me a cheeky wink that made me see exactly what Tansy had fallen for.

"Never mind STDs," he said, "next time I consider having casual sex with a woman I'm going to ask for a clean bill of psychiatric health before I so much as undo my shoelaces!"

Maybe Jack Fallow's experience is one that could serve as a warning to us all.

14th December, 2015

Northampton

Her mother said she should draw a line under the whole unfortunate incident, but she kept the lyndfordecho.com link on her desktop. The title and opening sentence of the article made her heart thump, and she could hardly bring herself to read on, but when she read the first few paragraphs she smiled with relief. Jake said he liked her and found her attractive; there, she knew it! She knew it! Her eyes did no more than skim the rest. It was written by that bitch Rachel; she'd have twisted Jake's words to fit the purpose of her article. Why spend time reading her stupid lies?

Her resignation addressed to Helen Morse crossed in the post with Helen's letter suggesting that it might be in the best interests of all concerned if she sought employment elsewhere. She assured her that any reference requested by a prospective future employer would concentrate on the excellent work she'd carried out for her team, but Tamsin was not fooled; having worked in HR, she knew about the carefully worded warnings slipped into the 'other comments' box on reference forms.

Being back with her parents was good, a safe, calming interlude, but she couldn't stay there. They treated her with irritating, over-cautious concern, as if she was ill. She had to get another job, and find her own place.

"Why not leave it until after Christmas?" her mother said. "Have a couple of months off. Firms don't take new people on at this time of year, anyway."

No, but in January all the media articles entitled *New Year, New You* came out, and people made resolutions about following their dreams. Staff returned to work, depressed to be back in the same-old-same-old after the jollity of the holiday celebrations. A percentage would pretend to have 'flu to extend those two weeks, or spend downtime scanning job sites, or just not come back; Tamsin had seen it all. The time to get her feet under the table, her CV ready, was now, before the New Year rush of restlessness.

She enrolled at several of the bigger employment agencies in the town, preferring to attend in person rather than seek work online. Success was all about that six-second first impression; workplace recruitment legend had it that whether or not a candidate remained memorable was determined as soon as they walked through the door.

Tamsin knew as soon as she saw the name that she'd found the right agency.

Extra Mile was a small outfit, staffed by Rick, Tracy and Joshua.

Tamsin felt at home there, and loved going in to chat about her prospects to professionals dedicated to finding the perfect candidate for each position, not just ticking boxes on target sheets. She especially loved talking to Joshua, who had, he told her, a passion for human resources. Often, she stayed at Extra Mile long after they'd exhausted the vacancies for the day. There was a real spark between her and Joshua; he asked her about herself, made suggestions, was genuinely interested in her job search. She felt safe to admit that she'd had a few personality clashes in her last job; could they skip the *Lyndford Echo* when it came to references? Josh winked and grinned; he understood.

It helped that he was gorgeous, too, of course. Sexy mouth, well dressed, always smiling. Eyes that looked into her very soul. He laughed at her jokes, hung on her every word.

One day, she'd bumped into him just as he was leaving work.

She'd actually been sitting in the coffee shop over the road, waiting for the office to shut, but he didn't know that. Dressed in a business suit, so she could pretend she'd just been for an interview.

"Not a position I found through Extra Mile," she smiled, coyly. "Can you forgive me?"

"As long as your job search is showing results, that's what matters," Joshua said.

Oh, those eyes!

She offered to take him for a drink, to say thank you for all his help.

"There's really no need, I'm just doing my job," he said, "but what the hell, why not? Thanks!"

Over a couple of Buds, he happened to mention his girlfriend. Tentatively. As if he was telling her they had an obstacle to overcome. She probed further; he didn't live with her. Tamsin wasn't worried.

If he was in love, he would not be sitting in a pub with another woman.

Their relationship just needed a kick start, and she had a plan. She would choose Christmas presents for all three of them, from a highly satisfied client, so that she wouldn't look like a stalker (she'd learned that lesson!), but something a bit special for Josh. Something that would say something to him, *I know. I know there's something between us, and I know that you know, too.*

This Christmas would be a happy one; every day she woke up with joyful expectation, imagining scenarios in which they would admit their feelings for one another, fantasising about his face on the pillow next to hers.

This time, she would take it more slowly, carefully. She would remember her mistakes with Jake (Jake! She could hardly remember why she had loved him, now.)

Even as she tried to put a check on herself, though, she knew it was too late for caution. Too late for either of them, the ball was already rolling down the hill, and it was a shame about his girlfriend, but in love, as in war, there was always collateral damage. Just in case, though, she'd take photos of him when he was in her bed. A security measure, to make sure he didn't have any crazy ideas about returning to the girlfriend.

This time, she was entering the battlefield armed and dangerous!

Shame she couldn't relate her love and war metaphors to Josh; he loved her sense of humour. Never mind, she would save them up for when their relationship began.

Actually, it might be rather amusing to email Jake Fallon to tell him how she was, and all about the new love in her life. There, that would show him!

She'd add a couple of the selfies she'd taken recently, too. Show him what he was missing.

Humming to herself, she opened her laptop.

Chapter Thirty

Juliet: The Wife

16th December, 2015

She'd got away with it.

Paul had no idea who'd gone to the police about him.

Which just proved that he hadn't a clue what went on inside her head.

After his ordeal at the end of October, he'd been subdued in a way she'd never seen before. Didn't want to tell her about the interview, or reveal how those awful hours had affected him. When she dared to ask who might have suggested his name to the police, he brushed her off.

"I don't know. Some labourer who's got a grudge against me, I should think."

Weird.

Paul didn't *let things go*. Such mild acceptance was completely out of character. The Paul she knew would rant and rave, kick things. Make threats. Not that she was complaining. If he investigated that group of labourers with grudges, he would come up with nothing, and the more people he eliminated the nearer he might come to guessing the truth.

He'd closed the door on it, apparently. But she hadn't.

Gary Dunlop might be in custody, but she still didn't know where her husband went at night.

Hours of his time remained unaccounted for.

Something else had occurred to her, too.

Paul wasn't the type of man to be content with a virtually non-existent sex life. Now she was emerging from her safe cocoon of denial she admitted that she wasn't happy with it, either. There wasn't even any real affection in the relationship; if there was, she wouldn't have minded about the lack of sex.

Their household was so quiet in the two months leading up to Christmas. *Quiet, too quiet.* Sam and Max were scarcely around (Max being away at UEA until December), but the tension between her and Paul was waiting to snap. Whenever they were in the same room, even if only drinking coffee with the Sunday papers, or getting undressed before bed, unspoken words hung heavy.

Hers did, anyway. There didn't appear to be anything *he* was desperate to say to *her*.

Lara said, "You've got to have it out with him, or you'll end up back on the loony pills."

She didn't want to start taking anti-depressants again. She'd stopped taking them after Dunlop was arrested and the withdrawal had been hard, even though she wasn't even sure they did any good. How could a silly little pill make your life okay when there was so much wrong with it?

So, she wasn't married to the Lyndford Strangler. But who was Paul? Her lover, her companion, her partner through life's stormy seas? He was none of those things.

I'm forty-nine, she thought. *Is this it? Feeling grateful for the not-too-bad days for the rest of my life? Not daring to ask my husband where he goes at night? Pinning my hopes for happiness and fulfilment on a jewellery-making course in the New Year?*

Maybe it was the looming 'big five-o', or the end of another year. Maybe it was the constant stream of pictures and articles about Gary Dunlop, his family and everyone who'd ever known him, that made her unable to put this past, terrible year to bed. Whatever the cause, this was no life. Not for Paul, either.

Didn't he *want* a better marriage?

She chose her time carefully, a night when Sam had gone out and they'd had a relatively pleasant, relaxed dinner. Afterwards, he'd flopped on the sofa in front of the television, saying he was tired. A good sign; at least he wasn't going out or doing whatever it was that he did in his office, leaving her to watch TV on her own.

A stranger walking in might envy them. A luxurious, comfortable home provided by a man who wanted the best for his family, made beautiful by a woman who loved her husband and sons.

That she was the only person who cared tuppence about things like switching on the Christmas tree lights after dark, or pinning up the vast pile of Christmas cards, would not be obvious to anyone.

She opened another bottle of wine and sat down next to him.

"Thanks." He actually gave her a smile as she handed him the glass, tired eyes looking up at her.

"Max rang me earlier," she told him. "He'll be home on Friday afternoon." Even her favourite son had chosen not to come straight home from university, spending the beginning of the holiday at a friend's.

"That's good."

"I'll go and pick him up from the station."

Paul didn't answer. Stupid thing to say in the first place, really; it was obvious she would do that. Boring. Was it really so difficult to make conversation with her own husband?

Yes, it was.

The silence yawned between them.

He picked up the TV guide.

The clock ticked.

The lights on the Christmas tree twinkled.

They could watch some programme that neither of them was particularly interested in, or they could have a proper conversation.

"Paul, there are a few things I need to discuss with you."

He drew back from her. "Okay. Shoot."

Dare she? Dare she ask? Deep breath. "Please don't be cross with me. But—look, I want to know where you go at nights. When you're out. Most of the time you don't tell me where you're going, or where you've been, and I think I have a right to know."

His face closed up. "Work. Business. That's all."

"Yes, but you're out until the early hours sometimes."

"So business can mean socialising, too. So what?" He shrugged his shoulders. "I don't tell you exactly where I've been or who I've been with because you don't know the people, it's not that interesting, and I wasn't aware I had to file a report."

Juliet looked down at the wine in her glass. If only she could find solace in drink, as some could; it helped a little, but she didn't like being drunk; it made her think too much. "Are you having an affair?"

His laugh was harsh. "Oh, that's it. I should have known. Typical bloody woman. Just because you don't want to spend every hour of every day with them, they accuse you of having an affair!"

"Well, are you?"

His face told her how little regard he had for her. "No."

She gulped down her wine. She may not like being drunk, but it did make her feel braver. "Well, we hardly ever have sex. I just wondered. If you're not having one now, have you in the past?"

"If I had, could I be blamed for it? I don't have anything very exciting to come home to."

His words hurt more than any slap. "That's not very nice." *Don't cry, don't cry.* She opened her eyes wide, picked at the hem of her skirt. "It's a really horrible thing to say, actually."

He flopped back. "Yeah, well, truth hurts, sometimes." His words were cruel but his voice sounded only tired.

"Paul, it's not fair."

"No. Life isn't. You asked, I told you."

The tears came. She couldn't stop them. "Am I really so awful? Such a dreadful wife?"

He rubbed his forehead. To her surprise, he took her hand and squeezed it, just for a moment. "No." Big sigh. "Of course you're not."

"People can't stay exciting, for years and years." She felt encouraged by the small show of affection. "I'm just an ordinary woman, I can't pretend to be anything else, but we have this house, the boys, our whole lives together—"

He drained his glass, put his glass on the table and stood up. "You're right, we do. It's a lot to be grateful for."

"Well, then, can't we make more of an effort to—"

His face grew hard. "No, you misunderstand. What I meant was, I've done all this for you, but apparently it's still not enough."

Oh no. It was starting.

"I'm sorry, of course I'm grateful—*please* sit down, Paul. Please. Let's put things right between us, it's almost Christmas, and—"

"Bloody women and Christmas," he muttered. "It doesn't matter, it's just one stupid day. It's only you who gives a fuck about any of it."

"You know what I mean; the boys will be back; we've got things arranged. Family, friends."

"Yeah. Well, I'm dreading it, if you really want to know. I hate it, every year. Can't wait for it to be over. All that palaver, all that money wasted." He reached for the coat he'd thrown over the back of a chair when he came in, and she panicked.

"I'm sorry you hate it. I try to make it fun. Oh, please, please don't go out. Not now. Stay here with me."

He sighed, flung the coat back on the chair, and turned to her.

The look in his eyes frightened her.

"Okay. You asked. I haven't always been faithful to you. Does that answer your question?"

The revelation didn't knock her for six, because she'd always known; she was surprised by the relief of hearing him admit it, at last. "Who with? Who is she?"

"There isn't any 'is', or 'she'," he said. "I've had a couple of flings in the past, that's all. Nothing important. Just a bit of deviation from the day in, day out routine. Twenty-four years is a long time to be with the same person."

"Who? When?" She really wanted to know, but not because she wanted to scratch the women's eyes out. His words cut into her, but didn't break her heart.

He was doing his coat up, reaching for his scarf. "No one you know. No one important."

"I want to know." She sat up, straightening her back. "I have a right to know. I'm your wife."

"And don't I know it. Well, tough, I'm not telling you." He picked up the coat again, and turned to walk out of the door.

"Please don't go out. Please. We need to talk. You can't just lay this on me, and then walk out, it's not fair!"

"No, we don't *need to talk*. There's nothing to talk about. Not ever. There hasn't been for years and years." He paused, his hand on the door knob. "I won't be late. And before you ask, I'm going for a drink. That's all."

And he was gone.

We don't need to talk. There's nothing to talk about. Not ever.

Those words mattered far more than his revelation (that wasn't a revelation at all, really) that he'd had meaningless sex with faceless women in the past. She'd like to do similar, if only she knew some men to do it with.

There was nothing else, just this life, here, now. And this life was nothing.

Juliet sat there for some time, staring into her empty glass. Eventually, she poured another. The alcohol warmed her, soothed the lump in her throat, but she didn't want to be a person who needed that crutch.

She closed her eyes, and Lara spoke. *Aside from his admission of affairs, aside from the violence, the years and years of making you feel as though you don't matter, there is something much bigger going on here, i.e. the fact that you thought he might be capable of murder. Doesn't that mean the marriage is over?*

Out of all the people in all the world, do you really want to live with this one?

Lara was right, of course. A little harsh though she may be, at times, she was always right.

Paul didn't like Lara, but that was tough shit, really, wasn't it?

Paul had rarely been in the same room as Lara, but on those few occasions he'd reacted to her so strongly that she'd been forced to keep them apart.

Now, though, she understood.

He hated Lara because he was scared of her. Because she wouldn't put up with his crap. He told Juliet she was weak and boring, made her feel pathetic, but he was only man enough for a weak, boring, pathetic woman. He didn't want her to be any other way; a tough nut like Lara would tell him where to get off.

Well, if he didn't like her, he knew where the door was.

Lara was here to stay.

Sitting in her chair with the glass of wine, she looked at the woman next to her, but she was no longer looking at Lara. Now she saw Juliet the victim, and she pitied her, but she was glad not to be her.

There's nothing to talk about. Not ever. There hasn't been for years and years.

She didn't need to drink. She would take a long bath, with lots of bubbles, and start planning how she would begin the rest of her life.

Lara Tully put down her glass and went upstairs.

Paul had not been entirely honest with his wife. He had not been faithful to her, but neither had he indulged in affairs.

Paul Tully had been using the services of prostitutes for years.

At first, he'd met them via 'escort' websites, but was never entirely comfortable with leaving a trail online.

The girls who worked Monk's Park had served his requirements for a long time, until he bought the property in Crow Lane.

The one rented to the Lithuanian boys. Karolis and Valter.

The premises stood tucked away round a slight bend at the far end of the Lane, separated from any functioning businesses by a stretch of unused, rundown industrial buildings. The front, a large area with a high ceiling, was a car repair business. Resprays, MOTs, reliable and otherwise. Fake number plates, though of course this wasn't advertised. 'Cut and shut' jobs, probably, too, but Paul didn't want to know.

Most people who ventured down that part of the long, winding, road during the day were those who wanted repairs done on the cheap, an easy MOT, a new look for a stolen vehicle. At night, though, when all the other businesses were shut, other visitors appeared. The back of the property, entered only via a discreet door opening onto a dark, narrow staircase at the side of the garage, led to the real source of the brothers' wealth. The huge first floor with its bricked-up windows, divided into cubicles where the girls worked.

Valter brought them in, from his home country. Naïve young women, some as young as sixteen, unworldly enough to believe the handsome, smiling young man who promised them a room in a hostel and a job as a chambermaid in a smart hotel; the pretty ones might be employed as dancers in nightclubs. Valter had all the contacts, he told them. Of course, they would have to pay back their travel costs, and Valter's fee (unspecified), but they could take English lessons and eventually get better jobs, in offices or shops. After they'd paid their debt, their money would be their own.

The hostel turned out to be two huge dormitories on the second floor, up another narrow staircase behind a door at the end of the rows of cubicles where they worked. There the girls ate, talked, washed and slept, until brought down for a customer who'd made his selection from their photographs. There was another exit, a rickety old fire escape, but it was hardly safe; one girl had tried to escape and fallen, breaking her leg. She disappeared the same night; the men had no use for a girl with a leg in plaster. In any case, the semi-qualified doctor they paid for treating STDs, gunshot wounds and minor ailments did not have the know-how to set a broken limb.

Paul knew all this because he listened. Years of working with immigrants meant he had picked up more than a few snippets of their various languages.

He suspected many of the girls were addicted to heroin, provided by Karolis and Valter to keep them dependent, but that wasn't his problem.

The Lithuanian girls didn't talk much, just smiled and did whatever he wanted. They told him he was handsome. They knew they must do whatever a customer wanted or tough guy Herkus and his two sidekicks would leave them in no doubt about their obligation to Valter, who had so kindly plucked them from a life of poverty to live in the west, where you could make your fortune.

Paul enjoyed a smooth working relationship with his tenants. They offered to supply him with cheap building labour if he wanted it, but he declined, politely; it didn't do for them to have a hold over him. He had other sources. He kept their rent low; they gave him girls at a discount price.

He suspected Valter and Karolis had other business sidelines, but he never enquired. The less he knew, the better.

Sometimes Paul still used the Monk's Park girls, but he visited Crow Lane once or twice a week. After he'd had sex with the girl of his choice there would be beer or thick, dark Turkish coffee and a game of cards with the men in their 'lounge', a small room containing ancient armchairs, two tables and a fridge for drinks, then he might visit the truck stop on the edge of Monk's Park, and buy himself a cheeseburger.

He hadn't been lying about the cheeseburgers.

They were delicious: hot, greasy, calorie and cholesterol-laden. Lately, every time he ate one, he thought, *fuck you, Juliet, Fiona, Oliver, Rob and your fucking boring dinner parties that I have to put up with in order to get where I want to be. Fuck the lot of you.*

He knew what a sham Juliet's world really was. Keeping up with the Joneses, the snobbery, the falseness; they pretended he was one of them, but he knew what they really thought of him.

Perhaps he was more like the Lithuanians, survivors from tough backgrounds who used their wits to get ahead.

Valter and Karolis knew nothing about his plans for the warehouse. Other developers like him were buying up the disused properties in Crow Lane, though he'd snapped up the best. The area was to be rejuvenated. Paul might have been snubbed by the Masons but he'd kept good his contacts;

thanks to Oliver whispering in his ear almost before the town planners had signed off on the idea, he'd got himself in on the ground floor while the properties were still as cheap as chips and no one else wanted them. Crow Lane's proximity to Monk's Park Industrial Estate was fortunate; within three years it would be a smart, characterless and lucrative expanse of manufacturing and small retail units.

Paul Tully's strategy was simple. The Lithuanians thought they were so clever, moving to Britain where everything was easy, where you were given houses and money to live on and could make your fortune outside the law. Stupid bastards. They laughed about the British and their lax attitude to 'economic migrants' (how funny they found this term!), but had no idea the party was nearly over. If they weren't prepared to move out when required, he would report them to the immigration authorities.

How shocked he would be to discover the brothel operating above the garage!

Karolis and Valter could not prove his regular patronage; they weren't even clever enough to install CCTV cameras to catch people like him making use of it. Thought having Herkus and his boys hanging around was all the protection they needed. The Crow Lane warehouse would become six spacious retail units, with storage or manufacturing space above. The plans were already approved.

Alas, what Paul Tully didn't know was that Valter and Karolis were not quite as stupid as he thought. They'd noticed the activity around the area, the men in suits and hard hats poking around the various empty premises, and they'd talked to other traders, who owned their properties. They had a good idea what was on the cards for Crow Lane, but had no intention of leaving until they had made enough money to finance their dream: smarter premises in London, a proper massage parlour. An 'in' with the drug lords of the East End.

They had a business plan, too, and it meant staying in Crow Lane for another year, at least.

What Paul Tully didn't know was that if he tried to force them, or made any threats about betraying them to the authorities, they would kill him. They drank with him, allowed him to win money from them, and when he left, they drew their fingers across their throats, and laughed.

Paul suspected nothing.

Often, over the past few months, he'd congratulated himself on the way everything was falling into place for him. Juliet featured in his thoughts no more than might an employed housekeeper; she was just *there*, to facilitate his day to day life.

The other thing he didn't know was that, approximately four months after the December night when he first admitted his infidelity, she would leave him.

With money from a bond left to her by her parents, she would buy a smart apartment in the upmarket north end of Lyndford, miles away from Monk's Park and Crow Lane. She would choose a property with two bedrooms, so that Max could live with her during his university vacations if he wished. Her jewellery-making course would be completed by then, and she would start work in a trendy arts and crafts café in the pedestrianised area of the town centre.

His former wife would be known by her middle name, in line with the range of jewellery she planned to make in her spare time and sell online; Max would set up Lara Gems for her, on Etsy.

Juliet had always preferred her middle name, because it was the key to the person she wanted to be. Lara was a brave, strong, passionate woman. Before, she hadn't known how to be her, so Lara had become her friend, when she had no one else. Now, each morning when she looked in the mirror, Lara smiled back at her, becoming more clear, more confident every day.

Juliet would not travel with her to the new apartment. Instead, her ghost would wander the rooms of the marital home, whimpering and sobbing, haunting Paul's every step.

Chapter Thirty-one

Steve: The Friend

Wester Ross, Scottish Highlands

23rd December, 2015

Steve stood at the edge of the loch, staring out over the huge expanse of still, dark water. The sky was overcast, the light failing, and the cold seeped through his padded jacket, wool scarf, hat and gloves, but he loved everything about it, the icy air sharp on his exposed cheeks, even down to his almost numb toes. He loved the crisp air, the silence, the feeling of being a part of nature, if that didn't sound too twattish. But out here, you were more aware of yourself in relation to the landscape. Just you, the land, the water, and the stars in the night sky. Up here the sky got *proper dark* at night, instead of that dull, dirty, deep-greeny-grey-mucky hue of the built-up areas in which he'd always lived.

He especially loved the silence.

He and Nina had been up at the holiday cottage owned by her aunt for six weeks or so, now. A short drive from Ullapool, and Loch Broom. Nina told him that in the spring they could wander down past the fields and see the new-born lambs as they struggled to stand on shaky legs, only half an hour into the world. Watching them had been her favourite thing as a child, she said.

The cottage was fairly basic, with unreliable internet, but that was fine. They had no rent to pay, which was more than fine, as Steve had yet to find work. Nina had a job as a receptionist for a small building firm; she said there might be labouring work for him in the spring, or maybe he could set up on his own, advertising himself as a fixer of computers. If they could sort out decent internet. In time, in time. Right now, they kept their outgoings as low as possible, but that was fine, too. Steve was happy up here. He wanted little, apart from peace, quiet, and Nina.

It was Nina who sorted it all out, but she seemed to like being in charge, so he let her carry on; they laughed about what a good match they were.

"A bossy one and one who doesn't mind being bossed: perfect!" Nina said, but he didn't feel bossed. She was more organised, that was all. He became too easily distracted; he'd be looking on the internet for Travelodges and Premier Inns, for instance, only to discover he'd somehow travelled five sites away via the interesting looking links, and was reading about an archaeological dig on a Greek Island.

They'd stayed in the King's Lynn Travelodge for a week, during which Steve talked to his employer and explained the situation. He'd worked at Lyndford Computers for eight years; he liked and respected his boss; there was no way he could just do a runner. Nina's parents arranged to put Steve's belongings into storage once he'd given them a list of his immediate needs. His flat had been placed on the books of an accommodation agency and rented out until he was in a position to sell. They'd already found him a tenant; the income was enough to keep him afloat. Although he knew he must find work eventually, he was in no hurry.

The loose ends were being neatly tied up; his old life tidied away, forever.

As soon as they were safely away from Lyndford, Nina talked to Cassie, and persuaded her to admit that AJ had threatened her to make her drop her complaint about Dan.

"There probably wasn't a strong enough case, anyway, but he told her she'd regret it, big time," Nina said. "Said he knew people who weren't fussy what they did for money. Talked about acid in her face, and Cassie was convinced he meant every word."

Steve felt on edge all week, hardly daring to leave the safety of the hotel, even though they'd told no one but the police of their exact location.

If no one knew, they couldn't be forced to give it up.

All the same, they both jumped ten feet in their air whenever there was a sound outside their room, every time their phones rang.

"We've just got to sit this week out, and we're safe," Nina kept saying. Her aunt's cottage was shut up for the winter, with amenities turned off. Steve would have preferred to stay nearby while it was made ready for their arrival, but Nina wanted to be near home, 'just in case', she said, though Steve wasn't sure in case of what; he suspected the real reason was her reluctance to be so far from her parents. He understood.

Not for the first time in his life he was glad to have no ties.

When they were at their most anxious, they told each other AJ was unlikely to go to the trouble of tracing them, even if he knew where to start. He didn't know Nina's surname or where her parents lived, and no one had a forwarding address for them.

Steve held on to the hope that Dan would want him to drop it. AJ was in the past.

"That'd be worth the expense of moving to another solar system, never mind a few hundred miles up north," he said. Making light of things helped his nerves. Sometimes.

Just when they thought they were in the clear, though, about half an hour before they left the Travelodge, Steve's phone began to vibrate.

There was something about the way it rang—

"Fuck." Steve picked it up and looked up at Nina, feeling the blood drain from his face. "It's Dan." He was annoyed to find himself shaking, uncontrollably. What was he, some kind of wimp?

"Don't answer it," Nina said, "it'll only be more of what AJ said to you."

"It's okay, I wasn't going to."

Steve Turner's phone. Please leave a message. Bee-ee-eep.

A couple of minutes later, a notification popped up: new voicemail message.

He looked at Nina, and she took his hand. He felt sick.

"I've got to listen to it."

"I know."

He put his arm around Nina, and tapped the phone onto loudspeaker.

"Steve? It's Dan."

The sound of his friend's voice provoked an emotion that he couldn't name; sadness, remorse, relief, fear, all mixed up into something so weird, so strong, that he felt short of breath.

"Yeah, right, well, you know what I'm going to say. I was gutted about what you did. AJ told me it was you. Doesn't matter if it was you or Nina, it's all the same. If it was her idea, you didn't stop her." There was a pause. "Heard you'd packed up and left, which confirmed it. You're right to be scared. Word of warning; don't come back. AJ's not the sort of bloke you want to piss off."

Bee-eep.

The message cut out. Steve and Nina sat in silence; sure enough, the phone rang again.

New voicemail message.

"Yeah. Anyway. As I was saying. You don't accuse your best mate of something like this and come back from it. It's over. Don't contact me again. Have a nice life, my old *buddy*." A click, and he was gone.

Steve turned to Nina, and held her tight.

"We will, won't we? Have a nice life, I mean."

She put her arms around his waist and snuggled her face into his chest. "It'll be brilliant." He stroked her hair. Holding her, he felt renewed with strength. No longer in Dan's shadow; because that was where he had been, for his whole life.

The next morning, they packed their bags and left for Scotland.

Now, as he turned and walked across the gravelled bank, away from the water, Steve felt warm with contentment. At home, Nina would be back from shopping in Inverness, last minute Christmas bits and bobs; her parents would arrive tomorrow. She was excited about seeing them, though Steve would be just as happy when they were gone, and he could be quiet, alone with his love. Their first Christmas together. Last year he'd sat round at Dan's dad's watching *Star Wars* films and drinking whisky until he could see three TV screens, wondering if Mr Thewlis would be offended if he left before tea time. He would never have dreamt that this year would turn out any differently, thought his life would always be just jogging along. Waiting, without knowing if whatever it was he was waiting for would ever happen, or if he'd still be sitting in his flat watching the Crime and Investigation channel, on his own, when he was sixty.

He wondered if he'd ever cross paths with Dan again. When they were older, when his life had changed, too.

Probably not.

Steve snuggled his face into his soft angora scarf (an early Christmas present from Nina), and hurried back across to his car.

Night was falling, and she was waiting for him.

Chapter Thirty-two

Maisie: The Teenager

23rd December, 2015

"It's so good to know that starting today, for ten whole days, nothing is going to *happen*," Maisie said. She frowned, examining her thumbnail, then looked up and grinned. "Long as I stay off the internet, anyway!" Sinking back into the huge cushions on Kate Brownlow's sofa, she picked up her mug of hot chocolate. "Oh, Kate, this is lush! The marshmallows—*ohh*!"

Kate laughed.

"I mean, I'm not *scared* of the stuff they say, exactly," Maisie continued, "but—well, you know, it does get to you a bit. Getting away is just *wonderful*!"

"Ah, it was actually Greg's idea for you to come here, so you can thank him, not me." Kate picked up her own mug. "I did drop subtle hints every five minutes, but I thought I'd let him be the one to suggest it."

"Well, it got us out of going to Spain! Two weeks with no one under fifty, and Gran would've wanted to talk about *him* all the time. We just want to forget it now, you know?"

She'd cried with relief when the Brownlows invited them to stay for the whole of the Christmas holiday, right up until January 3rd. Now, she gazed out of the window, unable to stop smiling. No snow, of course—she'd never seen a white Christmas—but at least the day was cold and bright, not dank and mild, as Christmas so often was.

"Do you think you can?"

"Dunno yet. It's not bad every day. Loads of people are dead kind. But then you get some arsehole—" Maisie put her hand to her mouth and giggled. "—sorry, I mean some*one*—shouting out 'murderer's wife' in the street, or beating on Zack in the playground." She gave a small, half smile. "The other day Mum was at work, and this bloke came in, asking her daft questions about all those weird cheeses they sell—I mean, he, like, took up *loads* of her time—and then said, 'you got any bodies in the freezer out the back, too?' Ran away laughing. Mum was well shook up."

Kate raised her eyebrows. "I don't know where people get off even thinking up stuff like that."

"Mum says it's made the deli mad busy, anyway." She leant her head back, staring at the ceiling. "I hope she's going to be okay. I mean, Zack gets stressed out when they pick on him at school, but it hasn't been as bad as they thought, and he's learning to fight back. Sometimes I reckon he even uses it to show off. I know that sounds a bit sick, but people want to know what Gary was like. It's made him a bit of a star in his class. And he's still not allowed on Twitter and that, so he doesn't see the bad stuff.

"That's good." Kate curled up on her chair, pulling a cushion onto her lap. "What about you? Is it still bad?"

Maisie didn't answer for a while. "It's all there if I want to look at it. But I don't."

She didn't want to tell Kate how hard it really had been. Bethany had decided that queening it at the gossip epicentre was more fun than being a supportive friend; she'd ganged up with the persecutors, agreeing that Pru must have been pretty desperate for a boyfriend if she'd gone out with the Lyndford Strangler. *She must have known something, mustn't she?* That was what they were all saying. Anything to be in the limelight; she'd started a blog and written posts on everything she could think of that might interest the vultures, the high spot being the time Gary Dunlop gave her a lift into town and tried to chat her up. She'd included photos taken on her phone of her with the family, including Gary, alongside various sexy selfies. Maisie heard she was tweeting it to various online news sites, hoping to 'get famous'.

She'd offered to give the lowdown on everything she knew about the Todds, but because of her age her mum would have to give permission for such an interview, and she 'didn't want to get involved', Saffron said. Shame this non-involvement didn't extend to making her daughter take the blog down; it was getting hundreds of hits every day.

When Maisie discovered that her best friend was one of the chief perpetrators of the gossip she was so overcome with anger, shock and pain that she locked herself in the bathroom and kicked at the door so hard she made a big hole in it—which upset Pru, and they had to pay out to get a new door, *and* she had to tell Pru why she was so angry, which upset her, too. Another lesson learned: she was no longer a child, and sometimes she needed to think first, act later in order to protect her mother, instead of the other way round.

Zack had been terribly upset too, and didn't understand.

"That little madam just wants her fifteen minutes of notoriety," Saffron's mother said, "regardless of who it hurts. Karma will get to her one day, when someone hurts her this badly; try to stay away, and don't let it get to you."

Easier said than done, sometimes.

The other shock was Pru's friend Wendy from down the road, the one who'd remarked many times that Pru had, in Gary, 'got a good 'un there'. She now hurried across the road if she saw them walking towards her, or became engrossed in something on her phone or in a shop window.

Maisie's sixteenth birthday fell during the dreadful weeks following Gary's arrest, but she was happy for it to pass by unnoticed by anyone except her immediate family and Saffron; there was nothing to celebrate.

The police had been so kind, once they'd ascertained that she and her family had known nothing. The nice detective called Cara said she was most impressed by the idea of checking Gary's mileage, and Maisie felt very proud (even though it was Kate's brainwave).

"You've got a good head on you," she said. "Do you want a leaflet about careers in the Force?"

As it happened, there had been little evidence to be found in Gary's car; a few times he'd committed his crimes in stolen vehicles so that his car wouldn't be picked up on CCTV, and to avoid forensic evidence. He'd worn different pairs of shoes to make different footprints, even taken cigarette butts from ashtrays in pub smoking shelters and scattered them around the dumping ground to confuse the police further; sadly, it had worked. Gary had never been so much as fingerprinted by the police before, and so many traces led them up blind alleys or the wrong ones altogether.

Charlotte had been charged, too, with perverting the course of justice; during investigation the alibis she gave Gary were proven to be false. The Family Liaison Officer explained that Charlotte knew nothing about what Gary was really doing. He'd given her the impression that his residence with the Todds was temporary, until he 'got back on his feet', and told her he was involved in 'an import-export business that wasn't always strictly above board', which sometimes meant he needed alibis for both the police and Pru; she was so besotted with him that she'd done as he asked.

As for Bobby, the bullying story was merely part of the fiction, and it was only when Charlotte learned the severity of the charges against him that she came clean.

She was an unworldly sort of woman, the Liaison Officer told them, who'd believed what she was told without question, and thought Gary would return to her once he had some money behind him.

Kate and Greg Brownlow had become true friends, with Kate their fairy godmother throughout. She'd proved to be of particular help to Pru, arranging a counsellor for her through her women's group.

"It's about learning not to blame yourself, and to help you find out why you allow men to chip away at your self-esteem," Kate told her, 'because, aside from everything else, Gary did just that, in such a subtle way, which is often the most dangerous. Don't worry, we've all been there." Pru had been dubious at first; still in shock, she was not open to anything except dulling her pain with white wine and said she didn't want to become some strident *independent woman*, because she liked having a man around, but slowly, gradually, she found herself able to talk about it.

"I feel so disgusted with myself that I ever let him touch me," she told Kate. "That's been the hardest thing; coming to terms with the fact that I was sleeping with a man who was doing what he did."

Maisie excused herself from the room when the conversation wandered down this road. Didn't want to know about her mother's sex life on any day of the week, but certainly not when it involved that evil piece of scum. Serious puke.

She'd been so worried about Pru for the first month, fearing the self-medication with Echo Falls might become too much of a habit, but Kate got it right, as usual.

"Sometimes the people who appear strong can't cope when the going gets tough, and the people you think will collapse come through with a strength that even they never knew they owned."

Pru was back at work within a month, and called a meeting with her staff in order to avoid awkwardness, and discuss strategy should they suffer any enquiries or abuse from the public.

She asked Maisie and Zack if they wanted to move away, start afresh somewhere else; the Family Liaison Officer had discussed with her the possibility of new identities. Zack thought this sounded cool and wanted to know if he could change his name to Luke Skywalker, until he realised it would mean never seeing any of his friends again. Maisie was surprised to find that she didn't want to go, either.

"If we run, it looks as though we're ashamed, and we didn't do anything wrong. And wherever we go, someone will always find out, won't they? 'Cause people just do."

Her school held a special assembly for her, hosted by Kate, which, she said, would bring the subject out into the open and nip any possible bullying in the bud.

Maisie cringed all the way through it, but didn't like to tell Kate how much she'd loathed the whole idea. Her greatest wish was that it would all go away so they could go back to their lives and pretend they had never met Gary Dunlop.

While he was still the talk of the town, she was in limbo.

Her worst fear was damage being done to their house, but this had happened only once, when someone spray-painted the words 'Murder House' in red, on the garage. She came home to find her mother in bed, in tears, the words still there for all to see; that was the worst day. Neighbours helped her clean it off, but not before someone filmed it before and during, and posted it on YouTube. Kate wrote an email of complaint to the site and got it taken down.

No one knew who'd done it, or claimed not to; people in the area *knew* them, her neighbours called into the deli, their sons played with Zack. How could they do that to them? For a while she felt sick with nerves every time she walked up the road towards her house.

Even up to the last day of that autumn term she'd been hounded by the press at the school gates, wanting to interview her. She started to leave with

Kate, via the teachers' car park, until the journalists got wise to it and followed them round there, too.

After the journalists came the lawyers, offering them the opportunity to sue for harassment, a swarm of them, after a picture of Zack appeared in a national: 'The boy who lived under the same roof as the Lyndford Strangler'. One of his teachers was assigned to accompany him home from school each day, which he hated.

The Family Liaison Officer advised them to speak to no one, put the phone down without comment, ignore emails. Even when they left to travel to Kate and Greg's isolated farmhouse, they'd had to leave via their neighbour's back gate.

"It'll stop, eventually," Kate told her now, "when they realise that they're never going to get anything from you. Or when Cheryl Cole gets married again, or one of the Kardashians puts on weight, or something."

Reaction wasn't all bad. They'd had some wonderful letters of support from strangers, including one lady who said that her heart went out to them because she'd had her own fears about the identity of the killer. She even sent them a present of some posh bath stuff; the letter made Pru cry. If an address was included, Pru and Maisie replied to every single one.

Pru said she wanted to get in touch with the support group for the families of murder victims, too, to see if she could be of any help.

"It might be too much for you," Kate advised. "They might blame you."

"I can cope, I think," Pru said. "Anything I'm suffering is nothing compared with what they're going through. If I can help, I will."

After two months, it was finally starting to calm down.

That night, after a long, lazy dinner, Kate and Greg left the three of them on their own in the living room, to watch a film; Zack chose *Spiderman*. They sat on Kate's huge sofa together, eating popcorn and enjoying the warmth of the real log fire.

Maisie loved Kate's living room, which was, she thought, like something off a film or a Christmas advert on telly. Lamps and scented candles, the fire, the tree with the white and gold lights, the presents underneath it, holly along the mantelpiece and even stockings for her and Zack pinned up by the hearth, like an old-fashioned Christmas card.

The smells of pine logs and the spices from Kate's mulled wine made her feel snoozy, warm, and safe.

As the film began, she did something she hadn't done for some years: she snuggled up to her mother, putting her head on her shoulder.

Pru took her hand. "Thought you were too old for that!"

Maisie sat up and smiled at her; Pru looked tired, but happier than she had for some time.

"I fancy being a kid tonight." She picked up a strand of her mother's long, fair hair. The darker roots were two inches long, and it hung lifelessly around her shoulders. "Why don't we get your highlights done, Mum? For New Year's Eve; Kate said they're going to have a party."

"Good idea. Yes—I will. We could both go." She dropped Maisie's hand and splayed her fingers out. "Get our nails done, too; look at the state of mine!"

"Will you two shut up?" Zack said, untangling himself from his mother's right arm. "It's starting!"

"Sorry." Pru gave his hand a squeeze and winked at Maisie. "I promise I won't talk again—" she reached forward and took the bowl of salted popcorn from the table"—as long as Maisie and I get to eat all the salted, okay?"

"Cool, as long as I get the toffee to myself!" Zack looked highly pleased with the deal. "Now will you be quiet?"

"Okay." Pru turned the volume up. "That Andrew Garfield's a bit cute, isn't he? If I was twenty years younger. What d'you reckon, Mais?"

"Mu-um! Gross me out!"

"Mum, shut *up!*"

Maisie and Pru laughed, settling back onto the sofa.

The logs crackled in the grate; a *countryish* sound, Maisie thought. It mingled with the scent from the rose oil in the burner on the table beside her, and that in turn echoed the golden glow from the candles on the hearth and the feel of the huge, soft cushions against her back, until all her senses merged together into one sensation: happiness. Then she thought about Ellie Kane's little sister, in the picture in the newspaper, and felt guilty for being happy.

Kate had told her that feeling wouldn't go away for some time, but she would learn how to deal with it.

Perhaps she could help with the bereavement group, too. There must be something she could do.

She wriggled her fluffy-sock-covered feet under her mother's legs for extra warmth; Pru looked up at her, and smiled.

She didn't say anything, but that smile made Maisie feel better than she had for many, many months.

I love you. We're going to be okay now.

With the help of friends like Kate and Greg, and Saffy and her mother, they could start to move on and forget the part Gary Dunlop had played in their lives.

Well, not forget; maybe just put into a corner and shut away, where it belonged.

Maisie felt as though she'd grown up ten years in the last few weeks. Bethany's betrayal had been a terrible blow, but right now the only thing that mattered was the three of them sticking together.

Spiderman swung between skyscrapers, and Zack looked on, wide-eyed, his hand moving popcorn from bowl to mouth. The next day was Christmas

Eve, the most magical day of the year, and they had a whole ten days here in the countryside before they had to go back home.

He was behind bars, where he could never hurt anyone else, ever again.

Maisie smiled back at her mother.

I love you. We're going to be okay now.

Chapter Thirty-three

Dorothy: The Mother

Christmas Eve, 2015

As she made final touches to the table, she found herself smiling. She'd been smiling a lot, lately.

A damn sight more than she had during the earlier part of the year, anyway.

Before, she had never known the joy that came from being part of a family—albeit a rather unusual one—who genuinely cared for each other. Of belonging, of being an important part not just of Orlando's life, but of others', too.

The old adage that you could choose your friends but not your family was wrong; you *could* choose your family. Family was a *feeling*, not a consequence of birth. She'd only just learned this, from Colin, who thought she was 'amazeballs'. Well, who'd have thought it, eh?

As she arranged the last napkin into a clever little fan shape (a new skill), anxiety beset her. No, not anxiety, exactly; nervous anticipation, because she'd never cooked for five people before and this meal had to be special, for Christmas Eve. Tomorrow she would be the guest, so tonight she wanted to neither overshadow (not much chance of that) nor disappoint.

She'd planned a relatively light meal so as not to overload stomachs; Kathryn's Christmas Day lunches were legendary, she was told. Tonight, then, she would serve a salmon mousse, rosemary-marinated roast lamb with steamed vegetables, and homemade mango and passionfruit sorbet for pudding.

Christmas with her new 'family'; wonderful.

September and October seemed a long time ago.

Orlando would never know of her fears. Reverend Green had been most understanding, not shocked at all, and had assured her that she had not committed any terrible sin; she would come to terms with it in her own time.

On that dreadful day back in October she'd made the hardest decision of her life, but from whichever angle she looked at the information in her possession, she'd known she had no choice.

If there was even a tiny possibility that her worst fears were justified, she had to talk to the detectives. So that they could reassure her, that was all.

Her heart had never felt heavier than on that bus ride to the station. At each stop she almost got off and went home. Only her memory of those young girls she'd seen the day before stopped her doing so.

Alas, the enormity of her decision was matched only by her confusion once the deed was done.

After the most distressing conversation of her life, she emerged from the police station in complete bewilderment. Her fears had been treated respectfully, and with patience, but that was all.

Had she gone through so much angst just to be given a cup of tea, passed a box of tissues (nasty, hard ones that made her nose sore), and pacified with kind words from a policewoman young enough to be her granddaughter?

"I do understand how devastating this must be for you," said the girl. Well, yes, it was, but Dorothy doubted the girl understood how she felt or, indeed, what the word actually meant. People chucked it about all over the place, these days.

"I doubt you do," Dorothy said, suddenly feeling no further need to cry. "Can you tell me what will happen now?"

"We'll keep a record of everything you've told us, and we'll certainly make enquiries," said the young PC, without conviction. Dorothy left the station feeling patronised, bemused, exhausted and angry.

It was only later that she found out why they'd treated her fears so casually; they'd already got their man. Gary Dunlop. Dorothy read in the paper about the family with whom he'd lived, and her heart went out to them; she sat down and wrote them a letter of support, care of the *Lyndford Echo*. As an afterthought, she went out and bought them a gift set of soaps and 'bath bombs' from that shop in the pedestrian precinct, hoping they wouldn't think she was a batty old woman, and that the present wasn't inappropriate.

She'd received a lovely letter back from the mother, Pru; perhaps they might become friends, too, one day.

When she returned from the police station, though, she'd lain on her bed and wondered if she would ever be able to behave normally again. Never before had she wished, so much, that she had someone to say *don't worry. I'll make everything all right.*

I'm not weak, she thought. *I can take care of myself.* But wouldn't it be nice not to have to, all the time?

She even prayed, but added a sentence at the end telling God that she would understand if He didn't give her prayer top priority, because if He could see into all their hearts and minds, He must know that she wasn't entirely sure He existed.

It was perhaps rather bad manners to ask at all, really.

Then she went downstairs and made a cottage pie, to take her mind off it. As if anything could.

Orlando came home and ate the cottage pie, they chatted about trivia, and then he went off to metal detecting club, or so he said. Took his gear, but after he'd gone, she went upstairs to his room and discovered that his trophy box had gone, too.

She just sat. Tried not to think.

At around nine o'clock she was staring at the television when the phone rang.

"Mum, I'm coming home early," Orlando said. Lots of noise in the background. Didn't sound like the metal detecting club. "I just thought I'd give you a warning in case you want to nip upstairs and put some lipstick on, or something!"

She frowned. "Why would I do that?"

He gave a little laugh, and she was sure she could hear female laughter in the background, too. "There's someone I want you to meet!"

Oh, the difference a moment could make. One phone call, and her anxiety floated away. She'd been wrong. All this time. Orlando had got himself a girlfriend.

The most obvious answer, and she'd talked herself out of it.

Fifteen minutes later she heard the front door open and she went out in the hall, her best smile in place, ready to welcome whoever was out there.

Her mouth fell open.

"Mum, I'd like you to meet Marla."

Eh? Was she going mad? What was going on? There was no woman there, no one who might be called Marla, just Orlando, and Colin from the art class.

Both of them were dressed as women. They looked ridiculous. Colin had foundation sticking to his stubble, and Orlando's strong, muscular legs looked like something out of—oh, a *Carry-On* film, in those tights. He was only missing the handbag on his arm and the grumpy expression. Wait a minute—his legs were *shaved*. He was wearing make-up, a long, brunette wig—oh, and that turquoise and silver necklace she'd seen in the trophy box—

What on earth was going on?

Wait a minute—they must be going to a fancy-dress party! Of course! But why had he pretended he was going to metal detecting club? Why hadn't he just come out with it, told her where he was going?

Orlando smiled. He had lipstick on his teeth.

"This is Marla, Mum. I'm Marla. And this is Silvana." He and Colin both smiled at her. *Beamed* at her. "You know him as Colin, but tonight he's Silvana."

Her laughter sounded slightly insane, even to her own ears. "Very funny. I thought you had a young lady with you—"

They glanced at each other. Still smiling, but Orlando was biting his lip, something he always did when apprehensive. Something wasn't right. She felt sick.

"This *is* fancy dress, isn't it?" She felt the smile fall from her face, and Orlando's cheerful expression changed to one of concern. He took her arm and guided her into the living room, while Colin bustled about getting cushions and pouring her a brandy for the shock, still dressed in that ludicrous blonde wig, remarkably steady on those high heels.

"I think maybe we all need one of these," he said, hand on hip, before taking two more glasses from the sideboard. He sounded even more effeminate than usual.

"This *is* fancy dress, is it?" she said, again.

"I'm sorry, Mum," Orlando said, sitting down next to her on the sofa and taking her hand. "I've been wondering how to tell you for so long, and, believe me, it's taken many nights of humming and hah-ing, and to-ing and fro-ing—"

"It certainly has," said Colin, handing her the brandy, "he's been all of a tizzy for months now."

He sounded like Kenneth Williams.

Colin pulled the pouffe close to the sofa, and sat down, arranging his legs in a most ladylike fashion. "It was me who persuaded him he really must tell you. I said to him, I said, Orlando, your mum is a *super* lady, she's understanding, she loves you, and isn't it better that she knows? Dorothy, he's hated lying to you. That's been the worst part, he said."

Why was Colin acting like this? Like a parody drag queen; he'd never been the most masculine of fellows and of course she knew he was probably homosexual, but this—

Gently, carefully, they both explained to her. That they were transvestites, or cross-dressers, which was something quite different from being a *transsexual*, or *transgender*, as those were the brave souls who felt the need for sex-change operations ('Ouch, no thank *you*!' said Colin), and cross-dressing didn't mean you were a pervert, or a homosexual (though Colin *was* homosexual; Orlando thought he actually might be asexual—which was not the same as bisexual—but that wasn't anything she needed to know about), and they weren't doing anything wrong—but Marla and Silvana were part of them, and they'd both felt happier since they'd been able to express their whole selves, which they did in the privacy of a club, in the company of like-minded people.

"It's becoming more important to me," Orlando told her, "and I'm finding that I want to be Marla more and more often, so I knew I couldn't keep it from you much longer."

Colin nodded. "This is the worst part. The wonderful bit is meeting those like us, and being free to be ourselves. We just hope it doesn't upset you too much; I told my family a while back, and they're fine with it now." He smiled. "Kathryn, my big sis, has even given me coaching on how to walk in high heels!"

Dorothy's mind swirled as she tried to take the information in, especially as they kept repeating about how being transvestite wasn't the same as transgender, and how even happily married men could be cross-dressers (*really?*), until her head ached with all this new information, and at last, at last, at *last*, all her questions fell into place.

Orlando's absence from metal detecting club.

His late nights.

The trophy box.

The trophy box.

She laughed at the very thought and every time she tried to stop, her lips twitched at the corners again, like when Orlando whispered stuff about Reverend Green and the lead piping in church. The brandy went straight to her head and, oh dear, the boys were looking a bit worried now. Sitting there with their funny wigs and make-up, Colin with his rough male skin showing through his caked face powder—

"Mum?"

She swallowed hard, almost choking. "I'm sorry, darling. I'm sorry, I'm not laughing at you, I promise, I'm laughing at myself." But she knew she could never, ever explain why.

"Are you sure you're alright, Mrs B?"

Dorothy held up her hand. "Yes, yes, I'm fine. Honestly." Her shoulders shook again, and Colin hastened over to the sideboard for more brandy. "Yes, I'd love another one, thank you. Shall we get drunk? I haven't been drunk in years!"

Orlando put his arm around her shoulders. He smelled of Coty L'Aimant. *Her* Coty L'Aimant, no doubt. "I'm sorry, Mum. I just couldn't keep pretending. I've hated lying to you."

All at once her laughter turned into tears, but they were not unhappy tears. She was happy, she was relieved, it was funny, no, more than funny, it was hilarious, but she mustn't laugh at them, she really mustn't let them think she was laughing *at* them. Because she wasn't. Not really. Well, perhaps at Colin, just a little bit.

She looked up at her son. "Can you tell me why?"

He smiled down at her, so sweetly (if you could get past the cherry-red lipstick); her Orlando, who she'd loved with all her heart since before he was born. "I can't really, Mum. It's just something that's in me; I tried to ignore it for years, because I felt silly." He looked up at Colin. "You know, ashamed. Terrified of being laughed at, or shunned—well, you can understand that, I expect! But then I met Colin, and he introduced me to others like us." He stroked her hair, and his eyes looked so kind, just as they always had. He was still her boy, even if he did want to wear Marks and Spencer Per Una floral separates; she recognised the outfit from the M&S website. Had he ordered it, or bought it from the shop? Had he tried it on in the fitting room? No, surely not.

"It's not something you shout about, especially not when you're a staid old civil servant," he went on, "but fear not, I am not about to turn up at the Department of Work and Pensions in a Jaeger skirt suit and patent stilettos!"

They laughed, but then Orlando took on a serious expression. "This is who I am, though. I'm forty-three; I'm fed up with spending my life denying that."

The second enormous brandy warmed Dorothy into a fuzzy blanket of unreality. Very pleasant. *Oh dear, he does look rather silly*, she thought. *But perhaps I can help him with that.*

"I know you must think I look completely ridiculous," he said, reading her mind. Just as he always did. "There's room for improvement, I know."

"Perhaps you can give him some tips, Mrs B!" suggested Colin, and leant forward to clink his glass against hers. "Bottoms up, eh?"

Dorothy wondered if Colin consciously put on this persona with his false eyelashes; oh well, never mind. She'd always liked the boy. And didn't she pride herself on her open mind?

"It's okay, it really is," she said, taking Orlando's hand and smiling at them both. "I can deal with it."

"You must have a lot of questions," Orlando said.

"Probably. We'll leave them for another time, though." The tears filled her eyes once more, and she looked into the dark, kind eyes of her beloved son. They weren't the eyes of a killer. How could she ever have thought they might be? "You've trusted me enough to tell me, and that's all that matters."

"I've told Marla she's got to take care when she's out," Colin trilled. "I said to him, I said, that Lyndford Strangler fella preys on gorgeous dark-haired girls, doesn't he?" He gave a little squawk, sounding even more like Kenneth Williams. "Mind you, he'd get a bit of a shock if he put his grubby mitts up either of *our* skirts!"

The curious, elated mood of that first night mellowed, and as the weeks passed, she experienced moments of concern, but these were for her son, rather than herself. He was still her baby; she didn't want him to suffer ridicule.

"I'm alright," he said. "One of the lessons I've learned by getting to know others like me is when it's safe to 'come out' and when it might be better to not to. At the end of the day it's no one's business but mine, so I'm still choosing my moments carefully, but knowing I can be Marla whenever I want makes me able to enjoy the Orlando days more."

She thought for a moment. "I understand that. I remember feeling better once I'd left my parents' house, even though I was on my own with a new baby. At least I didn't have to spend all my time trying and failing to please them, and I could enjoy visiting them because I knew I could leave."

"That's it. And, Mum, you know that being honest with you was the hardest but the most important thing of all, don't you?"

In fact, she rather enjoyed their secret. She smiled to herself about it, sometimes, when she was out shopping, or sitting in church observing the po-faced Angela Wykes and Mrs Gibson, wondering what they would say if they knew; would their supposed Christian tolerance of their fellow man extend to her son, or would they consider him a sexual deviant? Tempting though it was to tell them, just to observe their reaction, Orlando wouldn't let her.

They enjoyed their secret together. One Sunday, kicking up soggy leaves as they walked back from the mid-morning service in the late November mist, Orlando said he might ease them in gently by wearing his red suede ballet flats to church with his best suit, just to see if they could handle it.

"Angela Wykes has got pretty huge feet, actually," he said. "I was looking at them when she walked up to do the reading. Perhaps I could ask her where she buys her shoes."

He was quite low-key as Marla, not slipping into the camp, pantomime dame affectation of Colin; he was still himself, his mannerisms becoming only slightly more feminine.

"Might be because I'm not gay," he said, when she mentioned it. "I'm a straight bloke who likes wearing frocks and lipstick, that's all."

He promised to take her to his club after Christmas—if she felt ready to be fawned over by a load of drag queens, he warned.

"I think I'll take my time over that one," Dorothy told him. "I'm not saying no, just not yet."

She had, however, been introduced to Colin's sister, Kathryn and his father, Douglas, who'd had a terrible time coming to terms with his son's proclivities; maybe it was harder for a man. He still preferred 'not to have my Clarins True Radiance foundation shoved in his face', Colin said, but was now more accepting.

Perhaps she could help him; he must feel so alone, with no wife to talk to about it. Later on that night, maybe, after their Christmas Eve dinner, when their children were watching one of those programmes their generation liked. Arms heists, car crashes and undercover agents, with loud, intrusive soundtracks and ludicrous plots. She and Douglas could drink port together (he liked his port, so she'd bought a nice bottle of Taylor's, specially), and discuss their peculiar situation, if he wanted to. But only if he wanted to; he was a charming man, underneath, and, aside from anything else, it was so good, sometimes, simply to have someone of her own age with whom to chat. They had the same points of reference.

Her preparation finished, she stood back, admiring her handiwork. The room looked cosy, welcoming, the table worthy of the company, with its pristine white linen cloth, shining cutlery and fan napkins (Colin was a willing tutor on such things). She contemplated who would sit where; Douglas at the head of the table, she decided, and felt her lips curl upwards as she thought of him. She wanted him to feel at home, and not made uncomfortable by Marla and Silvana; Colin had dropped hints about a few spectacular outfits for Christmas. The mind boggled.

She was part of this extended family, now; Colin said that was what they were, now that the traditional two married parents and two-point-four children was a rarity, not the norm.

"Your family is whatever you decide it should be," he'd told her, and she liked this concept; it made her feel very modern and liberated. She was part of this strange, tolerant, mish-mash, twenty-first-century *family*.

She picked up a glass and checked it for smears. Orlando had mentioned, the other day, how well she and Douglas got on. How Douglas straightened his tie and smoothed his hair when he talked to her; these were all signs of the male of the species 'preening', her son said. Maybe, if she was open-minded enough to embrace her only son being a transvestite, she could consider the idea of not being on her own, a single woman against the world, for the rest of her life. It was all she had ever known, but maybe it was time for a change.

Maybe. Just maybe.

Epilogue

February 2016

Dora was determined, he had to give her that. He could see how hard she was struggling to keep her eyes fixed on his. Did she hope he would think of her face every night, before he fell asleep?

Sorry, love, in a week or so I won't even be able to recall exactly what you looked like, just the sensation of the moment.

Strangling someone was a hell of a job, and even more so when you had to make sure they didn't touch you. Having to be cautious made him feel almost resentful. Spoiled his enjoyment. But that last look, the one before they finally gave in to death, the acceptance in their eyes, gave him a fulfilment that could be found nowhere else.

Afterwards, it was just a matter of clearing up, as quickly, quietly and efficiently as possible. Body in the car boot, carefully lined with bin bags just in case. He drove out to Waterton, twelve miles away, and dumped the body in the river. Weighted it down well, this time, with bricks. Had to make damn sure it didn't get discovered; couldn't rely on the Lyndford Strangler to take the flak now.

He wasn't a fame hungry idiot like Dunlop. Had no desire to see his handiwork splashed all over the newspaper.

The watery grave was always a risk, but it was part of the ritual that made him feel complete.

He'd wrapped the body in the bin liners from the car boot but kept the head free because he liked to shine the torch on them, watch their hair spread out under the water as they sank; it was dreamlike. He never felt more alive than he did at this moment. *I decide whether you live or die.*

This was the ultimate.

He'd enjoyed reading about Gary Dunlop in the paper. Fucking moron. You had to have self-control in this game, not take normal girls, like Ellie Kane. Girls with families and friends who cared about them. The papers always had a field day when a respectable civilian was murdered. Stepped up the publicity.

Twice, they'd questioned him. Twice they'd let him go. Ha!

But the list of names of the murdered girls had put the wind up him good and proper.

She wasn't there. There was no Angelika.

He'd cursed, kicked and broken various household items when he read the list. Why wasn't Angelika there? Had they thought it was Dunlop but been unable to pin it on him? Said he'd confessed to the others but not to her. Seeing as he didn't do it.

Come on, Dunlop, couldn't you have said you did her, too? Wouldn't make any difference now, would it?

Pity he hadn't known about the 'slut' motif. Clever move by the cops, that, he had to admit.

He'd panicked, but not for long. There was no further mention of her in the article, and nothing to indicate, in days to come, that they were still looking for her killer.

She was a girl from nowhere, and nobody cared.

The case must have gone stone cold.

He relaxed.

He'd been so careful, as he always was, to leave no trace of himself on her. First move was to bind their hands above and behind their heads so they couldn't scratch him. He wore a polo neck, a balaclava, gloves. Condoms, obviously.

His strategies made him proud. He picked girls who could go missing without anyone giving a shit. Used to do the odd junkie teenage runaway, the type who moved from hostel to shop doorway to waste ground wino camp fire, but they were hard to find, and you never knew; one of them had turned out to be some rich bloke's daughter. When that one was splashed all over the papers it gave him a few sleepless nights, for sure. The illegals were better. There was no trace of them, and the guys who brought them in didn't want to waste too much time and energy looking for any who went astray.

"We write them off as spillage," Karolis had joked. "You're bound to lose one now and again, in this game. They disappear; they don't go to the cops because they're not supposed to be here in the first place." He shrugged his shoulders. "We write the odd card to their folks back home, supposedly from them, saying how well they're doing. Even send a bit of money. It's worth it to keep any problems at bay."

The day after Dora, he felt like the fucking *main man*. Those Lithuanian wankers raged about where she'd gone, how she'd got out, who helped her, and he laughed whenever he thought about them, unable to see what was going on under their stupid gyppo noses.

It was AJ who'd helped him see how the two of them stood apart, men with the courage to own the basic human instinct. Not that they ever spoke about it after that first time; they didn't have to.

One night, a couple of years back, they'd been sitting in his conservatory, jawing all night over Jack and coke. Coke with a small 'c'. They'd got into talking about sex and women, like you do, and he'd known AJ was testing him, by the way he kept revealing a little bit more and a little bit more. Judging his reaction.

He knew there was something else, and he bided his time, for hours, until it came out.

AJ had been getting it on with this mouthy tart, he said, who liked it rough ('heavy stuff, not just a bit of slapping about'). It got rougher than he'd intended, though. Accident, but it happened.

"Long story short, I suddenly realise she ain't breathing no more. Try to wake her up but—nah. Nothin' doing. So I leave her in the hotel room and get the hell out."

Coke rush had nothing on the buzz he felt when he heard that. "You never got caught, then?"

"No, I was down London. No-name slag in a no-questions-asked, cheap hotel." His eyes went glassy and he stared into space. "I nearly shat myself when I saw what I'd done, but it was kind of a thrill, too, y'know?"

Oh yes, he knew.

Dan Thewlis knew all about that thrill.

He didn't say anything, just nodded, allowed a hint of a smile to play around his eyes, and waited for him to continue. For what he knew was coming. The revelation that they were the same.

"I mean," AJ said, eventually, "that's what blokes do. It's our human nature to fight and rape and kill. Like, the law says we can't, *civilisation* says we can't, but it's still in us, ain't it? If we were born, I dunno, fifteen hundred years ago, no one would think nothing of it."

They'd looked at each other, nodded and grinned; no more words were needed. Dan broke the silence by racking up another line; it wasn't an uncomfortable silence, though. More one of conspirators who were in perfect sync.

Perhaps AJ had seen it in him, when they first met. Knew he was a kindred spirit. He was sure AJ had never revealed that story to anyone else, and that he knew his secret was safe.

Ever since then, there had been a bond between them. Words never said, but always there, separating them from everyone else, like they were on a pedestal looking down at the ordinary Joes who would be shocked by them, who didn't have the guts to know themselves. To follow through on their basic, primal instincts. Who didn't dare cross the line.

Sitting up on high like that was a good feeling.

One day they might talk about what else they'd done, but there was no hurry.

Shortly after that night, AJ introduced him to Karolis and his gang.

"Had to wait till I was sure I could trust you." AJ said. "You don't even tell Steve or Noel, right? You don't tell a soul."

AJ sold gear to Karolis and his men, and Dan worked a couple of nights a week as a bouncer in their shit-pit of a brothel. Easy money, just for keeping the punters in order, sorting out any who wanted to rough up the girls ('cause you couldn't put them to work if they were covered in cuts and bruises, Karolis said; no one wanted to see the handiwork of the guys who'd come before). Sometimes he just had to sit out the back, in a van, smoking and drinking a few beers, to make sure none of the tarts tried to escape. That was what he was supposed to do, anyway; Angelika he had let go, and Dora the same. There would be others, too. Just enough to keep his pecker up, once in a while. He wasn't greedy.

The tarts had one night off a week, rotated, and most spent it watching DVDs, but one or two sneaked out to try their luck on Monk's Park, to make some cash of their own. Once out there, they could easily be abducted by psychos like Gary Dunlop. Who cared? Nobody, that was who.

Dan didn't take them on the night he was on duty, because Karolis would give that big ape Herkus and his goons permission to administer the odd 'reminder' about who was boss if he wasn't working when and where he was supposed to be, but now and again he let the girls nip out and come back, safely, so they'd try it again. Dora told him that one of the other guys let them go out, too, if they slipped him a twenty and gave him *feliacija*. Was worth it; they could earn a hundred quid in just a couple of hours, she said, all big eyes. The men liked them because they were young and pretty. Innocent looking.

Dan kept his eye out for the runners. Cruised around Monk's Park to see if they were there. On the night he took Angelika he'd actually helped her get out; all he'd had to do was distract the guy on guard duty for five minutes so she could get down the fire escape.

He thought he might tell AJ about Dora. Break the silence. He thought he knew, anyway, though; something about the way he looked at him when Karolis was cursing and hollering about where the girl was.

He'd seen a hint of a smile about AJ's eyes, and when he returned it, the other man gave him a nod so faint that no one else would have noticed it, but a nod, nevertheless.

Dan whistled as he walked along the road to work the next morning. He liked to walk sometimes, when he was on a high. See the world around him, even if he'd be stuck under some stinking blocked sink later. He felt like a magician.

The bored, frustrated housewives flirted with him, never knowing what he could do to them, if he wanted.

The grimy aspect of his job didn't matter to him on days like today; his head was far above it.

He walked past Lyndford Computers, still with its shutters down. Pity about Steve, but it was good that he'd gone. Out of everyone in the world, Steve knew him the best, and he was a clever fucker. He'd known he was lying about Cassie, the perceptive bastard. Yeah, best that him and that witch he was shagging were out of his way. Shame, though. The legend was that people who did what he did had no feelings for other human beings, but it would be weird not seeing Steve.

He reminded Dan of being a kid. When the world was a simpler place, before he opened the door to his real self.

His very first was a punk girl they'd met down by the river, when he was just sixteen. Irish runaway. He'd got Noel to take the body away, in his car, and they burnt it on some waste ground out on the road to Kirton, but it got a bit messy; there was muck all over their clothes, they worried about the fire being seen, and someone found the remains. He'd sworn to Noel that it was an accident, but Noel had been a bit funny with him ever since; that was why he started working away, Dan reckoned. Only came back for his dad. They'd never talked about it, but it was getting easier as the years passed, and Noel spent time with him, these days, when he was home.

He'd often wondered what it would be like to kill someone, but he didn't have any plan to do the punk girl until it happened. They'd met her in the park, him and Steve, but it started to get dark and Steve said he had to go home (he had a bitch of a foster mother at the time). Dan stayed with the girl, and they'd drunk most of a bottle of cheap vodka she'd nicked from Netto, and started fooling around, but then she tried to stop him. Little cow kneed him in the bollocks, pulled his hair, and that made him mad. No bitch treated him like that.

Seeing that terror on her face, when she realised that she'd gone too far, made him want to shout with triumph. He hadn't known it would feel that good.

When it was over, he hid her under a bush until Noel could help him.

Afterwards, he thought about it all the time. He felt as though his life had been leading up to that point, and he knew he would do it again.

Noel looked scared, when he told him. Big brother, who ruled the roost, was wary of him. Twat even said they should go to the police, at first. 'Cause of the girl's parents. Dan had to force himself to cry and say he was scared of being sent away, and upsetting their dad, before he relented. All the while they were doing what they had to do, Noel kept shaking, and saying, 'you don't seem very upset', and 'this ain't a fucking game', stuff like that. Dan whooped when they lit the fire, and Noel hit him, knocked him on the ground and pinned him down, told him to shut the fuck up and behave.

His next one didn't happen until he was twenty-one, but the fuss about the punk girl was enough to make him consider his methods. The river was better. Not always the Lynden, either; sometimes he took them further afield. Yeah, and the trick was not to get greedy.

Dora was safe and sound on the bottom, out past Waterton. *He* was safe. One step ahead of the cops. They hadn't even taken a sample when he was taken in for questioning. Either time. That was what you had to worry about, these days. They could fit you up for any fucking thing, once they'd got your DNA.

"They can say they've got a match even if they ain't, that's what they do, y'see," AJ had told him, but Dan knew what he was really saying.

AJ had got Philip Landers down there the minute Steve and that witch got him picked up; the solicitor told them that unless his client was being formally charged, he was advising him not to supply a sample.

They complied without too much hassle; Landers reckoned they'd already decided Dunlop was their man.

In his head, he'd punched the air when he left the station.

All the same, he'd played it safe until now.

Until the need came over him again.

The high he got from taking Dora's life was better than any line of coke, any fist fight, any fuck of a mate's wife (even Roxy; that had been a thrill. Dicing with danger. AJ would kill him. Literally).

To be in control of whether someone lived or died: the ultimate.

He might have to pay Cassie another visit, too, the whining slag. This time, though, he would be more careful. This time, she wouldn't see him coming.

Dan Thewlis strutted, knowing nothing about three developments that took place over the next few days.

Only two days after he killed her, the bin-liner-wrapped body of Dora was discovered in the river at Kirton, not far from where Gary Dunlop had stopped Zack Todd from playing on the bridge ten months before.

The discovery was made early in the morning, and this time the police were careful to keep it out of the press; the public were still recovering from the revelations about the Lyndford Strangler.

The night after Dan put her in the river was one of fierce storms. He didn't know that the river was not very deep at the spot he chose. The flow of the water was accelerated by the force of the storm, and the body washed downstream, the rush of the water and impact of rocks with which it came into contact loosening the weights; the body's buoyancy was increased, and it floated upwards.

Despite his precautions, the force of his copulation with the girl had been enough to make the condom split, and semen found its way out. In the dark, with gloved hands, Dan had been unaware of this. There was not much, but enough to make a DNA match.

Or would have been, if the police records held one.

This problem was solved by the second development, just a week later, when Noel Thewlis was involved in a fight outside Cinderella's night club. He was not the thug responsible for the critical condition of the seventeen-year-old in intensive care, but, as there had been a gang of six men on one side and four on the other, and all claimed total amnesia about which punches had been administered where, DNA tests were requested.

Noel knew he had nothing to fear, and complied willingly. All he'd done was bend the nose of some ape who was bearing down upon him, and perhaps give him a bit of a shiner, before he got thumped himself. Getting into brawls was not usual behaviour for him, and he felt remorse about that night, appalled that someone might die; he was anxious to be eliminated.

At around eight p.m. a few days later, just as DI Cara Nolan was about to go home for the evening, she received a phone call.

The DNA sample from Noel Thewlis was a match so close to the sample taken from the unnamed body pulled from the River Lynden that the latter had to indicate the presence of either Noel or his sibling; it was too close a match to belong even to a parent.

Noel Thewlis had no criminal record and spent most of his time out of the area.

He had just one sibling, a nasty piece of work by all accounts.

Daniel Thewlis had been arrested for attempted rape, called in for questioning not once but twice during the Lyndford Strangler murders, and was a known close associate of scrap merchant Alan Jefferies, a suspected dealer in narcotics and person of interest in several minor crimes over the years.

He had also been likened to the original e-fit photo from the description given after the murder of 'Angelika'.

DCI Reddick was at a dinner party hosted by friends of his wife when he received the call; always keen to make an early exit from such an occasion, this time the haste with which he jumped up and grabbed his overcoat was little short of indecent.

"Wait till I get there," he told Nolan, as he shrugged it on. "I want to be the one to arrest this particular scumbag."

The third development occurred only six hours after DCI Reddick received the happy news, when Dan Thewlis was safely in custody.

A girl appeared at Lyndford police station in a state of extreme anxiety. Thin, unkempt, begging for some 'medicine', she pulled up her sleeve to reveal track marks up her inner arm.

Her name was Tiesa, but she spoke little English. Before she collapsed, the desk sergeant managed to extract brief, confusing details about a friend gone missing, and some men who would kill her.

She was taken to hospital where she was given a full physical examination and found to be undernourished and addicted to heroin. Methadone was supplied, her nationality determined, an interpreter assigned.

What she told the interpreter was enough to make the police officer call DI Nolan immediately.

Tiesa's sunken eyes made Cara want to weep. She sat down beside the bed and took the girl's hand, and Tiesa gripped it back as though she was holding onto a lifeline.

Via the interpreter, she told them that she had been kept captive in a big building down a long road, with many other girls. She'd sneaked out down the fire escape, and walked for many miles, asking the few people she saw where to find the police, eventually being taken pity on by a cab driver, who'd stopped out of concern for her state.

She was scared, she said, of Karolis and Herkus, because of what they made the girls do, of the drugs they gave them, yes, but much more frightening was the fact that her friend, Dora, had gone missing. She'd escaped to go to the place where the men came in their cars to pick the girls up, and had never been seen again.

Yes, she'd lived in the big building since she was brought over from Lithuania. The man called Valter had said he would get her a job in a hotel, but it was all lies. They made them have sex with the men, and kept them captive.

Another girl, called Angelika, had disappeared, too, a year before. She hadn't known Angelika, but some of the other girls talked about her.

Two of the men let them sneak out, she said. One of them was an English man called Dan.

The other one made them hand over some of their money and give him *feliacija*, but Dan just let them go because he was a nice man.

"We all like Dan," said Tiesa.

DS Nolan took out her tablet and brought up the e-fit picture produced after the murder of Angelika.

"Tiesa, I want to show you something," she said. "Is this your friend Dan?"

"Yes. Yes, that's him." She giggled. "Except he is more handsome in real life!"

Cara Nolan closed her eyes for a moment, and conjured up in her mind the photograph of Angelika. The clear, pale skin, the long, fair hair, the brutally marked neck, the closed eyes that would never open again. *I've got him*, she told the girl, silently, and she hoped all that afterlife stuff was true, and Angelika would look down from *wherever*, and know she hadn't failed her.

In his cell, Dan Thewlis smiled. As Philip Landers had said to him, all they could prove was that he'd had sex with Dora, not that he killed her.

"Because you didn't kill her, did you?" Landers said, his face expressionless.

"Course I didn't!" Dan laughed. "Whaddya think I am, some sort of psycho? Nah, I left her in perfect working order; she must've been bumped off by a punter who went with her after I did."

"Just admit to picking her up at Monk's Park, nothing else," said Landers, who was clearly worried about the discovery of Karolis and AJ's operations, too.

"Nothing else to admit to, mate. Told you."

Now Dan lay back. They had nothing on him. Nothing to link him to Angelika, or Crow Lane, or the drugs, absolutely fucking nothing.

He closed his eyes, the smile still on his face. He was home free.

DCI Reddick put the phone down after talking to Cara Nolan at the hospital, and this time he felt nothing but triumph.

He'd known there was more to Dan Thewlis than met the eye. Too cocky by half.

He remembered thinking what a shame it was that you couldn't keep a bloke in a cell just for being an obnoxious dickhead. Even now, that obnoxious dickhead was probably sitting there, as cocky as hell, sure he would get away with murder.

Reddick stood up and put his jacket on, ready to make the walk.

Not this time, mate, he thought. *This time, I've got you.*

THE END

Author's Note

Thank you for reading *The Devil You Know*. If you enjoyed it, I'd be very grateful if you would visit Amazon and write a short review. As an independent author, I'm reliant on word of mouth to publicise my work, and reviews help so much. Thanks!

You can follow me on Twitter, Goodreads, Bookbub, and my blog.

Other books by Terry Tyler:

The Project Renova Series (post apocalyptic/dystopian)
Tipping Point
Lindisfarne
UK2
Legacy
Patient Zero

The Lanchester Series (family drama/parallel history)
Kings and Queens
Last Child

Stand alone, full-length novels
The House of York
What It Takes
Full Circle
Dream On
The Other Side
Nobody's Fault
You Wish

Novellas
Best Seller
Round and Round

Short Stories
Nine Lives

Printed in Poland
by Amazon Fulfillment
Poland Sp. z o.o., Wrocław

43801555R00199